LOST IN REMEMBRANCE

LOST IN REMEMBRANCE

WRITTEN & PUBLISHED BY: Matthew J Richardson

Dedication:

To everyone that encouraged, supported, ridiculed, or belittled me on this journey…

…Thank You.

Chapter One

Crackle, crackle, crackle.

The faint sounds steadily filled my ears. It filled the darkness surrounding me with purpose, letting me know I was alive. The pressure on my cheek is hard and gritty, but not forceful or aggressive. I soon realize that the pressure against my face is also against my chest, arms, and my legs. The feeling was not a crushing or stabbing sensation, just consistent with the rest of me.

Crackle, snap, snap.

The slight mossy smell of dirt fills my nostrils with every trembling filled breath I took. Not a cold tremble, but an almost exhausted breath exits my lungs irregularly to the beats of my racing heart. The taste of mud graces across my top lip as a feeling of grit scrapes against my teeth. The slight dryness of my tongue scratches at the top of my mouth as the sides are still moist from the small pool of saliva forming in the corner.

Snap, crackle, snap.

The pain of every muscle in my aching body squeezed itself into the already well occupied space of sensations that are coming over me along with another, light. Streaks of light made cracks in the surrounding darkness of my vision. Colors of whites, grays, oranges, and browns flood over the dark, blurring together almost too quickly for my mind to make sense of. A thought molded itself in my mind. *Where am I?*

My eyes opened ever so slightly as to not overload my vision even more with these colors that formed into familiar and yet foreign shapes of recognition. The gritty feeling on my cheek pierces into my right eye, quickly forcing it to close tightly. My cheek promptly found sensations of scratching and digging feelings into my skin. *Why am I on the ground?*

Crackle, crackle.

The burning in my arms intensifies as I pushed on the ground with both hands firmly pressing on the dirt and gravel. The taste of mud in my mouth fades as my head lifted off the ground, leaving a small pool of drool in its wake. A quick spit of saliva onto the ground and the taste disappeared.

Turning to my side, I gently pulled my legs in front of my body, allowing me to be in a sitting position on the ground. I closed my eyes and started taking deep breaths to slow my breathing, reducing my rapidly beating heart from bursting out of my chest. Opening my eyes again, I glance down at my dark gray pants covered in the same dirt and mud that was all over my face. As I follow the outline of my body, I notice my dark blue long-sleeved button up dress shirt also covered with the same filth.

Snap, crackle, crackle.

I suddenly realized the tightness around my neck was from the dark gray diamond patterned tie, outlined with colors of reds and blues around the diamonds, hanging down in front of me. Reaching my hands up to loosen it, I can feel the dirt in between my fingers as I pulled on the tie's smooth fabric. At the last second, I decided to just take the entire dress tie off from around my neck and used it to brush the dirt away from my hands. As I became somewhat satisfied with the cleaning, I closed my eyes again, took one more deep breath, and slowly exhaled as I finally felt the pounding behind my sternum become lighter, lighter, calm.

Crackle, crackle, snap.

As I once again opened my eyes, I turned my head towards the direction the unrelenting sounds that seemed to surround me were coming from. I could feel a warm breeze from the same direction, yet I saw nothing specific. A fog seemed to be in that direction filled with colors of reds and oranges, yet I could not make out one object; not one recognizable resemblance to anything I have ever known, just the fog. *Where am I?*

I looked around for anything identifiable to me. I hoped I could spot something that would give me a better understanding of where I was or how I got there. Besides the dirt, which I quickly realized seemed to be some sort of road or path, there appeared to be tall fields of grass or possibly hay. The fields gave me a sense I was possibly laying on the grounds of a farm. Unfortunately, with no signs, equipment, or people anywhere in sight, there was no way for me to begin even remotely getting answers to my questions.

Suddenly, I felt my left ear perk up, as I could hear a very faint noise in the distance. Turning my head from left to right, I tried to find where the new sound was coming from, but I could not lock onto the location. *Is that someone's voice?* All I could see was dirt, grass, hay, and fog, followed by even more of the same; my eyes just could not find a prudent direction. *That is someone's voice!*

My searching became more intense as I quickly and forcefully began trying to pinpoint exactly where the voice was coming from. I forcefully turned myself over onto my knees as I looked around more and more furiously. *Is it coming from the hay?* I look towards the fields, nothing. *Is it coming from the fog?* I looked again with no success. My mind tried to listen to the actual, barely making sense of what they were saying. I tightly closed my eyes and tilted my head towards the ground. *What are you saying? What are you saying? WHAT ARE YOU SAYING!?*

"Hey!" I slowly opened my eyes and looked up to my right. Sitting only a few meters away sat a small light blue house. The house had a large double panned bow window on the front all the way to the right where the living room of the house would be. Smaller single hung windows in pairs were to the far left, showing the location of bedrooms. In the middle was a white painted covered porch with white banisters that stretched along the length of the porch separating it from the front yard. In the middle of the banister was an opening with two steps that led down to the ground. At the edge of the steps was a small walkway with four large, long concrete slabs placed end to end in the ground, leading to the edge of the dirt road. As I found myself still kneeled in the dirt, I felt confused as thoughts kept racing through my head. *Where did that house come from? Was it there this whole time? I could have sworn there was nothing there before.*

"Are you okay?" the voice said again as I stood up slowly, realizing that my legs still felt weak. As I walked closer to the property, I discovered the porch had a couple of large chairs sitting off to the left side of the porch with a small glass table sitting in between them. In the chair to the left sat a large dark figure, which I quickly realized was a person, a Black Woman. "How did you get out there?" The long silvery strands of her hair led me to believe she was an older woman. She wore what looked like a long dark green dress with accents of white, yellow, and brown and what looked like black rubber shoes covering her white sock covered feet.

I felt myself stop just as I reached the edge of the dirt road, right in front of the first cement slab. I glanced down at my feet as I saw my pair of black dress shoes lined up parallel to each other; their tips pointing at the edge of the concrete. Looking back up at the old woman, I hear her chuckle as she said, "Well, come on up here, dear." Another quick glance back down at my feet and they suddenly felt less heavy as one foot lifted, and I took a step onto the walkway; first the right foot, then the left.

As I approached the porch, I saw the small smile on the woman's face as she adjusted the pair of large, round lens, gold-colored eyeglasses up from the edge of her nose. She then placed her book she was holding down onto the glass table next to her chair. "Come up here dear," she motioned to me with her now book free hand as I climbed the two steps and stood now on the porch of her home. Her voice sounded foreign to me, but I could not distinguish exactly where it was from.

"Here, why don't you have a seat right here?" she asked me as she tapped the empty chair. The chair was a tall backed, maroon colored arm yard chair. A long yellow and orange striped cushion sat in the seat that covered the back and the seat of the chair. As I sat down, I realized that what I thought was wood was nothing more than plastic; but the chair was still much more comfortable than the ground I was just laying on moments ago.

As my body sunk into the chair, she sat up in hers, leaned over towards me and said, "Now dear, what were you doing out there on the ground?"

As I opened my mouth to answer her and tell her I had no clue how I wound up lying on the ground in the middle of what I could tell was nowhere, nothing came out of my mouth. The more I strained to talk, the more no noise would exit past my lips. Looking at the woman with a confused expression on my face, she must have known I was panicking because she placed her hand on mine and said, "Oh dear, I guess your words are all dried up. I tell you what, there is a tray over there with a pitcher of water and some empty glasses. Could you be a sweetheart and get us some drinks?"

I turned my head and saw a small, three-foot-tall table with wheels for feet at the bottom. The table comprised three aluminum trays equally spaced between four narrow, faded gold-colored legs. The bottom and middle trays were empty, but on the top tray I could indeed see a pitcher and a stack of empty clear glasses. I stood up reluctantly from my comfortable seat and walked over to grab the drinks she requested. As I came upon the tray, I noticed that there was not just a glass pitcher of water with ice cubes sitting to the top left of the tray with the stack of glasses in the middle, but then I saw another glass pitcher sitting to the top right. This pitcher appeared to be filled with what I assumed to be lemonade with its distinguished clear yellow coloring and the sweet smell of sugar wafting into the air. I could feel my mouth salivate for the sweet taste of the lemonade as I reached for the pitcher and suddenly stopped as I was about to grab the handle.

She asked me to get two glasses of water; she did not tell me to help myself to this. I better not. I pulled my hand back and reached out to the pitcher of water, filled two glasses, and returned the pitcher back to its resting location. As I walked back to the woman, I handed her one glass of water and sat down in my seat. "Good, you got us some nice cold water. You didn't want the lemonade?"

I took a long, cool gulp from my glass. "You didn't say to get lemonade," I answered, followed by a quick expression of shock and relief.

"Ah, there you are. Looks like you found your words after all." She sat back in her chair, took a sip of the water, and placed the glass down on the table next to her book. "So now, what were you doin' out there on the road?"

"I honestly have no idea where I am, let alone how I ended up dining at the mud pie buffet line."

The old woman replied with a side smirk, "Oh, you are a funny one. Well, how about an easy one then darlin'? What is your name?"

Finishing another long sip of the icy water, I said, "My name?" I paused and continued, "My name is…" I froze. I looked down at the glass of water, remembering how taking a sip from it allowed me to speak and thought maybe it would work again. I quickly lifted the glass to my lips and chugged the water until it was gone. Pulling the now empty glass away from my mouth, I looked at the woman and said, "My name? My name is… FUCK ME!"

She cocked her head to the side and, with a frown now replacing her smile, she said, "Well, now that is quite the vulgar name if I ever heard it."

A sudden sense of dread and confusion rushed over me. *How can I not know my name?* This was becoming too much, all coming at me all at once. I didn't know how I ended up in the middle of wherever I was. I did not know where I was going or where I was coming from, and now I could not even recall my name. "I'm sorry ma'am. I didn't mean to curse. I was just hoping that would work."

"It's not magic water, dear; it only helps when you need refreshment. Everything else comes afterward." As I placed my empty glass on to the table, the old woman reached out and squeezed my hand, trying to comfort me. "How 'bout I tell you what I can, you know, to get you started?"

"Started? Start what?"

"Well, on where you need to be."

I quickly cut her off. "I don't even know where I am!"

That all too familiar smile returned to her face as she calmly replied, "Where you are is exactly where you're meant to be, I think."

Sternly, I stood up out of the chair, feeling much of my strength returning. I turned back towards the old woman and asked, "But where is 'here'?"

"Everyone, everywhere, has places they want to be. Everyone, everywhere, all have places they had once come from. And then everyone, everywhere, has places they need to be. To remember who they are and what it is they want. Not everyone is the same, and not everyone gets what they must, but it is within everyone to take from what is in front of them. I think that is you now; whether you know or realize what is here for you, you know more than you may think. It'll come back to you."

As she sat back in her chair, I just scratched my head and stared off into the fields, "Ma'am, I do not know what you're talking about."

She waved her hand out in dismissal, "Oh, you can stop with that old ma'am business, dear. Call me Shaelynn."

I sat down on the banister, glanced back towards her and said, "Shaelynn? Wow, I know more about you than I do myself."

She laughed out loud, placing her hand on her chest over her heart. "I like you, dear. I really hope you find what you need."

I stood back up again, brushed myself off a bit more from the dirt that was still on my clothes, and rolled up my necktie before I placed it into my back pocket. "I guess there's nothing else you can tell me, is there?" I asked Shaelynn.

"Well, sure there is." She pointed out towards the dirt road. "Everyone always needs somewhere to start. For you, I feel *that's* where you should be."

I turned slightly towards the road as well and said, "What, dirt road highway? I don't even know how I ended up at face plant city and that is where I need to go?"

Laughing Shaelynn replies, "No dear, that's your path. Look, there are directions you can choose. Both may give you answers, but only one is going to help you get to where you need to belong."

With a big sighing breath, I stepped off the porch and started walking towards the dirt road once again. After several feet I stopped and looked back towards Shaelynn and said, "Thank you ma'am, I mean Shaelynn. I guess this is goodbye. I don't think we'll see each other again."

"Oh, I would doubt that, dear, if I were you. You never know where we will all end up in life," she shouted back, followed by a waving hand of farewell.

As I made my way back to my original resting place, I had two options to go. To my right was the orange and red-colored fog; the feelings of heat and those off settling sounds still coming from all around it. To my left was another layer of fog with colors of gray and blues entwined within its mist; the feelings of cold and silence coming from it. *I don't know which way to go.* After several glances back and forth, back, and forth, something drew me towards the gray. *I guess this is where I go.*

After several steps towards the dense fog, I heard Shaelynn call out, "Looks like you found where you need to go!"

Coming up to the edge of the fog, it almost appeared like it was this great wall separating everything from its other end. I slowly lifted my hand and pressed it into the fog; the cold shot up my arm and almost pulled me in before I quickly snatched my arm back. *Come on! It's just fog!* I took one last deep breath and before I walked into the fog I stopped, looked back and shouted, "Hey Shaelynn? My name… is Sam!"

Chapter Two

"My name is Sam. My name is Sam. Sam. Sam." Repeatedly I kept restating my name, hoping that I would somehow remember the rest of it if not anything else. "Sam. I am Sam. Sam." I had little else to do with my time other than saying my name out loud to myself since I had already soaked up all there was to see on this long road in front of me. It almost seemed like I had been walking for hours, though I could not tell since I had lost my watch; if I even had one since I could not remember that either.

The fog continued to stay the same thickness and consistency as I kept walking, giving me visibility only a few yards in front of me. Besides the fog, all there was to see was the dirt road, the green grass on either side of the road, and myself;

nothing more than that. So, I just continued, "I am Sam. Sam. I am Sam. Sam I am." I stopped suddenly in frustration and said to myself, "Great, I sound like a fucking children's book."

I was stuck on trying to figure out my full name because I had already exhausted so many other things I was trying to remember about my life. *Where am I from? Who are my parents? Were they still alive? Where do I live? What is my job? Am I married? Do I have children?* Question after question I kept asking myself and I kept getting the same thing, no answers, just more questions.

The other thing that kept crawling back into my mind was what Shaelynn had said about me "getting where I needed to be." *What did she mean by that, exactly?* In all honesty, I was probably overthinking the situation. Based on her appearance, she seemed to be no more than middle-aged, but she spoke like she was possibly much older than that. I just could not shake the thought; however, that she knew more than she had told me. *Stop thinking like that. There is no proof of that and you're trying to blame an old woman for your own amnesia, if that's even what this is.*

Scrape.

I suddenly tripped and stumbled a few steps as I felt the dirt under my feet become solid like I kicked a large rock sticking out of the ground. As I looked down, an expression of shock and almost joy came over me as I saw what my hazard was. I kneeled and placed my hand on the ground to make sure I was not imagining what was now in front of me. No longer was I walking on a dirt road made by wagon wheels, but a paved road of asphalt was now in my path. I looked back behind me but could not see where the dirt road ended; nothing but asphalt and fog. *Was I that distracted in thought that I never noticed?*

I stood back up sternly and began walking again, but with a bit more authority in my stride. After seeing my fresh change in scenery, I was determined more than ever to continue. I still did not know what was in front of me or where I was going, but I knew one thing for certain. *Where there are roads, there are towns. Where there are towns, there are people.*

I walked again for what felt like a few hundred more meters, when I could hear a very faint noise coming from in front of me through the fog. Very slight sounds of an almost clicking noise, but they were quick. As I got closer to it, the clicks became increasingly recognizable. The clicking became more in a tempo pattern and became more metallic in its rhythm until the clicks become undeniable. *I know that sound; someone's using a ratchet!*

In front of me and off to the right, I started making out a shape through the thickness of the fog. A long silver and brown object stretched from left to right in front of a faint bluish green box looking shape close to the ground. *The ratchet noise is coming from over there.* As I got closer, I slowed down my pace to a cautious crawl. A few more steps and I clearly recognized the silver and brown object as a rusty bumper. *It's a car.*

The bluish green box turned out to be the faded paint job of a car that sat on the side of the road. The roof of the car had a peeling white cloth top that had seen way too much sun. The wheels on the driver's side, both front and rear, had their hubcaps missing, while the passenger taillight shield had a large crack going all the way down with a small chunk missing, exposing the light fixture inside. The seats were of a darker blue fabric along with the color matching dashboard. Overall, the car was exceedingly long and wide, and incredibly old.

At the front of the car, the hood was open, and the ratchet clicks were coming from there. As I got closer to the front of the car, I could see a man bent over in the car working on something in the engine. He was a very skinny yet lengthy white man. The dark blue of his jeans covered the top of his very black boots, which had an extraordinarily strong shine to them. His white button shirt pulled from his pants as the sleeves fought to stay at their pushed position halfway up his arms as he played mechanic to the vehicle. His long black hair came down on either side of his face, blocking him from sight.

"Ah ha! I'm almost done with you now," he said out loud to only what I could assume was the engine. His voice was deep and raspy. It had a dark and stern tone almost molding itself behind years of experience. *I might have just found the second old person in this town.* He also did not have the same foreign accent that Shaelynn did, so I knew that would not help me narrow down where I might be located.

"Um, excuse me. Sir?" I said as I approached slowly as to not shock or scare the old man.

"Yeah, just a sec," he replied, lifting his right hand up in the air in my direction holding out his index finger. "So, you're going to be stubborn, I see. No matter, I'll fix you yet," he continued talking to the engine of the car. As he stood up from his engine bay, he placed the ratchet into one of his back pockets and grabbed an old red rag that laid on the frame of the car and began wiping his hands off from the oil and grease that was on his fingers.

"Now, what is it I can do for you?" he asked me. He was not as I pictured him before I saw his face. Although he had a very aged voice, his face did not have the same luxury. He had an exceedingly long face with a semi-large nose, deep-seated brown eyes and a very stern brow capped with an exceedingly long, stretched mouth. *Who's scaring who?*

"Hi, I'm sorry to interrupt you from working…"

"I would assume you are certainly not sorry," he scoffed, interrupting me.

I paused for a second, then asked, "Um, sorry?"

"I don't think you are. Cause if you were sorry, you wouldn't have done it now, would you?" He smoothed his long hair down the back of his head even though his hair didn't move.

Done? Done what? "I don't know what to say," I cautiously said, with a look of confusion on my face.

The man sternly stared at me as he slowly walked out from in front of his car and began taking a few steps towards me with an expression of aggression on his face. "I think you'd want to find something to say and find it quick," he hissed, with anger growling through each syllable.

I quickly put my hands up in front of me as I stammered, "Hey, no. Shit. Whoa, whoa. No trouble. No, um, hey, no!" while taking a couple of steps back from the man. "I just wanted to ask you…"

Before I could finish, the man let out an exceptionally large belly laugh as his expression of anger turned into joy. "Oh, don't worry boy, I'm not gonna hurt you." I breathed a sigh of relief. "Sometimes you just gotta pull a man's chain to know who you're working with."

"Jesus Christ, what was that? I think I just peed a little. Why would you do that to a perfect stranger?"

The man's expression turned quickly back to anger. "What? You don't find me intimidating? You don't know what goes on around here. What it takes. To make people aware of who's in charge; you can't be soft!"

I quickly put my hands up in front of me again in protest, "Hey whoa, I wasn't trying to offe… Let's start over. My name is Sam, and I just wanted to ask you some questions."

"Questions, huh?" His voice toned down to a low calm. "Well, Sam, doesn't everyone always have questions? And I suppose you want me to answer those questions?"

"I mean, if it's too much trouble, I can just…"

"Well Sam, I'll tell you what." He reached in through the driver's side window of the front seat of the car and pulled out a black jacket. *Of course, he has a black jacket.* "I've got some items waiting for me at the shop there across the street. Go grab them for me, and we can talk."

I smirked as I replied, "Shop? What shop? There's nothing around here? I'm almost surprised I found you."

Putting on his jacket, the man reaches into his left pocket and pulls out a blue box with white lettering on it, but I could not make out what the words said. As he opened it and pulled the long white thin cylinder-shaped object with the deep brown colored edge out of the box, I quickly realized the box was cigarettes. As he placed the cigarette into his mouth, he nodded his head in the direction behind me and half mouthed, "It's right over there."

I spun myself around to see a gas station with a garage and a convenience store attached to it. *What the fuck! Where did that come from? Was that there this whole time, and I didn't see it? Why does that keep happening to me?* Turning back around, I see the man holding an old gold and silver styled lighter in his hand. *Flick, flick,* were the sounds the lighter made as he lit his cigarette. After closing the top of the lighter with a loud *clank,* he placed it into the inside pocket of his jacket. I could only assume that's where he got it from. He then reached into his right pocket and pulled out a folded white piece of paper.

As he extended out his arm to hand me the paper, he stated, "Take this with you and give it to Ronald, that's who works there. He'll know what to give you."

I took the paper and asked, "Well, I'm pretty sure he's not gonna know who I am, so who do I tell him the parts are for?"

"Just tell him they're for William," he said the name with an almost snake-like slither that sent a chill down my spine.

"William? Got it." I turned and walked away slowly, only glancing back uneasily after a few steps as I saw William leaning up against his car, slowly taking one drag after another of his cigarette. I halted and called back to William, "Hey wait, am I supposed to pay for this?"

"Don't worry, it's covered!" he yelled back at me with a small but noticeable grin on his face. *It's covered? What in the world? Did I just meet the mob boss of this town?*

Walking onto the property of the gas station, it looked like it had serviced many people at one time. There were eight pumps covered by a large lit canopy, however, the pumps themselves looked like they had not been serviced in years. The parking lot leading up to and away from the pumps was paved but was slightly buried with sections of dirt all over. A very tall sign with the station's name on it was at the far end of the lot. The sign read '*S – Max*' though I did not think that was the actual name since some letters had fallen off. Below the name was a large white pasteboard section that the station would put specials or messages for passersby to read. All that was left attached to it were random black letters and numbers barely staying on. *All we need is a giant wheel of money and a blond co-host and we got ourselves a game show.*

The building sitting behind the gas pumps had the same under serviced appeal as the rest of the property. The building was a wet gray color with faded edges of reds, oranges, and browns all over. On the right, there were four garage bays that looked like they had not been opened in years to work on anyone's car. All four garage doors were painted red but were peeling badly and had four rows of four-square windows running from left to right and down so you could see which bays had a vehicle in them. The four bays were empty.

On the left of the building, it looked like a convenience store. Four large windows stretched across the front of the building, with a double entrance door next to them. Through the windows, you could see a handful of rows of shelves lining up and down the inside, with refrigerators at the far end on the left. Walking through the doors, I could get a better idea of the layout of the store. The shelves and refrigerators looked like they had not been restocked in a long time, almost all completely bare of any inventory. To the right of the doorway was a counter with two registers sitting on it. One for ringing out customers making their purchases and the other looked like for buying lottery tickets. Both of them, along with the counter itself, had a thick layer of dust covering them all.

All the way to the back of the store sat another long counter with pictures and posters of car parts plastered all over it. Behind the counter, I could see a man sitting looking through a magazine; not once acknowledging me. *That must be the man I need to talk to.* As I made my way back to the counter, not once did the man look away from his magazine. He was a skinny man with a small face but a large mustache under his nose that covered his entire upper lip. He had on a faded green mechanic's work suit with patches of dark green that stretched across the chest with a stitched white colored name badge written in script that read *Ronald.*

After several moments of being ignored, I deliberately cleared my throat to get his attention. He did not move. So finally, after waiting long enough, I said, "Um, hello?"

Without looking away from his magazine, he replied, "Please stand in line, sir. I'll be with you as soon as it's your turn."

Confused, I asked back, "What do you mean? What line?" He let go of one side of the magazine and pointed to my left. I turned to see a small roped-off section of floor space made with six four-foot-tall black polls and red fabric rope for people to stand and wait to be helped; there was no one waiting. I turned back towards the man and said, "There's no one in line."

Without missing a beat, he responded, "Sir, as soon as I'm done with my current customers ahead of you, I will help you. Please stand in line until then," and then turned a page in his magazine. Waving my hands in the air and shrugging my shoulders, I annoyingly walked over to the roped-off line and stood staring at him.

After a few more moments and two more pages turned, he closed the magazine, placed it on the counter and called out, "NEXT!" I immediately looked up at the ceiling and began to whistle softly. Looking left then right, the man again called out, "NEXT!"

I looked back down from the ceiling, obnoxiously placed my hand on my chest in faked shock and said, "Oh me? I'm so sorry. I wasn't sure you were talking to me with all these people in here."

As I walked up to the counter, the man let out an audible sigh and asked, "What can I help you with?"

I held the folded white paper in my hand and said, "Hi, Ronald, is it? I'm here because I need to pick some things up."

"You placed an order here?" he frustratingly asked, reaching out and taking the folded paper from my hand.

"Well, it's not for me. I'm supposed to tell you I'm picking this stuff up for William?"

Ronald immediately froze. He slowly looked up at me and softly asked, "William sent you?"

Confused, I replied, "Yeah, he's just out there across the street," as I pointed over my shoulder behind me out the window. Ronald slowly leaned off to the side of the stool he was seated on to look around me to glimpse William across the street; still leaning up against his car, still smoking his cigarettes. As Ronald straitened back up in his seat I asked, "Is there a problem with me grabbing William's things?"

"No!" he quickly replied abruptly. "I'll go grab them now. P-please wait right here." Ronald hopped off his stool seeming to shrink nearly a foot. He then marched himself through a set of double doors off to the side of the counter that must have had a spring on them because they closed by themselves immediately. After only a couple of seconds, Ronald returned, quickly slamming himself through the doors, carrying three packages in his hands. Two of the packages were boxes colored in red and blue with white lettering, while the third box was colored in white and yellow with black lettering. Since I honestly knew nothing about cars, I had no clue what any of the items even were; or even if they were indeed car parts.

"Here we go. Everything Mr. William asked for. Will there be anything else today?" Ronald asked nervously.

"No, I don't think so. He said these were already taken care of?"

"Huh? Oh, oh yeah. Yup, no worries. They're all set."

This was just too weird; why was he suddenly acting like this over the mention of William's name? Something in me could not let it go. "I have to ask," I started, "is everything okay? Is there something I should know about William?"

He looked right at me with a horrific expression on his face. "You don't know William?"

"I honestly just met the guy minutes ago."

Ronald paused for a second and took another look out the window at William before he nervously laughed and replied, "Oh no, nothing at all. There's nothing you need to know about. Ronald is a great guy."

"Ronald? You're Ronald."

"Right, right you are. I am Ronald, no, not William, there's no William here. You have a wonderful day, okay?"

"Wait, Ronald…"

"HAVE A GREAT DAY!" He slowly sat down on his stool as his expression returned to its blank stare as he opened his magazine back up and once again began reading away, ignoring me. Before turning around, I glanced down at the magazine he was holding and saw that he was holding it upside down. *What is going on? Is this guy seriously ignoring me right now?*

"Any problems?" William asked me as he flicked the butt of the cigarette he had just finished to the side.

"No, no problems at all. I guess THIS is what the chicken was doing," I replied as I finished crossing the street carrying the three boxes. William chuckled as he stood up from leaning against the car. "So, where do you want me to put them?"

He reached into his car and made a pulling motion as the trunk of his car popped open. "Just place those boxes right in there."

I looked down at the trunk and asked, "There's not a body in there, is there?"

"I don't know. What do you think, Sam?" he replied as he walked over and grabbed the side of the lid of the trunk without breaking eye contact with me. He forcefully lifted the lid to reveal that the trunk was completely empty. I breathed another sigh as he asked, "You disappointed?"

Placing all three boxes into the trunk, I quickly stood up and said, "Not at all."

He closed the trunk once I was out of the way and said, "Well, I guess we can answer your questions now? So, what would you like to know?"

Walking around from the back of the car, I asked, "Where are we? Like, what state are we in?"

William let out that creepy chuckle that I've quickly grown to recognize as he replied, "I'd say you're in a state of confusion, aren't you? But then, perhaps you're in a state of realization of your situation. Or even a state of reflection, or reincarnation from who you were or what you are."

"Fuck, you sound like Shaelynn."

"You met Shaelynn?" he asked as his smile disappeared into a scowl. "She give you all that nonsense about *paths*?" he continued as he walked to the front of the car and closed the hood; the hinges let out a loud howl. *Was that a scream? Hold it together, don't let your imagination run wild.*

"Nothing any less confusing than what you're giving me now."

"Ah ha," he said under his breath as he gnawed his bottom lip, looking at me up and down. "I tell you what, why don't you hop in, and I'll take you where you need to go?" as he opened his driver's side door.

Just like that? I don't even know where I need to go, so how does he? Something just did not feel right about this whole situation. *Something doesn't feel right about this whole fucking day!* After a second of thinking to myself, I replied, "Ah, you know what? Maybe I'll just walk a bit more. Try to figure things out for myself, maybe?"

William shrugged his shoulders and got into his car, closing the door with a hard slam. Leaning out the door, he said, "The city isn't that far off. Maybe we'll run into each other again. And when you come to your senses, we can have a proper conversation." He leaned back in and started his car. The roar of the engine sounded like a professional race car, as a red and orange glow seemed to emanate out from under the undercarriage of the vehicle. Leaning back out from his car, he added, "I wouldn't think of asking Ronald any more questions, though." *What? How did he know?* I turned to look back at the gas station to see a large, closed sign hanging on the doors to the store. "He's done for today," William added as he drove away.

As I watched the car get further and further away, it seemed to almost make the fog dissipate as, just a short distance down the road, a city came visible through the fading thickness of the fog. I took one last glance over at Ronald's gas station as all the lights on command shut off and the entire property became silent. Just as soon as the lights went dead, the fog almost seemed to swallow the gas station, covering every inch of the property until it was no longer visible. I took a deep breath and said to myself, "I guess you know where you have to go next Sam. Sam. Hines."

Chapter Three

It seemed like it took me almost an hour to reach it, but once I did, I quickly realized that this city was huge. Everywhere I looked, there were gigantic steel gray structures that had the appearance that they reached out and touched the very top of the sky. Street after street, block after block, there was modernization everywhere. Traffic lights and crosswalks, automated electric advertisement boards, holographic commercials, it was amazing. Nothing even remotely resembling the broken-down gas station or crop fielded farm I left behind just hours ago.

On the ground level, every building had all kinds of stores and businesses from street corner to corner. From restaurants to bookstores, liquor stores and smoke shops, to toy stores and cafes; you name it and this city seemed to have it. Each business appeared like they were busy and packed with people, though I could not see clearly into any location since it seemed they all had a type of fogged tint to all their windows and doors. I could see shapes of people, but I could not tell them apart from one another.

The sidewalks, too, were filled with people coming and going in all different directions. Some were going into businesses and shops, while others exited carrying packages or bags with the logos of the shop they just left. Some of them sat at tables at multiple restaurants and cafes. Some just carried on with their private conversations within their groups while there were those that looked like they were heading off to work carrying briefcases or messenger bags stretched across their shoulders, dressed in expensive suits or very pricy dresses. All of them going about their lives so fast that I could not focus on any one person to talk to, and they were too busy to even notice me.

Vehicles filled all the parking spaces on both sides of every street where space permitted it as well. All different shapes, sizes, and colored cars and trucks from several manufacturers and not a one looking like William's beat up sedan. Buses drove up and down the streets stopping at zones to unload passengers, pick them up or a combination of both every couple minutes almost as if to keep the flow of people moving so the city sidewalks did not overflow. Though I could not remember any specific city I had ever been to before, I could honestly guarantee myself that this was the most efficient I had ever seen.

Since I woke up what seemed like hours ago, the smells of dirt, pollen, body odor and old engine oil were the only scents that lingered in my nostrils. Now, ever since entering the border of the city, the sweet smells of fresh fruits, frying meats and vegetables, baked breads, and freshly brewed coffees that my stomach began to make loud noises. *Like I could pay for anything to eat anyway,* I thought to myself, since I knew I had nothing in my pocket except for a dirty tie. No wallet, no ID, no money, nothing.

Thud!

The sudden impact on my back was hard and staggered me as I felt myself falling forward towards the ground. I reached out and grabbed hold of a street signpost near the edge of the sidewalk to prevent myself from completely falling to the ground. As I returned to a vertical stance, I immediately turned around to see what hit me when, to my dismay, a group of girls walked past me having a conversation, laughing, and giggling the entire time.

"Ah, you can just say excuse me if I'm in your way, ya know?" I questioned the group of girls as they kept walking. The three of them did not look like they were any older than their mid-twenties. One had long blonde hair while the other two both had brunette, one of which was a little of a lighter shade than the other. All three of them had on summer outfits showing off their legs with different colored sun dresses all stopping just below their rear ends. "Hey, you hear me?" Again, they gave me no response.

Frustrated, I rushed towards them and, as I caught up to the girls, I darted in front of the group and called out, "Hey!" This time the sharp thud hit me in my chest as two of the three girls I stood right in front of collided right into me and pushed me off to the side as they just kept walking and never stopping or interrupting their conversation. They did not push me out of their way; they just walked through me as if I did not even exist. *What the hell?*

To the left of the girls walking in the opposite direction coming towards me, a man on his phone walked past the girls, then turned his head back towards them, shook his head, then kept on walking towards me. The man looked like he was in his middle thirties, clean shaven, with short black hair that was styled into an almost combed back spike look and dark sunglasses covering his eyes. He had on a lightly faded button up baby bluc long-sleeved shirt with the sleeves rolled up past his elbows, a pair of faded dark gray jeans and dark brown loafers with a faded dark brown messenger bag slung over his shoulder that hung across his chest resting on the opposite hip. *Oh yeah, he saw something.*

"Can you believe them?" I called out to the gentleman as he sipped on his white and green paper coffee cup, smiling. "I tell ya, these girls nowadays sure have their heads…" I stopped myself as the man walked right past me without even acknowledging me. *What the hell?!* "Seriously, you too? What? Do I have shit on my face or something?" The man again never stopped or looked back towards me to reply. "Hey, your hair color is running down the back of your shirt!!" I called out in frustration, trying to get a response. And again, I got nothing.

A powerful sense of confusion quickly came over me. "Excuse me? Excuse me? Ma'am, excuse me? Sir, could I ask you a question?" Over and over, I tried to talk to anyone and everyone that walked past me, coming and going in either direction. "Excuse me? Could you please? Excuse me?" Again and again, not one person replied to me. *Am I a ghost? Am I dead? No! I can't be! I can feel, I can smell. Then what the hell is going on?*

Suddenly, another thought ran through my head. *Smell? Wait… SMELL!* I twisted around to see a sandwich shop right in front of me with its own customers walking in and out its doors. Several feet above the doorway attached to the wall was a neon sign with the shop's name brightly lit up with red letters. Reading from left to right, the sign spelled out the shop's name with the letters from large moving down to small, then all the way back up to large again with the last letter. Next to the door were three enormous windows with different logos of the different meats and cheeses used in their sandwiches while advertisements of specials filled up the spacing in between. Just like the other businesses I saw walking through the streets, I could see people inside, but I could not make out their details. I moved towards the opening of the shop while dodging the pedestrians walking in every direction until I walked through the door.

Inside, I immediately noticed the layout of the shop. The walls were colored with what looked like a fresh coat of paint on them. The walls were divided with a bright green on the top half while a bright red took the bottom. In the middle, a thin white line separated the colors from touching. Around the shop sat several tables with customers enjoying their food as they had conversations with each other; some just finishing as they got up from their seats while others had just sat down and plenty more in between. Light sounds of music could be heard coming from the far back right corner of the shop. To the left of me were three standing coolers with glass doors on them with a wide variety of drink selections to choose from, while there stood a fourth cooler with a selection of fresh salads and desserts. Directly in front of me sat the counter with three enormous TV screens hung overhead with the menu of the entire selection laid out so people in line could make their choices easier.

"Hey pal, what can I getcha?" I quickly glanced at the man standing behind the counter as he glared at me, waiting for my order. He was not a very tall man, but he was overly broad; his frame appeared to be very muscular, but you could see his large stomach behind his stained white tee shirt and white apron. His white ball cap sat backwards on his head, just barely covering his short crew cut hair. I could not find a name tag anywhere to know his name.

"Oh me, yeah," I replied as I slid up to the counter, still glancing at the menus. "Yeah, I actually just have questions."

"About what?" he quickly said back. "We got all kinds of a meats an' cheeses you can get on ya hoagie. Hot, cold, you want it toasted? We got all kinds of a sauces, fresh ripe tomatoes, sweet peppas, what? We got you covered!"

Behind him were half a dozen workers all at different stations making everyone's food but without hesitation they all almost on command shouted out, "GOT YOU COVERED!

"Yeah, um, actually no. I have questions about this city?"

"City? We make hoagies here, pal. So, what can I get ya, pal?"

"Yeah, I just want to ask you a question."

"About what? You don't see somethin' on the menu up there," he said as he pointed at the menu.

"No, I see the menu, but I have a question about something else."

"What else is there? If it ain't on the menu, we don't carry it, so what can I get…"

I cut him off, shouting, "I don't want a hoagie!" I glanced my eyes over to behind the man in front of me and I see the half a dozen workers that were in the background all had stopped what they were doing, and all had their heads turned towards us and were now staring at me. *What have I done?*

"You don't want a hoagie?" I return my eyes back at the man in front of me. "What the hell ya here for, then?"

"Look, I'm sorry, but I need to know where…" He cut me off again.

"I told you if it ain't on the menu we don't got it."

"I just want to know where I am."

"Where you are is in the best hoagie shop on the block where we gotcha covered."

"GOT YOU COVERED!" shouted the half a dozen workers again.

Are they for real? "No, what city is this? What state?"

I can tell the clerk was getting frustrated because he began waving his hand in the air while shaking his head as he said, "If you ain't orderin' get outta here so I can help the next customer behind ya."

Stepping to the side to let the customer behind me step up to the counter, I asked, "Can't you give me any info at all?"

"If you want info, you gots to go to the Central Info Station," he replied as he pointed towards the door. "Now get outta here!"

I quickly turned and walked out of the door. *Okay, I need to go to the Central Info Station to get answers.* Suddenly, a blanket of dread fell over my shoulders. *Wait, where IS the Central Info Station?* Then it hit me as I slowly turned around. "Fuck, I gotta go back in there." As I walked back into the sandwich shop, I walked right up to the counter and before I could say anything, the clerk behind the counter stopped me.

"Hey pal, what can I getcha?"

Is this guy for real? "Hey, sorry to come back in here," he cuts me off.

"Oh, no problem at all. Welcome back. Everyone always comes back when they realize we got them covered."

"GOT YOU COVERED!"

"What is happening? No, I was just in here and you told me about the Central Info Station?"

The clerk looked at me, confused and a little annoyed, as he replied, "Man, I've never seen ya before now. So, what hoagie can I getcha?"

My anger boiled up under my skin, "I don't want a damn hoagie, just an answer to my question!" Again, the workers in the back behind the clerk all stopped and turned their heads towards me. *Dude, what have you done?*

With a furious tone to his voice, the clerk intoned, "What do ya mean you don't want a hoagie?"

"Hold that thought," I replied simultaneously, holding my hand up with my index finger pointing out as I turned towards the door and ran out of the shop. As the door closed behind me, I began thinking to myself, *okay, am I really going to do this?* Looking up at the sky, I started counting to myself. *Three, two, one.* I turned around and walked back into the shop a third time and got right into line.

Without missing a beat, the clerk behind the counter looked at me and called out, "Hey pal, what can I getcha?"

As I stepped up to the counter, I answered, "Hey man, afternoon. Real quick before I order. Which way is it to the Central Info Station?"

With a smile he replied, "Hey no problem, it's at the center of the city. Just head right outta here and you'll be on ya way. So, what can I getcha?"

"Hey thanks, I appreciate that."

I turned and walked towards the door when I heard the clerk call out, "Hey, ya gonna order somethin'?"

As I reached the door, I turned back and sarcastically replied, "Nah, man, I never eat here. You guys don't HAVE ME COVERED!" As soon as the words left my lips, the music instantly stopped playing as I once again saw the workers in the back behind the clerk stop what they were doing and turn their heads towards me in silence. With a smile on my face, I went to walk out the door but immediately froze in place. As my eyes glanced towards the other customers eating in the shop, I quickly realized that all of them had also stopped everything they were doing and were staring at me in silence. Every single eyeball was now glaring at me with anger burning from within. "Ah fuck," I said as I turned and ran out the door, turning to the right and racing up the street.

Once I felt I had gotten enough distance away from the shop, I slowed down to catch my breath. As I felt my fast-beating heart in my chest slowing down, I noticed strange things all around me. The buses were coming and going, dropping people off and picking them up, but not one car had moved. Not one person had gotten into a car, no one had started a car, and no one pulled into a parking spot, nothing. Just the buses were on the streets and nothing more. Then on the buses themselves, I could clearly see into the buses, but I could not see the passengers. I could see shapes of people, but I could not make out any of their details until they got off the bus. The same with the people getting on; no matter what they looked like as soon as they stepped foot onto the bus, all color and distinguishing features just seemed to disappear and just a dark outline was left.

Why didn't I see this before? What the hell is going on in this city? I started looking around for any signs or directions or even a posted map that could point me in the right direction to lead me towards the center of the city. I at last had a clue and knew I needed to find the Central Info Station to finally get answers. As I looked back and forth, I could locate nothing that was helpful. Turning around, I suddenly noticed a woman standing a short distance down an alley in between two of the buildings. She seemed to stand in the shadows, out of sight, but she was noticeable. With all the weird stuff going on in this town, I thought nothing of it and turned away before I heard a faint, "Hey!"

Turning back towards the woman, I heard another, "Hey," only this time she was now walking towards me with a stiff determination in her stride. Concerned, I took a step back away from the charging woman as she closed in on me and grabbed hold of my shirt with both of her hands as she shouted, "You can see me? You can see me?"

"Yes, yes, I can see you!" Her face, which had showed grief, quickly changed to an almost hopeful joy as she began to tear up. "Wait, you can see me and understand me?" I asked her, puzzled. With her tearful smile, she nods at me without letting go. As I stared at her for only a few seconds, a thought popped in my head that I could not shake. *Why do I know you?*

Chapter Four

A thought I had in my head was bothering me for several minutes, so I just had to ask. "What happened to your shoes?" The moment she confronted me on the street, we quickly made our way back to the alley from where she emerged. It was obvious that she was not from this city, just from her demeanor. She did not have the same seemingly carefree attitude that the other citizens had; and that she could see me.

Her behavior led me to believe that whatever happened to me had happened to her as well. She was a short woman, early to middle thirties. Other than her bare feet, she was fully clothed wearing purple yoga pants, and a black t-shirt and from what I could tell a black sports bra supporting her small breasts since the strap stuck out ever so slightly from the back of her shirt. *Damn it!*

Stop peaking at her like that, you creep! Yet the small spots of dirt and sweat all over her were a good indicator that she more than likely woke up on the ground as well. "I don't know. When I woke up, they were missing."

I still could not shake the feeling that I knew her, but for the life of me, I just could not remember where from. Though not just a few short hours ago, I could not even remember my name. I studied her face, trying to jump start some type of memory in my head. Her hair was a brunette with strands of what looked like dirty blonde pulled back into a ponytail with a red hair tie. She was incredibly attractive; she had green eyes with a small nose that had a tiny stud piercing in her left nostril, and a slight number of freckles that covered her nose and either side of her cheeks just under her eyes and thin lips for her mouth. *What do you want a date you ass? Stop it!*

"I don't know where I am, how I got here, nothing! All I know is my first name and even that I didn't remember right away." The small streaks on her face let me know she had been crying before, and it looked like it was happening again as she panicked.

"Hey, hey, it's okay," I said as I tried to console her. "Trust me; I know what you're going through. Here, let's start with that. What's your name?"

Wiping her tears with her hand, she looked at me and whimpering said, "Gina."

"Gina? Okay, good," I said to her with excitement, but her name did not sound familiar to me, so I still didn't know how I knew her. "My name is Sam. So, I guess we both are suffering from the same issue. I woke up in a field on what I guess was a farm, but my memory did eventually start to come back."

She wiped more tears from her face, but at least was calming down. She took a deep breath and asked me, "You woke up on a farm? I woke up in this city, just a couple of blocks away."

In the city? How did she get so lucky if you could even call it luck? "Do you remember where exactly that was?" I asked her curiously. "I'm not sure if it will help with our memories, but it wouldn't hurt." She nodded, sniffing back more of her tears. "Okay, but the first thing we need to do is get you something on your feet."

I turned around and started walking back towards the street when Gina called out, "Where are you going?" as she chased after me.

"This town is full of stores and shops, so there has to be a shoe store around here somewhere." As I got to the end of the alleyway, I started looking at each store front until I noticed a shoe store at the corner of the opposite street from us. “Look, there’s one over there.”

She grabbed my arm and pulled back on it while she said, “I don’t have any money, and how am I supposed to pay for them? Are you buying them?”

I did not really think of that. “No, when I woke up, I had no wallet either,” I answered her before looking back at the store. “We’ll think of something. Come on.” I grabbed her hand and pulled her behind me as we made our way through the crowds of people until we reached the crosswalk. I could feel her squeeze tightly against my grip, not to try and pull away but more like she didn’t want to lose me. Once clear of the alley, we crossed the street with other pedestrians until we stood outside the store.

I do not know how we are going to pay for this, but she can’t walk around in her bare feet, I thought to myself. Standing in front of the store, the two glass doors kept opening and closing automatically as customers walked in and out. On either side of the doors were giant glass windows where you could see people walking around inside the store, but just like all the other businesses, you could not see any details of the people. I took a deep breath and went to walk in when I felt another tug on my arm.

“Are you sure about this? These people don’t even notice we exist. How are we supposed to buy anything?”

"Have you actually tried going into any store yet?"

"No," she answered. "When I couldn't get anyone to help or talk to me, I just stayed hidden."

"It seems like the people that actually work in the stores can see us and talk to us." I paused a couple of seconds before continuing. "But even that seems to be limited. All I know for sure is that besides you, everyone here is not normal." The glass doors opened as I walked forward and the both of us entered.

The store was massive. Glass windows spread all along the exterior that faced the intersecting street corner with another entrance and exit door on the right wall in the middle of the windows. The far back and left wall that were not parallel to the street just had what seemed like an endless number of shelves with all kinds of shoes on them. In front of the walls, free standing shelves stuck out at angles every four feet, one after the other all the way down the length of the store, with more mirroring their position on the opposite side of the store in front of the windows. At all four sides of the store was a brown carpet with aisles of large white tile that formed into a giant cross or plus sign that met at the center of the store. Placed at the center, a large counter that shaped itself into a sizeable square was where the registers for the store were located. On all four sides of the counter, customers stood in lines waiting patiently to be checked out. Within the square, there were about six employees assisting customers.

I realized that the store was divided into sections between men's and women's footwear. Each section was then separated by styles between dress shoes, lounge and fashion, slippers, athletic sneakers and so on. At the end of some of the freestanding shelves were end caps that had selections of athletic clothes, like tee shirts, jackets, socks, and shorts that would match with selections of different footwear. *Best place to start,* I thought to myself.

We slowly made our way over to the women's athletic section where there were a decent number of customers shopping, but it also had a wide selection of footwear for Gina to pick from. As we made our way over, I eyed around four to five more employees walking around helping customers, so I tried to make sure not to make eye contact with any of them. "Find a pair," I said softly to her, pointing slightly at the shelves while trying to monitor all the employees.

"Which ones should I get?"

"Preferably ones that fit your feet." She looked at me, frustrated with my answer to her question. "Sorry," I whispered. "It doesn't matter. Just find something comfortable in your size and get yourself some socks, too." As I glanced over at the end cap with some of the athletic clothes, I added, "Grab a shirt or jacket, too." Just as I finished my sentence, I saw an employee walking over towards me, so I quickly walked away from Gina to cut him off.

"Hello sir, how can I help you today?" he asked me. He looked like he was maybe in his late teens or early twenties, medium height but well built, like he played a lot of sports in school. His uniform comprised of a navy-blue polo shirt, black pants and what I could assume was the latest and hottest sneakers with their bright colors of blues, reds, yellows, and black splashed stripes covering its white base. His name badge hung from a lanyard that dangled from around his neck.

"Yeah, hi," I said, glancing at his name badge. "George, is it? I have a question about those shoes you got on." He glanced down at his footwear before looking back up at me. "I'm sure those are good for running, correct?"

"Why yes, they are. These are our version eight nineties, and they are good for all outdoor sports."

"I see, but are they good for dancing?" His facial expression immediately changed from helpful to complete confusion. "I tell you what. Why don't you show me where they are?" He turned around and started walking away to lead me to where the shoes were on the shelf. As I followed close behind him, I glanced back at Gina to see her trying to frantically put shoes on. She glanced up to see me staring at her. I mouthed, “Calm down,” hoping she got the message and stop drawing attention to herself.

After a few minutes of talking with George about all there was to know about shoes, I saw Gina standing off to the side, trying to get my attention. “So, should we get you a pair of our eight nineties for you today, sir?”

“Excuse me?” I said, as I quickly looked at him.

“Should we get you a pair?”

“Hmm, they are kinda expensive, aren’t they?”

“They are a higher price than most, but if you compare the better material they are made from and the longevity you’ll get from them, they are totally worth it.”

I glanced back as Gina was now slightly hopping up and down, nervously waiting for me. I looked back at George and said, “I tell you what. Let me think on it and I’ll just take what she’s getting today.”

He glanced up towards Gina and smiled. “Okay, sir, I’ll tell you what. Here is my card. When you’re ready, just come see me and I’ll get you taken care of.” I looked at the card for a second, then took it from his hand. The card had his name on it, along with the store's logo and address printed on it. I quickly glanced at the address to see if it said the city and state, but all that was printed was the street name, nothing more. *Damn it, worth a try.*

When he walked away, I approached Gina while looking at the jacket she had draped over the top of a pack of socks with one pair taken out and the box the sneakers came out of. As I walked up to her, I could see the jacket she grabbed matched her yoga pants. I took the shoebox and tossed the pack of socks into the box. "Here," I said as I handed her the jacket. "Take the tag off of this and put it on."

She took the jacket from my hand and pulled the price tag off from the sleeve before handing me the tag back and putting it on. As she zipped the jacket closed, I walked over to get into a line as she followed me. "Sam, what are you doing?" she whispered frantically. *I have no idea.*

"Just follow my lead."

After only maybe a minute, we heard someone call out. "I can help you over here, sir," George said as he waved us over to the register he was standing at.

As we walked over, I could see Gina panicking. I turned to her and whispered, "Go walk out."

"What?" she loudly whispered.

"Just do it." She walked around me and started making her way towards the door. George followed her with his eyes when I spoke out, "Oh, she's just gonna wear those out. I got all the tags here." I sat the shoebox on the counter as George looked down at the box and opened it to see the pack of socks and the tag for the jacket before nodding and smiling in approvement.

He started scanning the items up into the register as I tapped lightly on the counter with my mind racing. When he got to the shoebox and scanned it, he paused and started staring at the box, confused. "Is there an issue?"

"You said your girlfriend was wearing the new pair, right?" I nodded as he continued. "Where's her old pair?"

"Oh," I said as I paused, trying to think of something. "She had a cheap pair of flip-flops that broke from *that* store on the other side of town, so we just threw them away."

He looked at me for a couple seconds, then smiled and replied, "Oh, I know that store. They do have cheap shoes. Tell her she's better off just shopping here with us." *Fuck me, that really worked?*

George finished scanning the shoebox and hit the total on the register, but before he could tell me the dollar amount, I reached behind me to my empty back pocket and said, "Shit. She's got my wallet. Let me go grab it really quick." I turned and started walking away towards the door where Gina stood waiting for me. As I got near her, I quickly whispered, "Walk out now."

She turned around and rushed out the door ahead of me as I heard George behind me shout, "Sir!"

Once we hit the street, I heard the door close hard behind me. Gina stood in front of me, but she was looking at the store with a scared expression on her face. As I turned around, the previous movement of all the customers inside the store that you could see through the windows was now motionless. Inside the building, all you could see was shape after shape of black shadows that looked like they were staring at us. I looked down at the business card still in my hand that George gave me, only now it was completely blank. When I looked back up, all the shadow shapes were now lined up in the windows, all next to each other like they were stalking us. I dropped the card as it disintegrated before it hit the ground.

Placing my hand on Gina's back, I said to her, "Let's get out of here."

Chapter Five

I was not sure what I was trying to look for. I was just hoping that something would jump out at me if I spotted it. Unfortunately, that just was not the case. We were standing in the back-alley intersection area of a cluster of industrial buildings, out of sight of the major streets. This was nothing like the primary area where all the locals in the city were.

The area was cold and damp, no lighted signs, no stores or restaurants of any kind. There were no buses carrying passengers to and from the area. In fact, there were no people at all. Just large concrete and brick buildings, some with docking bays for delivery trucks to load and unload goods. Off to the far left were three boxed trucks sitting parked with a red and green logo on the side that looked familiar to me for some reason, but I quickly pushed it out of my mind since I knew if it were local to this city then I would not understand what the business was. I walked around looking at the walls of the buildings, the light that crept in from the sun in between each of them casting shadows, the oily stains, and piles of dirt on the ground, and the spot where Gina said she had woken.

"And you said that you have no memory of anything before you woke up?" I asked her, even though I knew she was getting frustrated.

"Yes! That's what I said for the tenth time. Can you please stop asking me?"

I knew I was pushing her too hard. "I'm sorry Gina," I said as I walked over and sat down on a concrete docking bay sticking out in front of a large garage door. "I guess I thought that if you remembered any more that maybe that would spark something in my memory."

She walked over and jumped up onto the docking bay to sit next to me. "You can't force me to remember something that just isn't there." She paused for a second before continuing, "But I get it. I'm scared; this city is…"

I cut her off and said, "This city is bat shit crazy." She looked at me and started laughing a little, allowing her to calm down.

"So, what do we know about this place? What are we going to do now?"

I started looking around for a couple of seconds before I answered her. "Well, there apparently is this Central Info Station at the center of the city that can give us a bigger idea of where it is we are, and maybe allow us to get out of here." She looked away as I continued. "Though the way this city and these people have been acting, I'm not even sure if that's going to lead us anywhere."

Gina took a deep breath before she asked, "What other choice do we have?"

I jumped down off the dock before I replied, "Well, I'll tell you this; if a better idea reveals itself, we can do that instead." She nods her head and jumps down off the dock as well. "We better get going," I said as I walked away from the area. When I did not hear her walking behind me, I stopped and turned to see Gina as she stood and stared at the ground where she found herself. "You, okay?"

"Yeah," she said with a little tremble in her voice. "I just never want to come back here again." She jogged to catch up with me as we walked side by side. After several minutes, she turned to me and asked, "What about you?"

"What about me?"

"Well, do you remember anything other than your name?"

I immediately shook my head. I didn't want to tell her, even though I don't know from where or how, I couldn't shake the thought that we knew each other. So, I kept it to myself. "You were lucky. You knew who you were when you woke up. Me, I didn't even know that. It took a bit before that came back to me."

Her eyes opened wide. "That must have been terrifying?"

"It was."

She waited a minute before she asked, "Where did you say you woke up at? Was it close by?"

I shook my head again. "No, I found the city after I woke up. I was in the middle of a field on a farm on the outskirts of the city. I don't know how long I was walking for, but it felt like for hours until I made it. Wondering about this city, you wouldn't think there'd be nothing but farmland surrounding it. But that's all that is there. As a matter of fact, since you woke up back in that alley, you haven't had the chance to see the fog yet, have you?"

She looked at me, confused. "The fog?"

"Yeah, there's this weird fog that seems to surround the entire land of not only the farmland, but the city as well. And it's not normal fog either." When her confused expression did not leave her face, I continued. "I'm not really sure how to describe it. It looks like just a thick fog you'd see on the surface of a lake on a chilly morning; gray, cold, wet, and hard to see through. But then there are parts of it that are different. It was hot and had this almost terrible feeling to it. Almost as if the fog was filled with emotions of anger."

Her facial expression led me to think she did not believe me. "That sounds improbable."

"It's true," I replied, laughing. "In fact, out of miles of fields, there was one old lady that lived in a small house in the middle of everything that led me towards the city."

"Wait, she led you? She told you to come here?"

"Well, she didn't actually 'lead' me here. She told me I'd have to make decisions on where I wanted to go and deal with the consequences, or something to that aspect."

Gina quickly spoke, "But she actually talked to you? She saw you and everything?"

"Yes," I answered, smiling at all her questions. "Her name was Shaelynn. She wasn't the only person I met out there, either. There was this guy William, too. He was not so helpful."

"Really? Why do you say that?"

"I'm not sure, but I just got this really creepy vibe off him. Plus, he was fucking scary."

"Scarier than what we've seen?" she asked.

"By far. And from what I've seen, the people that will actually talk to you they seem to be afraid of him too." With that, Gina wrapped her arms around herself slowly, as if she were trying to warm herself up from suddenly getting cold. *Maybe it's best to stop talking about it for now.*

When Gina led me to the area where she woke up, it took us a little over ten minutes to get there once we left the main street. So, I figured that I would have around the same time to think about what we were going to do once we returned to the main street. After about five minutes had gone by, I was so deep in thought about our next move that I did not realize that Gina was talking to me until she slapped me on the arm. "Ouch," I called out, but as I was speaking, she was shushing me.

"Shh," she whispered with her index finger against her lips. "Do you hear that?" I looked up into the air, trying to listen carefully. Suddenly, I heard something. An opening in between two of the buildings revealing another alley led away to the right where the sound was coming from.

I took a couple of steps to the right towards the alley when Gina grabbed my hand. "What are you doing?" she whispered with her eyes wide open.

"I'm trying to figure out what that is," I replied, whispering as well.

"In this fucking city, who the hell knows what anything could be?" She pulled my hand towards our original path ahead and added, "Let's just go and forget about it."

I looked forward at the alley in front of us before I heard the strange sound again to our right, pulling my attention towards it once more. I could see she was scared, but there was something about the sound that was drawing me towards it. I squeezed her hand back and whispered, "I want to know what that is. We'll check it out quick and then we'll move on." She grabs hold of my hand now with both of hers as she shook her head, trying to convince me not to go. I squeezed her hands tightly while with my free hand I motioned for her to follow me while slightly pulling her behind me.

We did not have to walk extremely far before we heard the strange sound more and more. It did not take long before we realized that the sound was a person, a man's voice, to be exact. *What is he yelling about?* A little closer, we quickly realized that he was not yelling, he was screaming.

As we emerged from the alley, there was a stack of exceptionally large shipping crates off to the left, so we quickly ducked behind them to not be seen. Before too long, we saw a man down at the far end running in our direction. He was a gray-haired man wearing a heather gray polo shirt with black pants and black loafers as he struggled to stay upright while he ran. He kept looking behind himself as he frantically sprinted, calling out, "Please, no! Leave me alone!"

He suddenly collided with something as he was knocked over and landed hard in an enormous pile of trash bags and debris. "God no! No!" he screamed out as he struggled to pull himself up. I felt Gina's grip on my hand tighten as I kept watching. As the man freed himself from most of the debris, he was suddenly looking up at what knocked him to the ground. Surrounding the man were three gray shaped figures. They looked human, but there were no distinguishing features, no clothes, no facial features, just tall gray figures. The man looked up at them and said with fear in his voice, "I'm sorry, I'm so sorry. I didn't mean it!"

One of them walked towards him as the man screamed out, "Don't hurt me, please!" The gray figure kneeled in front of the man slowly. Since it had no visible eyes, I could not tell what it was looking at. Out of nowhere, something protruded from its hand as it stabbed the man in the leg. The man screamed out in horrific agony as blood leaked out from under his leg; the object sticking in his leg must have gone all the way through.

Without thinking, I went to stand up when Gina pulled me back. "What in the god fuck are you doing?" she hissed at me.

"He needs help."

"We don't even know what those things are. We don't know why they were chasing him." The man screams out again.

"It doesn't matter Gina; he doesn't deserve this." Her eyes slightly filled with tears while she looked at me with an expression of anger; I could tell she was terrified. "I'm going to help him. Stay here, out of sight." I pulled my hand from her grasp as I ran out from behind the crates and charged at them at full speed. The man's screaming distracted the figures because they did not notice me running towards them.

As I got closer, I noticed off to the left, sitting in a row, was a stack of metal garbage cans. As I ran by, I reached out and grabbed the lid off of one of them and kept running. Once I got close, I screamed out, "Hey!" and watched to see which one turned first. When the gray figure to the far left turned towards me, at full speed and strength, I pulled back and swung forward with the lid, striking it square in the head as it staggered backwards. I turned towards the one in the middle and pulled back to strike it, but it immediately reached out and grabbed me by the arm. In one motion, it pulled me hard and threw me across the alley. The lid flew from my hand as I slammed into a wall before falling into a pile of garbage. Striking the ground, my vision became blurry, and darkness filled my eyes as different images flashed through my mind as I tried to shake the impact off. It was only a moment before my vision could bring me back to the alley.

It took me a second to regain my composure as I looked up at the gray figure walking towards me. When I went to stand up, I felt my hand brush against a piece of wood. Once the gray figure was hovering over the top of me, I started to stand, then grabbed the piece of wood tightly and swung up. The piece of wood was much larger than I thought, but it struck the gray figure in the stomach then scraped up and contacted under its chin. The board cracked from the impact and part of the end splintered as the strange creature fell backwards to the ground.

I looked down at the figure that had stabbed the man and quickly realized that it was not an object that it used to stab the man, but it *was* its hand. It looked like the right hand of the gray figure altered or morphed itself into a small sword or knife at the end of its arm, which it used in its attack. It pulled its hand from the man's leg as it made a wet squish sound. He screamed out in pain once it left his body; blood poured from the open wound. The figure then stood up and turned towards me as I stood in front of it a few feet away, holding the piece of wood in the air like it was a bat. It looked down to the ground where the figure that I struck with the board lay twitching and convulsing until it came to a sudden stop.

The standing gray figure in front of me then raised its head, looking at me once again. "Come on, you piece of shit!" I screamed, trying to provoke the figure. From its blank, featureless face, a pair of glowing red eyes glared at me as it seemed to puff and flex itself making it look bigger.

Suddenly, from far behind me, I hear, "Sam! Look out!" I turned to see the third figure that I hit on the head with the garbage can lid was now walking towards me. I adjusted my stance and swung the board towards it, striking it hard. A loud thud echoed from the strike as its head snapped to the side with a sick twist before it collapsed to the ground once more. The top of the board broke completely from the strike and now had a splintered end at the edge of the board. The figure, just like the other one, hit the ground hard and started convulsing until it stopped.

"Sam!" I heard Gina scream out again, but it was too late. I felt a sudden sharp pain in the back of my arm as I realized that the lone gray figure had stabbed me in the back of it. I turned around to see it pulling its arm back to stab at me again when suddenly the man on the ground kicked his good leg out and struck the figure at the bottom of its ankle. It stumbled ever so slightly off balance, but it was the opening I needed. I swung my good arm that was still holding onto the board around and came across the front of the gray figure, slashing it across its chest with the sharp edge of the board.

A large gash opened as black goop leaked out from the wound. The gray figure let out a horrific scream that hurt my ears as it staggered backwards from the hit. Without warning, it leaped into the air at an incredible speed as I could barely follow it with my eyes as it disappeared over the roof of the building several stories up. I dropped the board and fell to my knees, trying to catch my breath.

As I heard Gina running up behind me, the man tries to crawl out of the garbage he had been laying in for the last several minutes. "Help me!" he cried out as Gina stops behind me and grabs my shoulder.

"I'm okay," I immediately said as I stood and walked over to the man with her close behind me.

Gina stops the man from trying to stand up. "Don't move. Let me look at this first." She looks down and grabs the slice in his pant leg and pulls it outward, tearing the fabric and exposing his injury. The gray figure did indeed stab right through the man's leg as the wound gushed blood from the top and bottom. "I need to find something to tie this off," she said as she frantically looked around the garbage.

I suddenly remembered and called out, "Here!" as I reached into my back pocket and pulled out my tie. She snatched it from my hand and immediately wrapped it around the man's leg just above the injury and tied it tight. She continued to tear the rest of his pant leg off and wrapped that around the gashes to stop the bleeding. The man kept crying out in pain every couple of seconds as Gina tied the makeshift bandage tight.

"This isn't going to be good enough; he needs a hospital or if I had a proper med kit."

I stood up and remembered those three boxed trucks earlier back. "Wait here. I'll hopefully be right back."

"Where are you going?" she angrily called out.

"I'm gonna see if those boxed trucks have a med kit in them."

"Wait, no!" she immediately yells out. "What if that fucking thing comes back?"

"I'll be right back," I assured her as I started running back towards the trucks. It did not take me too long before I came back upon the trucks still parked. I ran up to the first truck and pulled on the handle to find it locked. *Fuck, I left the board back with them.* I quickly glanced around and found a small piece of brick lying on the ground off to the side.

Picking it up, I turned towards the truck and threw it at the window of the driver's side door, shattering it instantly. I climbed up and unlocked the door from the inside as the door swung open. I searched frantically around inside the cab, trying to find a med kit, but found nothing. Picking up the brick piece, I jumped out and went to the second truck and broke the window of that door with the brick. Luckily, I did not have to repeat the damage to the third truck because as I searched inside the cab of the second truck; I found a med kit under the passenger seat.

With the med kit in hand, it did not take me long to run back to where Gina and the man were still lying on the ground. Running up to Gina, I handed her the med kit and said, out of breath, "Here, I hope this has what you need."

She quickly opened it up and, after rummaging through a couple of items, calls out, "Yes, this is perfect." She pulled out several items and laid them out in front of her as she undid the tie around the man's leg.

Still moaning in pain, the man asked her, "Do you know what you're doing?"

She looked right at him and answered, "Yes I do, don't worry about a thing." She then turned her head towards me and continued, "Though I'm not sure how I know."

Chapter Six

Night quickly made its way over us as the long day that finally seemed to end. The alley we were hiding in darkened as the light left the sky. Whatever those gray figures were, the one that got away did not return. The other two that I had killed appeared to have just vanished into dust, leaving small shadow stains on the pavement. Everything that happened today just brings more questions and does not provide a single answer in its wake.

It did not take Gina long before she was able to stop the bleeding from the man's leg, but I could tell that he was in terrible shape. The medical kit I had found in one of the delivery trucks contained not only medicine but the alcohol and material for her to make stitches to close off his wounds, yet she kept repeating under her breath that he was going to need a hospital soon to prevent infection. It was not long after she stitched the second wound that the man passed out from the pain. He was breathing, so we knew he was still alive. When she finished, we constructed a makeshift bed of cardboard boxes and scraps of cloth for him to rest. Soon after, Gina sat next to him to monitor his breathing, making sure he stayed with us. Meanwhile, I left the two of them by hiding out of sight behind the building to gather myself and my thoughts on this entire day. Down the side of the building, I found a small stack of crates and boxes to sit on.

The one thing that haunted me was the fact that not only did I bring myself to fight whatever those creatures were, but that I killed them. I still could remember nothing about my life other than my name but ending another living thing's life just seemed unimaginable. *It had to be done. I didn't have a choice. They were going to kill that man. I had no choice.*

The other thing that I could not forget was the images that seemed to have pushed their way into my thoughts during the fight. I had no recollection of any of the places or things in any of them. But the one thing that seemed to stick out the most was the image of a shadow, of a person. But the more I thought about it and tried to remember anything of detail about them, the more the image in my head clouded. My thoughts distracted me so much that I had not noticed Gina walking up behind me.

"How's he doing?" I asked her, but I got no response. She started to forcefully undo the crude bandage I had made from one of my sleeves that I had tied around the gash in my arm. "Hey, how is he?" I asked again and once again received silence. I could tell by her expression she was upset over something. As she finished removing my bandage, I pulled my arm away from her and turned myself towards her and asked, "What's wrong with you?" She took a step back, waited a second, then stepped forward and punched me right in the face. "What the… OW!" I called out, covering my cheek with my hand. *It's not that painful, but she does have a mean right hook.*

"Are you out of your goddamn mind? What the hell is wrong with you?" she said to me angrily. She was not yelling, but I knew then that she wanted to scream at me.

"With me?" I replied, rubbing my cheek.

"How dare you pull a stunt like that shit," she continued while waving her arms in the air.

"What was I supposed to do? If I had stayed hidden, that man might be dead."

She stepped forward and pointed her index finger right in my face. "And if anything had gone slightly different, then you *BOTH* would be dead!" I began to understand why she was upset as she continued. "You are the only person I have met in this fucked up city that actually helped me because we both are lost. We need each other, and it was selfish of you to put yourself in harm's way. We still know next to nothing about where we are, where we came from, or anything! For all we know, we are in fucking hell!"

I knew she had a point, but I also knew I did the right thing. "Okay, I get it. I'm sorry. But I couldn't just watch those things possibly kill him."

"Yeah, well, he might have deserved it for all we know." She turned her back and took a couple of steps away from me before stopping and just standing there with her arms crossed. I understood her anger, but also, I knew right then and there she would have been fine if I had died. She obviously knows more than she realizes, and I had this feeling she would have figured out how to take care of herself. But I also knew she had a point, and we needed to be more careful until we had a better understanding of our environment and situation.

She turned back around and slowly walked back to me. I raised my hands in defense, making her sigh slightly. "Put your hands down dumb-ass, I'm not gonna hit you again," she said as she placed both her hands on top of mine and pushed them back down. "I'm sorry I yelled at you like that; I guess I get angry when I get scared."

"I get it," I replied as I pulled her hands so that she sat down on the crate next to me. "I get why you're mad at me. Looking at the situation, that was completely stupid of me. I guess I just reacted instead of thinking first." I took a deep breath and sighed while letting go of her hands. "I don't know. Maybe that's who I am; maybe that's a part of my personality that I can't remember. I mean, look at you; maybe you're a doctor or something like that."

"Maybe," she replied hesitantly.

"I know we need to be careful around here," I continued, "or at least until we get a better understanding of exactly where or what this city is. But we can't just play it safe and hide all the time or we might never find a way out." I saw she wanted to say something, but I cut her off before she could get a word out. "But I will promise you this. We'll stick together until the end. We will help each other make it out of here. And we'll decide together, okay?"

"Okay," she said with a bit of a side smile on her face as she turned me around so that I was facing away from her as she began looking at my arm. The sting from the alcohol she used on my slash wound stung sharply, but not for long. Soon after she finished cleaning my arm, she redressed it with a fresh large bandage that must have been inside the med kit. Once she finished, she turned me back around to face her once more before she continued. "But just so we're clear, I will not stop being scared just because you say so. There's a difference between being brave and being reckless. You don't need to check with me to make a choice; you're a grown man."

"I understand," I said as she stood up.

"That should be good for now. You're lucky that thing didn't take off the entire arm."

I stood up as well and replied, "Don't I know it? I guess we should go check on our friend back there, huh?" She nodded and turned around as we both walked back towards the injured man. As we walked, I felt a smirk come across my face as I lightly asked, "So you were scared for me, huh?"

She quickly whipped her head around and stated with a fist, "You want another shot to that pretty face of yours?"

An urge came over me. I could not resist as I replied, "You think I'm pretty, huh?" Without hesitation, she cocked her arm back as she prepared to punch me yet again. I placed both hands up in front of me to block her while calling out, "Just kidding, just kidding!"

She let her fist open back up as she started walking ahead of me. Under her breath, I heard her say, "Ass."

Once we emerged from the side of the building, we saw that the man was awake and trying to sit himself upright. Gina quickly walked up to him while putting her hand on his shoulder, trying to get him to stay put. The second he saw me, he said, "Oh my lord, there you are," as he tried to straighten himself up more.

"Hey, hey. You need to stay still and not try to move so much," Gina quickly instructed.

I shuffled myself around to the other side of where he lay and sat down on the ground next to him. "How are you feeling?" I asked.

He smiled, chuckled a little and answered, "Like I got a giant hole in my leg." *A joke, that's a good sign, I think.* He continued by adding, "But that's a price I'm happy to pay for you saving my life. Thank you." He extended his hand out and gestured that he wanted to shake mine.

I reached out and obliged him by shaking his hand back. "I'm Sam, this here is Gina."

He turned towards Gina after setting my hand free and stuck his hand out towards her and said, "Gina? Thank you, my dear." She smiled and shook his hand as well.

"So, what's your name?" I asked him.

"Oh, my apologies. My name is Henry. Though I'm afraid I can't seem to remember much more about myself than that." Gina and I looked up at each other, which he noticed. "What? What is it?"

Looking back at Henry, I answered, "There's nothing wrong with that at all. In fact, it looks like we might have been meant to help you. We can't seem to remember anything about ourselves, either." He had a shocked look on his face, yet it filled with a sense of hope. He quickly turned his head to look at Gina as she confirmed with nodding her head in agreement.

Gathering himself again, he looked back in my direction and asked, "So, what does this mean?"

"That," I sighed before I continued, "is what we're still trying to figure out. The only things we know is we all woke up in a different location and we can only, so far, remember our names." The hope almost appeared to leave his face. "But we are holding on. We need to find out everything we can and hope we can learn a way out of here. Now, what can you tell us?"

"Like what?"

"Right after you woke up, like, where was it?" Gina asked him.

Henry took a deep breath, and he started his story. "I woke up in the middle of a park, inside a gated off area where basketball hoops were. It was maybe a half-hour walk from here. I was laying under some bleachers when I woke up. I do not know how I got there, and there was no one around to ask for help. At least, not at first."

"What do you mean?" I questioned, confused.

"After I pulled myself from under those bleachers, I probably walked for what felt like forever until I came upon a section of the city that was heavily populated. But everyone I tried to talk to just ignored me. No matter what I said, they just walked past me without so much as a word or even a glance." He groaned as he reached down and grabbed his leg as a shot of pain worked its way through his body.

I needed him to tell us more. "You said not at first. What did you mean?"

"What did I mean?" He pointed at the ground behind us where the dust shadows for the two gray figures still laid. "Not until those things showed up."

Gina crossed her arms tightly before she said, "Those things were terrifying. But Sam and I never saw them until they were chasing you. Why did they come after you?"

He sighed again, still holding onto his leg. "You didn't see them probably because they weren't them at first."

This is so confusing. "I'm not sure we're following. What do you mean?" I asked, even though I could tell he really did not want to talk about it.

"Because those gray… things, they're these city's people." Gina took a step back away before Henry continued. "As I said, I was trying to get someone to help me, but no one was paying any mind. I got angry and finally walked up to this man and grabbed him by the arm and begged him for some help." Henry let go of his leg and covered his face with both hands. Suddenly, we could hear him sob. "Those eyes, my god those eyes," he said through his hands.

This was becoming too much for him, but I still needed to know. Placing my hand on his shoulder, I asked, "Henry? Can you keep going?"

"Sam!" Gina shouted back at me.

I needed to know. "I know this is difficult for him, but this is also important. We need to know what we are up…"

"It's okay," Henry said, cutting me off as he removed his hands from his face and put them up in the air in between Gina and I to get us to stop arguing. As he took a few deep breaths, he continued. "I grabbed the man, and he looked at me with such hate. He pushed me away so hard that I fell instantly. As I got back to my feet, I tried to apologize and tried to walk away, but he followed me. Suddenly, there was a second man, then a third, all chasing me, as no one paid attention." He started crying as he added, "They just went on with their lives as these men chased me down with bloodlust in their eyes."

After a few more seconds of his sobbing, he wiped his face and continued. "I eventually ran down a back alley trying to get away from them or at least put some space between us, but it was a bad idea. They caught me and started beating me slowly and painfully. Then, I saw it with my own eyes. The men they used to be just melted away, and all that was left were these gray husks of their former selves. They weren't human. In my eyes, all I saw were demons."

Chapter Seven

It took Gina and I several minutes of silence before we said anything. During that period, Henry composed and gathered himself, allowing him to calm down. Afterward, Gina and I took turns telling our stories from the first time we woke up all the way up to that point. Neither one of us made Henry feel any better because, out of the three of us, his story was the most tragic.

We concluded it made no sense in trying to move at that point. So, we agreed we would wait until the sun came up before we tried to resume on our way. The best thing we figured was to sleep the night out. Or at least, try too anyway. Henry just continued to lie where he already was and fell asleep immediately. Meanwhile, Gina and I laid against the opposite wall so we could monitor Henry just in case he needed help during the night.

I went to take a quick walk around the area before I turned in, just to be sure we were still alone. The city had become extremely quiet. It was strange, there had almost seemed to be no wind down from the hustle and bustle of the day to now; just busy to silent. I walked out to the end of the alley to see the primary area of the city to find not only all the people had gone, but every single light was out. The silence was almost more disturbing than the busyness prior. I made my way back and finished inspecting the area around where we camped. It did not take me long before I made my way back to find Gina had constructed a small area on the ground with some flattened cardboard boxes and some old fabrics mixed in with some of the garbage nearby. She was using her purple jacket from the shoe store as a small blanket as she curled herself up in a tiny ball.

Keeping my distance and to give her some space and privacy, I sat down on the ground with my back against the wall several feet away. I moved my injured arm around in circles, trying to get some relief as I got myself as comfortable as I could. Before too long, I took a few deep breaths and closed my eyes. I tried to silence my thoughts, but I could not slow my mind. *Demons? Henry said those grays were demons. I don't think they're actual demons, but they are for damn sure something no one has seen before.*

After a while, my mind started to finally calm down, and I felt myself drifting asleep. All I could hear was the light sounds of

Gina and Henry breathing as they slept until there was nothing but darkness and silence. Suddenly, flashes of images began to quickly appear and disappear in my eyes. I could not make any sense out of what I was seeing. The only thing I could recognize from the images is they were like the images I saw when that gray threw me against the wall. Then, as the images kept rotating over and over, a strange but familiar scent filled my nostrils. *What is that smell?* I suddenly felt a hot sensation flowing over my head and falling to the ground. *Is this water?* The unfamiliar sensations were confusing me; was this a dream or a memory?

I clinched my eyes tightly closed, trying to almost reset my focus so I could figure out what was going on. But as I opened them, the sun blinded me as it shined down on the alley. My body felt like I barely got ten minutes of sleep, but the rays of the sun told me it was hours later. My mind turned back to my dream, and I could not help but have the same thought repeated in my head. *What was that all about?* Before I could move, I realized that Gina's jacket was covering me like a blanket. *Wait, how did this get here?* I looked down at the wall where she was sleeping earlier, and she was gone. I quickly glanced over towards Henry's space, and he was missing as well.

As I stood up, I could faintly hear the two of them talking in the distance. I walked toward their voices and quickly found out what they were discussing with each other. Gina was watching

Henry try to walk around while he was holding onto what appeared to be a wooden stick or a staff. As I got closer, Henry lifted his head up from watching the ground and called out, “Hey! Good morning.”

Gina turned her head towards me as well but said nothing. It looked like she had loosened the strap of the med kit and had it now slung over her shoulder, coming down across her chest and resting on her hip like a satchel. As I joined the group, I looked at Henry and said, “Good morning.” I turned towards Gina and whispered, “Hey.” She smiled and tilted her head up at me. Turning my attention back towards Henry, I asked, “So what are you guys up to this morning?”

“Well, since it’s obvious we can’t stay here, and you guys can’t carry me, we needed to figure out some way of getting me to walk.” He lifts the wooden stick up in the air and adds, “Broken broom handle. Gina found it mixed in with the garbage.”

“Nice,” I replied.

Henry started walking gingerly. The broken broom handle, when the end was placed on the ground, stopped right near his hip. As he walked, he had the end of the handle grasped in the palm of his hand. He supported himself with it, trying his best not to put much weight on his bad leg. As he walked back to us, he said, "It's not the best thing or the most comfortable thing in my hand, but it'll do. Just don't go expecting me to run anywhere."

Gina turned away from us and began retreating towards the alley. I looked at Henry and said, "Okay, why don't you sit for a minute, and we'll get moving as soon as possible." Watching Henry nod his head in agreement and sit down on a stack of crates, I turned and tried to catch up with Gina. As I get close, I call out, "Hey, wait." She stops and turns halfway back towards me without saying a word. When I stopped in front of her, I asked, "Are you good?"

She looks at me with her arms crossed in front of her and whispers, "I… I… I think I remember something."

Excited, I respond, "That's great!" Her expression made me think otherwise. "Maybe not?" I added. She turns nervously back and forth like she wants to say something but cannot. "Hey, hey, what is it?"

"I'm not really sure. It was more of a feeling than a memory. Like it was something terrible, but I can't remember what." She pauses for a few seconds and then continues, "It came to me while I was sleeping. It was more like flashes of images, but when I woke up, I had this bad feeling." She paused, then said, "And the first thing I see is you."

"Me? What about me? Is it about me?"

"I don't know. I just know that when I looked at you, I felt sadness and pain."

"You don't think I caused you harm, do you?"

"Again, I don't know. It's probably nothing." She said as she waved her hand at me dismissively. She turns her head and looks down the alley back towards Henry.

Noticing this, I asked, "Did you say anything to Henry?"

"He was already awake and trying to move around when I woke up. I checked on his stitches and re-wrapped his bandage before I asked him if he remembered anything when he woke up and he said no. That's when we started trying to find a better way for him to move around." She paused for another second before she added, "As long as we don't run out of painkillers from the med kit before we get him help, he should be fine."

We both stood in silence for a couple of seconds before I said, "I had some flashes, too."

She turned back towards me before she shockingly asked, "What?"

"I'm not sure if they're memories, but I saw these flashes of somewhere other than here. Plus, I could feel, I felt water on my face and body, and I could smell something that I can't put my finger on."

Gina's expression on her face looked like she was deep in thought. "Do you think that they're connected?" she finally said after a few seconds.

Shrugging my shoulders and shaking my head, I replied, "I'm uncertain. They could be, but until we both get better glimpses of what is in our heads, there's no way to know."

From the distance, we could hear Henry call out, "Are you guys ready to head out?"

"Yeah, we're coming!" I yelled back at him. I went to walk towards him when I remembered I had Gina's coat still in my hand. Handing it to her, I whispered, "Oh, here. Thanks." She took it from me as she removed the med kit and put it back on, smiling. As she zipped her jacket closed, she picked the med kit back up off the ground and began tightening the strap, making it smaller as she wrapped it around her waist and clicking it, so it now hung on her side like a fanny pack. I chuckled slightly at the image as we made our way back out.

Rejoining Henry, he looked up at us from his seated position and asked, "So, what is our next move?"

"Well, one worker from a shop told me about some Central Info Station in the middle of this city…"

Henry cut me off. "A central station at the center of the city?"

"Yeah, I know. They're real original here," I answered him before I continued on. "I honestly don't know if we will get any answers there, but at least it's a start."

"Wait, you talked to one of them?" Henry suddenly questioned, shaking his head in complete disbelief.

"Actually, two different ones," I replied.

Gina quickly added, "Actually, two of them are from two different stores. He talked to one before he and I found each other. Then, he talked with one in a shoe store."

Henry got incredibly nervous and stressed. "I don't know if I trust this. How do we know they weren't just tricking you? What if they just told you that so we'd go there so they'd kill us?"

I could tell he was panicking. Gina sat down next to him, placed her hand on his shoulder and said calmly, "I really don't think so. From our experience, the workers in the stores and businesses are only interested in their jobs."

"Yeah, that's right," I added. "The guy that was from the sandwich shop didn't care about anything other than taking an order from me. And when I walked away and returned, it was as if he had never seen me before. Once I figured out what made them tic and acted like a legitimate customer, he answered my questions." *But when I insulted him, the entire store looked like they wanted to kill me,* I thought to myself.

"And the guy Sam talked to at the shoe store, all he wanted to do was sell Sam the latest sneakers before we left. So, if we need to find help from somewhere possibly, we just have to go with the scenario of the business."

"This is a big chance we're taking, and if you're wrong…" Henry trailed off as he put his head in his hands. It was understandable that he was scared. After going through what he did, I would be frightened too. I said nothing to either of them, but I was scared. It scared me to run into one of those gray figures again; it scared me I would lead us to our doom. But I could not just stay hidden away in this city forever. I needed to move on. I needed to find out what happened to us. Most of all, I needed to find out who Sam Hines truly was.

Henry lifted his head out of his hands, sighed, and said, "Okay. You're right, we have to do something."

Gina squeezed his shoulder and smiled at him in approval as she stood up, then helped him to his feet. Holding onto Henry's elbow, she looked at me and asked, "So, how do we get there?"

Scratching my head, I said reluctantly, "You're not gonna like it, but we need to head back to the main street where all the people are."

Chapter Eight

It took us twice as long to get back to the main street than it did before when it was just Gina and myself. Henry understandably slowed us down so much because he needed to stop every so often to rest his leg. Gina gave him an extra dose of pain medicine to help with the pain. I knew she was going to demand that we look for a hospital before too long to get Henry the help he needed. But I also knew Henry would refuse if we suggested it, too. Justifiably, he did not trust anyone that lived in this city.

As I emerged from the alleyway, everything looked exactly the same. The cars parked in their spaces, the number of pedestrians walking up and down the street, the smells of the fresh food cooked from the restaurants, all of it. The other thing that I noticed was the fact that no one was paying me any attention. They did not care about me at all.

I turned back towards Gina and Henry while placing my hand up to give them the signal to wait at the back of the alley as I looked around. Gina nodded her head and helped Henry sit down on some steps in front of a side door to one business. I took a few more steps out onto the sidewalk, but I made sure that I stayed far away from the passersby to not interact or disturb them. To my left, I found the sandwich shop where I first heard about the Central Info Station. I knew I did not want to go back in, but I was trying to remember what the guy at the counter had told me the day before.

"Okay, so what was it he said? Head right out of the shop and I would be on my way." Turning to the right, I peered down the street as far as I could see, but I did not notice any signs for the Station. But for the moment, I knew I had a direction for us to travel.

Returning down the alley where Gina and Henry were resting, I wanted to give them the news. "So, I figured out which direction we need to go. If we head back out to the street and head right, we should then head in the right direction."

"Heading in the right direction? Why is everything a guess?" Henry questioned as he rubbed his leg.

Frustrated, I sarcastically responded, "I'm sorry that I forgot where everywhere is in this city. I should know better since I grew up here!"

Without looking at either of us, Gina replied, "For all we know, we DID grow up here."

Throwing my hands up in the air, I said, "Well, I'd like to hear someone else's idea of what we should do here. Go ahead, I'm listening." Neither one of them said a word. I turned away from them and walked across the alley to the opposite wall and leaned up against it angrily.

Gina stood up and took a couple steps towards the street before stopping and just looking at the bodies of different pedestrians walking by. About a minute later, she turned back around, walked up to Henry, and grabbed him by the arm to help him stand up. "Come on, let's get going."

Henry immediately responded, "What? Why?"

"Sam's right. We cannot just stay here, and I don't know about you, but I don't have a better idea. Do you?" Henry sighed and shook his head as he stood up. Gina looked at me and said, "Well, let's get going."

I stood up off from leaning against the wall and made my way towards the street. As I went to walk past Henry and Gina, without looking at me, Henry whispered, "I'm sorry, Sam."

I stopped and looked at him for a second before I replied, "Yeah, me too." As we got to the end of the alley, I looked slightly back towards them and instructed, "If we stay close to the buildings and make sure we stay out of the way of the walkers and not interact with them, I think we should be fine."

Gina nodded and started walking with Henry staying behind me. We walked down about two blocks before Gina called out, "Look, over there. That's the shoe store we told you about, Henry."

Henry quickly asked, "Why are they all standing there?"

I looked over at the store to see what Henry pointed out. Just like yesterday when we ran out of the store stealing Gina's sneakers and jacket, all the customers and employees in the store were still standing perfectly still. They were all still watching us through the clouded windows, not moving an inch. As I kept going down the street, I said, "Yeah, I don't think we'll be shopping there again."

As we continued walking, I looked back and forth across the streets, trying to find any directions that could lead us to the

Info Station. We traveled another two blocks before Henry called out, "Wait a minute, I need to rest." He walked over towards a bench that was stationed at a bus drop off and sat down. Gina looked at me with concern as she held onto his arm.

"Let him sit. Let's just try not to interact with any of the pedestrians." She nodded at me in agreement as she helped Henry sit down. From behind me, I heard what sounded like a slight commotion from within one of the shops. As I turned around, I saw it was a pub with its doors propped open. Taking a step towards the pub, I could hear what sounded like someone talking angrily from inside.

"Sam!" Gina called out to me. The constant noises of the city slightly muffled her voice. When I turned around, I saw her looking at me with concern and frustration on her face, almost telling me not to even think about going inside.

"Watch Henry, I'll be right back," I called out to Gina as I made my way into the pub. The paneling along the inside of the pub looked like it was made from dark stained oak wood. The lights that hung from the ceiling had shades around the bulbs of a dark green color. Items from all different countries, along with what appeared to be items from pop culture from different generations, hung on the walls as well. They all accented a large green flag that was draped off the wall in multiple locations all around the pub.

There were people everywhere; some were sitting in groups at different tables spread across the room, some were playing darts and shooting pool far in the back, some were gathered around watching a sporting event happening on a television hanging off the wall. Then there were a handful of people sitting at the bar of the pub. Two guys were trying to eat a meal, three were talking with each other, laughing about something, and then there was one lone guy kind of in the middle of them all, making a lot of noise.

"You call this piss beer? This shit is horrible," he said as he slammed the pint glass down, making the thick, dark liquid splash out and onto the countertop. He appeared to be a middle-aged man, maybe in his middle forties. He was medium built but a little taller than I was. His bald head partially glistened from the light that entered the pub from the doorway as he wiped it away every so often with the sleeve of his green shirt that had a small, strange logo stitched into it over top of the left breast of his chest. He kept sticking his hand in the back pocket of his dark blue jeans, almost as if he kept checking to see if something was still there. "Give me something better, damn it!"

"That's some of the best pint of brew I got here fella," the bartender replied to him. "What more do ya want from me?"

"Maybe something not so fucking thick." The bartender took the glass away from the bald man and placed it behind the bar. He walked over to the wall behind him and grabbed another pint glass and began filling it with another drink before returning and placing it down in front of him. I began to make my way over to the bar, zigzagging in between the other customers until I reached the bar and sat down next to the bald man. He turned his head and looked at me with a disgusted face before turning back and taking a big gulp of his beverage.

"Ah fella, what can I getcha?" the bartender asked me. The man behind the counter was a large muscular man with spiked red hair and matching red mutton chop beard. He had a white button-up shirt that barely held itself closed as he had both sleeves rolled up just past his forearms below his elbows and a towel draped over his left shoulder.

"Um, I'm not sure what's wetting my pallet just yet. Can I just get some water for now?"

The bartender smiled and answered, "Ah, ya seem to be a man dat's planin' on pacin' himself. I like dat." He walked back to the wall and grabbed another pint glass but filled it with ice water before setting it down on the counter in front of me. "Ya, just let me know when you're ready to step up your fancy," he said to me as he winked at me and walked away. Placing the glass to my lips, the cold liquid flowed down my throat with such refreshing comfort. *God, I didn't realize how thirsty I was.*

Placing the glass back on the counter, I said, "You look like a man that has a story to tell." The bald man turned and looked at me, confused. I add, "But you can't quite remember what that story is."

"The fuck are you talking about?"

"I'm guessing you've never been here before, am I right? And you can barely remember anything past your own name too, right?"

"How the fuck do you know that?" he asked me as he took another gulp of the beer.

"You have that look. Not to mention your colorful linguistic abilities far out reaches the average conversation of these people."

"FUCKIN' A, YEAH!" a guy yells out from the group off to the side that were gathered around the television as they cheered. We both turned our heads back towards the group for a second before returning to our own conversation.

"Alright, so I'm not from here. So, fucking what?" he asked me as he spun his glass on the bar.

"Look, I'm just like you. And there's more of us outside."

"So what?" he stressed again as he looked away from me more.

"So, why don't you come with us? I'm thinking that there may be a lot more of us around this city than we think. We should stick together and help each other."

Swallowing his last bit of beer, he aggressively bounced the glass on the counter as he put it down and he said, "What makes you think I want to go with you? Huh? I'm fine right here. I may not know where I am, but as long as I got a place to drink, I'll figure out the rest."

"Are you sure because from what we've…"

"FUCKIN' A YEAH!"

"Christ, are they watching a spelling bee?" I said as I shook my head.

Suddenly, the bald man stood up from his stool and said to me, "Look, will you leave me the fuck alone? I don't want your help."

Turning my attention back to him, I replied, "Are you sure about that? How are you even going to pay for your drink?"

He made a confused expression and said, "What are you talking about, dumb ass? I have money." He reaches behind himself to his back pocket and grabs a wallet. *Was that what he kept reaching back for?* He opened the wallet, reached in for a couple of bills, and threw them on the counter.

Maybe not everyone needs help after all, I thought to myself as he began to walk away when a loud slam came from the bar.

"Hey fella, what the hell is this?" Turning around, I see the bartender holding the bald man's money in his hands.

"What are you talking about?" The bald man answers. "I ain't paying for that first shit beer you gave me."

"Ya didn't pay for anyt'in'!" I glanced down at the money he was holding in his hand; all of it was completely blank.

"That's impossible," he demands as he opens his wallet again and pulls out a large stack of nothing but blank pieces of paper. The pub had become completely quiet. I started looking around at all the other customers and, just like everywhere else, the entire room of people were all looking at the stranger.

This is going to get bad quick. I stood up from my stool and said to the bartender, "Hey, he's sorry about that. No harm here." I turned towards the bald man and continued, "I told you, dude, you shouldn't have jumped into that pool in your clothes. See if you got anything in there for the man."

As the bald man went looking through his wallet, I looked back at the bartender and said, "The color must've washed off his money. I'm sure he's got something in there for you." He did not look amused. Turning back again, I whispered, "Hurry and give him money."

"I'm looking. There's nothing in here," he whispered back.

"What do you mean, there's nothing? You said you had money?"

"Yeah, I saw the paper and assumed it was money. I didn't pull it fucking out and count it all."

"Well then, you didn't know you had any money. Fuck." I turned back towards the bartender and smiled at him. He still was not amused. *Alright, time to get out of here just like the other stores.* Turning back towards the bald man, I whispered, "Okay, just start making your way towards the door slowly."

"What?"

Taking a step forward towards the bartender I said, "Ah hey, I'm sorry about this, but all his money got ruined, but our friends are right outside. So, we're just going to run out to them and…"

BANG!

The doors were slammed shut by two customers closing the both of us inside the pub. Every single person in the pub was looking at us with anger and fire in their eyes. As the bald man stepped back forward to stand next to me, I said to him, "Well, it's your time to figure out what to do."

"Fuck it!" he yells out as he turns towards the nearest customer and punches him in the face. The other men scrambled around the room as, one by one, they charged at us. The bald man began punching each one of the men that came at him, trading back and forth, left to right, between each fist.

As they started coming after me, the first man that approached me I kicked right in the knee, and he dropped to the floor. The second, I punched him on the side of his head, making him fall onto the first man. The third, however, punched me right in the stomach, making me back away to the counter, where I tripped over one of the bar stools. Getting back up quickly, I picked up the stool with both hands and swung it at the charging man, striking him with it. The blow sent him sailing over the bar counter, causing the seat of the stool to break off.

Looking towards the back, the men playing pool were making their way towards us with their cue sticks still in hand. Noticing that there were pint glasses all over the bar counter, I swung with the still together legs of the stool and hit the half a dozen pint glasses, shattering them all and sending a stream of broken glass and half drank beer flying in their direction. As they ducked for cover, it made them hold their advancement for the time being.

The bald man in the meantime was getting pinned to the wall by two of them as they kept punching him in the stomach. I ran towards them and chucked the broken stool at them, hitting them both in the back of their heads, freeing the bald man. He straightens himself off the wall then grabs a strangely shaped club with a thin handle and large rounded head that was hanging on the wall for a weapon. I armed myself with one leg from the now completely broken stool as we readied ourselves for the next wave.

Jumping over his counter, the bartender stood in front of us a few feet away. Two other customers walked up and stood behind him. The bald man raised the club up in the air and screamed, "COME ON, YOU FUCKS!" The bartender took a deep breath and began screaming in a very high-pitched tone. We both covered our ears, trying to block out the piercing pain. The moment the bartender stopped, the bald man yelled out, "What the fuck was that?"

"We are so fucked," I said softly, waiting for what I knew was coming next. Their eyes all glowed bright green then turning to a deep red, and I remembered what Henry had said about their eyes being terrifying before they changed. *He's not wrong.* I stood in fear as the three men seemed to melt away and all that was left were three gray figures. The bartender that stood at the front had a gash across its chest. It was a dead giveaway; he was the one that ran away after attacking Henry. *Hello my old friend.*

"The fuck is this? THE FUCK IS THIS!?" the bald man screamed as he charged ahead and swung the club in his hand at them. He missed the front standing gray figure but hit the one to the left, sending it falling over and slamming through the glass door of a free-standing refrigerator of to-go drinks, shattering the glass into many pieces. A large chunk of glass stabbed it in the head, causing it to fall to the floor, shrieking until it moved no more.

The front gray figure grabbed him by the face and, with a quick twitch of its arm, threw him all the way back past me as he bounced off the wall and hit the floor hard. The *Gray* then quickly stepped forward and swiped its other arm to the left, catching me in the face as it launched me sideways, tumbling over top of the counter and landing on the floor. As I tried to pick myself up, I saw it had cut me open on my face above my left eye as blood poured out of the fresh wound and onto the floor.

Suddenly, I heard a loud thump and turned around to see the gray figure standing on top of the counter, kneeling, and staring at me. The bald man was screaming as he picked himself up off the floor and was trying to keep the third Gray at bay while he swung wildly with the club. Glancing to my side, on the floor was a stack of empty beer bottles. I quickly grabbed one and chucked it up in the air at the Gray looking down at me, but I completely missed as it dashed out of the way with ease. The bottle hit the roof of the pub and exploded into tiny pieces of brown glass.

I quickly got to my knees and picked up a second empty beer bottle and chucked it towards the distracted third Gray as it shattered off its shoulder. This gave the bald man enough of an opening as he swung the club upwards and struck the Gray under the chin like an uppercut, sending it sailing backwards, shrieking as it landed on the ground with a sickening thud.

The last Gray jumped behind the counter and landed directly behind me. I pivoted my head around at the last second to see it had once again molded its hand into a stabbing instrument and lunged it down towards me. I barely fell forward out of the way as it just missed me and grazed the floor. I stood up sideways while almost falling over as I ran for the edge of the counter, moving past the stack of empty pint glasses, grabbing one, and throwing it at the Gray, which it easily shattered with its knife-like hand.

Getting myself back over the counter, I shout out, "Get out the door!" The bald man, without hesitation, ran for the doors, swinging the club and knocking over the two men that kept the doors closed. He ran for the refrigerator with the broken glass door, reached in, and grabbed something before pushing one of the exit doors open. I saw one of the broken legs from the stool I used as a weapon earlier lying on the floor in front of me. As I ran past, I bent down and grabbed it as I made it to the exit door.

Before I ran out of the pub, I noticed that in the refrigerator there were bottles of water along with six packs of fresh beers. I quickly sidestepped to the refrigerator and grabbed four bottles of water and ran out the door as well. Once we were outside, I yelled, "Close it!" as the bald man pushed the doors closed and we both leaned on them to keep them sealed. Just as expected, the pedestrians walking on the sidewalk paid no attention to us.

"What the hell is going on?" Gina called out as she watched us while she still stood next to Henry on the bench. I dropped the bottles of water onto the ground as I took the broken leg and pushed it through the two handles of the doors to keep it closed. The doors began to be forcefully rammed from the other side as we could hear heavy pounding along with the familiar yet muffled high pitch scream echoing out.

"That's not gonna hold them." The bald man said as we stepped back.

"As long as it stalls them, that's all that matters." I replied as I picked the water bottles back up off the ground.

Gina ran up to me and screamed, "Sam, what the hell? Why are you bleed…?"

Before she could finish scolding me, I handed her the bottles of water and said, "Not now. Run!"

"Run? What do you mean, run?" asked Henry, as he hobbled out from the other side of the bench.

"We got to go, Henry. We got to go now," I said as I approached him to help him move faster.

As I reached under his arm to wrap it over my shoulder so he could lean on me, he frantically asked, "What? Why are you bleeding? Sam, what is….?"

"Henry, unless you want to say hi to our old gray friend, shut up and lean on me so we can move!" Immediately, Henry got a terrified look on his face. He quickly leaned over my shoulder, putting most of his weight on me as I began to speed walk down the street while Gina and the bald man were several feet in front of us.

As we got several yards from the pub, the bald man yelled back towards me, "Where the fuck are we going?"

We all stopped at the intersection as the timer for a crosswalk was counting down, stopping the buses from crossing. I glanced up at the street sign hanging from the traffic light fixture that read *Center Street.* I shouted, "There! Turn left and cross." Gina was the first to cross, followed by the bald man, then Henry and me. Once we got across the street, we kept making our way down the road as the buildings of the city started turning older and not as kept up and quiet, with no pedestrians heading in our direction. We quickly realized as we ran further down the street, we were alone.

Chapter Nine

"Jesus Christ, you are such an asshole," Gina said as she stitched my head wound closed.

We had been running for some time on Center Street before Henry called out, "I can't anymore. I need to stop for a minute." Gina started looking around and found another alley leading down in between two buildings. She started walking down the alley, then signaled for us to follow her. Once we reached near the end of the alley, it opened to a very dark back area that was much grungier and dirtier than the alley we had been in the night before. The sunlight did not reach this section as most of the ground was wet, and it had a slight scent of mildew that filled the area.

As soon as we felt it was safe, and we were not being followed, Gina took Henry from me and led him to an area where he could lie down and put his leg up. She also pulled out some more painkillers and gave them to him, as well as opening one bottle of water for him to have. Trying to catch my breath, I leaned my back against one wall and slid down it until my ass hit the ground with a thud. Gina ran over from Henry to check on me, dropping to the ground as well. She opened the med kit again, pulling out a white cloth before opening another bottle of water and poured some of it out on the cloth.

I closed my eyes before I suddenly felt a slight pressure on my legs that felt distinctly familiar. As I opened my eyes, I saw Gina straddling over my legs so she could look directly into my face, trying to clean the blood away. Once she was done, she pulled out all she needed to close the gash in my head. "You know that, right? You're such an asshole."

"Yeah, I know," I answered her softly as I made my eyes look away from her as she tried her best with the stitches. After a minute, I looked back at her and softly added, "Thank you."

She lowered her hands from my face and sat back so that her butt was resting on my thighs before she asked, "So, are you going to tell me how in the world you did this in only a few seconds?"

"What?" I asked, confused. "I was in that pub for at least fifteen to twenty minutes before we got out of there. And I almost thought we weren't gonna get out."

"That's impossible. You walked in, the doors closed and then a couple seconds later they opened and out flying came you and," she paused before she turned partially around towards the bald man and asked, "What's your name?"

"Whatever you want me to be, sexy," he answered in a sarcastic and almost flirtatious tone. He sat on some steps that led to a platform for the back of the building we were hiding behind before it turned into yet another dock for the business that was inside. I didn't realize it at first but from the refrigerator at the pub he had grabbed a six-pack of beer, which now he was drinking one of them.

"Seriously, dude? After all this, you can't even be polite enough to tell us your name?" He shrugged his shoulders as he took another sip from his bottle. "Or maybe, you can't remember it yet. Is that it?"

He frowned with a disgusted curl to his upper lip before answering, "I'm not a fucking moron." He quickly chugged away at his beer as if to distract himself from saying any more.

"Here, this is Gina. I'm Sam, and the gentleman over there is Henry."

"Got it." He pointed at Gina and said, "Sexy bitch," pointed towards Henry and said, "Cripple," then pointed towards me and said, "and fucking dumb ass."

"Oh my god you are such a dick!" Gina called out as she turned her attention back towards me.

"Yeah, you can see it when you're done riding him, sweetheart," he said, laughing as he takes another sip of beer.

"You saved this guy?" she whispered to me.

"Yeah, I'm really regretting it," I whispered back.

After a few seconds and another sip of beer, he finally said, "Fine. It's Danny."

Gina slowly turned back towards him and said with a smirk on her face, "Dickhead, got it." His sarcastic smile turned into a frown as he shook his head and went back to drinking. Turning her attention once again to me, she asked, "He did this to you?"

"Not even close. It was more Grays."

"More?"

"Yeah, and one of them was our old friend, *Slash*. At least I'm assuming it was the same one from when we saved Henry because he had the exact mark across his chest that I gave him." She pulled a small bandage from the kit and placed it on my head over my eyebrow as I continued. "But I learned a bit more from this. It seems that if we interfere with their designed, or maybe assigned job, they turn into the Grays."

"My god Sam," she whispered with a tremble in her voice.

"Henry interrupted them when he was trying to get help, so they attacked him. And now when Danny couldn't pay his bill at the pub, it made them attack." The sting in my eye hit hard as she pressed the bandage firmly to get it to stick. As I sucked air in quickly and held it in, I continued and said, "But I suppose they don't know who we are until they become a Gray. I figure since Slash was the bartender of the pub, he was friendly, just like all the other store workers, until they turned and attacked."

Gina lifted her eyebrow before she asked, "But wait, what about the shoe store? How come none of them turned, as you say, into those Grays when we ran out?"

"I'm not sure honestly. It's just a theory I have, but maybe we left the shoe store before their change could take place. It might also explain why that associate's business card just vanished after we were outside and why they seem to be just stuck in place the second time we passed by."

"How is this even possible?" Gina questioned as she tried to make sense of it all.

"I'm not sure. But what I know is the Grays are extraordinarily strong and fast, but they are vulnerable. They get hurt just as easily as we do. So, if we have no other choice but to encounter them, we can defeat them."

"If we *have to* face them? Are you out of your mind? Stay the fuck away from them, Sam. You have fought them twice now and both times you nearly lost your life!"

"I don't want to fight them. I'd be fine if I never see one of those things ever again. But at this point, this city seems to be adamant on hurting us, so I'm sure we are going to, at some point, have no choice."

"There's always a choice, Sam." Gina said angrily as she stood up off my legs and walked a few steps away before sitting down on a curb. As we sat in silence for a few moments, she finally looked at me and said, "Tell me something about yourself?"

Confused by her request, I replied, "What do you mean? We can't remember anything. What do you want me to say?"

"Just make something up, I guess. I don't know, just tell me something that has nothing to do with this place."

I sat there looking at her for a few seconds, unable to speak. I looked out the alleyway and sighed as I heard her do the same and saw out of the corner of my eye that she looked like she was getting ready to stand up and walk away. "I don't know what I could tell you. I wish I could; I wish I could tell you I lost my parents at an early age and grew up living with my grandparents. I wish I could tell you that all my personality and humanity came from them." She sat back down and focused on me as I continued.

"I wish I could tell you I went to college, graduated with a degree, but found my calling in another field." Grabbing my shirt by the collar, I jokingly added, "Probably business." As I let go of my shirt, she started to smile more, so I continued my story. "I want to say that while in college, I met the most beautiful girl with a heart of pure gold."

"Is she pretty?" Gina asked softly.

Chuckling, I replied excitingly, "Super models wish they had her looks." Gina giggled as she leaned forward a bit more. "And that I have a lot of cars. I live in a big house and I'm totally rich."

"Do you have any kids? Can you tell me if the two of you have any children together?" she asked me.

"I wish I could tell you that all of it was true. I just really don't know."

Gina frowned as she leaned back before she said, "That all sounds amazing, Sam. Maybe some of it is true." She stands up from the curb and walks away, heading over towards Henry. *Maybe I should ask her to tell me something about herself.* As I opened my mouth to ask, a voice spoke out from across the other side of the alley.

"Ah, is it finally my turn since you're done with limp dick there?" Danny asked as he threw his empty bottle of beer on the ground in the corner of a building.

Gina stomped over to Danny and stopped a couple feet in front of him, sniffed loudly and said, "Yup, you're fine." As he gave her a dumbfounded look, she turned away and returned to Henry's side.

"You all are a bunch of fucks. I was better off at the pub before you showed up and fucked things up," he stated as he pointed at me.

"Yeah, you're welcome, by the way," I said as I tapped the bandage to make sure it stayed put. "So, you mind telling us how you found yourself at the pub in the first place?"

"Nothing really to say," he answered as he grabbed another beer and opened it. "Found myself in this fucking city, so I thought to myself, Danny, you need a drink," he smarmily said as he placed the bottle to his lips and began drinking once again.

"Yeah, but where did you wake up?" I asked, trying for him to give us more.

"At the pub. Well, right behind it, actually."

"Behind? And then you just walked to the street, turned around and said, 'Ah fuck, a pub' and went in for a drink?" I asked, getting frustrated.

"You got it, dumbass," and again another sip.

You know what, Gina was right. I am an asshole for helping this dip shit. I waved my hand in dismissal towards Danny as I put my head back against the wall and closed my eyes to the exhaustion that came over me.

The steam in the shower felt so good, along with the hot water that was running down my body. It was a weird feeling in my hands; between the heat of the water and the cold from the tiles along the wall as both hands were pressed against the wall as I leaned under the showerhead. I could see the last of the soap that had been washed off my body circling around the drain before getting washed away with the water. I thought to myself, *how long have I been in here?*

The shower itself was a delicate design. From the floor all the way to the ceiling were square tiles of a solid cream coloring with splashes of browns, grays, and oranges. The dark brass colored shower head was exceptionally large; it reached out on a short arm from the wall before a giant circular head hovered above me with different rows and patterns of spray holes for the water to stream from. Attached to the side was a flange for switching the water flow from the shower head to a hose of the same coloring with a smaller handheld shower head one could use to reach areas of your body for better cleaning. Below there were two nobs that came out of the wall. One with a large red 'H' and the other with a large blue 'C.'

On the left were small lips indented in the wall where the soaps and shampoos sat safely stored in arms at reach, along with a bar, just in case needed for support. To the right, half the length of the opposite wall, was another wall and then an opening to step out of the shower and enter the rest of the bathroom. At the bottom of the opening was a small lip that came up out of the floor so to trap water in the shower and not let it leak out onto the floor.

Reaching down to the hot and cold knobs, I turned them until the water finally stopped. Glancing around, I could see that the different shower soaps, shampoos, and conditioners that were sitting on the lips in the wall left me know I was not the only person who used this shower. After the water was completely off, I stepped over the lip on the floor and out of the shower. To my left, a small towel bar was attached to the wall where I reached and grabbed my towel to dry myself off.

The bathroom was impressive. To my right, on the other side of the wall where the shower stall was, sat the toilet and a large closet that looked like it stored all the extra bathroom supplies and the clean, unused towels. In front of me, on the opposite wall placed under two large sky windows in the ceiling, was a large tub that looked like it could be a jacuzzi. It had two small steps that you would need to climb up to step in. Next to the tub was a large mirror on the wall and a long countertop and dual sinks that had another assortment of soaps, skin care products, toothbrushes and more.

Everything on the counter looked familiar and, in its place, except for two things. Sitting in between the sinks sat a lit candle and a piece of paper next to it. As I approached the sinks, the smell from the candle was extremely sweet and triggered a nostalgic feeling, but I could not remember why. I turned my attention to the piece of paper.

Looking at the paper, I realized it was a note with familiar handwriting on it. The note read, *"Come out and open your gift."* I then realized that sitting at the top of the note was a small silver key that I had never seen before. The head of the key had three small circular holes that came together and shaped like the club suite from a deck of cards. Looking at the key, I said to myself, "What is she up to?"

I picked the key up off the counter, draped my towel over my shoulder, and walked towards the door of the bathroom. As I reached the door, before I opened it, I placed my ear close to the door. On the other side, all I could hear were the very faint sounds of a small, muffled voice. I reached down to the door handle, turned it, and opened the door.

My eyes quickly opened as I gasped for air like I had not taken a breath for some time. As my breathing slowed, I noticed that the day was new again as the light from the sun had shifted and was rising once again. *Did I seriously sleep the entire day away? Was that another vision or flash of images? Wait, was that a memory?* Looking over at the dock, Danny laid on it with his back to me and empty beer bottles sprawled all over the ground.

I suddenly felt a warm pressure on my right arm as I looked over and saw Gina was lying against the wall next to me. She had herself pressed up against my arm like a pillow with her jacket once again covering the both of us. I did not know when she sat down next to me, but I could not pull myself to look away. As I stared at her, I noticed the unique patterns under her eyes that her freckles made on either side of her small nose that had a small piercing in the left nostril. As I studied her mouth, I recalled the few times that she smiled at how adorable and attractive she looked.

I began thinking about the first time I saw her and how incredible her body was. The clothes she wore helped to accent her figure from her chest to her small waist to her hips and down. I even thought about when she had her brunette hair down past her shoulders, how there were strands of blonde streaks that I didn't know if it was from hair coloring or naturally from the sun.

The more I thought about her, the more I realized I had an extremely tight and uncomfortable feeling quickly growing in my pants. *Oh my god, I'm getting hard.* "Shit," I quickly whispered as I bent my knees upwards, raising my legs and blocking the noticeable bulge in my pants just as Gina opened her eyes and looked at me.

"What?" she said to me half asleep as her green eyes barely opened.

"Huh, oh no nothing. Ah morning." I quickly said to her, trying to keep her attention away from my crotch. "Did you sleep okay?"

"Yeah," she answered as she stretched. "I got really cold last night, so I hope you don't mind; I stole some of your heat." She reached down and grabbed my wrist and checked my pulse. "I was getting worried about you since you fell asleep so fast last night and with you being so warm, I was hoping…" She paused and had a concerned look on her face.

"What is it?"

"Are you feeling okay because your pulse is racing really fast?"

I quickly pulled my hand away from her grasp and replied, "Oh yeah, I'm good, I'm good. Hey how is Henry doing?" As I tried to change the subject, I looked over to where I remembered Henry was the night before and found him no longer there. "Wait, where is Henry?"

Gina gets up off the ground and puts her jacket back on. "He was asleep when I laid down next to you."

I looked left and right, trying to find any clue where he could have gone, and there was nothing. "Danny? Danny, wake up," I called out as I walked over to Henry's sleeping area, but Danny did not respond. "Danny! Fuck it." I started walking out and up the alley to get to the front of the building and to the street to see if I could try to find him.

"Sam, where are you going?" Gina asked as she started following me from behind.

"I have to see where he might have gone. I just hope one of those damn Grays didn't get him in the middle of the night." As we reached the street, I quickly and frantically looked up and down the streets to see if there were any type of clues where he could have vanished. "Shit, shit!" I screamed out as I ran my hands through my hair, feeling mountains of stress washing all over me.

"It's okay Sam, we'll find him. We will find him," Gina said, trying to calm me down.

I turned back and went back down the alley. I knew I needed to get Danny up and we needed to go search for Henry. Something in me kept telling me something was wrong, and I needed to help him. Just before we reached the back-alley area again, from behind me I could hear a faint but familiar voice from the distance.

"Sam. Sam," the voice called out. Gina and I turned back around once again and ran out to the front of the building, running towards the voice. Once we reached the street, we saw it was none other than Henry. "Sam," he called out again.

"Henry? What the hell, man?" I asked as we walked towards him. Once we reached him, Gina immediately got to his side so he could place some of his weight on her. She started leading him back into the alley and out of sight. "Where did you go?" I asked, walking beside him on his other side.

"I felt the need to be helpful and you all were sleeping there on the ground together. I didn't want to wake you." Gina glanced up at me and saw that I was already looking back at her as Henry continued. "I figured I would try to go look around a bit to see if I could find anything." Once we reached the back alley again, Gina helped him sit down so he could rest.

"Did you find anything, or was it all still the same?"

"Nope, I found something that I think is especially useful. If we wake up sleeping beauty over there, I want to show you."

Shaking my head, I said, "Why don't you just tell me what you found, and I'll go so you can rest."

"No, unacceptable," he quickly argued. "We're all going because it's going to be much safer than here, anyway."

Curious, I nodded my head in agreement. Gina walked away towards Danny. As she got to him, she raised her hand in the air and gave him a big smack to the back of the head. He immediately put his hand on his head to cover the spot she hit and sat right up. "What the fuck?" he called out.

"Oh good, you're awake," Gina replied to him sarcastically. "Come on, we're leaving. Get yourself moving." As Danny gathered himself, complaining the whole time, we waited a couple of minutes before letting Henry lead the way. Once again, just before we left the alley for the last time, I glanced back and studied it before moving on.

We walked for roughly twenty minutes, but with Henry's speed and bad limp, we weren't traveling a great distance. The entire way Gina kept trying to hand him pain pills, but he kept brushing them off. "I want to make sure I have a clear head, so I remember exactly where we need to go."

"Do you even know where we are going?" Danny called out from the back of us, but we just ignored his complaint.

After turning what seemed like our seventh corner, Henry stopped and smiled. "There it is. We are saved." As I watched him hobble away with a massive smile on his face, he walked towards a building that was halfway down and across the street. The building was old and looked like it was falling apart with its faded blue siding, some of which were cracked. It had several concrete steps at the front of it that led up to its double doors. At the top of its peaked roof, all the way to the front edge, stood a small tower that did not appear to be any over four feet high and maybe three-square feet round. Hanging in the middle of the tower appeared to hang some object that looked like the shape of a bell. On the left and right of the building were small two-foot-high metal fences that seemed to block off small areas of grassy yards with a large tree growing sky high at the middle of each area.

As we all stood at the bottom of the steps, Henry immediately began climbing, eager to get inside. "I told you, what do you think?"

As I take another look at the building, confused, I replied, "It's a church."

Chapter Ten

How is he walking so fast like this with that leg? We could hardly keep Henry from running through the entrance of the church as he pushed them open. The inside of the church had a unique appeal than it did on the outside. First walking through the doors there was another opening that led you directly to the nave and sanctuary. To the left was a small table against the wall with some pamphlets on it, a coat rack with a few dozen empty coat hangers loosely dangling on the pole, and a set of stairs that led down. On the right was another small table, also holding pamphlets, a small bathroom, and another set of stairs that led up.

Every wall of the small narthex was painted white, while the floor had large square glossy black tiles. As we walked into the nave, the walls and ceiling were also painted white, while a thin black and red carpet covered the floor. On both the left and right walls stood eight large stained-glass windows of all assorted colors, as they depicted discrete events from the religion's history. On either side of the nave were rows and rows of dark stained wood pews in the aisles. Halfway up, Henry slid himself into an aisle and sat at a pew staring towards the sanctuary.

At the front of the church where the sanctuary was, a large platform sat with three long steps. You could walk up from any side you approached it. At the top of the platform sat a wide table with a long white tablecloth covering it. Hanging from the front of the table facing the mass was a wooden cross that was stained with a cherry finish while two large golden candle stick holders sat on top at either corner with long white candles sticking out of them. A few feet back from the table was a wooden podium with a small desk light attached that was also stained with the same cherry finish as the cross. From the right of the table, all the way to the left, at the corner of the room was yet another platform that had three rows that were inclined upward, with eight chairs in each row with a piano and organ sitting in front of them. Behind the podium hanging from the ceiling was an extraordinarily large cross that looked like it was made of silver and gold that was surrounded by multiple spotlights that shined on it from every angle, making it almost glow.

As I stood in the middle of the church looking around with Gina standing next to me, I quickly realized that Danny was nowhere to be seen. "Where is Danny?" I asked as we both turned around to look towards the front doors. I suddenly saw someone I was not expecting.

"Sam?"

"Shaelynn?" She stood there drying her hands off with a faded yellow towel wearing a long light blue flowered dress with a white apron tied back around herself. Gina and I took a step back as I slowly raised my arm in the air, blocking Gina behind me. "I was definitely not expecting to see you here."

"Nor was I Sam. But I'm glad you made it here." Her accent had changed and was very different. It no longer sounded foreign, but homier and had a bit of a twang to it. She glanced down and looked at my arm guarding Gina. "Is there something wrong, Sam?"

"You can say that. After what we have been through, I'm having a bit of an issue trusting people from this city."

She smiled as she exhaled and began nodding her head. "I see. But as you know, I'm not from this city. My home is far away from here."

"Then what are you doing here?" I asked sharply.

She tucked the faded yellow towel into a pocket into the front pouch of her apron. "Well, this is my church, Sam. I have it here to help people like yourself if they need it."

"That doesn't make me feel any safer, Shaelynn. Why didn't you warn me about this city?"

"No! Not here!" We could hear Henry shouting at us from the pew he was sitting on. "This is a place of worship Sam, there will be no violence here."

"After everything we've seen, how can you sit there and say no violence?" I yelled to him, while not looking away from Shaelynn.

"Because she's the one that told me we'd be safe here." I could feel Gina grab hold of my arm with both her hands and tighten her grip.

"Sam," Shaelynn started, "I know you have been through many things these last few days, but you can trust me. You can trust my church." She turned herself around and walked away before she stopped and said, "You all look so hungry. Come down to the kitchen. I have hot food I just finished making." She then walked away and headed towards the stairs leading down.

Once she was out of sight, I turned around and power walked towards Henry as he got himself up out of the pew. "What the fuck, Henry?" I asked him angrily.

"Do not curse in this house of worship," he replied to me, not happy with me cursing.

"But Henry, how can you trust anyone that isn't us? Especially after you were attacked by people from this city," Gina said as she tried to plead with him.

He pushed his way past us as he began making his way after Shaelynn. "There is no anger in the eyes of the lord, only forgiveness and sympathy. If she wanted to be our enemy, she could have killed me when she found me sitting outside this church earlier. I DO think she's here to help us, and if she is indeed the person you say you met when you first woke up, then I don't see how you couldn't trust her."

As he moves on his way to catch up with Shaelynn, I sit down in one pew and just slump over the one in front of me, feeling defeated. Gina sat down next to me and said nothing. After a few minutes, I lifted my head up off my arms and said, "Is he right? Am I not able to trust anyone from this city? Am I just trying to be overprotective because I don't know what's going on?" I shook my head and placed it back on my arms.

Gina leans forward slightly and asked softly, “Can we trust Shaelynn?”

Thinking about it, I once again lifted my head, looked at her and said, “I want to. But after everything else… I don’t know.”

“Well, she was the one that helped you get on your way to the city, correct?”

“Technically, yes.”

“Okay, and you said she wasn’t like anyone else of the city dwellers that we’ve met either, right?”

“Yes.”

“So, maybe we can trust her. Maybe she can give us a better idea of what we need to do to get out of here and finally regain our memories.”

She’s right. That is the goal in the end. I sat back in the pew and thought for a few seconds before I looked at her and said, “Okay. We are still lost here, but if there’s at least someone that can point us in the right direction, then so be it.”

Gina began smiling largely after hearing what I said. “I was really hoping you’d say that, because that food smells delicious.” She stood up from the pew and took a few steps back before she turned around and began making her way to follow the others.

When she was out of sight, I stood up and began making my way after the others as well. Yet just before I went to walk down the stairs, I glanced out the window next to the front doors and saw Danny sitting outside on the banister, just kind of staring into the distance. I shook my head and went down the steps.

The stairs were not exceedingly long at all; only eight steps lead down to a basement-like area. Once I made it down to the last step, I realized this basement was underneath the tree that was fenced off to the left of the church instead of being directly underneath the building. The room was massive, with the walls all just like upstairs painted white. The roof was a dropped ceiling with cream-colored rectangular tiles covering the entirety with light fixtures every three spaces. To the left, there was a large kitchen with a half wall separating it from the rest of the room with a cutout in the wall for a counter so you could see into the kitchen. Shaelynn was there placing large aluminum trays on the counter while Gina helped her to remove the aluminum covers of the trays.

On the right looked like six small rooms because six doors ran along the wall, separated by about four feet before the next door. At the center of the room, rows, and rows of long tables with chairs on either side of them. The spacing looked like it could fit over one hundred people if it needed to. Henry seated himself at one table with his injured leg stretched out underneath it. He rested it on a chair that was on the opposite side from where he was seated. At the end of the room, all the way on the other side of me, was another small altar with a wooden podium that was not stained, and a small wooden cross attached to the wall. Just below the cross, a long table with a white tablecloth was placed with two more golden colored candlestick holders with short, thin candles sticking out of them.

"Don't be shy Sam. Come, fix yourself a plate," Shaelynn called out from the kitchen. As I approached the counter, Gina had already walked away and brought a full plate of food to Henry. There was so much food spread out across the counter. The selection of food ranged from chicken, ham, mashed and sweet potatoes, mixed green salad, corn and green beans, sage dressing, fresh biscuits, and even brownies.

"You made all of this?" I asked, surprised.

"The way Henry was talking about you, it sounded to me like you hadn't eaten in ages," Shaelynn replied.

"This is just so much food, though."

"Well, darlin', then you'll have more for later if you get hungry again."

Hopefully, we won't be here much longer to think about eating later. Hopefully, we will be on our way home. At the far left of the counter was a stack of white plates with three red plastic cups, each containing a different utensil; one had spoons, the next had forks, and the last had knives. After grabbing a plate and silverware, I made my way down the row, scooping out small portions of the different selections until my plate was full.

I made my way over and sat next to Henry, one seat away, as Gina sat on the other side of the table directly across from me. Henry had already eaten half of his food off his plate and looked like he already wanted seconds. I stared at the food on my plate while holding the fork in one hand and the knife in the other, with the spoon resting to the right of the plate on the table. It was not the fact that I was not hungry because I was starving, nor was it me not knowing what I wanted to eat first, but it was the fact that I still did not know if I could trust Shaelynn. Gina, still watching me, whispered, "What's wrong?"

"I don't know. I don't know if I can trust her." I glanced over at Henry one more time as he had now almost finished his food completely as I can see the hint of a smile as he chewed his food. I cut a piece of ham and held it on the edge of my fork as I stared at it for a few seconds. I slowly placed it in my mouth and chewed as the savory juices swirled around hitting every one of my taste buds on my tongue. Grinning, Gina pulled a piece of her chicken apart and ate her selection.

As I swallowed the ham, I did not think about trusting Shaelynn or about the city and its inhabitants. I did not think about the crazy store workers or the unhelpful street pedestrians. I did not think about the gray figures that died or the ones that still lived and were possibly hunting us. The only thing I thought about was just eating more of the food, because it was delicious.

As we all finished our second servings, I placed my silverware down on the plate and leaned back in my chair, feeling completely stuffed. Gina and Henry were also sighing and stretching in their chairs as we all looked at the empty plates on the table. Shaelynn walked out of the kitchen and approached the table standing at the end next to Henry. "Did y'all have enough to eat?" she asked us.

"Oh my god, I couldn't eat another bite. That was so wonderful, thank you," Gina complimented.

"Yes, thank you. It felt like I hadn't eaten a meal in years," Henry added.

"Good, I'm so glad you liked it." She looked at me and added, "Sam, can I have a word with you?"

I looked at Gina and slowly stood up as Shaelynn walked back towards the kitchen, removing her apron. As we stood at the end of the counter, I said, "I want to apologize. I've seen some things these last few days that I just can't explain, and I've also seen horrors I don't think anyone could imagine, and finding someone that...," I paused a second and took a deep breath before continuing, "I just want to say, I'm sorry for the way I acted."

She smiled and placed her hand on my arm just below the shoulder and gave it a quick rub. "There is nothing to apologize for, dear. From the moment I saw you, I knew you were going to be in for some difficulties. And so far, I was right."

"Right?"

"I was right in that you were going to figure things out on your path." She turned and threw the apron on the counter.

"My path? I really wish you would've warned me about what I was going to come across on my path."

She smiles and replies, "People learn in many ways. Some people learn from books, some people learn by someone else showing them, and some people learn by themselves by just figuring it out for themselves. We are all different. By telling you what you would need to learn wouldn't have helped you learn and grow dear. I would've just been pointing at you, and you would've just walked and learned nothing."

I'm so confused. "I mean, I guess but…"

She cuts me off by saying, "Now I need to get going. Y'all are welcome to stay here if you need to until you figure out where you need to be. The door is always open. This place is safe if you treat it right. Don't let evil in willingly or it will not protect you."

As she made her way up the stairs, I asked, "You think we'll run into each other again?"

She stops and turns partly around and answers, "I'm sure we will go down the road at some point if time allows it. Stranger things have happened in Remembrance."

Confused, I asked, "Remembrance?"

"This city. The city of Remembrance." She paused for a second before she raised her hand and added, "Be safe, Sam." She turned towards the steps and walked the rest of the way up the stairs and headed out the front door. As I stood there, I thought about what she had just said. *Remembrance? That's the name of this city? That's a start, but where in the hell is that? I've never heard of Remembrance. One question down, so many more added.*

As I returned to the table, Gina asked, "So, what's our next move?"

Sitting back down, I answer, "The plan is still the same. Get to the Central Info Station and go from there. That still seems to be the only lead I have now to help us learn where it is we exactly are, and even perhaps how we lost our memories." Turning around and looking towards the stairs, I added, "Though I wish I would've asked Shaelynn if she knew what it was and maybe where it was exactly."

"Are you going to take me with you?" Henry asked.

"No. I don't think you coming along would be the best thing for you. Stay here in the church where it's safe. Hopefully, we can find some more help and even maybe a doctor or a hospital."

"I was hoping you'd say something like that," he said. He pointed over towards the small rooms and added, "Shaelynn said there were beds in those rooms that we could sleep on. Maybe it is best if we slept here tonight and then you three continue going in the morning. Besides, we should probably clean up our mess for Shaelynn."

You three? Oh shit, Danny. "That's right, Danny is still outside." I said, as I remembered seeing him before coming downstairs.

"Why did he stay outside in the first place?" Gina asked as she began gathering the dirty plates and silverware before taking them towards the kitchen.

"I really don't know. But I suppose I should make a plate up and take it to him since we stuffed ourselves already."

"Might as well, there is still so much left here I'm not sure where I'm gonna find room to put it away," Gina replied from the kitchen as I could hear running water and the sound of dishes clanging together.

I stood up from my chair once again and made my way over to the counter, grabbed a plate and some silverware, and filled the plate with a selection of food before heading up the stairs. As I reached the top, I glanced over at the window and saw that still sitting on the banister was Danny. I walked up to the door and opened it just as Danny turned around. As soon as we looked at each other, he said, "Hey, who the fuck was that black woman that left here?"

"A friend. Why are you sitting out here and didn't come inside with us?"

He turned away, almost avoiding the question before he said, "Churches aren't my thing. I don't need to be in there."

"But there's shelter and beds, and even food." I handed him the plate as he turned back around and looked down at it. He took it from me and without another word began devouring the food on the plate. He just used his hands and did not bother using the silverware I brought for him. From the chicken to the potatoes, the green beans, and sage, he ate everything with his hands.

"They got beer in there?" he asked as he shoved more potatoes into his mouth.

"Dude, it's a church."

"So, wine then?"

"Water, they have water." I shook my head. "Well, if you want more, just come…" I paused myself as I saw something in the distance run down the street. Danny looked at me curiously.

"What?" he asked as he pulled the plate away from his face.

"I'm not sure, but I think I just saw a little girl run down the street."

Chapter Eleven

"A little girl? What do you mean, a little girl?" Gina asked as she immediately stopped straightening the kitchen upon hearing what I said. I stood at the bottom of the steps as Henry stood at the entrance of one room on the right, leaning against the door frame, while Gina walked out of the kitchen and stood in front of me.

"I'm not even one hundred percent. That's what I saw. Danny was there with me too and he didn't see her. I'm not even sure if I even saw what I thought I saw."

"Well, we have to find out now!" Gina ordered, as she had an expression of concern on her face.

"Gina, wait a second," Henry said. "We haven't seen a single child since we woke up and now there is a little girl that just happens to walk around outside for Sam to see. Think about it."

She shook her head in disagreement. "If Sam says he saw her, then she must be there!"

"But that's just it," I interrupted. "I'm not sure that's what I saw. She was way off in the distance, and she was crossing the street, heading away from here. Plus, since it was just her, that meant she would've been alone, which is highly unlikely that a child would be alone."

Gina quickly cut in, "But we all were alone when we woke up in this city. She might be part of where we came from." Before Henry or I could say anything, she continued, "And I don't give two shits if that drunk bastard Danny didn't see her or not. If she's out there, we need to find her!"

"Okay, okay," I said to her as I grabbed her by both arms. "We'll go looking for her in the morning."

"The morning!?"

"Gina, the sun is setting again and there is an even bigger lack of light than the main street section; it's just too dark outside," I tried reasoning with her.

"If she's out there, we won't find her until the morning anyway," Henry tried adding.

She broke the hold I had on her arms and looked at us both with disgust. "I can't believe you two." She walked towards one room, entered, and slammed the door closed.

I walked over and sat down at one table as I leaned forward and placed my head in my hands. Henry limped over and sat in the seat across from me. We sat in silence for a minute before I asked without looking up, "Are we wrong?"

He sighed and said, "That's one of those questions that doesn't have a right answer. Say this child you saw, you REALLY saw. If we go looking for her now, it's more than likely we won't find her until after daybreak, anyway. And if you didn't really see her, then we waste an entire night looking for someone that didn't exist." He paused for a second before he continued, "If we wait until the morning, more than likely we'll find her quicker. And if not, at least we could still make our way to the station, anyway."

I lifted my head from my hands and said, "But that's just it. Danny and I were standing there on the steps of the church, and she just went running down the street like nothing. Not running like she was being chased or if she was trying to catch up with someone. Just running, like she was playing or something. That's what makes me so confused. Nothing in this fucking city is normal, or anything like someone would think is normal, and yet here we are experiencing these crazy things." I place my head back in my hands.

"And with that Sam, is it so crazy that a little girl would wonder around this city all alone?"

I lifted my head up out of my hands and looked back towards the room that Gina ran into. I could hear her slightly sobbing. "I really hope we aren't making a mistake."

Everything on the counter looked familiar and, in its place, except for two things. Sitting in between the sinks sat a lit candle and a piece of paper next to it. As I approached the sinks, the smell from the candle was extremely sweet and triggered a nostalgic feeling, but I could not remember why. I turned my attention to the piece of paper.

Looking at the paper, I realized it was a note with familiar handwriting on it. The note read, "*Come out and open your gift.*" I then realized that sitting at the top of the note was a small silver key that I had never seen before. The head of the key had three small circular holes that came together and shaped like the club suite from a deck of cards. Looking at the key, I said to myself, "What is she up to?"

I picked the key up off the counter, draped my towel over my shoulder, and walked towards the door of the bathroom. As I reached the door, before I opened it, I placed my ear close to the door. On the other side, all I could hear were the very faint sounds of a small, muffled voice. I reached down to the door handle, turned it, and opened the door.

As I pulled the door open, I clicked the light of the bathroom out so the only light in the bathroom was that of the candle. Once the door was all the way open, I stepped into the bedroom as light from the night filled the room with a calming blue hue. As I stood in the bedroom, I looked around at everything in the room.

The room's walls and ceiling were painted white with a mocha-colored fan at the center of the ceiling with the lights off, but the fan blades spun at low speed. The left wall was a wall of windows and a sliding door that led out to a small deck that gave me a view of the beach from the bedroom. The wall directly to my left next to the bathroom had a dresser on it, with a handful of pictures and odd items. Then at the far end of the room was another dresser, and a television attached to the wall and a walk-in closet.

To the direct right was a lounge chair sitting in the room's corner. Along the right wall was the king-size bed with nightstands on either side of the bed with small lamps on each nightstand, but they were off. On the bed, there *she* was. She was kneeling on the corner of the bed closest to the bathroom. She was completely naked apart from a small red thong that was tied in small loops at either side of her hips and a pair of black strappy stiletto heels. Her hands were handcuffed behind her back, and she had in her mouth a red ball gag that had black satin straps tied around behind her head.

Completely taken back by the image before me, I couldn't look away as her green eyes locked onto me as they slowly and sensually blinked at me. I took a step closer and asked her, "Baby, what is going on?"

"Sam, Sam." My eyes opened to see the ceiling of the small room in the church's basement. The small twin bed was not the most comfortable thing I have ever slept on, but it was much better than the ground I have used as a bed the last two nights. As I sat up slightly, my mind kept thinking about what I just saw; or was it a dream? My crotch ached as my dick pressed against the inside of my pants as I had a complete hard on after the dream; or was it a memory? *Who was that?*

"Sam." As I placed my hand on my crotch, I could make out the outline of a person. Jerking back, startled, I hit the back of my head against the headboard with a loud thud.

"Jesus Christ!" I called out as I started rubbing the back of my skull, trying to keep the lump that was sure to form from coming too quickly.

"Sam, calm down. It's just me." As my eyes adjusted a little better to the darkness, I could make out that it was Gina.

"Gina? What the hell, man?"

"I'm sorry, I'm sorry. I can't sleep."

What does she mean by that? Why are you telling me? "What do you mean, you can't sleep? What's wrong?" I asked as I sat up on the edge of the bed.

She sat down next to me. "I can't stop thinking about that little girl. I can't sleep thinking she's out there. We need to go find her."

"Has the sun even come up yet?" I asked, trying to get the sleepiness out of my eyes.

"I don't know, but I can't wait any longer. I want to go find her."

Before I replied, I sighed. "Seriously Gina? You can't wait until we are rested?"

"I'm not asking you; I'm telling you I'm going to look for her. If you want to come with me, that's fine, or you can just stay here with the others. But I AM going."

I stretched myself out a little before I yawned, then sighed again. "Alright, fine, we'll go now." Gina immediately jumped up off the bed and opened the door to the room. The light from the basement blinded me as I walked out into the dining area with her.

I knocked on the door that Henry was in before I opened it. "Henry, Henry wake up."

"Wha…what?" he mumbled as he laid on the bed.

"Gina and I are going to go look for the little girl I saw."

"What? You are?"

"Yeah. We're going, but you stay here where it's safe. Regardless of whether we find her, we will be back in a few hours."

"Ah ha?" he mumbled, as I could tell he had quickly fallen back asleep. We climbed up the stairs and went to the front door. I stopped her just before she opened it.

"Have you seen Danny?"

She shook her head. "No, he never came inside last night?"

"No. I gave him a plate of food that he had devoured. But he never stepped foot in the church at all that I saw. Maybe he's still outside?" She opened the door, and we both walked out to see something that confused us but did not surprise us. Danny was nowhere to be found. *Now, where in the hell did he go?* Looking down at the ground was his plate. Some uneaten food was still on it.

"He's not here," Gina pointed out as she was looking around the corner of the one side of the church.

"I don't know. Maybe he went into the church after we all went to sleep. Then that's fine. That means Henry won't be here alone."

"Then let's just get going," she said as she ran down the steps leading down to the street. Once I caught up with her, she asked, "Okay, where was it exactly that you saw her?"

I pointed to the left of where we stood, about a block away. "She was running down the cross street over there, heading east."

She turned around and started jogging towards the street with me not too far behind. Once we made it to where I saw the little girl, we both looked down the street in the direction the little girl was running. We couldn't see too far as it was very dark, with almost no light. I could hear an unnerving rumble in the far distance.

"That's where she went?" Gina asked as she hesitantly pointed towards the darkness.

"Yeah, that was the way. Do you want to wait for the sun?"

Lowering her hand, she said a resounding, "No."

Chapter Twelve

It takes us almost no time at all after wandering in the darkness for several minutes that we had become completely lost. The near zero light from any direction made me realize we had jumped too soon into searching for the girl. The dark rumbling sounds we heard at the front of us had now surrounded us from all directions. But it didn't discourage Gina as she continued pushing forward.

I could barely make out any shapes of the objects that were on either side of the street as we walked down the middle. The only things we could make out were the actual buildings themselves, but we did not know the colors or structure designs used in the blackness. There was no fear of traffic since we had not seen a single bus bringing passengers through this area of the city since we entered it the day before. At the lack of light from the streetlamps compared to the main section of the city, my guess was there had been no one down these streets for some time.

"Where is she? Where is she?" I heard Gina keep saying to herself under her breath. I was not sure why she was so driven to find this girl when I said that I was not even sure I indeed saw the child. It might have been my mind playing tricks on me or even a shadow of something else. Not to mention Danny was there with me and he said he saw nothing, either. *Am I going crazy? Has this city finally broken my mind?* I had a hard time believing my own thoughts that kept running through my brain on repeat as we continued walking.

"Where is she? Where is she?" I became worried about Gina.

"Are you okay?" I asked her as I reached out and grabbed her arm, making her stop.

"Yeah, I'm fine. I just need to find her."

"You NEED to find her?"

"We need to find her, yes!" she snapped at me, questioning her.

"Hey, sorry. Just why is this so important to you?"

"Because she's just a little girl in this fucked up city and if we are barely surviving, then what is a little girl going to do? How is she going to survive if she encounters a Gray?" This is really upsetting her. I could tell I was making her feel worse. *There's something more about this than she's letting on, but this isn't the time to question her about it.*

"Okay, again I'm sorry. Let's keep going." I let go of her arm as she immediately turned and started down the street again.

We continued down the road in silence for another few minutes before I heard her sigh. She then said, "I'm sorry, Sam. I didn't mean to be so sharp."

"Hey, don't worry about it," I replied as we kept walking without looking at each other. "I've been cut a lot lately and dropped a lot of blood. You may have been sharp, but you didn't draw any blood, so we're good."

I could hear her smirk as she said, "Okay, then. Hey, I wanted to ask you, how did you know it was east she went?"

"The little girl?"

"Yeah."

"Well, based on the way the sun rises and sets here, I just used standard bearings. But now that I think about it, this city is so screwed up in all reality, even though I said east she could've gone west, or north, or fuck she could've gone potato."

Gina started laughing. *That's good. Hopefully that helps her ease her tension.* Suddenly, we heard a loud high pitch screech in the distance to the right that was all too familiar. I grabbed Gina's arm again, hard to make her stop moving. Whispering to her, I said, "Fuck, that's a Gray." We quickly crouched down slightly and made our way over to the left of the street, trying to find anywhere to hide. We bumped into what looked like a beat-up old car half-assed parked on the side of the street, but up on the sidewalk.

We quickly got behind it and pinned ourselves to the side of the car. I slid myself down along the side until I got just barely to the rear of the car as I attempted to peek around the edge to see if I could spot the Gray. After a second or so, I soon saw it walking by itself out from between two buildings. It stood there for a second before it let out another one of its screeches. Soon it was joined by another that came out from another corner, then another that jumped out of a window from the second floor of the building next to the group.

CRASH!

Out of nowhere, a fourth appeared, landing directly on top of the roof of the car we were hiding behind, causing the roof to slightly cave-in and the windows to blow out from the front and back. We both dropped to the ground as Gina jumped sideways and rammed into me, knocking us both down. Before she could scream, I quickly placed my hand over her mouth to keep her from screaming as my other arm wrapped around her chest, trying to pull her close so she wouldn't move. I could hear her whimpers through my hand as she grabbed my hand over her mouth with both of hers. I placed my lips up against her ear and every so lightly said, "Shh."

The Gray stood on top of the roof of the car for several seconds looking left to right and back before it leaped off the car and traveled across the street, landing next to the other three. *Holy shit! Four of them!* The group turned and walked back down the alley that the first appeared from out of sight. As soon as we could not hear them anymore, I slowly lifted my hand from Gina's mouth while I still held onto her. Her breathing was so intense, I could feel her heart pounding so hard inside her chest.

Once another minute went by, I lifted my other arm off her chest and whispered, "I think they are gone for now."

Gina turned around and was now straddling my pelvis. She had her hands on the ground on either side of my head, supporting her up while she looked me directly into my eyes. "Grays? There are Grays in this section of town too?" she whispered back to me, just inches from my face. I turned my head and looked in their direction underneath the car. Seeing the coast was still clear, I turned my head back towards her and nodded. "What the fuck, Sam?" she whispered to me as she began climbing off me.

Sitting up against the car once again, I replied to her, whispering, "Okay, so we know they're around here. As fucked up as this sounds, that might be a good thing."

"What the fuck do you mean? It's a good thing?"

"If Gray's are around, then there's a really good chance that there might be more stranded people just like us."

I could barely see her face, but I could tell her eyes got wide when she replied, "Which could mean the little girl?"

"It's possible. But either way, we need to be careful." We both stood up from behind the now destroyed vehicle as I looked at the roof of the car. I then glanced up towards the roof of the building that was behind us. *Did that fucking thing jump down from the roof?*

Gina took a few steps out from behind the car forward and said, "Looks like we're gonna get some light. The sun is coming up." I looked off into the distance and sure enough, the small rise of orange and yellows filled the sky. As we looked at our surroundings, it became apparent that my previous thoughts about this section of Remembrance being abandoned were true.

The buildings themselves looked like no one had lived in them for years. Cracks in the foundations, vegetation growing everywhere, and many of the windows shattered and blown out. Anything painted had its coatings chipping and peeling away from weathering and neglect. Piles of garbage laid everywhere on either side of the sidewalks against the buildings and on the street itself.

Strangely enough, as the light filled the streets, the smells returned as well as foul disgusting odors of rot quickly filled our noses. "My god this is so disgusting," Gina said as she placed her hand over her mouth and nose.

"Hopefully, we can find more survivors and get the hell out of here quickly." We began making our way forward down the street again, only this time we paid attention to the alley the Gray's walked down to ensure they didn't pop back out again and surprise us. Before I could say anything, I heard Gina gasp in horror. Turning towards her, I could see her looking down a side street to our left as she dropped to her knees.

As I looked down the side street, I couldn't believe what I saw. Several people laid on the ground dead. Their bodies torn apart. The smell we were inhaling wasn't from the garbage, it was from the carnage. I dropped to my knees right behind Gina as I could hear her weeping. From what I could see, there were about a dozen people. Eight women and four men. The Grays must have killed them and moved on for more.

"There is no sense to this," I said out loud, not necessarily to Gina, just in general. But if one of the Grays jumped out of one building and from the roof of another, then there were probably more dead bodies in those buildings as well. Before I could get a word out, I heard Gina state something through her tears.

"There are no children." I looked at the back of her head, but before I could say anything to her, she continued. "There are no children here. They're all adults." She was right. Amongst all the deaths that were in front of us, all the victims were adults; not one of them was a child, let alone the little girl I possibly saw. "Sam, we need to find her, and quickly." She turned around and grabbed onto my shirt with both of her hands. Her tears had made little streaks of dirt run down her face. "Sam, we need to find her, please."

"Okay Gina, we'll find her, and we won't stop until we do." I did not know why I made that promise to her. I knew in the back of my head that if there was a possibility of a little girl being here, then the Grays might have already found her. But when Gina looked into my eyes with her sad green eyes, all I wanted to do was give her whatever she wanted. She reached out and hugged me so tightly as her sobs slowed down. It took her another minute for her to calm herself before she let me go.

As we both returned to our feet, I looked back toward where the Grays had disappeared. "It's probably not going to be a good idea to check where the Grays have been. But, since it seemed like they were still searching for more people, that means we might have a better chance of finding more survivors if we look where they haven't been."

Wiping her face clear from the last of her tears, she said to me, "Wait a minute. You want to follow them?"

"Not at all," I replied. "But if we can go around them and maybe get a head of them, then we might find more survivors."

"Okay, let's do it," she replied as she stood back up on her feet. We quickly made our way across the street and hid along the wall to the left of the opening to the alley the Gray's walked down. They were nowhere to be seen, so I knew they already had a gain on us. We ran up the street until we reached the next cross section, then turned down the street to the right. We continued running down that street, only stopping at each side street and alley to peer down, trying to spot the group of Grays.

It took us running and stopping for two blocks before we finally caught up with them. They didn't seem to move in any specific pattern or formation. They almost just appeared to be trying to spot any irregularity in the surroundings. One of them kept yelling its high-pitched screech every bit, which made the others follow it. *Perhaps that one is the pack's leader?*

I quietly crossed the opening to the side street from the right side to the left of the opening without making a sound. Gina looked at me as she prepared to do the same. I looked at the Grays, making sure they were not looking in our direction before I looked at her and without a sound mouthed the words, "Be very quiet." Once she nodded, I looked at the Grays again, making sure they were still unaware. I finally looked back at Gina and silently mouthed the words, "Three… two… one."

Gina began running and slipped on a pile of small stones that were on the ground, making a sliding shuffle sound before she fell into my arms. We heard one of the Grays screeches quickly as I pressed her against the wall. Slowly, I edged my head out to get one eye around the side of the building to see down the street. A lone Gray was looking up the street towards us, but he was just standing still.

Pulling myself back, I looked at Gina and said, "We need to get going. Be ready to move when I say." She nodded her head, but I could see she was pissed at herself. I looked around the corner one more time, but the Gray was no longer there. "Shit."

"What?"

"It's not there." I noticed that there were steps leading up into the apartment building just next to us. I pointed at the steps and pushed her lightly towards them so she would climb them quickly. As she reached the top of the steps, Gina tried the door and it opened. As we stayed crouched down, we entered the building and just before the door closed, we heard a thunderous crash right in front of the steps as the Gray stood on the now cracked pavement of the street. *This bastard jumped from the roof again,* I thought to myself as I closed the door quietly.

The door had a glass window on it I tried to see out while looking from the bottom of the door at the Gray as it turned and began searching the area that we were just hiding at. Gina tapped on my shoulder to get my attention. As I turned around, before she could point, I saw what she wanted to show me. At the far end of the hallway, you could see at the very end that there was a doorway that led out to the back-alley area that the other Grays were searching for. The problem was the door was completely missing and we could see the top of the heads of at least two other Grays. "God fucking dammit," I whispered.

Turning back towards the window of the door, I looked out again to see what the other Gray was doing and witnessed that it was looking at the stairs to the apartment building. I quickly ducked down below the window again. "Shit, shit, shit, fuck, shit." I whispered in anger.

"What do we do now?" Gina whispered, though she had a bit of a tremor of fear in her voice. On the left side of the room, there were stairs that went up to the higher floors of the building. I pointed at the stairs as Gina turned her head to look at them.

"We go up." We both made our way up the stairs but remained crouched. As we got to the first landing before ascending the next level of stairs, I glanced down at the door and saw through the window that the Gray was standing directly in front of the door. Without warning, the door blasted open with such force it shattered into splintered pieces. "Go, go now," I whispered loudly as we both ran up the stairs.

We climbed four floors, checking each floor's entrance until we found an unlocked door. Running onto the floor, I pushed the door closed, but there was no latch. I pressed Gina down the hallway as we tried to find any of the apartments that could have been unlocked. Door after door, there was nothing unlocked as we turned two corners, going into a square, trying to find anything. Attempting to bust open a door would be pointless because the Gray would find us just as easily.

"What do we do? Where do we go?" Gina shouted in a panic. As we kept running, I noticed down the third hallway at the end was a window that was busted open.

"There!" I shouted as I pointed at the window and ran to it.

"We're five stories up; you want us to jump?" Gina questioned in disbelief. Once we made it to the window, I looked out to see that the building that was next to the apartment building had a small landing that was a floor down, with a maintenance door that was propped open.

"No, we're not jumping to the ground. We're jumping to that roof there." There was at least a six-foot distance between the two buildings, but with the angle down, we had a chance of making it.

"You're out of your fucking mind!" As she finished her sentence, we heard a slam and then an immediate screech; the Gray found us.

"Look, just jump as hard as you can and you'll make it," I said as I helped her out the window. Outside the window was a foot-wide ledge that looked like it went all the way around the building. There was barely room for someone to stand on the ledge, let alone a running start. As she hugged the wall with her back, Gina shimmied along the ledge until she was directly in front of the other building's roof.

"I can't do this!" she screamed in fear.

"Yes, you can!" With another screech, the Gray was at the end of the hallway. It spotted me and immediately charged towards me. "Jump Gina!" I screamed as I ran towards it to cut it off from her. Off to the left was a fire extinguisher hanging on the wall. I quickly grabbed it and threw it, missing but forcing the Gray to dodge to the right. As it neared me, its right hand molded into a stabber as it lunged forward at me. I moved more to the left, but it was not quick enough as the Gray's hand sliced the side of my stomach.

Rolling onto the floor, I could hear Gina screaming my name. The Gray turned its attention to the window as it looked outside and found Gina. As I lay on the floor, sitting on the floor next to me was a dead plant with a large vase and a large plate underneath the vase that it sat on. I quickly tipped the plant over and grabbed the heavy ceramic plate and threw it like a frisbee at the Gray as it shattered on its shoulder.

Pulling itself back inside the building, it screeched at me again before making another charge at me. I got up off the ground and tried to run away, but I knew it was just too fast for me. Spotting the fire extinguisher, I dove to the ground at it, grabbed hold of it with both hands and as I rolled on the floor, tossed it sideways at the Gray just as it sliced its hand downward at me striking the extinguisher.

BOOM!

As the Gray struck the fire extinguisher, it exploded, filling the hallway with a giant cloud of white foam and powder. It screamed as it spun around, trying to escape from the cloud. I could barely make out the Gray through the thickness, but just caught a small glimpse of it. Quickly getting to my feet, I charged full speed at it, striking it with my shoulder, then we both fell to the ground as I bounced off the floor with a hard thud.

The Gray, still screeching, made its way to its feet quickly as I noticed that the arm that it struck the extinguisher with had been blown completely off just below the elbow. I also spotted that it formed its other hand into a stabber as I just barely made it to my feet and began climbing out the window. "Sam, what is happening?" I did not answer her as I shimmied my way over to her and grabbed her hand.

"Jump!" I yelled as the Gray smashed the other window to our left. We both leaped off the ledge and soared through the air, just making it to the roof of the other building as we both slammed onto the roof with the Gray screeching at us from above. As I lay on my back, I looked up in the sky and saw someone looking down at us from the roof of the building another four stories up. *Wait, who was that?*

I looked over at the Gray standing in the window as it slowly stepped backwards, pulling itself further into the apartment building. I immediately knew what it was going to try. As we both stood up, I pushed Gina forward as she ran through the open maintenance door first with me quickly behind it as the Gray leaped through the broken window and landed on its feet just inches from the door as I pulled it closed. This door had a latch as I immediately turned the dial, locking the door instantly. On the other side of the door, the Gray began pounding on it, trying to break it down.

"Wait a second," I said, stopping Gina from running down the stairs.

"What is it? We need to get out of here."

"I know, but we need to go up to the roof."

"What? The roof?" she asked with a strained and confused look on her face.

"Yes, just trust me," I said as I went over and began climbing the stairs as we heard the Gray screeching from the other side of the door. As we climbed to the last floor, another steel door that pushed open to the roof of the building met us. I immediately started looking around for whoever it was I saw on the roof.

"What are you looking for?" Gina asked as she gasped for her breath.

"I saw a…" Before I could finish my sentence, I was tackled from my left and taken to the ground as my right side struck the roof floor, sending shock waves of pain through my side from the opened wound on my stomach.

Before I could turn my head and look, I heard Gina scream out, "Hey, get the fuck off him!"

"You led them to us," a deep man's voice came from the person who was lying on me.

"We're here to help you, jackass," Gina barked as she tried fighting the man.

I suddenly called out from the bottom of the skirmish, "Us?"

The man pushed Gina to the ground and grabbed hold of my shirt and said, "Yes, us! And now we got those things on us because of you." Suddenly, a screech echoed out from behind us as two Grays jumped onto the roof, one of which was the injured one-armed Gray. "Fuck!" the man called out as he got up off me and ran away.

Gina ran back towards the door to the roof as I lay on the ground. As both Grays started walking towards us. I made my way to one knee as Gina ran back into the building through the door. *Please get away Gina.* Both Grays got closer, and I knew I had nothing left to fight them with.

"Sam!" I turned my head to see Gina standing in the doorway as she threw something at me. As it landed on the ground in front of me, I could see it was a short steel pipe that must have been used to prop the roof door open at one time. I picked it up and swung it at the first Gray in front of me, striking it in the knee as it collapsed to the ground screaming.

A sharp pain came across my face as the one-armed Gray kicked at me, striking me in the head and sending me coasting across the roof until I hit an air conditioning unit. As I sat up, I saw the Gray charge at me again with its stabber molded from its other arm at full extension. I fell over to my side just as it reached me as its stabber hand sliced right into the air conditioner and got itself stuck. The Gray kept kicking and stomping on me trying to get itself free. I grabbed the steel pipe again and swung backwards, striking it on its side, causing it to fall over while still stuck.

"Run!" I heard the man shout as I crawled away from the air conditioner. The other Gray had made it back to its feet and was approaching the man and what looked like a few other people. They were attempting to cross from one roof to the other, using some thrown together bridge with materials that were lying around on the roof. The Gray was approaching them so fast, however, that they weren't all going to make it before it reached them.

Getting to my feet, I quickly made my way over to them as fast as I could while screaming, "Hey, you son of a bitch, over here!" The Gray paid no attention to me as it got closer and closer to them. As it reached them, three of them still had not made it across the bridge. The Gray stood over them and raised its arm in the air to cut them down as they screamed out in terror.

CONCK!

Swinging the steel pipe down, I struck the Gray in the back of the head as its skull split open. It screeched so loud as it tipped over and collapsed to the ground, dead. I dropped to my knees in exhaustion as the three survivors looked at me, including the black man that tackled me. Gina ran over and immediately dropped to her knees as she said, "Sam, oh my god, are you alright?"

I shook my head and said, "We need to get out of here." The survivors quickly began making their way across the bridge one by one as I got back to my feet. As the last survivor made it to the other side, I turned to Gina and said, "Get across the bridge. We need to go."

Disagreeing with me, she shook her head and said, "No, you are first."

"Gina, please don't argue with me. Just go, now!" She stepped away and walked to the bridge just as the Gray that was trapped in the air conditioning unit screamed as loud as it could, got back onto its feet, and freed itself. As it charged at me, I turned to see that Gina had made it to the other side.

I began backing up onto the bridge, keeping the Gray in my sight. Once I made it to the middle of the bridge, I felt it bend down. "This thing wasn't meant to hold you up like this," the black man shouted. As I backed up a little more, the Gray stepped onto the rickety bridge as it bowed even further. I swung the steel pipe, trying to keep it back, deflecting its swing attempts with its stabber hand.

I glanced behind me at the edge of the bridge and saw that it was being held onto the ledge by two small metal pieces. I turned back towards the Gray and shouted, "Pull the bridge up!"

"What? No, Sam!" Gina screamed from behind me.

"Do it!" I shouted again as the Gray lunged forward at me again as I barely deflected its attack. The man grabbed the bridge and immediately began trying to lift it.

"No, don't!" Gina screamed at the man.

"Pull it up!" I shouted again, deflecting another attack. I could hear the man struggling and straining as he lifted the bridge.

"Sam!" Gina cried out.

"PULL UP!" The man screamed out loud as the bridge cracked and broke in the middle where the Gray and I were standing. The Gray screamed out as it began falling through the broken aluminum and brittle wood. As I fell also, I reached backwards and just got my hand on the ledge of the building as I felt the black man grab around my wrist with both of his hands. My body slammed into the brick of the building with a sickening thud. Hanging there, I looked down as the Gray screamed all the way to the ground, landing directly on its head and making a sickening, squishy thud. Dangling from the edge of the building, I again shouted, "PULL UP!"

The man began lifting me as Gina grabbed my other hand as they worked together to pull me over the edge. Once I was safe, Gina grabbed me and hugged me, crying as I lay on the ground. I looked over at the man as he sat on his butt looking at me with a grin on his face. After a few more deep breaths, he asked, "So, you're here to help you say?"

Chapter Thirteen

The screeches of the remaining Grays slowly faded as we put further distance between them and ourselves. We got very lucky that the remaining Gray's never came searching for their missing companions before we had gone. As we made our way down from the roof of the building to the street, it was apparent that there were fewer people in this group of survivors than I thought. There were at least a dozen people gathered in this small group. *How did they find each other?*

We listened for several minutes for the screeches of the Grays behind us until they had all but disappeared before we ducked ourselves away into another building to hide and regroup. I helped the black man that tackled me earlier barricade the door closed before we retreated to the upper floors with the others. As much as being higher up was a disadvantage with the Gray's ability to jump and climb with ease, the advantage of seeing more of the streets clearly outweighed the hurt.

Once inside the large room, I collapsed in the corner, leaning against the wall, and sliding to the floor in a heap. The black man kneeled in front of me and asked, "Are you doing okay?" The man was not a large man, more tone and broad but not very tall. He wore a white button up short-sleeved shirt with black epaulet patches on both shoulders, black dress pants, and black glossed dress shoes. He had a gold watch that looked like the face was broken and a pair of thin gold framed eyeglasses that stuck out of the left breast pocket of his shirt, but I couldn't tell if those were broken as well.

"Did you play football as a kid? You fucking hit harder than the Grays." I said as I winced, grabbing my side. Gina came over and dropped to her knees as she frantically searched through the med kit, trying to find something to help me. "How is everyone else?" I asked Gina.

The room was an exceptionally large apartment. The area we were in was the living room with a kitchen at the far back with large windows all the way to the right where three other survivors looked out scouting the street. To the far left was a hallway where I saw some survivors come and go, which made me think there were at least one to two bedrooms and a bathroom. The apartment was, unfortunately, nearly empty of all furniture and what was there was old and worn down, some of which was falling apart.

"Everyone is good. A little worse for wear but happy they got away from the Grays," she said as she pulled out the last of the patches from the kit. "Take your shirt off."

I waved my hand at her dismissively. "I'm fine Gina, really. I'm tired, that's all."

"So, he said your name is Gina?" the man asked as Gina nodded her head. Looking at me, he continued, "And you're Sam?"

With a slight cough, I asked, "Do you think we could have the pleasure of your name?"

The man sat down on the floor against the wall to the side of us and answered, "My name is Austin. And I'm sorry for tackling you before."

"I get it," I replied tiredly.

"We do?" Gina whispered as she leaned over towards me before she pressed herself against the wall next to me.

"Yes, I get it. You were just trying to keep safe all these people."

"That's right," Austin agreed. "I feel, for some reason, responsible for them all." His demeanor changed to grim before he continued. "And after seeing what those Grays as you call them, did to so many people that I could not bear to see it happen to anyone else." We were silent for a few seconds before he said, "How were you able to kill them like that?"

"It's not easy," I said as I tried sitting up straight against the wall but grimaced as Gina tried to help me sit up. "It was honestly an accident."

"An accident? How in the hell do you figure something like that out by accident?"

"We've had run-ins with them already. I had to fight a group of them as they attacked another survivor. We barely survived, but one of them retreated."

"Retreated? Are you fucking with me?"

"No. And then he had to fight more to save another survivor, and they barely made it away then too. Sam could only kill one of them that time," Gina defended.

"And now you killed two more. Pretty soon they're gonna come looking for just you." I knew Austin was making a joke, but he had a point.

"They are extremely fast and strong, but their bodies are weak to attack. It's just not a guarantee that you can hit them." I grimaced again as I grabbed my side, feeling the wet through my shirt from the blood. Taking a deep breath, I asked, "So, how did all of you find each other when you woke up?"

Austin turned his head and looked at all the survivors scattered around the room. "I'm not exactly sure. I woke up in the middle of a parking lot in front of a grocery store, but when I went to go in for help, it was closed. As I wandered around the city, I stumbled across groups of the others little by little. There were nearly thirty of us before the Grays found us trying to break into a closed restaurant. Without warning, they just started slaughtering us one by one. Some people tried running in different directions, but they were dropped without mercy." Tears began running down his face as he tried to hide them, wiping them from his eyes.

I paused for a minute as I watched him gather himself before I asked, "So, every building or store you tried to get into was already closed?"

"Yeah, why?"

"So, you never made it to or seen the main section of the city?"

He shook his head. "What do you mean? There's another section of this city?"

"It's strange, but there is a part of this city, the section we're in now, that is dead and run down and unpopulated. Then there is the other part that is full of life and modern and full of people," Gina explained.

"Wait, there's a section of the city that has people in it and not Grays?" Austin excitedly asked.

"Well, unfortunately, not exactly."

"Well, is it, or isn't it?"

"It's full of people, but those people are the Grays in disguise. The people ignore us because we aren't part of the city. But if you interfere with them at all, they turn into the Grays." Austin slumped back against the wall in disbelief as I continued. "But what I don't get is we have seen none of the citizens in this section of the city. So, why are the Grays wandering around almost patrolling the apocalypse section? Are these Grays this city's law enforcement or some shit? I don't know."

"But we didn't provoke them, they just started killing people," Austin spoke out in anger. "If that were truly the case, they didn't even try to restrain any of us. They just began murdering us!"

"We know, nothing makes sense to us either," Gina said as she tried to calm Austin. "We're not saying that's what they are. We don't know what they are other than they are NOT human." It did not seem to have calmed Austin down as he rocked back and forth against the wall, still in anger.

"There is no reasoning or understanding what drives the Grays. The only thing I know is that they are dangerous, and we need to stay as far away from them as possible." Austin forced himself to calm down as he began taking deep breaths. "Now, if everyone is up for it, there is a church not far from here that has housing and food. There are already other survivors there. You think everyone here is up for another walk?"

Austin looked at me, frowning, before he looked at all the other survivors in the room again. Without looking at me, he said, "I think they will do it whether or not they are ready." He turned and looked at me, "Thank you Sam. Thank you Gina."

Austin stood up from the floor and before he walked away, I stopped him and asked, "Hey, can I ask you one more thing?" As he looked down at me, I asked, "Was one survivor in your group a little girl?"

"A little girl? No, I have seen no children. I've talked to nearly everyone here and none of them mentioned a child either." He turned and looked at the small group before he added, "We lost a lot of innocent people today, and some that got away from the first attack aren't here now. So, I can't say for certain if anyone has seen a child or not. I'm sorry."

I nodded my head as he walked away and started talking to the other people in the room. I closed my eyes and placed the back of my head against the wall as I sighed in frustration. After a second, I turned my head to look at Gina as she sat next to me, looking at the floor. I lightly whispered to her, "We are going to find her, Gina."

Looking at me, I could see her eyes filling with tears as she whispered back, "No, we won't."

It took Austin maybe twenty to thirty minutes to talk with everyone and get them set to leave the apartment and head for Shaelynn's church. It wasn't so much as they had to pack since they had no belongings, but to give them all the time to rest and prepare for the journey. Once everyone was ready, we headed down from the apartment and headed for the street.

Gina and I knew the way back to the church, but the problem was we were unfamiliar with the streets for us to head back. We ended up needing to backtrack to where we ran from the Grays to find the right streets to get back. Austin was not happy about it. To make things safer, I ended up going ahead and checking all the streets and areas, listening for any more of the Grays in the area before going back to the group and moving them.

It was a slow and methodical process. The thing that scared me more, as I made my way back and forth between advancing and back tracking, was the fact that the streets were completely silent. There were zero sounds other than my breathing and the shuffle of my feet as I ran. I found myself constantly looking up to the rooftops trying to see if there were any lingering Grays watching us; there was nothing.

We eventually arrived back at the apartment buildings where we were recently attacked. Austin kept everyone back, hiding in the side alley as I crossed the street to scout the area. Approaching the side street in between the two buildings, I looked up once again and saw pieces of the poorly constructed bridge still dangling from the roof ledge. And then, on the ground, just like all the other dead Grays I had killed, a pile of gray dust in a wet spot circled around on the street where the Gray had landed. As I stared at the ground, I listened again for any signs of the other Grays. There was nothing.

Looking over at the apartment building front door to the right, I saw the wide-open doorway with shattered pieces of the door still hanging from its hinges. I signaled for Austin to bring the others out from hiding. As they approached, Austin walked up to me and asked, "How much further?"

"It's not far now. Three more blocks straight ahead, then we make a left." Austin signaled everyone to keep going as we all moved down the street without hiding. After about a minute, I said to Austin, "You might want to warn them, though."

"Warn them of what?"

"We must go back past where the others were killed. I don't know any other way around."

Austin looked angry. He shook his head and said, "Why did you wait until now to tell me that?"

"I'm just trying to warn you and prepare you. It's going to be a painful trip to get to the church for everyone. They are lying in an alley off the street. If everyone sticks to the street and doesn't separate from the group, they won't see them. But I was so focused on trying to make sure everyone was safe getting to the church; I'm sorry." After another few seconds, Austin closed his mouth, biting his bottom lip, and nodded his head.

Soon enough, we reached the end of the third block as Austin gathered the group together and began telling them that the journey to the church was almost done, but they were going to need to travel back past the recently deceased. Gina walked up behind me as members of the group began weeping and gasping in shock. "This has been such a nightmare to everyone." I had no words to respond to her. I just stood in silence.

Austin walked back over to us and said, "Okay, I told them. We are ready."

"All right, all we have to do it…" I suddenly stopped, stumbling my words in the middle of my sentence as my ears perked up. I could hear the faint sound in the distance. I turned to the right and started walking towards the noise. *What is that?*

"Sam, what's wrong?" Gina asked as she approached me, grabbing my arm from behind.

Is that what I think it is? "Do you hear that?" I said as the sound seemed to get further and further away.

"What sound?" Austin asked as he walked up to my other side.

Gina soon panicked and breathed sporadically as she, without warning, jumped into a full sprint, running after the sounds. "Gina, wait!"

"What is going on?" Austin asked, totally confused.

"I have to go after her," I said in a panic.

"Well, what about all of us?" Austin asked, even more confused and panicking himself.

"Just get to the church!"

As I ran after Gina, Austin called out, "Well, how the fuck do we get there?"

I spun around and shouted, "Just go eight blocks straight that way and then make a right and it's a block and a half and you'll see the church on the right!" As I got the last word out of my mouth, I ran after Gina, trying to catch up as quickly as I could. My side burned with so much pain that I tried to ignore it. Gina was in a full sprint as she kept getting further away from me. It was two blocks before she finally stopped and kept looking left and right.

As I eventually reached her, she kept saying to herself, "Where is it? Where is it?"

"Gina, wait," I gasped as I tried to suck more air into my lungs.

"No Sam, I won't stop. I won't give up." I knew she would not. Not after just giving up less than an hour and a half ago, and now she was so close. I stood up and before I could get another word out, we heard it again. "There!" she screamed as she darted down the street to the left.

We ran another block and a half before coming to a stop at a side street. We pinned ourselves to the side of the wall next to the opening. Gina looked down at the side of the building we pressed against and quickly pulled back. "I can't believe it," she whispered, as we could hear it clear as day. I traded places with her as I tried to look down the street myself.

The scream was terrifying as I waited a second and looked to see a little girl pinning herself against a wall, screaming in terror, but at what I could not tell. As I pulled myself back, I whispered to Gina, "That looks like her. But I can't see what she's screaming at."

"It doesn't matter, Sam. We need to save her," she whispered as she panicked. The little girl screamed again as I closed my eyes and tried to think. My body was in no shape to take on another battle with a Gray, let alone take it on and win. If I do not, she is good as dead. *You know what you must do, Sam.*

I pushed Gina back. "Stay here Gina."

"Sam, no. You can't fight another Gray. I'll help…" I cut her off.

"No Gina. I'll distract it so you can get her out of here."

"But Sam?"

I looked around quickly for some type of weapon, but there was nothing. I took a deep breath, then looked at Gina. She kept shaking her head, but I just mouthed the words, "Three… two… one." I ran around the corner and down the street in a full sprint towards the little girl. As I got closer, the little girl screamed again at her attacker before she spotted me out of the corner of her eye. She tried to shift herself sideways to back away from my charge as well.

As I turned the corner as soon as the street opened, I ran for where I thought her attacker was. I screamed, "Get the fuck away from her you son of…" I suddenly stopped in place, frozen in confusion. I could not make sense of who I was looking at.

Gina ran up behind me as I stood there, and she stopped in place too. Utterly confused, she angrily questioned, "Danny?"

Chapter Fourteen

It took Gina several minutes to get the little girl to calm down. Every time she tried to get closer to her, she kept backing away. Eventually, the little girl backed up so much that she was trapped in a corner, unable to move anywhere. Gina continually kept talking to her in a soft and friendly tone. “It’s alright. We’re not here to hurt you, we’re here to help. It’s all right. Calm down, it’s okay.”

I stood between them and Danny as I refused to take my eyes off him as he paced back and forth, shouting at me. “What are you looking at, you fucker? Stop glaring at me. What’s your fucking problem?” No matter how much he cursed at me and paced around like he wanted to hit me, I stood my ground.

After a bit more coaxing, the little girl took a step forward towards Gina. Gina, who by this time was on her knees in front of her, reached her hand out for the child to freely grab onto. Another step forward, and the little girl reached out and grabbed Gina's hand. She pulled the little girl closer and inspected her for injuries or any signs of trauma she might have encountered.

"Is she okay?" I asked, while keeping my eyes on Danny.

"She seems it, but I don't know for sure. I want to get her out of here, though, and get her back to the church." The little girl was no more than maybe four feet tall and very skinny. She might have been no older than possibly eight or nine. She had long brunette hair and a small, round face. Her flower-patterned outfit that comprised of a red t-shirt and matching red shorts fit her comfortably, along with her red sneakers that almost matched the entire ensemble.

Taking two steps forward, I asked, "What in the fuck are you doing here, Danny?"

"The fuck you mean. I was looking for the girl."

"Don't give me that shit, Danny! You said you didn't see her, and then you take off saying nothing to us?" I took another step forward. "And why in the fuck is she screaming at the top of her lungs at you like you're one of the fucking Grays?" I asked, while talking in a low tone. I knew after my encounters with the Grays from a few hours ago that I had next to no strength to get into a fight with Danny, but I hoped he did not test my bluff.

"I was protecting her from Grays you dickhead. There was no time to wait for your pussy asses to make a move. She just got scared of them." He had next to no signs of fighting a Gray, no bruises, no cuts. The only signs he showed were that he was sweating and that could've been nerves, or from running, or hell, from all the alcohol he'd been drinking the day prior.

"You said you didn't see her. I asked if that was a little girl and you said you didn't see shit." I got right into his face and said, "And now I'm supposed to believe that you came to find her on your own accord?"

He took a step back from me as he said, "You believe what you fucking want." He pointed stiffly at the little girl and added, "She's there and she's alive, and that's because of me."

I turned towards Gina and the little girl and Gina was still holding her hand, but she was now standing. I glanced down at the little girl, and she was looking at Danny, but with a terrified expression on her face. "We need to go, Sam," Gina said as she guided the two of them out of the back alley towards the street.

I turned back towards Danny and said, "I don't know what the fuck your problem is. Stay here or come back to the church. It doesn't matter to me anymore. If I can't trust you, then you're on your own."

I turned and began walking away as I heard him shout from behind me, "Well fuck you then!" As I reached the street, Gina stood there holding onto the little girl's hand, but the little girl looked like she was not as frightened anymore.

I bent down a little and looked at the little girl's face and asked, "Are you hungry?" Without a word, she looked up at Gina as Gina smiled and nodded her head. The little girl looked back at me and began slowly nodding her head as well. "Okay, we're gonna take you somewhere safe." As I stood back up, Gina walked with her slowly down the street. As they got a couple yards in front of me, I looked back down the side street, as I could hear Danny still yelling and cursing. The sounds of items crashing onto the ground echoed out of the alley. Shaking my head, I began walking after Gina and the little girl, but stayed back a bit to give them space.

As we backtracked a couple blocks to return to the main road, Gina and the little girl turned right and kept going as I continued to keep my distance but held them in my sight. After another couple of blocks, I looked back behind myself and spotted Danny walking not too far behind. *Son of a bitch is coming back after all.* I had a feeling that he would find his way back to the church because there was no other way for him to find food in this city unless he tried to find another bar or pub to trespass in. *Not my problem if he does anymore.*

As we walked another couple of blocks, I saw that Gina and the little girl were having a small conversation with each other, but I could not make out anything they were saying. My side was killing me as I placed my right hand over my side as the bleeding was getting worse and my shirt just would not soak up anymore of my blood. *When we get back, I need Gina to look at this.*

"Sam, where are you going?" Gina asked as she turned right down a street while I kept walking straight.

I looked ahead of myself before I turned towards her and replied, "We're heading to the church, aren't we?"

"Yeah," she answered. "It's this way."

"But we only walked six blocks from the apartment buildings."

"Right, and now we turn down this street to get to the church." She turned back down the street with the little girl in tow.

I looked back forward again. *Wait, what did I tell Austin?* I followed the two of them another almost two blocks and sure enough, there was the church. The two of them walked up the steps and went right into the church, closing the door behind them as I sat down on the steps at street level.

As I tried to catch my breath, I began thinking about everything that had happened over the past few days. I had woken up in the middle of a strange open field with an old woman that turned out to be Shaelynn. She showed me kindness and helped me get to this city, the city of Remembrance, where I end up meeting other people with the same memory loss as I had. The only thing we all seem to know is our names, but nothing else about our lives. None of us knew how we got here or why, for that matter. Then there is this city. Remembrance looks like any other major city and yet all its inhabitants are so off-putting. Shaelynn showed me kindness and compassion, but everyone else that lives here just wants to ignore us or kill us.

I looked up at the street and saw Danny standing at a corner, waiting for me to go in before he made his return to the church banister. As I shook my head, I stood up and made my way up to the door. *I want to talk with Austin, anyway.* Opening the door and stepping in, the church was quiet. I wondered why I did not hear any of the other survivors talking or see them perhaps sitting in the main room. *Are they all downstairs?*

I turned to the left and headed down the steps to the basement to see Gina sitting next to the little girl and Henry sitting across from them at one table. Both had enormous smiles on their faces as they watched the little girl eat. The little girl was helping herself to a large cut piece of a brownie as her plate looked like she ate half of her vegetables and a quarter piece of chicken. I walked over to their table and stood at the end; Henry and Gina looked up at me, but the little girl never looked away from her brownie.

"Welcome back, Sam," Henry said to me. "I don't mean to be disrespectful, but you look like hell."

"Hey Henry, has everything been good here?" I asked him.

"Yeah, it's been quiet. I didn't know when you two would be back. I never saw Danny; did he go with you?" Gina's face turned into a frown.

"No, but he's outside, keeping his distance."

"Oh," Henry said, confused. "Did you tell him to come inside?"

"I wouldn't worry about him right now." I turned and looked at our little guest. "I want to talk to this one here." I walked around Henry and sat in the chair next to him. The little girl stopped eating her brownie and sat back in her chair. "What's your name, sweetheart?"

She slowly looked towards Gina as she nodded at her, letting the little girl know she could talk to me. In a light and almost embarrassed voice, she said, "Angel."

"Angel. I like that. Well, you already know Gina and Henry here." Henry waved with a big smile on his face. "My name is Sam. I'm so happy we found you out there. Do you know how you got out there in the city?"

She looked at Gina again before looking back at me and shaking her head. "I was looking for my mom, but I couldn't find her."

"That's okay," I told her. "As long as you're safe, that's all that matters." I could see her wiggle a little in her seat, as I could tell she kicked her legs in the chair. "Well, if you're hungry, make sure you eat up as much as you want. We've got lots more."

She wiggled a bit more in the chair and looked towards Gina. Gina immediately said, "Oh, I know what that is."

"What? What is?" I asked.

Smiling, Gina stood up and said to me, "Nothing to worry about. We'll just be right back." She reached out and took hold of Angel's hand as the two of them began walking up the stairs.

Where are they... oh, never mind. I leaned back in my chair and took a deep breath as the pain in my side hit me again. Henry turned to me and said, "It was dumb luck you found her out there, wasn't it?"

"Dumb... or perfect timing. That damn Danny was after her."

With a concerned look on his face, he asked, "Wait, Danny was after her? I thought he said he never saw her?"

"That's what I asked him, but he claims he wasn't going to wait for us to discuss it and apparently went off after her and saved her from some Grays."

"He fought Grays? Is he okay?"

Shaking my head, I answered, "I don't think he fought anything; he was perfectly fine. Not a scratch on him." As I took a deep breath, I grabbed my side. "I don't know what his game is or why he lied about it, but as long as the girl... Angel is safe, that's all that matters." I winced as the pain increased more.

"You have Gina look at that yet?" he asked as he pointed at my side.

As I groaned, I replied, "No, I was more concerned with her helping all the other survivors first."

"What survivors?"

I looked at him confused as I said, "What do you mean, what survivors?"

"What do you mean what do I mean?"

"Henry!"

"What?" he replied with a nervous laugh. "You keep mentioning these survivors, but I'm telling you no one showed up here since you left days ago except you."

Days ago? We were only gone for several hours. I stood up from my chair in a panic as I walked to the middle of the room, holding my head in one hand while holding my side with the other. "No, no, no. What happened to them?" I kept asking myself. *What did I tell Austin? Did I give him the wrong directions? Did I say six or eight blocks?* Upset with myself, I stopped pacing and looked right at Henry and asked, "Are you absolutely sure that no one showed up here? I mean, it's hard for you to get around; could you've missed them, or the door was locked, and they couldn't get in?"

"Sam," Henry replied as he put his hands in the air and motioned them to calm me down. "The door has been unlocked the whole time."

"SAM!"

We both looked at each other as we heard Gina call for me from upstairs. I dashed towards the steps as I called out, "What is it?"

"Just come here. There's someone at the door." *Someone at the door? Is it Austin?* I ran up the handful of steps, skipping some to reach the top quicker, as I saw Gina standing near the bathroom with Angel standing next to her as they both looked at the door.

I glanced out the window next to the entry to see if I could spot anyone, but there was no one I could see. Please b*e Austin, please be Austin, please be Austin.* I walked up to the door and opened it. Standing in front of me on the other side was Danny. "What do you want?" I asked him, annoyed.

"Come on, man," he replied as he made a sideways gesture. "I'm fucking hungry. You got any more food in there?"

"Are you serious right now? What makes you think you have any right?"

"Look, I'm sorry I didn't tell you I went after the girl, alright? But she's here now and she's safe. So how 'bout you stop being a dick and let me fucking in?" I turned towards Gina as she still had her arms wrapped around Angel as she shook her head with a worried look on her face.

After a deep sigh, I turned back towards Danny and said, "Alright, but you do anything that makes anyone in here uneasy, I will personally kick your ass worst then any Gray could."

With a crooked smile on his face, he reached out and lightly tapped me in the chest with the back of his hand and said, "Like you could." He came inside the church, closing the door behind him. As he turned around, he spotted Gina and Angel standing off to the side and he chuckled a bit. As Gina squeezed her arms tighter around Angel, Danny winked at them both before turning towards me and said, "So where's the food?"

"Down those stairs. Just ask Henry." He walked past me as I saw him looking at me from the corner of his eye before he made his way down the steps.

"Sam, what the hell are you thinking? I don't trust him," Gina whispered to me, furious.

"I don't think I trust him, either." Suddenly, another knock at the door rang out, startling the three of us. I turned around and grabbed the handle and said, "Hopefully, this is Austin and the others." As I opened the door, I was shocked at who I saw on the other side.

"Hello Sam," the deep raspy voice said to me.

I answered back, "Hello, William."

Chapter Fifteen

"Well, are you going to invite me in or you just going to make me stand here?" William asked as he stood in front of me, smoking one of his cigarettes. Looking down at the street behind him, I could see his old car parked right in front of the steps. Still, no signs of Austin or any of the other survivors.

"So, I guess you got your car fixed up?" I stated cautiously.

He turned around and glanced at it a quick second before he turned back and said, "Yeah, got those nice new parts installed. She's running like a queen now." He took a big puff from his cigarette as he blew the smoke out of the side of his mouth slowly.

"You can't smoke in here," I said, pointing at his cigarette. "This is a cancer free church."

He laughed patronizingly at my comments as he took another exceedingly long drag from the cigarette and threw it to the ground without stepping it out. As he held the smoke in his mouth, he turned his head and blew it out in a long stream of dark smelling smoke. As he finished, he looked back at me and smacked his lips together like he just took a long drink and said, "Ah!" He raised his arms in the air, shrugging his shoulders before he said, "Is that better?"

"It's a start," I replied as I stood my ground in the doorway.

"Can I come in now, or are you going to leave me out here like a filthy animal?" I turned my head towards Gina and Angel as they both had scared looks on their faces. William spoke out again as he said, "I promise, I come in peace."

I really shouldn't trust him since he lives in this city. But I should hear what he has to say. I stepped back and to the side, putting myself between William and the girls. "All right William, in peace." He grinned and let out a light giggle as he straightened his black jacket's collar and stepped into the church.

As he closed the door behind himself, he looked around at everything inside the church. Laughing, he said, "I've never been in this building before." He took a few steps forward and turned his head towards Gina and Angel. Immediately he bent forward towards Angel and said, "Well, hello there, little one. Aren't you a slight problem and a half?" Angel quickly took a step back and hid behind Gina as Gina stepped to the side, blocking William from her. Amused, William stood back up straight, laughing.

He walked into the nave and took everything in. He walked halfway up towards the altar, chuckling to himself. "Shaelynn really knows how to fancy shit up, doesn't she?"

"I'm not sure I follow?" I said, as I trailed him into the main room a few steps behind.

"Don't act stupid Sam, I know you're smarter than that. I know this is Shaelynn's church. I know this is the place she's been keeping hidden from me." My heart sunk into my stomach when he said that.

"Well, we needed someplace to stay, since everyone in this shit city is trying to kill us."

He put his index finger out and pointed at me. "No, no, it's not. It is not shit." He lowered his hand and continued. "No, you have just been such a headache. Cutting out my Justices, interfering in the city's operations."

"Your Justices? You mean those Grays?"

"Grays?" He began laughing ridiculously hard at the name we've grown to know our attackers by. "That's cute, Sam, I like that. Grays!" He sidestepped into a pew and sat down, looking up at the religious markings and images hanging off the walls. "I employ my Justices throughout this city to keep everything moving the way it's meant to. Anything that disrupts that flow," he snaps his fingers, "they remove the issue." He takes a deep breath and points to the pew across the aisle next to him. I slowly walked up to the pew and sat down. "And then you come along and FUCK with my city." His outburst caught me off guard.

"Well, in my defense, all you said to me was to come see you to have a conversation. You said nothing about, 'Hey, the people in the city will kill you if you talk to them, so make sure you don't'." He didn't seem amused by that. I could hear noises from behind us. I turned to look and saw that Gina and Angel were up in the rafter area that was right above the opening to the main hall. *So that's where those steps on the right lead to.*

"And yet you never came to talk with me, Sam. I thought higher of you. I thought you'd have the common decency to ask for a cookie if you were hungry, not break the cookie jar." He started looking around the room again with a malevolent smile on his lips. Without looking at me, he said, "All you little rodents running around in my city, trying to steal my cheese. And now I gotta clean up all the shit you left on my floor? That's not the way my city works."

"What are you talking about? I'm sorry your *Justices* are dead, but do you know how many innocent people they killed, too?"

William slammed his fist on the bench of the pew and said, "No one is here without a reason, Sam. No one is here without me. This is MY city." He stood up from the pew and walked back into the main aisle. "If you are still interested in that conversation we should have, then come to my complex at the center of the city."

"I don't understand anything you're saying, William. I don't even know how to get to your complex. Where was the giant sign at the beginning of the city that said, 'If you are looking for William, just follow this yellow brick fucking road'."

William shook his head as he sighed. "Maybe you're not as smart as I'd hoped. You were already on the main road multiple times. Center Street? Just follow that and you'll reach it." As he started walking away towards the front door, the church started becoming darker and darker. *Is night coming already?* As he reached the opening to the nave, he turned back and said, "Now I gotta go deal with another pack of rodents you left wondering my city." He pulled his pack of cigarettes out of his pocket, shook it once, and pulled a cigarette from the box with his mouth before tucking it back into his inside pocket. He pulled out his lighter from his side pocket and lit the cigarette, took a big drag, and blew the smoke into the air.

"Hey, I said no smoking in here," I barked as I stood up from my seat in the pew.

"Sam!" I glanced up at the rafter to see Danny with his hand wrapped around Angel's arm as she screamed while he was pulling her away from Gina. *When did he get up there?*

Laughing, William said, "Looks like you got your own fucking rodents to deal with." Glancing down at the pew to my right, I saw one of the many scattered books that was tucked into the little storage space on the back of it. Quickly grabbing hold of the hefty book, without thinking, and threw it as hard as I could up towards the rafter and before he could see it striking Danny on the side of his head.

"Danny!" I screamed as he let go of Angel and placed his hand on the side of his face and looked at me in shock. At that moment, in one motion, Gina grabbed Angel and pulled her back away from Danny as she kicked sideways into his stomach, causing him to stumble backwards and fall down the stairs. Once he stopped, he picked himself up off the floor and ran out the door. "Danny, you piece of shit!" I screamed out, but he was gone.

Laughing so hard, William clapped his hands together and loudly said, "Well, goddamn, that was fucking beautiful. Maybe there's hope for you after all. And if not, maybe he does."

"William, what is going on?"

As he took another long drag from his cigarette and blew out the smoke, he placed the cigarette in his mouth and said, "See you soon, Sam, if you make it there." He turned around and made his way towards the door.

"What the fuck does that…" I stopped my statement as I heard a very loud screech noise come from outside the church. *He can't!* I ran towards William just as he opened the front door. "Hey, you son of a bitch, you said you came in peace?"

He turned around and with that same malevolent smile on his face, he said, "I did say I came in peace. I said nothing about leaving," and pulled the door closed. Shaelynn's voice popped into my head as I remembered what she had told me earlier. *This place is safe if you treat it right. Don't let evil in willingly or it will not protect you.* Suddenly I heard one screech, then another, then another, and another. Soon, the horrific sounds acted like they were surrounding the church.

"Sam!" I ran back into the nave and looked up to see Gina holding onto Angel from the rafter.

"Hurry and get down from there!" Just as I finished my statement, a crash came from one of the stained-glass windows, then another as two Justices jumped into the church through the windows. One of them immediately kicked the pew that was in front of it and sent the pew sailing through the air and slammed against the wall. The other jumped over the pews in front of it and landed right in front of me as I tried to back away. With a quick swing of its hand, it backhanded me across my cheek, and I went flying across the room to the right, crashing onto the floor.

"Sam!" Gina screamed. Before I could even make sense of what happened, the second Justice was standing in front of me and picked me up with ease. With no effort, it threw me all the way across the nave to the altar as I crashed into and through the large table. Everything on the table scattered everywhere as I rolled and finally stopped when my legs slammed into the wooden podium. "Sam! Get up! Run!" As I tried to move, I could feel a piece of the smaller wooden cross under my arm. *It must have broken when I went through the table.* I glanced over and saw one Justice quickly approaching. *Well, it worked before.*

Just as the Justice climbed the steps of the altar and stood right over me, I went to grab the wooden plank of the cross, but my hand wouldn't grasp the board. *Oh my god, is my arm broken?* The Justice reached down and grabbed me by the throat and lifted me in the air with ease. I did everything I could to loosen its grip; slamming my fist into its hand, trying to kick it, but nothing was working. "Sam, no!" The Justice was suffocating me, as I could not breathe. I felt myself getting weaker and weaker. I glanced over at its other hand as it molded itself into the stabber. As it raised its arm in the air, my eyes closed as I could not breathe anymore.

Out of nowhere, the other Justice screeched loudly. The Justice holding onto me dropped me to the ground and spun around to see what was going on. I opened my eyes and gasped for air as I looked towards the other end to see the far Justice spin around, then collapsed to the floor as Henry barely stood there with a knife from the kitchen in his hand. The Justice standing over me screeched towards Henry as he backed up, terrified. With my good hand, I grabbed onto the board and swung up as hard as I could, striking it in the back of the head. The Justice stumbled forward and turned around quickly, only to be struck again on the right side of its face as I nailed it with a second swing from the plank. The force from the blow sent it stumbling to the other side of the room. It crashed into the organ as it made a loud groan of air as the organ fell apart. I charged over to the Justice laying in the pieces of the musical instrument and before it could try to move; I raised the board above my head and brought it down like a hammer, striking it directly in the face as a loud thud and crush noise filled the church.

"Sam!" Henry called out. As I turned around to look at him, a crash and explosion of wood pieces from the front door went flying everywhere. Another Justice stormed in through the door and attacked Henry, sending him flying to the left and down the stairs to the basement.

"Henry!" I began limping after him when suddenly one more Justice jumped through yet another stained-glass window and landed on the rafter with Gina and Angel. The Justice screeched at the two of them as Angel screamed at the top of her lungs in horror.

"Fuck you!" I shouted as I threw the board in my hand up at the rafter and missed the Justice, but it turned its attention towards me. This gave Gina just enough opening to reach out and grab a folded chair from a stack of them stored there, and she hit it in the back. It fell over the edge of the railing and landed on the floor right in front of me. I saw that lying on the floor at the opening of the main room was the knife that Henry was holding.

I attempted to run around the Justice on the floor and grab the knife, but it reached out and grabbed hold of my ankle, causing me to fall to the floor. I screamed out as it felt like it was twisting my ankle to the point of snapping it when suddenly a folded chair landed on its head. It looked up to see another chair hit it, then another as Gina was throwing anything she could get her hands on down on it. After the fifth chair hit it, the Justice released my ankle, giving me enough time to leap forward and grab the large knife.

I flailed the knife backwards, catching the Justice in the arm as it screeched out in pain. I then sliced it again, hitting it in the chest, followed by another swipe, slicing its leg. Just as it went to stand up, I jumped forward and stabbed it right in the face as it collapsed to the floor. I fell back onto the floor, but then remembered Henry as I heard him scream out in agony.

With what energy I had left in my body, I stood up and made my way towards the steps and tumbled down into the basement. As I looked up, I saw the Justice had Henry pinned under some tables as they had crumpled from Henry falling over them. I picked myself up to my knees and shouted, "Hey, ugly!"

The Justice turned around; it already molded one hand into the stabber. "Sam! Help me!" Henry called out from under the tables.

"Yeah, you. I've seen better looking piles of shit from an elephant with diarrhea!" The Justice screeched at me as it took a few steps towards me. "Nah, you're probably too stupid to understand what I'm saying," I said as I enticed it closer and closer. As I tried to stand up, I immediately fell over to the left towards the counter of the kitchen as I caught myself on the edge to hold myself up. As the Justice got almost right on top of me, it raised its stabber arm back. I looked right at it and said, "You know what you fucking shit?" I spit an extensive amount of blood onto the floor. "Duck!" The Justice drove its stabber forward at me just as I fell to the floor, exposing an electrical outlet on the wall behind me as it pierced it.

The lights immediately flickered, and sparks of electricity came shooting out of the outlet while the Justice screeched and screamed out in agony. As it struggled to free itself, the smell of burning flesh and meat filled the basement. I crawled away from the Justice as fast as I could as suddenly its arm burst into flames as it cried out one more time before it fell to the floor.

"Henry!" I called out as he crawled out from under the tables as well.

"Sam, I'm okay!"

I turned towards the steps and shouted, "Gina! Angel!"

I faintly heard, "We're okay!" As I continued to crawl across the floor, I bumped into a lone chair in the middle of the floor that I used to prop myself back up. I stumbled over to Henry and helped him to his feet as well as I draped his arm over my shoulder as we headed for the stairs to go up. As we reached the top, we saw Gina and Angel standing in front of the disintegrated door.

"We need to get out of here. This church is no longer safe," I told them as I made my way towards the door with Henry still in tow.

"Sam, wait a minute," Henry said as he freed himself from my grasp.

"What is it, Henry? We need to get going," I said as I watched him reach his hand up and clutch the side of the door frame to hold himself up.

"I'm staying here Sam."

"Henry, what are you talking about? We need to get away from here before more come…"

He cut me off. "This is where I belong, Sam. It's okay. You all get out of here." He turned and looked back into the church. "I don't know what it is, but I feel like this is where I need to be. I'll just slow you down. Just go, and Sam, take care of these two." He let go of the door frame and took two steps forward while sticking his hand out.

I looked down at his hand and placed mine into his as we shook them. "Are you sure about this?"

"I've never been surer." He released my hand and waved at Gina and Angel as I turned and started going down the steps in front of the church.

"Take care Henry," Gina said to him as she waved at him as well. Henry turned himself around and limped back into the church just as a thick fog formed inside the church as it surrounded Henry. "Sam!" Gina screamed out as she pointed up towards Henry.

"No, no, no!" I screamed as I quickly ran as fast as I could back up the steps but as I reached the fog, it turned from the cold gray color to a hot orange, red, and yellow stopping me in my tracks. "Son of a bitch!" I screamed out at the top of my lungs, as there was nothing I could do. I slowly turned around and made my way down the steps until I reached the street, where I collapsed to the ground. "He's gone." I said lightly.

Gina stood and watched me as I laid in a slumped pile on the ground. In the far distance, faint screeches from the Justices could be heard. She reached down and grabbed me by the arm and pulled on me to get up. With tears in her eyes, she said, "We need to go now."

Chapter Sixteen

We got ourselves a good distance away from the church as the sounds of more and more Justices echoed through the night sky. They kept converging on the church looking for us, not knowing we were already gone. Angel walked in front of us as Gina had my arm over her shoulder as she tried to help me in our escape. I kept glancing back behind us and saw no glimpses of Danny in the distance. *That son of a bitch didn't help us, and now Henry is gone. What the fuck is his problem? What is it with Angel?*

I still didn't understand what happened exactly. Once the fog filled the church swallowing Henry, Gina asked me, "Is that the fog you saw outside the city?" All I did was nod in response. At that moment, all my energy seemed to exit my body. All I kept thinking about as we walked was that feeling of heat and the orange glow that came through; was he burned alive, or did it just end him instantly and without suffering? I just did not know.

My body hurt all over. I've had my head busted open, blood dripping on the ground, my arm and side sliced open, I could not move my hand, and bruises and cuts covered almost every inch of my body. I felt like all my energy was exhausted, but Gina refused to let me fall asleep. Every time I closed my eyes for more than a few seconds, she yelled at me to open them back up.

We walked for what seemed to be several blocks until Gina told Angel to make a right down another street. Suddenly, I heard Gina call out, "Angel, over there. See if the door will open." I lifted my head and saw that we were walking towards a large and fancy-looking hotel. The tan building looked to be at least fifteen floors tall, not counting the lobby. Besides the multiple double doors, the entire front comprised multiple large windows. At either side of the entrance, tall twin clay statues stood on either side of the entryway like guards to the hotel. Looking up at the building on each floor, the windows for each room had a rose painted border around them. The lights all seemed to be out and the vegetation at the front was all overgrown, but the front door opened without trouble.

As we entered the building, Gina leaned over at a cushioned bench and left me to flop onto it. The lobby had the same tan paint on all the walls and ceiling as multiple circular padded benches sat in the middle for customers to sit on as they waited to check in or out. To the far right was a wide-open area with tables and chairs with a stage at the far end of the room, like it was home to a conference before everyone needed to make a massive exit. To the far left was a large counter with multiple computers on it that the staff must have used to help their customers with their rooms, along with four separate elevators to allow access to the upper floors. Straight ahead from the entrance was an enormous set of carpeted stairs that went up to an upper level that led to more conference rooms. A walkway with a banister on the outside of it went all the way around the edge of the lobby at that upper level.

"Angel, honey, keep an eye on Sam while I check a few things." Angel nodded and stood right next to me as Gina quickly made her way over to the counter and climbed behind it. Once there, I heard her say, "Okay, well, there is power." She started typing on a computer that was sitting there and started sliding door keycards through a reader to activate them. Angel turned and looked at me as I lay there on the bench as she reached out and placed her small hand on mine. As my eyes closed, she shook my hand to wake me up.

As soon as Gina had multiple cards, she jumped back over and made her way towards a stack of suitcases and duffle bags that were lying on the floor. She picked up a black bag, opened it, and dumped all the clothes out onto the floor. She then returned to me and handed Angel the bag as she said, "Here, hold on to this for me." Angel took the bag from her, and she then helped me back up to my feet. She carried me off to the side as she made her way towards a set of double doors that had painted on them in white lettering, 'Employees Only.'

As they pushed the doors open, Angel looked up at Gina and asked, "What are we looking for?"

"We're looking for the kitchen so we can get some supplies and food." We walked halfway down the hall before Gina said, "There. Those doors over there." She walked up to a set of double doors that were painted white but had silver kick plates at the bottom and windows at the top on both doors so people could see if someone was on the other side before walking through. Gina backed into the doors with me still slumped over her shoulder, then we all entered the kitchen.

It was massive, with multiple stations throughout the entire room. Every counter and tabletop were stainless steel as the fluorescent lights reflected off every surface. At the far end of the room, in the middle of the wall, were two large doors that led into walk-in refrigerators. On the opposite wall stood large cupboards that ran along the entire wall. Gina turned towards the wall next to the doors and leaned me against them as I slid down along it until I hit the floor.

"Over here honey," she said to Angel as they together walked over to the cupboards. Gina opened each cupboard one by one as she pulled out all kinds of dry foods, bags of snacks, breads, cookies, and more off the shelves as they hit the floor and moved on to the next. Once she reached the last cupboard, she walked over to Angel and took the bag from her quickly as she dropped to her knees on the floor. Opening the black bag, she began grabbing item after item and stuffed them into the bag. After the tenth item, she looked at Angel and said, "Do you see what I'm doing? I need you to grab as much as you can and put it into this bag. Can you do that for me?"

Angel nodded her head and immediately began grabbing items and doing as Gina asked. Gina placed her hand on Angel's cheek and caressed it as she stood up and ran across the room to the exit of the kitchen. "Where are you going?" Angel called out.

"I'm going to grab some more supplies to help Sam." Angel turned to look at me and a second later turned back towards Gina and nodded her head. Gina quickly turned and ran out of the room through the farthest door from me so the door would not swing back and hit me on the recoil. As Angel had the bag almost full, Gina walked back into the kitchen carrying three or four med kits as she dropped them to the floor next to Angel and stuffed them into the bag and zippered it closed. "This hotel's Nurses Station has plenty of supplies to help Sam. We'll take these for now and come back if we need more."

"Is he going to be, okay?" Angel asked.

Standing to her feet, she looked at Angel and said, "I don't know, but we're gonna do everything we can for him." Grabbing the strap of the black bag she adds, "You think you can carry this?"

Angel grabbed the shoulder strap, picked it up and slung it over her shoulder, lifting the bag only a few inches off the ground. "I can do it."

Gina turned towards and approached me as she began lifting me up off the floor. "Come on Sam, we're almost there." She looked back towards Angel as she had already placed the bag back on the floor. "Okay Angel, let's go." Angel picked the bag back up once again as she followed us out the doors and back to the lobby.

Once in the lobby, Gina looked out the windows to see if she saw anything of worry before she walked up to the elevator call buttons and pressed the up button. After several minutes of waiting for any of the elevators to come, she called out, "Shit!

They must be not working." She looked to the far end of the room and saw all the way in the corner on the other side of the large, carpeted steps was a door that had red letters painted on it that read 'Stairs.'

"I guess we're taking the stairs." Angel sighed as we all ran towards the door as Gina kicked it open and we entered the stairwell. "We need to go up four floors," she said to Angel as she began climbing the stairs while trying to maneuver me up them as well. After we climbed one flight of stairs, we could hear the bag Angel was carrying hit the ground and then dragged across the floor before it thumped against each step, she climbed behind us.

As we reached the fourth floor, Gina reached out and opened the door from the stairwell and let Angel walk through first before following behind her, letting the door close by itself behind us. Walking down the hallway, she counted the door numbers. "412, 413, 414," until we reached the end of the hallway with a lone door along a separate wall. "Here, 417." We approached the door as she took one keycard from her pocket and slid it through the reader as it blinked red. "No, don't do this." She tried again and again it blinked red. A third attempt and again, it blinked red. "Come on!" she screamed at the top of her lungs as she tried it for a fourth time. The lock flashed green, and we could hear a click from the door. She grabbed the handle and turned it as the door pushed open. "Angel, go in quickly."

Angel, with the bag still dragging across the carpet on the floor, entered the room and let go of the bag after we all entered. Gina left the door close behind us on its own. The room was massive; there was a large couch and two large recliners on either side of the couch as they pointed towards the wall where a massive television was attached to it. Off to the left was a large dining table with six chairs surrounding it next to a full-size kitchen. On the right were three doors, two of which were already open, and they both led to large bedrooms with huge queen-sized beds in each, while the third door must have been a bathroom.

"Angel, honey, can you peek in each bedroom quickly and tell me which one has the bathroom in it?" Gina asked.

Angel ran over to the farthest room first, then immediately ran out to the second bedroom before running back out, looked at Gina and said, "This one."

"Thank you, sweetheart." Gina carried me just a bit further into that bedroom and once we were standing next to the bed, she let me go as I collapsed onto the mattress, bouncing as I hit while my legs hung off the edge. She hurried around the side of the bed and grabbed me, pulling me further up onto the mattress so I was completely on it. Turning to the bathroom in the bedroom, she ran into it, turning the light on, and said to herself, "Please have water, please have water, please have water." She turned the faucet on, and water came shooting out. "Yes!" she shouted as she turned around and added, "but no fucking towels!"

She ran out of the private bathroom and went to the other bathroom, grabbing every shower towel, hand towel and wash cloth she could find before returning. As she returned to the bedroom, she dropped all that she had brought on the floor. She then turned to Angel and said, "Remember those red packages I put inside our bag? I need you to grab those for me as quickly as you can."

"Okay," Angel said as she turned and ran out of the room to the black bag, opened it, and returned with the med kits.

"Thank you, honey. Now, I need you to go out to the other room and close this door behind you. I need to help Sam."

"But I want to help him too," she answered as she reached out and grabbed Gina's hand.

Gina squeezed her hand back and added, "I know you do, and you are so amazing because you want to help. But Sam is in a lot of pain and it's going to get really scary in a minute. I promise, once the scary part is over, I'll let you back in so you can help."

"But I…"

Gina cut her off. "Please Angel. Close the door, quickly." Angel, with a frightened look on her face, turned and ran out of the room, closing the door behind her. Gina then turned her attention to me as she quickly unbuttoned my shirt and then removed it from one sleeve, then the other. As she pulled the shirt from the arm with my bad hand, I immediately screamed out in pain. "What's wrong?" she asked me.

With almost no volume to my words, I said, "I… can't… move my… hand."

She immediately started examining my hand, then my arm to my shoulder. Once she finished, I heard her state under her breath, "Damn it." She walked over and grabbed a handful of shower towels and a hand towel before returning to me.

"What… is wrong?" I breathed.

"Your entire arm is out, dislocated." She began wrapping the towels around me and around my arm. "I need to reset it; it will not feel good." She quickly pulled her jacket off and tossed it across the room.

"Well, I all… already feel… like… shit."

She folded the hand towel into a small rectangle, making it thick, and placed it into my mouth. "Bite down on this." As I closed my mouth down onto the towel, she lifted my hand and used the towels as an almost pulley system to help her. "When I count to three, I'm going to set your arm, then your wrist. Don't tense up." I nodded my head as she steadied herself in place next to the bed. *Okay, don't tense, don't tense…*

Without warning or counting, Gina immediately pulled on my arm and the towels as I felt a humongous and painful pop in my shoulder. I screamed out in agonizing pain before closing my eyes and passing out.

Chapter Seventeen

The steam in the shower felt so good, along with the hot water that was running down my body. It was a weird feeling in my hands; between the heat of the water and the cold from the tiles along the wall as both hands were pressed against the wall as I leaned under the showerhead. I could see the last of the soap that had been washed off my body circling around the drain before getting washed away with the water. I thought to myself, *how long have I been in here?*

The shower itself was a delicate design. From the floor all the way to the ceiling were square tiles of a solid cream coloring with splashes of browns, grays, and oranges. The dark brass colored shower head was exceptionally large; it reached out on a short arm from the wall before a giant circular head hovered above me with different rows and patterns of spray holes for the water to stream from. Attached to the side was a flange for switching the water flow from the shower head to a hose of the same coloring with a smaller handheld shower head one could use to reach areas of your body for better cleaning. Below there were two nobs that came out of the wall. One with a large red 'H' and the other with a large blue 'C.'

On the left were small lips indented in the wall where the soaps and shampoos sat safely stored in arms at reach, along with a bar, just in case needed for support. To the right, half the length of the opposite wall, was another wall and then an opening to step out of the shower and enter the rest of the bathroom. At the bottom of the opening was a small lip that came up out of the floor so to trap water in the shower and not let it leak out onto the floor.

Reaching down to the hot and cold knobs, I turned them until the water finally stopped. Glancing around, I could see that the different shower soaps, shampoos, and conditioners that were sitting on the lips in the wall left me know I was not the only person who used this shower. After the water was completely off, I stepped over the lip on the floor and out of the shower. To my left, a small towel bar was attached to the wall where I reached and grabbed my towel to dry myself off.

The bathroom was impressive. To my right, on the other side of the wall where the shower stall was, sat the toilet and a large closet that looked like it stored all the extra bathroom supplies and the clean, unused towels. In front of me, on the opposite wall placed under two large sky windows in the ceiling, was a large tub that looked like it could be a jacuzzi. It had two small steps that you would need to climb up to step in. Next to the tub was a large mirror on the wall and a long countertop and dual sinks that had another assortment of soaps, skin care products, toothbrushes and more.

Everything on the counter looked familiar and, in its place, except for two things. Sitting in between the sinks sat a lit candle and a piece of paper next to it. As I approached the sinks, the smell from the candle was extremely sweet and triggered a nostalgic feeling, but I could not remember why. I turned my attention to the piece of paper.

Looking at the paper, I realized it was a note with familiar handwriting on it. The note read, "*Come out and open your gift.*" I then realized that sitting at the top of the note was a small silver key that I had never seen before. The head of the key had three small circular holes that came together and shaped like the club suite from a deck of cards. Looking at the key, I said to myself, "What is she up to?"

I picked the key up off the counter, draped my towel over my shoulder, and walked towards the door of the bathroom. As I reached the door, before I opened it, I placed my ear close to the door. On the other side, all I could hear were the very faint sounds of a small, muffled voice. I reached down to the door handle, turned it, and opened the door.

As I pulled the door open, I clicked the light of the bathroom out so the only light in the bathroom was that of the candle. Once the door was all the way open, I stepped into the bedroom as light from the night filled the room with a calming blue hue. As I stood in the bedroom, I looked around at everything in the room.

The room's walls and ceiling were painted white with a mocha-colored fan at the center of the ceiling with the lights off, but the fan blades spun at low speed. The left wall was a wall of windows and a sliding door that led out to a small deck that gave me a view of the beach from the bedroom. The wall directly to my left next to the bathroom had a dresser on it, with a handful of pictures and odd items. Then at the far end of the room was another dresser, and a television attached to the wall and a walk-in closet.

To the direct right was a lounge chair sitting in the room's corner. Along the right wall was the king-size bed with nightstands on either side of the bed with small lamps on each nightstand, but they were off. On the bed, there *she* was. She was kneeling on the corner of the bed closest to the bathroom. She was completely naked apart from a small red thong that was tied in small loops at either side of her hips and a pair of black strappy stiletto heels. Her hands were handcuffed behind her back, and she had in her mouth a red ball gag that had black satin straps tied around behind her head.

Completely taken back by the image before me, I couldn't look away as her green eyes locked onto me as they slowly and sensually blinked at me. I took a step closer and asked her, "Baby, what is going on?" With another sensual blink of her eyes, she slowly tilted her head to the right of her as the light from the moon reflected off her face, revealing the freckles on her cheeks under her eyes.

I quickly realized that she was pointing her head towards the dresser along the wall as I spotted sitting on top another lit candle burning. As I approached the dresser, I noticed that there was another note folded in half sitting next to the candle. I dropped my towel on the floor and picked up the note, as I could hear her light moan as she watched me. As I opened the folded piece of paper, I read to myself the long-handwritten words.

Sam,

Thank you for everything you do for us to give us this beautiful life we live. Thank you for waking up every day and doing what needs to be done without question or thoughts of return. Thank you for working for a job that I know you don't like so that I can achieve my goals and live my dreams. Every single day, I miss you every single hour we're not together. Tonight, let me show you how much I appreciate you, how much I love you. Tonight, my body is yours.

Closing the note, I returned it to the dresser, laid the key on top of it, and made my way over towards the bed. As I approach, I can hear her breathing intensify, as if she was preparing herself for me to attack her. Yet as I now stood directly in front of her, I raised my right hand and placed it next to her left cheek allowing my thumb to, ever so gently, slide across her soft skin along the top edge of the satin strap of the gag. After several soft brushes of my thumb on her cheek, she locked her soft green eyes onto mine as I placed my index finger behind the strap and lowered it slowly, removing the ball gag, allowing it to rest around her neck. Before she could say one word, I quickly bent over and locked my lips onto hers in a passionate kiss as our tongues wrestled with each other's.

After several seconds of our embrace, I pulled myself away from our kiss and grabbed the ball gag, returning it to its place in her mouth. She let out a moderate moan as she knew I knew if the gag were in her mouth, there would be no hiding her pleasure. She locked her eyes back onto mine as she watched me reach out, grabbing onto her and lifting her off the edge of the bed, allowing her feet to touch the floor so she was now standing. Even with the stiletto heels on, she was still a whole foot shorter than I was.

Reaching out with both hands, I took hold of both her breasts and began gently massaging them, playing with her nipples in between my fingers. She moaned lightly as she closed her eyes as I bent down and began kissing her neck. As I felt her body tremble, I let go of her breasts and began slowly gliding my fingertips of my right hand down and back up along her stomach, gradually getting lower and lower each time down until I was gracing the edge of her thong. A stiff moan escaped from her lips, passed the gag as my fingers crawled in between her legs and began teasing her.

She could not hide her ecstasy as she moaned so loudly through the gag. I lowered myself to my knees in front of her as the smell of her excitement was present for me. I reached out with both hands and slowly untied both sides of her thong, as it fell to the floor in between her legs. Once she was completely exposed, I returned my fingers to their place of playing with her, except now they were completely free to massage her, tease her, please her. As I kissed her inner thigh, my fingers continued dancing around, getting so wet as they began slipping inside her as she screamed out.

Before too long, her passionate moans of rapture filled the room as her body trembled and almost collapsed, unable to resist my touch anymore. I quickly jumped up and caught her in my arms, keeping her from falling to the floor. It took her a second to regain herself as she glanced up at me while breathing so heavily, drool leaked out from the edges of the gag. "Are you okay, baby? Do you want to continue?" She straightened herself back up and looked me right in the face as she nodded her head.

I walked back over to the dresser and retrieved the key for the handcuffs. As I returned, I placed the key on the edge of the mattress and slowly turned her around and pulled her close to my body with her back against my chest and her hands still clasped rested just north of my crotch. Reaching my arms around her, I began slowly rubbing her stomach again as my hands made their way down, massaging in between her thighs, then returning up. Meanwhile, I kissed her neck while every so often, in between kisses, I lightly nibbled on her ear as she let out a quick scream as her brunette and blonde hair softly draped down me against my chest.

As this is happening, I could feel her slowly twisting her hips back and forth, rubbing her ass against my crotch, slowly from her right cheek to her crack, to the left cheek, then back. With her hands still in their bindings, her fingertips softly made crawling motions against my lower stomach muscles as they tried to reach for me but could not move. To torture her more, I moved my left hand up to her breast while my right hand reached down in between her legs again. Moaning so loudly, she wrapped her right leg around my leg as she trembled. The more she squirmed against my body, the more I pleased her until she once again exploded in passion, screaming out as I held her tight.

Once I felt her gather herself once more, I backed away from her and grabbed the key off the bed. Placing the key in my mouth, I reached up and untied the ball gag, removing it from her lips as she drew in a deep breath as I tossed it to the floor. Taking the key out of my mouth, I then unclasped both her hands from the handcuffs and tossed them to the floor as well. Once freed, she immediately turned around and got so close to my body as she reached down with her right hand and grabbed hold of me as I was at this point completely fully hard and erect.

With her left hand, she reached up and quickly ran her fingers through my hair as she pulled me down and locked lips with me in such an intense kiss. While she stroked me slowly with her right hand, after several seconds of our kiss, she pulled herself back. Looking me directly in my eyes, she moaned out softly, "I need you inside me, Sam." I intensely reached out, grabbed her, and lifted her up in the air. She wrapped both arms around my neck while she also wrapped both her legs around my hips as I held onto her by her ass.

Turning around towards the bed, I took the couple of steps to reach it and slowly lowered her down onto the bed. Once she touched the sheets, she crawled back until she was in the middle of the mattress as I crawled with her, keeping myself in between her legs. As she stopped crawling, I got within inches of her face as we began kissing each other again passionately as she laid herself back against the mattress until I was over top of her. As we pulled our lips away from each other, I placed both arms on either side of her shoulders to balance myself. She placed her fingers against her mouth and spit a little into her hand, then reached down in between both of us; she started smoothing her saliva up and down on me until I was nice and slick.

Once she was satisfied, she guided me between her legs, closer and closer, teasing herself with the edge of my fully erect dick as she let out a quick moan. I could feel the tip of me sliding into her as she moaned and whimpered with every inch. Spreading her legs out, she reached her hands up around my upper back, just under my arms, and pulled me forward, letting me know what to do. I lowered myself slowly as I felt myself moving more and more until I sensed her trembling. As I eased myself, filling her as much as I could, she let out such a passionate scream as she dug her nails into my back.

I began moving my hips back and forth slowly as our eyes stayed locked on each other. Her hands went from behind my back to the sides of my face as I kissed the palm of her right hand. Before too long, I could feel her muscles tighten around me; I moved my hips a little faster as my breathing became quicker. As my tempo increased, she moaned out with every other motion of my hips.

The sounds of our love filled my ears with such excitement as I moved in and out of her as the sensations felt like shock waves that spread all over my body. Every time her muscles clinched around me, and she screamed out, it sent chills of such ecstasy up my spine. The washed over expression of passion and pleasure all over her face as I kept moving just drove me more and more. Before too long, I felt myself swell inside her, as I knew I had a little longer to last.

As I looked into her passion drunk eyes, I whispered to her, "I can't hold it any longer."

She wrapped her legs around my back tightly as she replied to me, "Give it to me, Sam. Give it all to me." Hearing that made me move my hips back and forth so fast and hard as she screamed with such pleasure as she reached to her sides and clinched hold of the bed sheets so hard her knuckles were turning pale. Faster and harder I kept moving until I finally felt myself explode as a grumbling moan exited my mouth and she intensified her grip with her legs around me, not letting me pull away from her.

After a couple minutes, as we both began regaining our breath, she slowly released the grip around my back that her legs had as I gently removed myself from her and collapsed on the bed next to her. She turned to her side and placed her leg on top of mine. Facing me, while looking deep into my eyes, she whispered to me, "I love you, Sam."

Smiling at her, I replied softly, "I love you too…"

Chapter Eighteen

My eyelids fluttered randomly as they slowly opened, revealing a blur to the room. As my eyes tried to focus, my entire body felt so stiff that I could barely move. I lifted my arm out from under the bed sheets and rubbed my eyes to help them clear. Once I finished, my eyes focused as I stared at the beige colored roof. Throwing the covers off me, I quickly realized that I was completely naked. I suddenly felt a shift in the bed as I turned my head to my right and saw Gina sleeping on the other side of the bed. She was on top of the bedcovers but was under a separate blanket.

What the hell is going on? As I turned back around, I grabbed at my side to feel the slice in my stomach was covered up by bandages. In fact, all my cuts were patched completely up, and my right arm was wrapped and held close to my body. *That's right, now I remember. She told me it had been dislocated.* Looking around the room, this was a genuinely pleasant bedroom. The bed was at the center of the room, with the headboard attached to the wall. On the left side of the room there was a caramel-colored nightstand with a gold-colored lamp on it with a frosted shade at the top and a digital clock that just kept blinking 12:00. At the far wall was a doorway that was open to a small bathroom that had white towels lying on the floor. Even though the light was out in the bathroom, I could still see the towels were stained with blood. To the right of the bathroom door was a tall standing shelf that seemed to have multiple med kits stacked on it with different pill bottles, ointments, and bandage wraps, along with more folded towels and what looked like clean folded clothes.

To the far right was a long dresser with eight drawers, two columns of four, which had different opened packages of food and empty water bottles strewn all over the top. In the room's corner, a large flat screen television that was attached to the wall near the roof pointing down towards the bed. Looking towards the front of the room where the door to the bedroom was, on the floor next to the doorway, I could see a pile of clothes that used to be mine. They looked as though they were completely torn apart. Yet next to that pile were my shoes, then Gina's sneakers, and then a pile of clothes that were the clothes she was wearing.

Wait, did we? Is she naked under that blanket? My mind then quickly remembered the vision, or memory, or was it a dream? I could remember every little detail except the woman. Nearly everything about the woman reminded me of Gina, but I could not say definitively that it was Gina. All I knew was it was so real, the feeling of her breath against my face, the touch of her skin. Everything about her was Gina, and yet it was not.

I spun myself to the left gingerly as my legs dropped from the mattress, letting my feet touch the floor. I heard a soft moan come from behind me and then an immediate jarring of the bed as I knew Gina had popped up. "Sam!" she called out as I felt her stand up from the bed.

"Hey there," I said weakly. I heard her footsteps hit the floor as she dashed from the right side to the left side of the bed. As she stopped right in front of me, I saw she was wearing different clothes. Not just different, but much less than before as she had her hair pulled out of its ponytail as it dropped onto her shoulders, a larger t-shirt that had cartoon characters on it and the hint of her underwear as I could see the red panties that just barely covered her in between her legs. *It's more than what I got on.*

"How are you feeling?" she asked as she placed her hand on my forehead.

"How do I feel? Like I just called Larry Holmes a pussy."

"Who's that?"

"Wha… how do you… nevermind. I feel like shit, but I'm alive. I have you to thank for that, don't I?"

She removed her hand from my forehead as she answered, "Well, it was rough there for a minute. You were burning up and had a high fever that seemed like it didn't want to break."

Rubbing the pain in my shoulder, I replied, "I don't remember any of that."

She handed me an opened bottle of water and some pills and said, "I'm not surprised. You were unconscious for a while."

"Unconscious?" I asked, placing the pills in my mouth, and taking a sip of the water to help me swallow. "Then how did I get like this, sporting my fancy birthday suit?"

Taking the bottle of water from me and setting it on the nightstand she said, "I needed to help cool you down, not to mention all of your injuries that I needed to mend, I had little choice, so I got you out of what was left of your clothes then cleaned you up and kept putting cold compresses on you to help your fever."

"Wait," I blurted. "You keep saying I had a fever. How did you know I had a fever?"

"There were thermometers inside the med kits. I just used one to get your temp."

"Okay, I get that. But if I was unconscious, then how…" I halted mid-sentence and looked at her with a blank stare.

She frowned at me as she cocked her head to the side. "Be an adult. I needed your temperature, and you were already naked."

Swallowing hard, I sighed, "I was really hoping you were going to tell me that pain was me falling down the stairs."

Putting her hand on my face and pushing my head to the side playfully, she said, "You're an idiot." She reached over and grabbed a wrapped bar off the nightstand and handed it to me. "Here, eat this." As I opened the package, it was a granola bar that had dried fruit mixed into it. Taking a bite, it was a little hard, but my taste buds immediately tasted the sweetness of it.

"Not bad," I said as I swallowed slowly.

"It's not Shaelynn's cooking, but it's better than nothing." She walked over to the one shelf and grabbed the stack of folded clothes and showed them to me. "Angel and I found clothes that might fit you. There are a few choices to pick from if you want to get dressed." After placing the clothes back on the shelf, she turned back and grabbed my bandaged arm. "Can you move this arm without any issues?"

After I threw the wrapper of the bar into a small waste basket next to the nightstand, I lifted my arm in the air slightly. The pain shot through it like lightning but looking at my hand able to open and close was a relief. "It hurts like hell, but I think I'll manage as long as I don't have to use it to carry hundreds of pounds."

"Okay, good."

As she turned and walked back to the other side of the bed, I asked, "But wait, you said you guys found clothes?" I shifted slightly to turn around as I just caught sight of Gina facing the wall, taking the large t-shirt off and exposing her bare back. Now, she is almost completely naked except for the panties, which I realized was a red laced thong. I quickly spun myself back around before she noticed I had seen her.

As I listen to the rustling sounds behind me, I quickly realize she was getting dressed. "Yeah, as you slept, Angel and I explored this hotel and we found lots of suitcases full of stuff. We found new clothes for her, you, and me, along with more food and extra med kits." As she came back around to the other side of the bed to stand in front of me once again, I saw her new outfit. "I was really surprised we found anything for Angel. With her so far being the only child we've seen; I wasn't betting on there being a single thing usable in her size. But there was plenty for her to pick from."

As she put her hair back up into a ponytail, she was now wearing black and brown patched yoga pants and a more figure fitting brown t-shirt with the same patterns matching the pants. She threw a hooded maroon sweatshirt onto the bed that looked like it had gold lettering of some university. She dropped to the floor in front of me as she began putting her sneakers back on. "Anyway, what I was trying to say to you was if you needed help to get dressed, I could help you."

"I think I can handle it; I have been getting dressed myself my whole life."

Grinning, she said, "Yeah, but you've had the use of both your arms back then." *She's got a point.* As she finishes tying the laces of the sneakers, she stands up and grabs the pile of clothes and brings them over to the bed and sets them down next to me. As she backed away in front of me, she pointed at the pile of clothes and said, "Just look through what we found and see if there's anything that fits."

I knew she was right. I turned a little and started looking through the clothes they had found for me. Most of the items weren't bad looking at all, some of them were fancy and felt expensive. *If I have any more encounters with the Justices, these expensive threads are going to do me no good at all.* I set a heather blue t-shirt that seemed to reference retro video games to the side, along with a pair of blue jeans and a pair of black ankle socks. They also brought me boxers and briefs. *I'm not really thrilled about putting on someone else's drawers, but I have little choice.*

As I sat down to the side what I was going to put on, I grabbed the covers to pull them off me, but I stopped and slowly looked up at Gina as she stood in front of me watching. "What is it?" she asked, confused.

"Um, I know you undressed me to help, but I don't feel you watching me get dressed is proper bedside manner."

"Oh," her eyes glanced down towards my crotch, "OH!" She flapped her hands in the air and pinched her eyes closed in a manner that I could not help but laugh. "Yeah, sorry. I'll just go over here." She walked back around to the other side of the room and sat down on the bed with her back to me.

As I threw the bed sheets off me, I saw I was standing up, fully erect. *Fuck, it must've been when I caught a peek at her changing.* My eyes widened in shock and covered myself up again as I looked behind me to see if she was indeed not watching me. *Well, at least I know that still works. I'm so lucky she didn't see that.* I removed the covers from across my legs once again and grabbed the pair of boxers and put them on as quick as I could. As I lifted my legs up one after the other and began putting on the socks, I said, "So, I'm assuming you slept in here to watch me sleep?"

I could feel her twitch a little as she sat on the bed. "Yeah, I mean no! I mean, I needed to monitor you, so it just made sense for me to sleep in here in case you went downhill." *That makes sense. Although, if you were sleeping nearly naked, I'm surprised you didn't just sleep under the covers with me.* She added, "But the way you were burning up, it made me so hot that I had almost no choice but to sleep on top of the covers."

But nearly naked? I decided not to press the matter any further. She saved my life, and that's all that matters. "I didn't realize I was that bad, thank you Gina." I paused for a second before I continued. "So, what else did you two do while I was sleeping?"

Gina sat up straight and said, "Well, as you know we found food, and clothes, and more med kits but we were lucky we didn't need to use those immediately. But we also found why the elevators weren't working and got them moving again, turned out they were just switched off. Let's see, we also found the pool that this hotel has, so we swam for a little the one day."

"Wait, the one day? How many days have I been out?" I asked as I pulled the jeans on and buttoned them.

"It's been three days."

"Three days!" I suddenly remembered William talking about taking care of more *rodents* and immediately thought about Austin and the other survivors. "Shit! I need to find William's place and hope the others are still alive." As I quickly tried to put the shirt on, my arm had pain shoot through it from my shoulder all the way to my hand as I bent over in pain.

Jumping to her feet, Gina quickly ran around to the other side of the bed. "Here, let me help." She took the shirt from me and bunched it up as she guided my arm through the sleeve until it made it to my shoulder and repeated the same for the other arm until she pulled it over my head.

"Thanks, I think I got the rest," I whispered. Once I pulled the shirt all the rest of the way on, I looked down at the floor and went to grab my shoes.

"We found you sneakers, too." Gina said as she walked over to the other side of the room and bent down, grabbing something from the floor. As she returned upright, she turned around and had a pair of brand-new sneakers, from what I could tell. All I knew was that if they were not brand new, they were hardly worn. The sneakers were black high tops with red accents all around it with red laces and a red swoosh on the outsides of both sneakers. I quickly noticed the small patched stitched to the heels on both sneakers with a three-digit number on them. *Hey look, a pair of eight nineties!*

"Oh wow, those will be much better than those damn things I had. Thank you." I took the sneakers from Gina and sat down on the bed as I began putting them on. Once I had both sneakers on and the laces tightened and tied, I stood up and was amazed by the amount of comfort they had compared to my dress shoes. Looking at Gina, she had such an enormous smile on her face, like she had just given me the best birthday gift of my life.

"How do they feel?" she asked.

"They feel great, again thank you." I turned away from her and began walking out of the room as Gina followed behind me.

"What are you doing?" she asked, concerned.

"Like I was saying, I'm afraid William has Austin and the others, and I need to get to his complex before he kills them."

"But you don't know if he found them. They could still be in hiding, just like we are."

"It's possible, but the way he said rodents leads me to believe otherwise. And if it's not Austin and the other survivors, there could still be the chance that it's someone else. So, I need to get back to Center Street and find my way to where his complex is."

Gina turned around and went back into the bedroom and grabbed the hooded sweatshirt. As she quickly tossed it on, she said, "I think I know how we can find it." She turned towards the second bedroom and opened the door, revealing Angel sitting in the middle of the bed. An opened bag of pretzels sat next to two stuffed animals and a camera as she drew in a book. As she looked up from her book, Gina said, "Angel, I'm heading up to the roof again. I need you to stay here, okay?"

She leans a little to her left and spots me standing behind Gina. "Sam!" she shouted as she jumped off the bed and ran out of the room. As she approached me, she stopped just short of me as I lowered myself gingerly down to her. "You're awake!"

"I am. I needed the nap."

"I helped Gina take care of you. You were really hurt."

"You helped? Well then, thank you so much for taking care of me. I definitely got better because of you both."

"Do you like the shoes?"

Glancing back at the sneakers for a second, I said, "You got me these?"

“Yeah, I found them in a shoebox under one of the beds when we were exploring. I didn’t know if they were gonna fit you.”

“Well, not only do they fit, but they are super comfortable. Thank you, Angel, you are too good to me.”

She reaches out with both her arms and hugs me as tightly as she could. Her little arm pressed against my bad shoulder, but I did not let her know she was hurting me. “Thank you, Sam. Thank you for saving Gina and my life from the monster, and me from the other monster.”

Monster? She must mean the Justices from back at the church. I lifted my good arm and wrapped it around her, returning the hug. “You’re very welcome, sweetheart.” As she let me go, she took a step back while I returned to my feet.

“So, like I said, I need you to stay here and we’re going to be right back. Okay?”

“Okay.” Angel turned around and went back into her room and back up onto the bed. Gina walked over to the door and pulled it open, allowing me to walk out before she pulled the door closed. Just outside the room, diagonally to the left, were two elevators. Gina walked over to the panel and hit the up button as you could hear a brief clang sound from the other side of the door before one door pulled itself open. Stepping into the elevator, Gina pushed the fourteenth-floor button as the doors closed and the elevator began moving.

"Three days. You all have been up to a lot."

"Well, yes, and no. I went back to the lobby and looked up all the rooms that still had people listed as checked in and we just went to those rooms looking for what was inside."

"How did you figure out the elevators were off?" I asked.

"As we looked for more food and supplies, I found the maintenance area and found the panel for the elevator control. In an emergency, they automatically turn off, so once I turned the switch back to on, they worked."

"I'm honestly surprised anything works here."

"It appears this hotel has its own power generators on the roof if the normal electricity goes out. How long has that been? I don't know for sure, though." The elevator stopped at the fourteenth floor as the doors opened. "Come on, we have one set of stairs to climb, and we are there."

As we both stepped out of the elevator, I asked, "Any problems with the Justices?"

"Surprisingly, no. I thought I was going to need to barricade the front door or something, but I haven't heard a sound from them since we got away from the church." I didn't say another word as I followed Gina around the hallway to a set of doors with a glass reenforced window with a red border around it. Through the window, you could see a set of stairs that went up. Gina pushed the door open and began walking up the stairs as I followed until we reached a simple silver metal door that had white lettering painted on it that simply said 'Roof.'

She pushed the door open, and we both stepped outside. The air was very crisp and cool as it cut through me, giving me instant chills. *Even being this high up, it shouldn't be this cold up here.* "Now I know why you have that sweatshirt on." I said as I crossed my arms for a second.

"It's not because of the roof. Two days ago, the air in the city got cold, and the nights got longer, almost as if the season changed from Summer to Autumn without warning." She took a few steps towards the center of the roof. "Okay, so the entrance to the hotel is over here." She pointed to the side of the roof. "Center Street was a half a block that way." She pointed a little to the left. "And where did William say he was?"

"He said he was up Center Street." I walked over to Gina and began scanning the other buildings as I slowly turned. As I stopped turning, I walked to the edge of the building and saw a large round building with an almost dome-like roof to it. "There, I bet that's the one."

The roof was molded steel with black and gun metal coloring to it. The beams almost seemed to be formed in a crossover pattern, forming a very secure connection. The walls were painted with the same gun metal coloring, but I could not tell if it was also steel or concrete. And above all, it looked as though the building was only six more blocks from where we were. "That's where I need to go."

"Sam, you are in no condition to fight. Guaranteed, William will have a fuck ton of Justices there guarding that building."

"I know, but he kept saying he wanted to have a conversation or something, which leads me to think he doesn't want a fight."

Gina immediately added, "But he also said he came in peace at the church and look what happened there."

"Yes, I get it. William is a piece of shit; I'm not defending the guy. But he might be our only way out of here. He might be our only way home."

Gina again quickly spoke out. "You don't even know where home is!"

"No, I don't. But I know it ain't this! This can't be home! Does this feel like home to you?"

"I don't know Sam! I don't know." She paused for a few seconds before continuing. "I don't know what home is for me. I know what I feel, I know what I want. But I don't know what is for certain."

I was confused by what she said. "What did you mean when you said what you feel? What you want?"

"It's nothing. Let's just get back downstairs and… and we'll figure out what's next." She turned and began walking away from me as she headed for the door. I quickly caught up to her as we went back down the stairs and to the elevator. Getting on the elevator, she hit the button for the fourth floor and leaned back against the side of the elevator without looking at me at all.

As the elevator descended, I kept thinking to myself about what she said. *What did she mean? Is there something she's not telling me? Did she maybe have one of those crazy visions, too? I'm so confused I don't know what to think.*

As the elevator stopped on the fourth floor, the doors opened, and Gina immediately stepped off again without speaking a word to me as she made her way towards the door to our room. As she pulled the keycard out of her pocket, she paused. "What's wrong?" I asked her.

"The door is open." I glance at the door and see that it is slightly open and not latched. Gina races towards the door and pushes it open as she screams, "Angel! Angel!" As I enter the room, I see her race into Angel's room, still screaming, "Angel!" She runs back out of the room and with a panic look on her face, she screamed, "She's gone!"

Chapter Nineteen

Sprinting out of the room and down the hallway, Gina screamed out, "Angel! Angel!" She did not get a response. I shortly followed behind her as I grabbed the handle of each hotel room and tried to open their doors one by one with no success. As Gina returned, she said to me in a panic, "She knows not to go anywhere without me. She's never gone off without me."

"Is there anywhere she would've gone?" I said, as I tried to calm Gina down.

"No, there's nowhere. We had enough food; she had lots of stuff in her room to keep her occupied. There's no reason for her to leave." I turned around and went back to our room, but stopped just short at the door as I inspected it. "What are you looking for?" she asked me.

"I'm trying to see if the door was broken into."

"Oh god, oh god!" Gina immediately panicked more as she realized what I was trying to figure out. "They haven't tried to come into this building at all. Why would the Justices come now? And why would they come to this room specifically?" I could tell she panicked even more as she kept walking in circles as she held her head with her left hand, trying to think of what to do.

As I looked closer at the door, I said, "I don't think it was a Justice."

"What? How do you know that?"

As I stood up, I turned around towards her and said, "Do you not remember what they've done to doors in the past? Any of the Justices can just blow a door off its hinges if they wanted to. This door isn't even broken a little." As I turned and looked at the door a little more, I added, "Either they opened this door with a keycard or Angel opened it herself."

I followed Gina as she ran out of the room and straight for our bedroom and looked in the nightstand's drawer. As she reached in, she pulled more keycards out of the drawer and said,

"All the key cards I made are still here. If Angel left on her own, there would be no way for her to get back in."

"Did she know about the keycards?" I asked as I stood in the bedroom doorway.

"She knew that the only way to open the door was with one of these; she's seen me do it enough times." Gina suddenly threw the keycards onto the bed and dropped to the floor as she cried. *Why did Angel open the door?*

"Gina, we can't panic now. I need you to think of anywhere she could have gone," I said to her as I turned around and made my way to the other bedroom.

With tears running down her face, she said, "Maybe she went to the pool, but she isn't a good swimmer, so I don't think she would've gone there."

"That's good. Keep thinking," I said as I looked around in Angel's room. I did not even know what I was looking for, but I was hoping to find either a clue or perhaps Angel left us a note. As I looked around, I suddenly smelled a familiar scent that made me worry.

"I just don't know," I heard Gina call out from the other room.

"Gina, when you were exploring the hotel, did you find a restaurant in the hotel?"

"Yeah, but I already told you we had plenty…"

I cut her off. "No, I know you did. But did the restaurant have a bar in it, or alcohol?"

"What the fuck are you? Yeah, it had alcohol, but I wasn't going to bring that up here. Why are you asking me that?" As I looked at all the things on the bed that I remember seeing before, I noticed the camera was no longer on the bed. Leaning to my left, I noticed a small red glow on the floor in between the bed and the nightstand.

"Son of a bitch," I hissed to myself as I kneeled to the floor and saw what the glow was coming from.

I heard Gina get up off the floor in the other room and make her way over to Angel's room as she asked, "Why did you stop…" She immediately became quiet as she saw me on the floor. In my hand was the camera that Angel was playing with. It was still recording.

I pressed the stop button and immediately went to playback. Gina ran over and grabbed my arm so she could see the small view screen as well. As the video started playing, we saw what Angel was recording.

The video starts with Angel pointing the camera at the two stuffed animals on the bed. We hear her voice in a high-pitched tone and a low grumble as it sounds like she is giving voices to the two animals. We see her little arm reach out from the side of the screen and pick up one of the stuffed animals as she wiggles it left and right like it was dancing or jumping towards the other animal. Suddenly we heard a low knock come from in the distance. "What was that?" Gina asked as she gasped.

The image then shows the camera being placed down on the bed and we could see Angel sliding off the bed and walking out of the room towards the door. "Oh my god Angel," Gina said as she held her breath. Without warning, the still image of the bed echoes Angel's scream as she runs back into the room and tries to close the door. We then see at the edge of the video her trying to push and hold the door closed as hard as she could. Suddenly, she falls backwards into the side of the bed and her arm hits the camera as it drops to the floor. Her screams filled the room with terror. "Oh my god, Angel!" Gina screams as she turns away from the camera.

I can hear Angel fighting and struggling until the sound of a loud slap can be heard, then Angel's screaming goes almost silent. I can hear sounds of the bedsprings and more rustling noises until a pair of black dress boots and the bottom cuff of dark blue jeans. Without so much as a word, the pair of boots turned and began walking away, and two seconds later, we no longer heard anything. I threw the camera down on the bed in anger and screamed at the top of my lungs, "That son of a bitch!"

"Sam, what is it? Who took Gina?"

Turning towards her, I immediately said in anger, "Where is that restaurant?"

"It's down off to the side of the lobby, but what…"

Cutting her off I said, "Take me there, now!"

"But Sam?"

"Gina now!" Taking a step back, she turned and began walking briskly towards the door. As we exited our room, we ran down the hallway past the elevators next to our room and made our way all the way to the other side of the floor to the main elevators. Pushing the down button, I said nothing to Gina as she paced back and forth, staring at me. As the doors to one elevator opened, we both went on as Gina hit the button to the lobby.

Once the doors closed and the elevator started moving, Gina softly looked at me and said, "Sam, what is it?" I didn't reply to her question. I just watched the red electronic screen above the doors as it counted down until it got to a "L."

As the doors opened, we stepped out and I turned to Gina and asked, "Which way?" She quickly began running towards the one large conference room and made a left past the doors and then a quick right down a small hallway until we reached a thick set of black stained double doors with large gold handles. As she pulled the door open, we stepped into a massive restaurant. Booths lined around the edge of the walls of two-thirds of the restaurant, while they lined large tables up and down in the center of the room. They divided the last third of the room between a visible kitchen where customers could see their food being prepared, large windows allowing you to see to the outside parking lot along with a counter for checking in to be seated, and a bar.

I raced to the bar and spotted several empty beer bottles on the bar top. Turning towards Gina, I asked, "Were these here when you explored before?"

She looked at the bottles with a confused expression before answering, "I… I don't know. They could have been. Why are you asking me about beer bottles?" I walked up to the bar and picked up one of them. The condensation was still present as there was a water ring on the bar left behind by the bottle.

"Fucking damn it!" I yelled as I threw the bottle across the restaurant as it smashed into a wall and shattered.

"Sam, what the fuck was that…"

"Danny! It was fucking Danny!" I turned and walked a few feet away from her.

"Danny? But where did he come from?"

"He must have followed us here and hid in this hotel just like us." I turned and kicked one of the dozen bar stools as it toppled over and hit the floor hard.

"But I don't understand. Why would Danny do this? Why is he so interested in Angel?" I thought back to when we first found Angel and how terrified she was. Danny was standing there with her, but she was still so scared. I remembered how Danny told me how he was protecting her from the Justices, but Angel seemed more afraid of him.

"Fuck!" I screamed out with a long breath as I pounded my fist onto the bar. "He followed us back to the church when we found Angel. The Justices attacked us, and he never came to help. He just tried to take Angel again, and when he failed yet again, he fucking ran away and left us to die!"

Gina covered her mouth with her hands. "Oh, my god."

"Then he followed us here when we escaped. But he must have been following Angel and waited for the moment where he could get her. The moment where we wouldn't be around." I turned towards the bar and kicked another bar stool as a few more tipped over and hit the floor, including the one next to Gina as she jumped backwards out of the way.

"Jesus Christ, Sam, I need you to calm down and help me figure out where he would've taken her," she said to me, furious.

"Well, I'm almost guaranteed he would've taken her from here since it wouldn't make any sense to hide her in the hotel with us still here. But why? Why would he take her?"

"Sam, I don't give a shit why? I need the *where*. Where did he take…" She stopped mid-sentence as she looked down at the floor. "What is that?" As I tried to see what she was looking at, she walked up to where the bar stool was standing, bent down, and picked up a falling apart brown leather wallet. I immediately recognized it.

"That's Danny's wallet. I remember it from the pub." Gina opened it and started looking at all the cards in the slots before looking into the main pocket. She flipped through what I assumed were the blank pieces of paper that at one time could have been cash until she found a thick folded card and pulled it out. She threw the wallet onto the bar and unfolded the thick card and immediately started screaming as she held it in her hand.

"What? What's wrong?" I screamed as I ran to her as she had her arm extended out with the card in her hand. I took it from her and looked at it quickly, realizing that it was not a card, it was a photo.

"Oh, my god! Sam, oh my god!" Looking at the photo, I instantly felt the blood leave my face. The photo was the picture of a child, a young little girl. The photo was a picture of Angel.

Chapter Twenty

My anger boiled under my skin as I tightly held onto the photo. I began screaming at the top of my lungs as I crumpled the picture in my hand and threw it across the bar. Gina took a couple of steps back from me as I kicked the side of the bar. "That son of a bitch!" I yelled out to no one. My anger was not at Danny; however, it was at me.

From the moment I found Danny, I had an uneasy feeling deep in the back of my head, but I ignored it. I ignored it because I wanted to help as many people as I could that were in the same situation as I was. I wanted to help as many people as possible because I thought that if I had, then it would help me figure out what had happened to us all. Even after Gina and I found him with Angel the first time, I knew then that there was something not right with him and his story about fighting off the Justices and saving Angel; and even with her terrified face, I still overlooked it and let him into the church. I gave him the benefit of the doubt and it possibly cost Henry his life. And now possibly Angel's life as well.

"Sam," Gina said to me as tears ran down her face, "Sam, I need you to calm down." She took small steps forward towards me as she tried to get me to quiet down my anger. I turned my head towards her as I leaned against the counter of the bar with my hands gripping the edge, holding myself up. As I looked at her, more thoughts ran through my head. *Gina, you trusted me. You trusted me with your life and Angel's life. You trusted me when you were terrified, and rightfully so. I let you down.*

"I'm a fucking idiot!" As she moved closer to me, I added. "I knew he was a fucking scum bag and I still let him near you."

She grabbed my arm with both of her hands and said, "Sam, no, you're not. You're not an idiot." Her tears were still rolling down her face as she tried her best to get my mind back. "Danny betrayed you. He betrayed all of us. I should've locked or barricaded the front door to keep him out, but I didn't. This isn't your fault. This is mine." She squeezed my arm tighter before she added, "But I need you to come back to me. I need you to calm down and help me."

"Help with what? They're gone in a city with everything living in it, wanting to kill us." I pulled my arm out of her grasp and walked a few steps away from her. "She's gone!" As I stood there, I could hear her drop to the floor as she is now fully crying even harder. I knew at that point I had failed.

No! No, I refuse to accept that! Another thought entered my head as I spun around and grabbed Gina by the arms and lifted her in the air, raising her back to her feet. She jerked herself free once on her feet and said, "Don't touch me! If you give up, then I do too!"

"Gina, we might not be too late!" I blurted. She suddenly started calming down as she looked at me, confusingly. "How did you get keycards for the rooms in this hotel?"

She thought for a second before responding, "I made them at the check in terminal, why?"

"If you did, then maybe Danny did, too. Maybe he took her to another floor in this hotel!" She thought for a second before turning around and immediately running out the double doors we came in. Running after her, we made our way back to the lobby as she hurried behind the counter and started accessing the system.

After a dozen key punches, she pulled up the guest list. "Fuck!" she screamed as she smacked the side of the monitor.

"What?" I asked as I saw her look of hope fade away yet again.

"The last keys made were the handful I did days ago."

I turned around and stared out the large window of the lobby, trying to think of where he could've gone with Angel. "Think Sam, Think!" I said to myself. "So, it's obvious that he was hiding in the bar then this whole time. He can't get into any room without a key unless he planned on breaking down a door." I turned and looked right at Gina before I continued. "He's not completely stupid, so he must've known we'd go searching for her… unless that's what he was expecting us to do."

"What are you thinking, Sam?" Gina asked me as I started pacing back and forth in a few steps.

"He had to have known we'd be doing exactly this, and we would eventually find him, unless…" I stopped and walked towards the elevators.

As I stood in front of the call buttons, Gina asked me, "Unless what, Sam?"

Quickly turning around, I said, "Tell me which floors the elevators are coming from."

"What? How am I supposed to do that?"

"Stand back and watch the screens above the doors. When I push the call button, the elevators should say which floor they're on."

As I pushed the button, she began shaking her head as she said, "But Sam, we road down on one of these elevate…" She paused as the doors to the elevator we took down to the lobby opened immediately, as well as the doors to the farthest elevator opened as well.

I took a few steps back as a look of shock came across my face. I turned my head towards Gina for a split second before we both looked towards the front door of the lobby. "He took her from the hotel," I said before running towards the door.

As I pushed the doors open and ran outside, Gina right behind me asked, "But where would he have taken her?" Suddenly, the screeches of the Justices resonated in the distance. "Oh my god, they're back," she whispered.

"They're back, or they never left."

Confused, she looked at me and said softly, "What are you saying?"

I glanced up towards the sky as I looked at the sun overhead shining brightly down on us. Swiping my hand across my forehead, I wiped some sweat off my head. "You said that it got cold, and the days got shorter, right?"

"What?"

"And that you had not heard or seen a single Justice since you got into the hotel, right?"

"I don't know, yeah, but what does that have…"

Cutting her off, I continued. "I don't know about you, but it seems pretty hot and bright out here to me."

"Sam, what are you saying?" she asked me quickly as she frantically looked around, trying to spot any of the Justices in the area.

Glancing down at the ground, I saw a spot of blood that had dripped on the ground. As I bent down, I touched it with two fingers and looked at them to see that it was still wet. The way it was splashed on the ground, it looked like it was heading towards the hotel. "This is my blood, isn't it?" I asked Gina as I stood back up. "From days ago?"

"What? I don't know, maybe. Sam, please, tell me what it is you are trying to say to me?"

Turning towards her, I grabbed her shoulders, looked her right in the eyes and said, "Don't you remember? When I saved Danny in that pub? Remember how you said to me I walked in and a second later I walked out with Danny?" She nodded her head before I continued explaining. "I was in there for at least fifteen to twenty minutes fighting those Justices before we escaped."

"But Sam, what does that..." I cut her off again.

"Back at the church, I was talking with Henry about Austin and the other survivors. He said to me that even though we had been gone for several hours, he had said we were gone for days. Gina, don't you see?"

She had a completely confused look on her face. "Inside the buildings, time moves differently compared to outside." I could tell she started realizing what I was saying. "The pub, Danny taking off from the church, Henry saying we were gone for days. Time advances differently inside these buildings than it does outside."

Shock crawled across Gina's face as she said, "So, if he left the hotel, he might be still close by?"

"Exactly!"

As I let go of her, she asked, "Okay, but where would he have taken her?"

"There's only one place I could think that he might go if he wanted to get out of here."

Another feeling of shock and panic came across her face as she knew what I was thinking. "But why would he take her there?"

"Why wouldn't he? If he wants out of the city, who else would you talk to then the guy in charge of everything," I paused for a second before I said, "He's going to see William."

Gina stared at me for a few seconds before she said, "But that doesn't make any sense. William would just as soon kill them both, then even listen to anything that shithead has to say."

"I know, but maybe he thinks he can sweet talk him or something. Danny must know that William wants to talk to me, maybe… maybe he's going to make William spare him and Angel instead."

"We have no idea if that's what he's thinking!" she yells at me in a sudden panic.

"We don't have any other options in front of us. Danny was there when William was at the church, so he must have heard William say how to get to his complex. If you want to stay here and keep looking for Angel somewhere in the hotel, knowing she isn't here, then stay here. But I'm going to go to William's complex and hopefully stop Danny before it's too late." Screeches from the Justices could be heard closer than before as we both quickly turned towards them.

"Okay, okay! Fuck, let's hope you're right." After nodding at her, I turned and began running back towards the main road before heading up the street towards the complex we saw from the roof. *I really hope I'm right,* I thought to myself.

Chapter Twenty-One

My heart raced as we ran up the street. The screeches were sounding out all around us as we got closer and closer to the complex. My side ached so intensely as we rounded the corner and saw the building in front of us. Seeing the complex from the roof of the hotel did not do the building justice, as it was massive.

The gray up close was so cold with the steel pillars and support beams that stretched all around it. Just below the rounded dome roof were large windows that went all the way around. At the bottom, there was another enormous set of windows tinted dark with three sets of double doors at the front to enter. Justices surrounded the building at multiple spots spread out as they appeared to be guarding it.

We quickly ducked behind a concrete sign that was at the edge of the parking lot to stay out of sight. As we tried catching our breaths, Gina said to me, "Do you see them?"

Leaning out from the edge of the sign, I quickly scanned the area before ducking back behind the sign. "No, but that doesn't mean they're not here." After a few deep breaths, I added, "I'll bet he's hiding around here too, trying to figure out how he's getting inside as well."

She shook her head and said, "So, what are we going to do now?"

"I honestly don't know. There is easily at least a dozen plus Justices out there. We can't fight them all." Looking at the surrounding buildings, my mind spun in circles, trying to think of something. After a minute, I said, "I guess I can just give myself in to William."

"Jesus Christ, Sam, no! How is that going to help us?"

"William said he wants to talk to me, right? If I walk up to the door, it's not like he is going to kill me?"

"Sam, think about it," she took another deep breath before she continued, "if that were true, he wouldn't have tried to kill you back at the church." She had a point. I remembered what he said as he walked out the door of the church. *See you soon Sam, if you make it there.*

"The church was a test."

"What?" she asked with such confusion in her voice.

"The church, I think, was a test to see if I could survive. To see if I could handle the stress. That's the only thing that makes any sense to why he did it."

Gina gripped my arm and said, "Sam, you are out of your mind if you think I'm letting you just walk out there."

Turning so I could examine her face, I said, "Do you have any other options that I can't see? Do you have any better ideas? Angel is still with him, and I know he's waiting just like we are. Soon enough either he's going to tire of waiting and do something that's going to get them both killed or, the more likely, he's probably going to use her as a distraction to save himself… and get her killed." Gina's eyes filled with tears, but she held back from crying as I continued. "If I go out there, it will distract the Justices enough that they won't notice you."

Squeezing my arm more she asked, "So, what exactly am I supposed to do while you are just giving yourself up?"

Glancing over at one building, I pointed at it and said to her, "When the Justices are dealing with me, make your way over to one of those buildings and watch for Danny to make his way out."

"But what am I…"

Before she could finish her sentence, I cut her off and added, "Find something to use as a weapon. A pipe, a board, anything. You see that son of a bitch? If it's safe, you knock his fucking head off." I gently pulled my arm from her grip and turned my attention back towards the building.

Closing my eyes and taking another deep breath, I think to myself, *I really hope I'm right about this.* I stand up and before I walk out from behind the sign, I turn my head and look at it and see in giant maroon letters on a white backdrop the name of the building, "Central Info Station."

"Son of a bitch," I whisper to myself as I walked out into the open and towards the building. Within seconds of me taking several steps, the screeches of the Justices began ringing out and filling the air with their calls as more and more of them began converging on my location. I place my hands into the air at either side of my head, showing that I am not aggressive and that I am surrendering. The closest Justice that reached me, without warning or provocation, swung its right arm across, backhanding me in the face. The force sent me flying to my left several feet before slamming into the ground.

As I rolled across the asphalt, the pain in my side shot through my body as I lay on the ground gripping at my side. I glanced my head up to look at Gina as I noticed her standing up like she was going to run out from her hiding spot. With my free arm I wave it, trying to get her to go away, but I make it look like I'm trying to get my balance as I stand up. As I made it to my feet, another Justice, or the same one I was not sure of, struck me again on the other side of my face as I immediately dropped to the ground.

As I once again tried to slowly lift myself to my feet, I see I am quickly surrounded by multiple Justices as their screeches rang out into the air. "That's enough!" A familiar deep raspy voice echoes out from a loudspeaker coming from the direction of the building. I turn my head slightly and see three Justices standing over top of me with their molded stabbers ready to impale me. "Let him up!"

The Justices slowly retreated a few steps away from my flopped body as I began lifting myself up, spitting a large splash of blood onto the ground. As I reached my feet, cringing, I called out, "William?"

"Sam, you made it after all!"

Spitting again, I reply, "Yeah, well, if I knew this was the conversation you wanted to have, I would've just text you!"

His deep laugh filled the air, hurting my ears before he said, "Text me, huh? That's good Sam!" The loudspeaker goes silent for a few seconds before he calls out, "Let him in!"

The Justices take several additional steps back as two of the three that hovered over me allowed their molded stabbers to return to hands, but the third watched me with its stabber still out at the ready to strike. "You heard what he said ugly. Go stick that up your ass if you want to use it so bad." The Justice screeched at me in a different tone like it was angry at me. *Yeah, Sam, that was really smart.*

Holding onto my side, it took me a couple of minutes to make it to the doors. Before I entered the building, I took a slight glance behind me as I saw Gina racing across the lot as she entered one building without being seen. Once inside and the doors closed behind me, I studied the inside of the building. The walls were all painted with a plastered white paste while the floors were large square waxed tiles in a dark stone color. To the right of me, a large hallway that was roped off and had large maroon curtains that draped down from the ceiling of the hallway to the floor blocking access, as none of the lights in the hallway were on. To the left, an extensive set of steps went up with about four banisters spread out to allow many people the ability to use them at once.

In front of me was a large desk with a woman sitting behind it. She was typing away at a computer with her long blonde hair pulled back into a bun. As I approached the counter, I could see that she was wearing an all-white pants suit with large shoulder pads. She also wore a tight black halter top barely covering her breasts that peeked out from the struggling to stay closed jacket of the suit.

"Hello Mr. Hines," she said to me as I approached the desk. "You are just in time for your appointment with Mr. William."

"Mr. William? William William?" I asked, confused. "Boy, I guess his parents were really original, huh?" I paused as I tried to search for a nameplate or badge, but there was nothing that stated who she was other than the building's receptionist. She did not respond to my wisecrack.

"To my right, just make your way up these steps and follow the hallway on the left to make your way to the conference room," she said as she pointed towards the stairs next to the desk. While still pointing, I glanced at her wrist to notice the very masculine and very expensive looking watch she was wearing. It stood out more than anything because it just didn't match the rest of her.

"Have a nice day." She turned away from me and began typing on the computer once again.

"Up the stairs, right?" I asked her. I got no response. As I climbed the stairs, I could slowly see different floor displays scattered around the room of different architecture projects made of white clay and plaster on different stands and tables. Some buildings I recognized as I saw one model was the Central Info Station itself, another was buildings from the busy section of the city. There was even one at the far end of the room, that was a fancy hotel. But then there were many buildings and structures that I did not recognize, nor did I see anywhere in the city. *They could be around; I didn't get to every part of Remembrance, to be honest.*

As I walked past the displays, I saw shop after shop from small food stands to merchandise stores, clothing shops and more. It quickly dawned on me that this complex was an arena or stadium of some sort. As I made my way around the hallway as instructed, I stepped to the right and looked behind one of the maroon curtains along the side of the wall and saw I was correct. A large stadium with seating surrounding a large rectangular center was hidden out of sight from the main hallway. The air bit in my lungs as I breathed in and realized something. *Is this an ice rink?*

"I think you have kept me waiting long enough, Sam." I let go of the curtain and straightened up as I looked to my left and saw William standing outside the doorway to a large room. Two Justices stood on either side of him, guarding him.

As I made my way towards William, I said, "You don't make it really easy to get an appointment now, do you?"

Chuckling under his breath, he replied, "In my line of business, Sam, you need to be careful of who you let in. I need to make sure that the people I want to bring inside are worthy." As he finished, he stepped to his side, clearing my way into the room.

Just before I walked past him, I stopped next to him and looked at both Justices on either side of me. "Are Nit and Wit going to be joining us, too?"

William laughed as his deep voice echoed throughout the hallway. "No, I don't think so. They have other things to attend to." He nodded at both Justices, signaling them to walk away as they continued down the hall and out of sight around the corner. "Is that better, Sam?" he asked.

I didn't reply to him, I just entered the room. It was a large square room with an equally large cherry wood-stained table in the middle of the room with large marooned cushioned executive chairs surrounding the table. Across the walls on the left and the right of the room were multiple large, wide screened televisions attached to the upper portion of the walls. Each one of the televisions had a different camera shot of different sections inside the stadium and outside the building. At the far end were large glass sliding doors that looked out at the stadium. On the other side of the glass doors, a small balcony with descending seats; three rows with four seats per row on the left and the right, with a center aisle separating them.

"Have a seat, Sam," William said to me as he made his way to the opposite side of the room and sat at the head of the table. The chair he sat down in was much larger and a different color, as it looked like it was a black leather seat with a high back. Looking down at the chair in front of me, I grabbed the back and pulled it away from the table, but before I could sit, William raised his hand up and said, "No, not there, Sam. That one there." I looked at where he was pointing to and seen it was the chair that was directly across from him at the other end of the table.

Pushing the chair I had pulled out back into its place, I made my way over to the chair he wanted me to sit in, pulled it away from the table, and sat down. "Would've been easier if you had just said to sit here in the first place, don't you think?"

"Perhaps. It honestly doesn't matter where people sit… unless I want to discuss business. Then, I want to look them in the eyes." His voice curled as he finished his statement. "It's been a long time since I've come across someone like you, Sam. It made my palms itch."

Snickering, I replied, "They make ointments for that kinda thing you know? It's always best to just wash your hands once you're…"

Cutting me off he continued, "You have been nothing short of remarkable and a pain in my ass, Sam. But I knew you were special. Do you remember what I told you, Sam?"

"Eskimo kisses are the best?" I sarcastically replied. *What? Am I trying to piss this man off?*

"You are in a state of confusion, Sam. This entire time, running around my city, trying to save all these little rodent shits. You tried so hard to keep everyone alive that you fell behind. And how did that work out?" I said nothing as he continued. "My Justices wiped half of them out. And the other half, in due time, they will be dealt with as well." *The other half? Austin and the others?*

He stood up from his seat and slowly started making his way towards me. "But you, Sam, you are more than they are. You have so much potential that I can taste it. This can be your moment of resurrection, Sam; this can be your moment to join me in Remembrance. You can be the missing piece to complete my glorious masterpiece. You, Sam, can finally fix what all these other failures before you could not accomplish."

"Failures before me? What do you mean by that?"

"Come on Sam, you can't tell me you didn't notice?" He walked over to one television on the wall behind him as it flipped to an image of the city. "I have been working on creating the perfect living organism of success. I've been trying to put together the best living organism in a city that I can just sit back and watch its perfection." As he continued to speak, the images on the television changed pictures on its screen to add visual aid. "The people, it's blood; the shops, its organs; the Justices, its immune system; and me at the top of it all, running everything as its brain. But I cannot do it all by myself, Sam." He turned back towards me. "I need someone that understands my vision and can help me wriggle out the imperfections while supporting the ever-growing perfection."

I looked at him with an expression of loathing. "Are you out of your mind? A living organism?"

"Do not mock me, Sam! I have no problem of just getting rid of you, but I'm giving you the chance to join me and be part of success."

I was silent for a second before I asked, "You mentioned others? What happened to them? Did you kill them too?"

"Sam, ending everything is no way to handle things, no matter how easy it is." He walked back to his seat at the other end of the table and sat down. "If someone doesn't show the proper motivation to complete their responsibilities, I simply demote them to allow them to prove to me I was wrong and give them another chance."

"Demote them? So, what happens to them?"

He started chuckling as he said, "Well, some of them became citizens, some shop workers, a few become Justices." He paused for a second as the door to the room opened. "Just like this gentleman right here." I turned my head and was surprised to see the bartender from the pub walk through the door, staring at me with anger on his face. He walked over to the other side of the table and stood next to William as he chuckled to himself. "I believe you too have been formally introduced before?"

"Ya, Mr. William, dis fella and I know each other really well." His spiked red hair represented the hate I saw in his eyes as he answered William.

"That's an understatement. That is like saying I've been formally introduced to my jock itch."

"Ya listen here fella…" William put his arm up as the bartender took a step forward to halt him in place.

"That's enough!" William barked.

Looking at the bartender as his expression of anger seemed to stay put from being stopped in his place by William, I leaned back in my chair, drawing my finger in a straight line across my chest, and said to him, "So, how's the chest feeling? I guess I left a lasting mark on you, didn't I?" His face turned bright red, almost matching his hair color.

"Sam don't mock his failures," William said in an underhanded tone as he looked at the bartender in the eyes.

The room became uncomfortably silent for a few seconds before I asked, "So this guy used to be someone that helped you? So, what happens to the city when they fail?"

The bartender's lip curled up as he snarled at me. William sighed before he said, "Unfortunately, the parts of the city that have been a… disappointment, they are shut down and we start over again with a new section. Once the new section is perfected, then we move on to other aspects."

"So, wait, let me get this straight. These abandoned sections of this city are areas where you just shut it down because it wasn't what you liked?" I could tell William got uneasy in his seat as he struggled to stay comfortable.

"Why keep it going when it's a failure?" He glanced over at the bartender as he said that before he looked back at me and continued. "That's why I want you to join me. Help me end this trend and finally achieve the perfection in my city."

I glanced over at the screen that showed the images of the city on it before I said, "So what happened to all the citizens, the 'blood' if you will? Did you just move them over to the new section?"

"If they continued to be a vital contribution, then yes."

"And if not?"

"Come on Sam. You can't save everyone from the inevitable. If they are not contributing to the perfection, then they need to be removed." The bartender smiled slightly as William said that.

"So, kill them? You just kill them, just like that?"

He slammed his fists on the table and stood up quickly before he said, "Oh, come on, Sam! Don't make it sound so dramatic! To achieve perfection, you need to surround yourself with people that believe and want to contribute. I don't run a charity. I want perfection, not the best efforts. And if they can't cut it… I cut them."

"You make it sound like they are here voluntarily. You forced me here against my will and I'm fairly sure you did the same to them too!"

He laughed so hard. "Are you sure about that, Sam?" he asked me as he sat down again. A sense of confusion and dread filled my head. *What is he trying to say to me? Is he right? I still can't remember everything. Am I here because I want to? No, I don't believe it.* "People chase success by any means they can achieve it. If someone is a visionary, like me, that has a plan and a goal, people will come willingly and even forget who they are to succeed. People will change who they are to make something of themselves from the pathetic, retched, globs of nothing to actually be someone important. Everyone had their own reasons to be here. I just gave them the opportunity. You're no different from them for coming to me, but you. You, Sam, could very well be my best yet."

"But I… I can't… I don't," I tried to speak, but what he said had me so twisted inside my head.

"Sam, Sam, Sam. The truth is, you wanted to be here just as much as anyone else did before you. But you have the potential to finally help me achieve what we must do for Remembrance to reach its perfection. Are you willing to take that step with me, Sam?"

I was so lost as I looked at William slowly, shaking my head. *Is this why I was here? Was this the reason I went through everything? The pain, the suffering, the loss?* Looking at William, I straightened myself in the chair and asked, "What is it I need to do?"

Chapter Twenty-Two

William started clapping while looking at the bartender. "You see? What did I tell you?" he asked the bartender as he walked around the table and stood right next to me. "Sam here is the ultimate piece I've been waiting for."

"I'm happy for ya," the bartender said as he smiled slightly while still looking at me. William stuck his hand out to shake my hand as I backed the chair away from the table and turned it towards him. As our hands grasped each other's in the handshake, I realized that his grip felt cold, and his skin felt almost fake and leathery.

"We have so much work we need to get started on Sam." He let go of my hand and walked back around to the other side of the table where his chair was and sat back down, excited. A small black and gray intercom switch sat on the table off to the side that I didn't notice before. He pressed a button on the switch and said sternly, "He said yes, set it up."

"Yes sir," a voice said back before cutting off. *Set what up?*

"So, again, what exactly is it you want me to do?" I asked him.

He looked at me for a second, and as he smiled, he said, "Well, help me fix my city, Sam. There are so many problems that your predecessors implemented that are so wrong that I can't fix them. I want you to rip it all down and rebuild it from the bottom up, getting everything right from the get-go."

"You want me to demolish entire blocks?"

He started laughing before replying, "If you want to think of it that way, then sure. I want each section of my city to be so efficient that I don't even want to look at it. I want it to just work and aid the perfection."

Nodding my head, I said, "I think I might be able to handle that. I'll need to figure out exactly how to go about doing it, but it shouldn't be too much of a problem."

"See, that's what I want to hear, James," he said as he slapped the side of the bartender with his right hand. "He's already thinking of ways to make things run better."

"Well sir," James said, "a plan isn't exactly the actual job, is it? He's gonna need to show some actual progress. Until then, it's not'in more than words."

William turned towards James and tapped his fingers on his chin. "You have a point, James?" He turned his chair back towards me before he said, "I like your spirit, Sam, but James is right. You're going to need to prove to me you are prepared to take the job and all the responsibilities that come with it."

"What do you mean?" I asked.

"I need to be sure you can do what I need to make Remembrance reach its goal. I need to know that you are going to do what's required without hesitation." He stood up from his chair and began to slowly walk towards me. "As I said before, Sam, if people here do not fit in, that they do not meet what is necessary to reach my ultimate goal of perfection, then I cut them out."

Standing in front of me, he leaned down and placed both of his hands on the arms of the chair I was sitting in and put his face very close to mine. As I looked into his eyes, I noticed the whites seemed almost stained and yellowish while his breath smelled of burning compost. *If I knew what burning flesh smelled like, this would be it.* Softly he said to me, "I need to make sure you are willing to also do what is needed. I need to make sure that you can cut out what, or who, isn't working."

"You want me to kill someone?" I asked as a slight tremor creeped out with my words.

He began chuckling again as he stood back up. "I told you, Sam, you don't need to be so dramatic." He took a couple of steps towards the glass doors before he stopped, looked back at me, and said, "Follow me, Sam."

As I stood out of my chair gingerly while holding my pain filled side, James was already standing next to me as William slid one of the glass doors to the side, opening the balcony that was just outside the conference room. He walked out and went all the way to the ledge as he looked out at the empty arena. James raised his hand towards the balcony, allowing me to walk out ahead of him as I walked up to and stood next to William. I heard the glass door slide close behind me as James shut it before he joined us, but he kept his distance.

William took a deep breath, sucking in an extensive amount of the cold air before blowing it back out. "You see this Sam," he asked as he pointed out to the ice rink. "Even though there is nothing happening out there yet, everything works efficiently with no effort put in by me. The ice of the rink is still cold and remaining solid. Everything is being illuminated by the lights. The seats are folded closed, keeping warm until they are needed. Everything here is working without me telling it to do its job." He turned towards me and added, "That's what I want. I want you to set everything up so I can see it working to perfection without me actually saying it."

"I get what you're saying, but people differ from lights, seats, and ice."

"And that's the beauty of it, Sam. You make it that way. You can get everyone on the same page and work towards my, no, towards our goal of perfection. And if they interfere with that goal, you have the power to get them out and put someone else in."

I placed my hands on the side of the balcony and leaned over the edge slightly. "I understand what you're expressing, William, truly I am. If I came here to be a part of this; however, I still can't remember. If I came here to be successful, I could only go by your word." I stood back up but turned around and sat down on the edge of the balcony. "Everything you are saying feels so familiar and almost Déjà vu, I can't question you. I can't sit here and say you're lying to me because it doesn't feel like a lie." Before I continued, I crossed my arms. "I've seen the imperfection you mentioned as well. What needs to be fixed, what needs to be tweaked, what needs to improve," I turned my head and looked right at James and added, "and what needs to be removed."

James frowned at me as one of his fists clinched tightly. Turning back towards William, I said, "But the thing that I cannot accept is all the senseless killing that has been going on."

William shook his head. "My Justices may take their jobs a little too seriously. I will agree with you on that." He glanced back towards James before he added, "They love their job and I appreciate that of them. But perhaps that is also something that you can improve if you can get everything else working." James kept his eyes fixed on me.

"Well, that's just it, William. If all this senseless killing was simply because of the overreactions of your Justices, I don't know if I can accept that. If you are in control of everything here, then you oversee the Justices, too. Which means their killing of people is on you just as much as them."

"Sam, Sam, Sam. That's why I need you next to me. I need you to fix what I have missed, my boy." He placed his hand on my shoulder and squeezed it so hard. "It took me a long time to realize that I can't do it all by myself. But it took me just as long to realize that I couldn't surround myself with just anyone because they failed me. But you, you are the first prime piece to my perfection in my city that will help me surround myself with the right pieces."

Standing up from the balcony and removing myself from his grasp on my shoulder, I turned around and sat down in the seat that was directly across from me. "If that were all true, then why try to kill me? Why not just tell me about all of this when we ran into each other at the gas station days ago? Why make me go through everything I've had to endure when a simple, 'Hey, I want you to work for me,' would've been enough?"

He sat down in the seat next to me on the other side of the aisle as James took a couple of steps forward slowly, but he, again, remained a distance back. "Sam, I told you, I needed to make sure you were truly the right one. I just got done telling you I've had too many slackers around me. I needed to be very selective about who I wanted at my side."

"And what about all the other people here? Gina? Danny? All of them?"

He shook his head while laughing. "Sam, do you think you were the only one that I wanted to see? What better than to have an extensive selection of candidates for a position up the rankings? A competition for the best candidate, which you are the one in the end."

"So, I was competing with everyone? I was helping my competition?" I looked out at the empty arena, feeling completely confused. "I competed with other people that had no idea they were my opponents?" I slumped back into the chair, feeling defeated.

"Sam, it's nothing to feel ashamed about. You helping your competition just showed me I made the right choice. Willing to help your enemies while still achieving the right result shows me you have what it takes. But knowing when to leave your enemies behind is a major attribute too."

I had so many thoughts racing through my head. *This feels so right, and yet it also feels so wrong. What he's saying is making me feel strange, yet willing to follow him. Is he lying to me? Is all of this simply just a misunderstanding? Am I here to fix all of what is wrong here? I just don't know!*

"But we are getting ahead of ourselves, Sam," he said to me, snapping me out of my head. "There is still one more task that I need you to do before I can officially make sure you are the one that I want. I need to make sure you can make the tough decisions when they are needed."

"What are you saying?" I asked him, as I saw his smile turn into an evil snarl. Without a word, he turned towards the rink and sat back in the seat as the maroon curtains blocking the aisles and stairs of the arena opened all at the same time. A loud screech echoed out, bouncing off all the walls as one after another after another, the arena seating began filling with Justices. A sea of gray figures swarmed all around us as the far end of the arena opened, revealing a tunnel to a lower area. "What is going on, William?"

He continued to ignore me as he kept looking out over the ice rink as pairs Of Justices marched out onto the ice two by two until there were around ten standing in an almost circular formation. Another screech echoed out before I heard a scream come from the tunnel the Justices just came from. Suddenly, a person runs out from the tunnel and falls on the ice as he slips and slams on the ground. Shortly behind him, more people came out from the tunnel as they were all corralled into the middle of all the Justices.

"William!" I shouted as I stood up from my seat. "What is going on?" I asked sternly again before I felt James grab hold of my shoulder and squeezed it so tightly that it felt like his fingers were going through my skin. I glanced at the group of people again and then I saw near the side trying to protect the others was Austin. *Oh, my god! It's the other stranded!*

"I told you, Sam, I need to make sure you can do what is needed."

"What is needed? What the fuck are you getting at here?"

"Oh, come on now Sam, do I have to spell it out for you? These people here are not contributing anything towards my city. They are nothing more than dead weight that are just costing me. I want you to get rid of them."

"What!" I shouted at William as James's grip got even tighter. As I screamed out in pain, I could hear someone's voice from the group on the ice.

"SAM!" Austin called out.

William slammed his hand on the arm of the seat he was sitting in. "Great, when you get to know the people, you need to get rid of, it gets so much harder to do what is necessary. Don't think I'm not sympathetic to you, Sam. But this will not change my mind. I still want you next to me, but you need to show me you deserve to be there."

I tried to move my arm away from James's grip, but I could not get it free. Looking at William, I shouted, "I told you; I refuse to kill anyone!"

As he shot up out of his seat, he got right in my face and shouted back, "I told you stop being so fucking dramatic Sam! Don't stand there and pretend like I don't know what you've done to some of the other Justices in my city! You're more capable of doing what I require of you than you act like! But as I said before, if you don't feel comfortable doing it yourself, that's what the Justices are for." I looked back at James as I saw him finally smile.

"No William, I'm not telling the Justices, or Grays, or Strawberry Shortcake here to do anything to those people. They did nothing wrong." The grip on my shoulder became so intense that I could feel James squeeze even harder as it felt like the bones of my shoulder were shattering beneath my skin thanks to me insulting him again.

"Nothing wrong? They wasted so much of my city's resources just by keeping them around! They are nothing more than a waste in MY city." He turned and looked at the crowd of people as they all looked up at us on the balcony. "But perhaps there is still a chance, Sam, that you will make the right decision."

With the wave of his hand, suddenly the other side of the arena opened to reveal another tunnel right below us. Again, two by two, the Justices walked out onto the ice until they formed another circle. As I watched, I was quickly filled with horror as the first circle was filled with Austin and the dozen stranded. Only three people filled the second circle. Danny, Angel, and Gina. *Oh my god, no!*

"There, Sam, I gave you a better choice. Now, instead of just cutting a group of people, you have your choice of groups.

Choose one, and they will go on; the one you don't choose will be cut away from Remembrance, forever."

Chapter Twenty-Three

James still held onto my arm as he led me around the rounding hallway, heading towards the ice. After William wanted me to make a choice between Austin and the other stranded or to pick Danny, Gina, and Angel, he thought it be better if I made my decision from the ice itself so I could look them in the eyes. What I did not account for was that James would make sure I made it there by almost dragging me down.

As we got to a flight of stairs, it felt like James threw me forward as I rolled down the concrete and tiled steps until I hit the first landing. "Come on fella, dere's no need to be knockin' yourself out before we get to da good part," he said to me with a smile on his face as he walked down the stairs gingerly before helping me back to my feet.

"Well, Jesus Christ there James, maybe if you quit using me like a fucking medicine ball, we'd get there faster. You think William would like it if you off me before I'm even one day on the job?"

James grabbed hold of my arm and forced me forward down the next set of stairs. "I don't give two fucks if ya make it, fella. I hate that he even brought ya here, and now I got to make nice with the likes of ya? The hell with that!"

As we made it to the bottom of the stairs, he forced me through another door as we entered the circling hallway. "Oh, so that's it. You're jealous. So, was it your job that I'm taking?" I asked with a sarcastic tone to my voice.

He quickly tightened his grip on my arm as he pulled back and spun me around to face him. Without warning, he placed his right hand on the side of my face and shoved hard, throwing me across the hallway as I slammed into the concrete wall, shoulder first injuring it even further. "Now let's get one thing straight here fella, ya ain't replacing me. I'll be damned if I end up in that pub again, ya hear me?"

Sliding myself up the wall until I'm standing on my feet again, I looked at him and said, "So it's the unpaid tab then? That's not mine." He pointed down the hallway and I without a word began walking again. Before too long, we emerged from the hallway as we walked out onto the ice. The sight of the Justices filling every seat in the arena was a terrifying image as I looked around the giant oval. Hearing someone crying, I glanced over to my left and saw Austin and the stranded still gathered while the Justices remained surrounding them.

Looking to my right, Danny, Angel, and Gina were still grouped together, while being guarded by Justices. Angel stood near Gina, holding her hand as Danny seemed to pace back and forth, every couple of steps he would slip on the ice. The air was much colder than it was higher on the balcony as I saw my breath leaving my lips.

"It's time, Sam," William called out from the balcony. "It's time you showed me your worth. To show me your dedication to perfection."

"Sam!" Gina called out. "What is going on?"

"It's going to be okay Gina," I replied, but was cut off by William.

"So, you've already made your decision!" William called out.

I quickly spun myself around, trying not to slip and fall, and shouted up at William, "No, I've made no decision yet! I need time!"

"You can't drag this out, Sam! Don't waste my time! If you can't decide, then perhaps James…"

"No!" I immediately screamed back at William before turning my head and looking at James. He stood there smiling as he rubbed both hands together in almost anticipation. "Before I make my choice," I shouted up at William, "I need to talk to both groups to know who I'm going to choose!"

William stood silent for a few seconds before he replied, "Very well. But don't take forever or I'll make the choice for you!"

"That won't be necessary!" I began walking towards Gina but stopping only a couple feet from her as a Justice stood in front of me and screeched into my face. "To the side whiney," I said to the Justice while waving my hand to the edge as the Justice stepped to the left.

"Sam, what the fuck is going on?" Gina whispered to me as Angel stayed close to her leg, still holding her hand.

"Are you okay?"

"Yeah, I'm fine, but what the fuck is he talking about? What choice?"

I didn't answer her. I slowly kneeled on the ice as I looked at Angel and waved her to step closer. She slowly stepped forward out from behind Gina's leg but still stayed at her side and continued to hold on to Gina's hand. "Are you okay, sweetheart?" She nodded slowly, but her eyes looked down, ashamed. I noticed a bruise on her cheek.

As I raised my hand in the air to touch her face, Danny shouted out, "Hey, don't fucking touch her!" I glanced at him for a second, as I could feel anger creep up my spine before disappearing.

Looking back at Angel, I asked, "Did he do this to you?"

She nodded again before reaching up in the air with her free hand and grabbing Gina's hand now with both of her little hands. "I'm sorry Sam. He knocked on the door and I thought it was you all," she said to me in a very sad tone.

"Hey, hey, hey, don't worry about it, Angel. It's not your fault; you did nothing wrong. I'm gonna get you out of here soon, okay?" She nodded her head again as she stepped back behind Gina.

As I stood slowly back up, Danny shouted out at me again, "Hey, you fucking piece of shit, come over here!" I, again, glanced at him for a few seconds, then turned my attention back to Angel and Gina.

"What happened?" I asked Gina softly.

"I hid in one of the surrounding buildings, just like you said. All the Justices seemed to disappear once you entered the building, as I watched the arena closely. Soon enough, I saw Danny and Angel sneak out from an alleyway across the lot." She looked down at Angel before she added, "He was dragging her by her arm as she tried to pull away from him." Looking back at me, she continued. "I ran out of the building after them to help, but before I could kick the son of a bitch in the back, the Justices swarmed us out of nowhere." A tear started falling down her cheek.

"It's okay, don't worry," I said as I wiped the tear off her cheek.

She leaned in closer to me and whispered, "Sam, what is going on?"

"I'll be back," I said softly to Gina. She tried to say something again, but before she could get the words out, I had already turned around and was walking cautiously across the ice. Once I reached the other group, none of the Justices gave me any resistance and stepped to the side to allow me to talk to them.

Austin approached me and said, "Sam, what the fuck, man?"

Shaking my head and without looking at him, I said softly, "Austin, I'm so sorry. I told you the wrong street. I sent you down too far and now you're here and I'm just so sorry."

"Sam, what are you talking about?"

"When I told you how to get to the church, I accidentally told you to go too far. I told you eight blocks, but it was only six. Because I fucked up, you and the others here got caught."

Austin shook his head and said, "We never made it to the church because we only went two blocks before Justices swarmed us."

Lifting my head to look at him, I asked, "Wait, what?"

"I thought we were dead, but they just brought us here now."

I was so confused for a second, then I thought back to my conversation with William in the church. *He said to me he had rodents to deal with. I thought he had captured them because of my mistake. But that son of a bitch had them all along!* "Damn it, William has been playing me."

"Who's William?" Austin asked.

"Grumpy McSaggybottom up above," I replied sarcastically. Austin glanced up towards the balcony as the closest

Justice screeched out, almost as if it were laughing. I looked at the Justice for a second and a thought came to my mind. *That was strange, almost like it heard and liked what I said.* As Austin looked back at me, I said, "Okay, hopefully this is almost over. I'm still trying to figure everything out."

"But what exactly…" Before Austin could finish his sentence, I felt a strong grip around the back of my neck as I was yanked backwards and thrown halfway across the ice, sliding to the side before slamming the back of my head against the barrier wall.

"Enough stallin' fella, make your choice!" James yelled at me as he stood next to Austin.

"James, leave him alone. He will make the right choice!" William called out from the balcony.

"The fuck does he mean a choice?" Danny shouted out.

"A choice Danny? You know, like when you choose beer over water, or when you choose to use the left hand or the right to stab someone in the back." As I got up off the ground and supported myself on the ice, I continued. "Or when you choose to lie about seeing a little girl, when you lied about going after a little girl, and when you lied about saving a little girl!" I walked closer to Danny as another Justice stepped out of my way. "She is terrified of you and wants nothing to do with you! And yet you, at every opportunity, tried to harm her for whatever reason we couldn't figure out. That is, until you drunkenly left your fucking wallet at the bar of the hotel, and we saw the picture!" I clinched my fist so tightly that I could feel my fingers getting numb.

"Fuck you, Sam!" he shouted at me as he took a step back like he was going to swing at me but before he could the Justice standing next to me raised its arm in the air and backhanded him knocking him to the ice.

Shocked, I unclenched my fist and felt my heart beating faster and faster as I began breathing quickly, trying to slow it down. As Danny sat himself up, he looked right at me with such anger and hate in his eyes. "Talk!" I screamed at him.

"Yeah, okay fine. I lied. Are you happy?" As he got back to his feet, he said, "I knew if you people found her, you'd just keep her from me."

"That's not good enough, Danny. Who is she to you?"

"She's my fucking daughter!" I glanced over at Gina as the expression of disbelief on her face matched my own. I then looked at Angel and saw that she began to cry as she coward behind Gina even more. *That explains the picture in his wallet, but something still isn't right.*

"Your daughter? That frightened little girl there doesn't look like the emotions a daughter would have around her father," I said to Danny as I pointed at Angel.

Angel leaned out from behind Gina and screamed, "You're not my daddy!" She then ducked back behind Gina.

"You fucking right I'm not your daddy!" He screamed back at her.

I became even more confused when I asked, "Wait the fuck up. You just said she was your daughter? So, what is it, are you or aren't you?"

"Fuck you, Sam!" He turned away from me and took a couple steps towards Gina and Angel, but Gina backed the both of them away as he walked past them while looking up at the balcony. "William, is it? Look, I don't know what you and shit face have going on here, but if you just give me and the girl a free pass out of here, then I'll take care of whatever it is you want from him."

"Danny don't! You don't know what you're saying!" I yelled at him.

Turning towards me he shouted, "Fuck you!" Looking back up towards William he asked, "So what do you say?"

William rubbed the bottom of his chin like he was actually thinking about Danny's offer before he called out, "Sam is the one that I am interested in, not a child abuser."

"He's a what!" I shouted as I looked at Danny. "Is he right? Danny?" I stormed over towards him as a Justice sidestepped in front of me before I could reach him. "Danny, answer me!"

"Hey, I am no such thing!" Danny shouted back up towards William.

"Oh please, I can smell the alcohol all the way up here. And how did the child get that mark on her face, hm? You disgust me."

"Danny! You better start talking right now!" I screamed at him.

"The fuck you want me to say?"

"The truth!"

"The truth? The fucking truth? The truth is yeah, I'm not her dad; I'm her stepdad. I married her mother, but I couldn't have kids of my own. So, I tried to adopt her, but the little bitch didn't want to be my daughter. She wanted to keep her original father's name!" He turned and looked at her before he said, "She disrespected me at every turn, and I just couldn't take the bullshit anymore. So, I disciplined her, and I'll keep disciplining her until she gets that she's mine!" Angel tries to hide behind Gina more as she cries out loud.

"What the hell is wrong with you Danny!" Gina screamed as she kneeled to hug and console Angel.

"I want my mommy!" Angel cried out as she wrapped her arms around Gina's neck so tightly while her pain filled tears ran down her cheeks.

"Oh, shut the fuck up!" Danny screamed towards Angel and Gina. "Your mother is a bitch, too. Always saying to me, 'Why are you drinking so much? Why are you angry so much?' Fuck that fucking shit! Maybe it's because this entire family is worthless to me! Maybe the more I try, the more you both just piss me the fuck off! When I finally get out of here, so help me fucking God!"

From all the way across the ice rink, Austin called out, "Hey, what the hell is going on over there? What's with all the screaming?"

Danny turned towards the group and screamed, "Hey, you shut the fuck up! Nobody cares what you have to say!" He looked back up towards William and shouted, "Alright fine, fuck the girl!

Fuck her mother! What do I need to do to get out of here? Name it!"

William scowled down at Danny with an angry look on his face as he replied, "If it were up to me, I'd cut you out of here right now. But I told Sam that it was up to him." He turned his gaze towards me and added, "So Sam, what is your choice? Who is it going to be?"

I walked towards the center of the ice, as I couldn't help but feel so many emotions all at once. I was angry; I was hurt; I was confused; I was so many things. Glancing over towards Austin and the others, I could not help but rush a few thoughts through my head. *This is not fair to them; they are completely innocent. If I don't choose them, then they must suffer being killed for doing nothing wrong but getting trapped in this city. But if I choose them, they get to go free, and the others get killed.*

I turned my head and looked towards Gina, Angel, and Danny and more thoughts came through my head. *And then there are Angel and Gina. They saved my life. They have stuck with me every step of the way. Even when we lost Henry, they still believed in me. I honestly don't care what happens to Danny, but can I really let them get hurt because of me? But if I choose them, then all those people on the other end. What the fuck am I going to do?*

Suddenly I heard James shout out from behind me, "Hey, come on, fella! Hurry and pick someone!"

I felt myself get knocked out of my thoughts as I turned my head slightly towards him and I asked, "Say that again?"

"Say what? Just pick someone already?"

I turned completely around so that I was facing him, and I said, "Someone?"

"Did I finally knock some screws loose in ya head, Sam? Yeah, someone!"

I turned back around quickly while trying not to slip on the ice. Looking up at William, I said, "Okay, I've made my decision!"

"Well, 'bout time Sam. It's not like I had all day for you to come to your senses. Okay, so who is it going to be?"

"Well, first things first, though. You said that I had to not only decide, but I had to do it too, right? I had to cut them out?" I shouted up to him.

"Yes, Sam. And I also said that if you couldn't do it yourself, then you could have the Justices do it for you. That's just as acceptable. So, who is it?"

"So that means I get total control of the Justices, right? I tell them what to do and they must do whatever it is I tell them, right?"

"Yes Sam, Jesus Christ! Why is this so hard for you? Just tell me already!" William said as he started getting angry with all my questioning and insurances.

"Then say it!"

"Then say? The fuck! Say what?"

"Say it so all these Justices hear it. They have to do what I say!"

James quickly piped in and said, "The fuck ya doin' here, fella?"

Quickly pointing back at him, I bark out, "Shut the fuck up, James! Right now!" Turning back towards William, I again shout up to him, "I need you to say it!"

"Alright fine Sam! If it will make you feel better!" He looked out towards the arena with all the Justices still stirring in their seats, he raised his arms wide in the air and shouted to them, "As Sam here has correctly stated, whom ever he states to be cut out of my city, you will follow his direction completely!" The Justices all started screeching out as loudly as they could reach.

Gina and Angel, along with Austin and the others, all quickly covered their ears to block out the noise. As the screeching got quieter, William looked back towards me and said, "Now Sam, I want to hear it. Who is it going to be?"

With a grin on my face, I looked towards Austin and the other stranded for a few seconds as they all looked at me scared. I then turned my head and looked at Gina and Angel as they, too, looked terrified. I returned my head to center and while looking at William, I smile even bigger and said, "I choose… me!"

Chapter Twenty-Four

The pain in my side exploded throughout my body as I slammed into the barrier wall way behind me. As the words, "I choose me," exited my mouth, James had grabbed hold of my shoulder and yanked me backwards, sending me sailing across the ice until I hit the wall with a loud crash. Glancing up above me, I see James pointing at me while two Justices walk towards me with their stabbers at full extension. I tried to get myself up, but it was no use. They were over me in no time. I could only watch as both Justices pulled their stabbers back to drive them through my body while Gina, Angel, Austin and so many others screamed in horror.

"Fucking stop!" The deep, raspy voice echoed throughout the arena with an almost destructive vibration. The Justices on cue straightened up and retracted their stabbers as they molded back into hands. As they both stepped to opposite sides, I looked at James as he looked frustrated, throwing his arms in the air in disgust. "What are you fucking doing?" the voice echoed out again.

James, turning towards the balcony that William was standing on, looked up at him and answered, "I'm just doin' what he said."

"Not you, you moron! I'm talking to you, Sam!" I draped my arms over the edge of the barrier as I pulled myself back to my feet. *I can't take much more of this abuse.* As I turned around to face towards William, he again shouted, "What in the fuck are you doing?"

"It's called sacrificing myself. I'm using myself as tribute so that these innocent people," I stopped for a second and pointed towards Danny, "and Danny, can go on with no more threats from anyone!"

"Fuck you!" Danny shouted at me. I ignored him.

"No Sam, that's not how this works!" he shouted at me in anger.

"Well, you said…"

He cut me off as he replied, "I said you are here to fix the problems in my city. Which means you cannot give yourself up to allow the problems to continue!"

"But none of these people are what's wrong with this city! None of them are part of the infrastructure your *'city'* is designed around!" I yelled to him as I air quoted the city. He stood there as if he was listening to my analysis, so I continued. "You said to me you designed this city yourself, right? And it was glorious but flawed! You soon began bringing in different people to help you fix what was wrong! And after some time, you kept seeing more flaws, so you cut those people out or moved them to other areas and demolished what was standing to start anew!" I paused for a minute as he stood there staring at me.

Finally, he crossed his arms and shouted down, "I'm listening, Sam!"

"Okay. So, the more people you brought in, the more you started over and raised your city until the flaws returned, and you again cut those people out, and then you started again!" I walked so gingerly towards James as I continued. "And you repeated the pattern over and repeated," placing my hand onto James's shoulder, I added, "and always the same result!" James shrugged his shoulders so my hand would fall off him.

I could tell William was getting frustrated. "You need to get to the point, Sam. What does any of this have to do with your choice?"

"That's just it William! I told you that the task you set before me was going to be difficult and I'd need some time to figure everything out!" I chuckled a little before I added, "The funny thing is, it took me less time than I thought!" While looking up at William, I took a few more steps towards the other barrier. "I've figured out everything that needs to happen to Remembrance, how to fix it all, how to stop this shitty cycle, and yes, get your perfection."

He leaned over the edge of the balcony and glared at me with excitement. "Well, come with it Sam, tell me! Tell me what you need to fix!"

I turned around and looked at everything. I looked up at the sea of Justices stirring in the stands. The Justices that were standing on the ice, tensed their bodies as they waited for me to speak as well. I glanced over at Austin and the others as they stood crowded together, terrified. I turned my head and looked at Angel and her frightened face, at Danny and his disgusting expression, and then at Gina. I stared at Gina as her face filled me with calm and determination as a warmth filled my lungs, making me feel just, confident, and powerful.

Turning back around, I looked up at William and said, "I have made my decision. If I can't choose myself, then fine! If I must choose someone to cut, then fine! I still have total control of the Justices, right? I tell them who needs to go, and they'll take care of it?"

"Yes! Yes Sam, you have total control of the Justices! Tell me! Tell me now! How do I fix my city?" he begged me.

"My choice, and how I fix this fucking city, is you!"

"Is? WHAT!" he screamed at the top of his lungs.

"You are the single reason this city couldn't reach its perfection! You are the reason so many people before me couldn't hold up to your expectations! You are why this city constantly fails!" The Justices in the stands screeched and became restless as William straightened himself up. "I choose you!"

"No! You can't do that! You can't choose me, you idiot!"

"Wrong! You wanted me to figure out why the city kept failing! You said it yourself, you started the city, and it failed, you brought in people, and it failed, you moved people and cut them out and it still failed! That leaves only one logical conclusion." I turned and looked at James as a look of disbelief washed across his face. "William is my choice!" The Justices in the stands began running for the exits and flushed themselves down the aisles and hallways while others began leaping across the ice to the other side of the arena as droves of them made their way towards the balcony.

William backed up slightly before he charged forward and looked back down at me. "No! You can't do this! You listen to me! I am not the problem! He is the problem here!" he screamed as he pointed at me, but none of them seemed to listen. As more and more Justices approached the balcony, William suddenly tore his jacket off and threw it to the ground before he crossed his arms across his body and swung them out as he screamed, "No!" A shock wave flew out from the balcony as gray puffs of smoke and ash filled the arena in a humongous burst as every single Justice that was in the stands and the hallways exploded into nothingness. The only remaining Justices that were left were the handful still standing on the ice, including James.

William, exhausted, fell over onto the floor but caught himself on the edge of the balcony. Through his weakened breaths, he said, "You son of a bitch, you've ruined everything. They're all gone; my city is ruined. Remembrance is ruined. My perfection is ruined!"

"Remembrance had a chance to succeed. This city could have been something glorious I have no doubt. But you and your greed and pride ruined any chances it had and ruined so many of its inhabitants as well." As I spit a glob of blood from my mouth onto the ice, I added, "It ends now."

"I'll have your hide for this. James, get him!" he screamed down at us as he struggled to pull himself back to his feet. I turned and looked at James as he just stood there, staring at me, and not moving. "I said get him now! Do it now James!"

He slowly cocked his head to the side as he looked up towards William's depleted body and said, "Sorry fella, ya said I'm supposed to listen to this guy right here! That I'm supposed to take care of whoever he picks to get cut out!" He looked back at me and said, "Isn't that right there, fella? I mean, sir."

"What? No, James, you can't do this! You are my…"

James cut William off as he screamed back, "I'm your what? I had this guy's spot, and you tossed me to a bar? You tossed me like I was nothin'! And then not only that, but then I gotta take orders from him? So that's what I'm fixin' to do here!" He looked at me once more and asked, "So, that's your choice, then?"

"Yes, that's what's going to fix this city, James," I answered.

"That's all I needed to here." A deathly screech cried out of him as he melted away to his horrifying Justice form, showing off his scar across his chest. Gina and Angel screamed in fright along with some of the other stranded on the other side of the ice as he leaped up into the air and came down onto the balcony.

"No! James, no!" William called out as James's Justice form disappeared from our sight. Out of nowhere, as he gripped onto the edge of the balcony, Justice James yanked William backwards, screaming. "No! James No! Oh god no!" William's screams of pain and horror echoed out as his grip on the ledge slipped slowly away until he was no longer visible to us. All we could hear were his cries of pain and terror echoing from the balcony for several seconds until without warning there was nothing.

Looking down towards Austin and the others, I called out, "Let them go!" Without hesitation, the Justices that surrounded them stepped away from the group as they walked across the ice towards me. Looking at the other Justices surrounding Gina and Angel, I said, "You too." Again, with no hesitation, they all backed away. Gina and Angel walked towards me and once they got near, they hugged me. After a couple seconds, I glanced towards Danny as he started walking away and I called out, "Except him!"

Danny quickly turned around as multiple Justices surrounded him, blocking his escape. "What the, hey fuck you!" he screamed out, but the Justices just screeched right back at him.

"Mommy!" Angel screamed out as she let go of me and began trying to run towards Austin and the other stranded.

Suddenly, one woman dropped to her knees and screamed, "Angel? Angel!" As the two grabbed hold of each other, the woman could not help herself as she cried uncontrollably. I glanced over at Gina as she cried as well.

Austin stood in front of me and said, "What the hell was this all about?"

Smiling, I said, "A horrible dream. But it's over now." Shaking his head. He smiled and stuck his hand out as I took his hand and shook it.

"So, what's next? Are we safe from these, um, Justices?" he asked as he pointed towards some of them.

"Yeah, they aren't going to be a problem for us anymore, I think."

"So, who was that guy?" Austin asked me as he pointed towards the now silent balcony.

Shaking my head, I replied, "The cause of all this. Someone that tried to rule without consequences or compassion and his arrogance and addiction got him in the end."

Gina then asked, "But what did he mean by calling all this his city?"

Sighing, I said, "It's really a long and sad story from what I gathered. But he tried to get too many people to chase this crazy dream of his and trapped them here. Call it magic, call it dark arts, call it whatever you want. He was just a man that lost his humanity to accomplish his goals." Looking back at the balcony myself, I added, "And he almost did it to me, too." I turned towards Gina and asked, "Do you think you can help everyone get back to the hotel?"

She began nodding her head and said, "Yeah, absolutely."

"A hotel?" Austin asked with a confused look on his face.

Gina looked at him and said, "Yeah, it has food, and beds, clothes, running water, medicine, everything we need."

He looked at her, confused, and said, "Everything we need for what?"

"Everything we need until we figure out what's next for us to get ourselves home," I said to him as I tapped him on the shoulder. As he shook his head in confusion, I said, "I know, I know, where is home? We'll figure that out." I took a step back and shouted out, "Okay, everyone, not a Justice, head for the exit!"

Austin called out to everyone to follow Gina as they made their way into the tunnel and quickly vanished out of sight. All that remained in the arena besides me were a handful of Justices standing around and Danny still being guarded. I heard a rumble above my head as I turned around to see Justice James jump from the balcony and land on the ice, cracking it from the impact. As he straightened up, his Justice form faded away and the pale skinned, red-haired prick was back.

"Is it done?" I asked him.

"Ya fella, ya don't need to be worryin' about him." As he approached me, he said, "William was very powerful here. But I never thought of that move you just pulled fella. I was wonderin' if you were gonna try and fight him with your fists."

"The thought crossed my mind at one point."

"I would have given you your respect, but he would've killed you on the spot. You had no shot. But out thinking him, smooth." As we stood for a second in silence, James asked, "So, what's next?"

"I don't know. Guess I'm in charge now, huh? I never ran a city before."

James crossed his arms and leaned forward a little before he said, "Well, ya could always just give it to me."

Smiling, I replied, "That is a thought. But don't you wish you went back to your old life?"

He straightened up with a ponderous look on his face. "I never really thought it was an option. I mean, I suppose, but what about the rest of ya's?"

"Well, that little move William did to get rid of the other Justices. What happened to them?"

"Oh, they're gone, fella. He cut them all out."

I shook my head in anger. "Damn it, William." I glanced over towards Danny as I saw him glaring at me with such hate on his face. "What about all the other people in the city? What about them?"

With a crooked smile on his face, he said, "Fella, they all gone. The only people left in this city are us right here and your people that just left."

"So, no matter what, unless I pick up where William left off and bring more unsuspecting victims here, this city is done?"

"Sounds to me like ya got it all figured out, fella."

I stood for a minute as I looked around at the emptiness in the arena as I took a deep breath and slowly left it all out. "Then maybe, maybe we just call it a day."

"What?" James asked, confused.

As I turned and faced him, I said, "The rest of you are free to return home. This city is no more. There's nothing left for you to do." James stood in shock as I could see his brain started thinking about what it meant to be free. To not have to be a Justice anymore, to not have to work at one of the stupid shops. To be free.

"Hey! You fucking piece of shit! I want out of here!" We both turned to look at Danny as he began to almost bounce around in between the Justices that were guarding him.

"What about that fella over there?" James asked as he pointed at Danny. We both walked across the ice to where Danny was being guarded as he stood ready to fight.

"You let me go right now. I want out of here," he said to me with such disdain in his voice.

"So, you can do what? Go hurt Angel again, go hurt your wife again? Or you run off like the piece of garbage you are and find a new family to hurt and torment? No, I don't think so," I said as I clinched my fists at my sides.

"I already said before that I don't care about them anymore. And what I do with my life is none of your business. But you move these fucking freak bodyguards away from me and I'll fucking pull your tongue out of your mouth and shove it up your ass!"

Spit flew out of his mouth and landed on my face. James giggled as I wiped it off my cheek. "That's pretty funny there, fella," James said as he laughed.

"Really? That you find funny?" I asked James as I wiped the rest from my face.

Still chuckling, he replied, "Hell yeah. Not cause he spit on ya, but because he's got no idea how much shit he be in."

I could feel the muscles in my face tighten as I turned my attention back towards Danny. "Alright, that's fine. Just answer me this; why did you abuse Angel? Why would you put your hands on her?" I asked.

Snickering, he replied, "Because neither one of them learned. They didn't learn that I was in charge and what I say goes. People in my life never learn, so I had to force them to learn. Did they get hurt, perhaps? But eventually they got it, or it was the last thing they did." I took a step back from Danny, as I could not believe what he had just said. *Is he saying what I think he's saying?*

"Damn fella, ya some kinda psycho aren't ya?" James asked as he shook his head.

"Psycho, nah. It's just the way of the world. The strong are in charge and the weak need to fall in line."

"Jesus Christ, Danny, you sound like you enjoy it!" I shouted at him.

"Maybe a little. I'll enjoy it a lot more when I find the next woman that doesn't learn right away. Maybe I'll see if Gina wants me to teach her a lesson."

The anger in me boiled over as I charged forward, but James stopped me as two of the Justices screeched at Danny, forcing him to step backwards. "Fella, fella, fella, come on now. Ya don't want to be doin' that like this, do ya?"

As the Justices stared at me, I stood back for a second. I pushed James's arms away from me and said, "Yeah, you're right." I turned my attention towards Danny and said, "Alright then, you've made your case, Danny." I looked at the Justices guarding him and ordered, "Let him loose."

As the Justices stepped to the side, Danny raced forward towards me. "Yeah, I'm gonna fucking make you…" Before he could finish his sentence, when he was close enough, I quickly cocked my arm back and swung forward, catching him right on the chin as he stumbled to his right.

"James!" I screamed out.

Without missing a step, just as Danny stumbled past him, James screamed out, "Bro!" He jumped in the air and pump kicked Danny in the back of his head sending him flying to the ground and sliding across the ice several feet until he came to a stop at the feet of several Justices.

I walked up and stood next to James as we both watched Danny slowly turn himself over in a daze. "That was a nice shot," I complimented James.

"Ah, it ain't the first time I had to kick a fella in the skull. So, what do we do with him now?"

I stood for a couple of seconds before I said, "I told you that the rest of you are free to go home; that you're no longer needed here."

"That's right, ya did say that."

"Unfortunately, I might have lied to you."

Shaking his head and crossing his arms across his chest, he replied, "Oh, that's not good, fella. Ya don't want to upset the likes of us now, do ya?"

"No, I most certainly do not. That's why I'm being honest with you now."

Shaking the cobwebs from his head, Danny looks up at us and, with slurred words, said, "Hey, what the fack? What you tolkin' about?"

"I have one more thing for you to do, James; get rid of this piece of trash," I ordered.

As some Justices started screeching, James asked, "What ya want us to do with him?"

"What? What? What's goin' on?" Danny questioned as he frantically looked around at each Justice as they stepped closer to him.

Thinking for a second, I replied, "What was it he said? If I let him go, he was going to do what to me?"

Smiling, James answered, "I believe he said he was gonna pull your tongue out of ya mouth and shove it up your arse."

"What the fuck Sam!"

"Hm, maybe if he learned what that felt like, he wouldn't threaten people with it. Don't you think so, James?"

"Sounds like an excellent lesson to learn dere Sam."

"Then I'll leave you to it."

James's voiced deepened slightly as he said, "Hm, maybe you're more like William than I thought."

As I turned and began walking away, I didn't look back. I could hear the Justices all screech as Danny called out, "Sam! Sam, no! Fuck you, Sam!" His words were quickly replaced by his screams of pain and agony, followed shortly by mumbles of the same pain and agony. As I made my way further down the tunnel, I quickly saw the doors that were left opened by the others. Once I reached the doorway, I noticed that the screeches from the Justices all stopped, and everything became silent.

Once I reached halfway across the parking lot, that is when I finally turned around and looked at the building. All the life, all the activity, all seemed to just vanish from it. The lights went dark, and the building went cold. Suddenly, I watched as the fog that shrouded this entire city quickly hovered over the building and seemed to swallow it until I could see the building no more.

As I made my way down the street towards the hotel, James's last words to me filled my head. *Maybe you're more like William than I thought.* My head filled with thought after thought clouding my brain so much that they forced me to stop. *What the fuck did I just do? Oh my god, I just told them to kill a man! What have I become? No, that's not me. That was what William wanted me to become!*

That wasn't me! I will make sure William never gets his way. I will never become that. That will never become me. Ever.

Chapter Twenty-Five

The streets seemed like they all have even less life to them than before. Even when Gina and I were walking in the pitch blackness of the night, the darkness still seemed to have a pulse. Now, with the departure of William and the Justices, the streets and buildings just appear to be empty shells. It gave the walk towards the hotel a larger sense of eeriness. The lights of the hotel filled the twilight sky as I got closer to the building. I purposely took longer to walk back because I could not forget the feeling of shame from my mind from what I had just done not too long ago.

The last conversation with Danny haunted me, as I could not shake it. It disturbed me how he could just talk about abusing Angel like it was nothing; like it was just a part of life. Or how he talked down about his wife, Angel's mom. What drove him to the point of acting this way I would never know. But the thing that bothered me more, and the thing I did not realize at first, was that he remembered. He knew that not only was he Angel's stepfather, but that he abused Angel, that he could not have his own children, his whole life, he knew it all.

I could remember nothing, and yet Danny could remember what he called disciplining a little girl and his wife. But it was not just him; I never realized it before, but Angel knew everything as well. She knew who Danny was, that he was her stepdad, even from the very first time we found her. When she found her mom, she knew who she was. She knew all of it and I never noticed. I quickly pushed these thoughts to the back of my mind, as I was only mere yards away from the hotel.

It felt like an hour had passed, but it could have been thirty minutes or two hours for all I knew. As I crossed the parking lot, I could suddenly see everyone moving around inside the hotel. No longer were there just gray shapes hidden behind fogged glass. *That probably means the time break error has stopped with William's end as well.*

Entering the hotel, the atmosphere in the lobby differed from when Gina and I left it. Many of the survivors were standing around, some talking with one another, some were hugging each other, while others were heading off into an elevator or heading for the restaurant for food. The overall feeling was calm and relieved. Looking over at the counter, I could see Gina handing out keycards to survivors so they could have their own rooms to rest and recover. *I should leave her alone.*

I made my way towards the restaurant, heading down the hallway and through the double doors once again. Standing at the entrance, I could hear some people in the kitchen cooking and laughing while three or four sat at a table in the middle of the dining area also laughing. Glancing over at the bar, I spotted Austin sitting at the bar, a beer sitting in front of him as he sat on a stool leaning over the counter. All the bar stools that I had kicked over in anger earlier were now all standing back up. *Did he clean up my mess?*

Making my way over to the bar, Austin turns his head and spots me as he smiles while turning the bottle in his hand slowly. Once I reach the bar, I see at the end of the counter sat Danny's wallet folded closed. As I reached out and picked it up slowly, Austin asked me, "Do you know who that belongs to?"

I go behind the counter and walk halfway down the bar until I come upon a garbage can. Dropping the wallet into the garbage, I reply, "A son of a bitch." Looking at Austin, I add, "I need a drink." Austin picked his bottle up and pointed at a pair of glass doors to a refrigerator with the head of his own beer as I opened one door and pulled out my bottle. Closing the door, I turn around as Austin is already holding out a bottle opener for me as I take it and pry the cap off the bottle and place it down on the counter.

I returned to the other side of the bar, where I sat down on the stool next to Austin as I put the bottle to my lips and took a long gulp of the cool alcohol. As I pulled the bottle from my mouth, without looking at him, I asked, "Has anyone told you you look like a pilot?"

Grabbing his sleeve between two of his fingers, he replies, "Is that what this outfit is for? Fuck, I was really hoping I was the captain of a lover's cruise ship." The two of us laughed as he took a drink from his bottle of beer.

Mimicking him, I placed the bottle in my mouth once again and took another long gulp of the beverage. After pulling the bottle away and smacking my lips together, I sat the bottle back down on the bar top and said, "Yeah, you know I really don't like beer."

Austin chuckled as he too took a long gulp, sat the bottle down next to mine and said, "Yeah, me too." We both laughed, but my laugh quickly ran away. "So, what troubles you?" he asked me.

Slowly shaking my head, I replied, "Nothing and everything."

"I've seen that look before, don't ask me where, but I know that means you're feeling troubled. And that's understandable. What we just went through; what you just went through. Shit, I'm surprised you're even still standing."

"Me too," I said as I grabbed the bottle and just held it as I watched the small droplets of sweat form on the brown glass.

"So, those things, those Justices, you called them?"

"What about them?"

"Well, are they going to follow us here? Or are they staying at that stadium?"

Looking at him, with a half-smile on my face, I said, "You asked me that already."

"I know, but I want to be sure. We've come so far and survived so much; I just need to know everyone here is finally safe."

I shake my head. "They will not be around anymore. They are all gone."

With a wide-eyed look on his face, he asked, "How the fuck did you manage that?"

"I guess… I guess I fired them?" I took a sip of the beer and slowly swallowed it before putting the bottle back down once more.

"Fired? How the hell do you fire monsters? What does that even mean?" Austin asked. "Are they or aren't they…"

"They're gone Austin," I said, cutting his question off. "You don't need to worry about them." Austin watched me as I took yet another large gulp of the beer without looking at him as I placed the bottle on the counter once more. He watched as my face grimaced as I was determined to let the alcohol take its effects on my body.

"Okay," he said softly. "I believe you." He slowly turned forward once again as we both just stared at the wall. We sat in silence for almost a minute before he turned to me again and then asked, "What about that guy you were arguing with? What was his name?"

Without looking away from my beer, I replied, "Danny."

"Yeah, was it just me, or was he really that much of a creep?"

"He was definitely not a good person, if that's what you're asking." I take yet another large gulp from the beer as I finish the bottle before I added, "But then again, neither am I?"

"What? What do you mean by that?"

"He's gone because of me."

"Because of you? I don't believe that for a second."

"Well, believe it Austin. I'm just as much of a fucking bastard as he was."

Austin slapped his hand on the countertop, making me jump a little as he leaned in close and said, "The fuck are you saying? I don't believe that for a second!" I turned to look at him as he continued speaking. "Do you not see what I do? Right now, this hotel is full of people that almost gave up on themselves; almost gave up on their own lives. You came along and all of them not only pushed on but are now safe and ready for another day. It's because of you that this hotel right now is full of survivors of some of the wickedest bullshit anyone has ever seen. You put yourself in harm's way over and over to save complete strangers, and you have the scars to prove it. Few people can say they did that."

"Well, Danny sure can't. Because of me, he's gone," I whispered as my eyes watered.

"Sam, the way he was acting, talking all that crazy, stupid shit, putting his hands on his family, he was going to get himself killed, eventually. As far as I can see, you stopped him before he could hurt another innocent person ever again." He placed his hand on my shoulder as I winced from the pain in it and added, "Yeah, it sucks that you did it. I get it. But you are still a hero, even if you don't think you are."

Turning my head to look at him, I said, "Thanks Austin, I get what you're trying to say. It's just, I don't think I can get past it like that easy."

Letting go of my shoulder, he stood up and walked around to the other side of the bar. "No one expects you to," he said as he took the empty bottle from my hands and threw it into the trash. As he dumped the rest of his beer down the drain of the sink behind the bar, he added, "But you can't get over it drinking this shit." Once he finished emptying his bottle, he tossed it into the garbage as well and, while smiling, said, "You think they got some energy drinks around here?"

As I laughed, I reply, "I honestly don't know."

As he walked back around from behind the bar, he said, "I'm gonna go see what snack food they got in this place and sleep for like twenty-four hours." As I laughed again, he leaned in and said, "You should go see what Gina's up to. But get this self-doubt and loathing out of your head. You are a good person." He slapped my stomach with the back of his hand and chuckled as he walked away into the kitchen.

Looking behind the counter, I see my reflection in a large mirror that was against the back side of the bar, against the wall. Looking at myself, I see all the scars, scratches, cuts, bruises, but above all, I see myself. I do not see this image of a monster, the image of a murderer, or the image of a vile person. I just see me. *No matter what anyone says to me, what I did was wrong, and I must live with it. But I can live with it, and if I must pay for it down the road, then I'll live with the consequences.*

Standing up from the bar stool, I make my way back out to the lobby. As I reach the now nearly empty hall, Gina is just handing the last keycard to another stranded couple as they walk away from the counter and head up in an elevator, smiling. I sit down on one of the padded benches across from the counter as Gina sighs, fixes her ponytail, then gingerly walks out from behind the counter as she makes her way over to me. As she gets closer, I study her walk as she approaches and just think how amazing she is.

"You know, I can't figure you out."

"Oh," she said with a small giggle.

"You have all this medical and first aid knowledge, so I think you might be a doctor or a trauma nurse. But then you just quickly punch those keys on these computers and then I think you could run your own hotel, or maybe you're just some tech genius." She smiles bashfully as she is now standing only mere inches from me. "I just can't figure you out."

"I could say the same for you, Sam," she replies with a smile.

"Really?" I reply.

"Yeah. Like today, for example. Like how in the world did you figure out how to take control of the Justices? How did you know your plan was going to work?"

"Truthfully?"

"Yeah!"

"Honestly, I had no idea. I didn't know because it wasn't my plan. My plan was I was going to sacrifice myself for you."

"What!" she said as she yelled at me and took a step back. "That's not funny Sam."

"It's not a joke, Gina. At that moment, I saw no other option in front of me. William was making me choose between the two groups. Whoever I chose got to live while the others died.

So, if I chose myself, I hoped that I'd die and the rest of you would live on." Leaning back against the back of the bench, I took a deep breath while she slowly walks up and sits next to me. "It was the only thing I could think of to save everyone's lives."

She reached out and grabbed hold of my hand as I added, "I wasn't going to be the reason you got hurt."

"Me?" she asked softly.

"You, Angel, or anyone else. It was only after James, you know, the big red-headed guy," Gina started to laugh as I explained with my arms to show how big James was. "Well, when he said that I had to choose someone, I thought to myself if there was ever an opportunity, that was my chance. I hoped William would've been so obsessed with his perfect city idea that he would release enough control of the Justices that I might trick him into letting all of us go. I never imagined it would go as far as it did honestly."

I glanced down to see that Gina was holding my hand with one of hers but was rubbing the top of my hand with her other hand, softly stroking her fingers across my skin on the back of my hand. "No matter what you planned, Sam, you saved everyone here. All those people that I gave keycards to all were singing your praises. They weren't thinking about the Justices, they weren't looking over their shoulders for the next attack. They were saying

Sam saved us. Even Angel to her mom; she kept saying how you saved her from the monsters!"

"And in that moment, when you all left, I felt that power that William had, that control," I said to her in stunned emotion. "Right before I left that arena, I felt it in my body and my mind, and I felt so strong and insanely in command." As I shook my head, I added, "And also, I felt so dark."

With such concern in her eyes, she asked, "Dark? What do you mean?"

I did not want to tell her because I was afraid of her reaction, but I needed to get it out. "Right before I left that building, it was myself, the remaining Justices, and Danny. He was talking all kinds of crazy shit and such anger and violence. He kept saying something like he was going to discipline more people, or another family, or something like that. And then he threatened you, and I just felt this immense power and…"

"And what Sam?"

"I told the Justices to handle him. And then, I said that they were no longer needed, and I just walked away."

"Oh my god," she said softly even though we were alone, so that only we could hear it. "I'm so sorry Sam."

"What? Sorry for me?" I asked, completely bewildered. "Why are you sorry for me? I'm the one that is still here?"

"Sam, you just got done saying that he was going to hurt someone else, if not Angel or her mom again, right?" I nodded at her. "So, you did what you had to do to save more people from pain and suffering by stopping him?"

"But, but I don't…"

"You did what you had to. That's all that matters right now. Was it a horrible thing? Yes, and no one should have to make that decision. If anything, you used William's Justices to actually deliver Justice."

"But Gina I…"

Gina placed her hand on my cheek. "Stop trying to make me angry with you. I already told you it was a horrible thing that had to be done. Danny was an evil person who put his hands on women and children for no other reason other than pain. Instead of trying to help you or Henry at the church, he tried to kidnap Angel again in the middle of the chaos. I don't feel bad for him, and neither should you."

The whole time I was hating myself for what I had done, two different people told me it was not as horrible as I made it. Danny was indeed a bad person and if the situation had been more normal, I would have called the authorities. But these past several days have been anything but normal. He threatened me; he threatened Angel, Gina; if I had let him go, we'd probably still be having issues with him. It's going to be a long time for me to forgive myself, but so far it seems that everyone I've talked to has already forgiven me.

"What about the control I got from William? What if it turns me into someone like him?"

Frowning, Gina replied, "Didn't you say you dismissed the Justices?"

Nodding my head, I said softly, "Yes."

"So, didn't you then release the control you had by getting rid of what it actually controlled?"

"I don't know."

Sighing, she then said, "Okay, well, you obviously feel horrible after using the power, right? I think that guilt, if you indeed still have that power, will keep you from using it again, don't you think?"

I pulled my hand away from hers and turned my head away to look out the windows in the lobby. *I can't believe I'm thinking this, but I think she's right. I'm beating myself up inside over something that I have no desire to use ever again. I'm feeling sorry for myself for doing something that needed to be done to save lives. She's right, after all.*

As I turned my head back towards her, she said, "I think the best thing for you now is to rest." She gets up from the bench and stands right in front of me. I feel her press the outside of her knee softly against the inside of my thigh as she reaches her hand out towards me. "Come on, let's get you to bed." I reached my hand up as I joined it with hers while she squeezed it firmly, pulling me off the bench as we walked towards the elevators.

Pressing the button to call one of them, she did not turn around to look at me, nor did she say another word in my direction. She just kept facing forward. As the elevator dinged, then opened its doors, Gina walked into the elevator while still holding onto my hand as she led me to the back corner. She pressed the button for the fourth floor and the doors closed. Once the elevator ascended, while still holding onto my hand, she slowly backed up until she was pressing her back and butt against my chest and legs, pinning me to the wall of the elevator.

"Hey, what are you doing?" I asked her softly with a smile on my face. She did not respond to my question, she just continued to press against me and hold my hand. Once the elevator stopped at the fourth floor and the doors opened, Gina stepped off the elevator, pulling me behind her as we made our way down the hallway towards the room. However, we are met in the hallway by Angel and her mother.

"Gina! Sam!" her little voice called out as she hurried up to us with her mother not far behind. She held in her hands all the items she had found throughout the hotel. Everything except for the video camera. *She must have wanted to get all her stuff from our room since she'd be staying with her mother now.*

Gina kneeled on the floor and asked Angel, "Did you get all your stuff you wanted?"

"Yeah, here you go." She hands Gina a keycard as Gina smiles and places it into her pocket. "I'm so glad you guys helped me find my mom."

"Yes, and I can't even begin to thank you both for looking after her and protecting her. It means everything to me," her mom said to me.

"It was no problem at all. I'm just so glad we could get you two reunited. I'm just sorry it took until now." I could tell she wanted to say something to me. While Gina talked with Angel, her mom nodded her head off to the side and I took a couple of steps backwards while she followed me.

Before I could say anything, she whispered to me, "No really, thank you. Thank you for having the courage to protect her from that horrible man of a husband. I was so afraid of him for years that I let him control us." As she turned her head to look at her smiling daughter, she added, "But, seeing her never so happy, let me know I failed her."

"Danny… was not a good person for sure. You're right about that. But think of now as your opportunity to truly give Angel the life she deserves, and you the same."

She turned her head to look at me and said, "He's gone, isn't he?" I was caught back for a second by her comment, so I just nodded. With a sigh, she said, "That's fine. I don't want to know, nor do I care to know. The love I had for him at one time has long since left. He's gone and Angel's safe. That's all I care about now." She reached out and hugged me for a few seconds before she let me go and walked over to Angel and said, "All right, let's let them go, honey."

"Okay mom," Angel said with a sigh as she hugged Gina. She then walked over to me and stood in front of me, waiting for me to bend down. Once I did, she hugged me around my neck and squeezed awfully hard. I didn't have the heart to tell her she was actually hurting me. "Thanks again for saving me from the monster," she whispered into my ear.

Rubbing her back, I replied, "You're welcome." She let go of my neck, then walked over to and passed her mom as they made their way towards the elevator and got on. It finally dawned on me that the monster she kept mentioning was never the Justices. It has been, and always will be in her eyes Danny. As I stood up, I turned around to see a very intimate look on Gina's face as she smiled at me. Reaching out her hand, she took hold of mine once more as we made our way down the rest of the hallway until we stood outside our hotel room. Still saying nothing to me, she then unlocked the door with her keycard, opened the door, and pulled me inside.

Chapter Twenty-Six

The darkness of the hotel room was slightly diminished by the night sky as it shined through the large window in the living room. As I push the door closed, Gina turns on a small lamp on a desk at the corner of the room. As I walked over to a light switch to turn more on, she said, “No, don’t. Leave them off; this one is enough.”

“Okay,” I replied with hesitancy as I left the switch down. Walking over to the couch, I sat down in the middle seat, letting my body just collapse as I rest on the soft cushion. Gina walks over behind me as she places her hand on the back of my head, running her fingers through my hair. At the touch of her fingers, I let out an involuntary sigh and moan as I closed my eyes.

"Do you want to get cleaned up before bed?" Gina asked me softly. *I am so weak and tired, and in so much pain, but I guess I could use a shower before bed.*

"Yeah, that sounds like a good idea," I said back to her.

"Before you go in, do you mind if I get in there first?"

"No, not at all. Go right ahead," I answered her.

I felt her remove her hand from the back of my head and walk away. "Just wait here. I'll be right out," she said to me as the door to the bedroom closed. As I am now alone in the room, I keep my eyes closed as I laid my head back against the cushion of the couch as I felt for the first time since I woke up in the dirt field, I could finally relax. After a minute, I lift my head off the couch and open my eyes to look directly at the large television in front of me. *I doubt it, but I wonder if there's something on tv?*

I looked around for a second before I spotted the remote control on a small table next to the window. Every inch of my body was so tired as I stood up and walked over to the window. As I picked up the remote, I looked out the window and just glanced at the top of all the abandoned buildings throughout the city. I could not help but let my mind wonder in thought. *I still don't know how many times William restarted this city; how many individuals' lives he affected. All those people that he tricked into coming here with promises of success and riches to ruin their lives. He can't do that to anyone anymore.*

As I returned to the couch and sat down, I could hear running water through the wall. *Gina must've really wanted to take a shower first. I don't blame her for that either. I guarantee once I get in there, I'm gonna just let that hot water run down my whole body; I'm gonna turn myself into a prune.* Turning on the television, I am immediately greeted by a green screen with different icons and images of different shows and movies to choose from. As I scrolled through the options, almost all the programs looked familiar, but nothing was jumping out at me to watch. I finally saw what was on now as I hit the "Watch Live" option, but I am met by an error message that said, "We are having a problem showing you this."

"That's what I thought," I said to myself as I turn the television off. I suddenly realized that the water was no longer running in the bathroom from the shower. "Is she done already?" I asked myself. As I threw the remote to the right of me on the couch, the door opened to the bedroom as I heard Gina walking out, slightly sliding her feet across the carpet on the floor.

"You finished already?" I asked her.

"Yup," she said to me as I saw her walk around to the front of the couch. I noticed she was wearing her oversized t-shirt that she had sported to sleep in once again. She had no pants or shorts on, as I could see her bare legs to her bare feet. She was carrying a large plastic bucket that was filled with hot water as she set it down in front of me slightly off to the left of her.

"What's that for?"

"You said you wanted to get cleaned up before bed, so," she said as she pointed to the bucket as I then noticed she had a wash rag, a towel, and extra bandages in her other hand.

"Well, yeah but I…"

She immediately cuts me off by shushing me. With a smile on her face, she then asked me softly, "Stand up for me?" I stood up slowly and carefully as she dropped the rag into the hot water while the towel and bandages, she placed on the couch. She walks in front of me and looks me right in the eye as I look down at her. I suddenly felt her fingers around the bottom of the shirt I was wearing as she grabbed hold of it and lifted it up in the air until it was high enough that she could pull it off me. She threw the shirt across the room as I heard it brush against the wall before it rested on the floor.

She kneeled and grabbed the rag in the water as she dunked it in and out of the water as I see soap suds form in the bucket. "You remind me of my father," she said to me, as I was totally shocked. *She remembers! Oh, my god!* "He was a good man, a good father. He died when I was incredibly young; he was a police officer, and he was protecting a group of people and sacrificed his life to save theirs. That's how you remind me of him." She squeezed the extra water from the rag before she returned to standing as she rubbed the warm, lathered, and wet cloth slowly across my chest and neck. "From the moment I saw you here, you have gone out of your way to save so many people, including me multiple times, and not once did you think of the consequences." Dropping the cloth into the bucket, she picked up the towel and patted it on the areas of my body that she had just cleaned before returning it to the couch.

As she kneeled back down, she reached into the bucket and dunked the rag in the water again, then continued. "But it's not just that, Sam, it's so much more. After I lost my father, it was a while before my mother married again. But he was nothing like my father. He was a terribly angry man, he drank a lot, and he hit my mom and me." She stood up again and rubbed the cloth slowly across both of my arms and hands. Once finished, she drops the cloth into the bucket again, then picks up the towel and pat dried my arms. I soon realized that each pat of the towel she made on my body sent incredible chills throughout from my head to my toes. Once done, she again returned the towel to the couch.

"It was years that my mother and I lived in constant fear of him, and then one day, he was just gone. I don't know if he abandoned us, or his anger got him killed, but I simply just did not care. But, because of him, I put up such an immense wall that if anyone tried to get close to me, I kept them at a far distance." She bends down to the bucket again.

"I had an awfully hard time trying to make friends because I just couldn't trust anyone. But I had a fascination with medicine, so that's what I wanted to go to college for. But I still had my walls up, so again I had a hard time getting to know anyone in my classes." She stood up once more and motioned her hand in a circle to let me know to turn around. Once I was facing away from her, I felt the warm rag slowly running up and down across my back.

"And then I met you."

"Gina?" I breathed, but she ignored me. Once again, I felt her soft pats of the towel on my back. At the same time, it almost felt like she was standing even closer to me as I felt her soft exhale of her breath just graced the skin of my back.

"We met each other one morning on the campus pavilion; I tried to give you the cold shoulder, but you refused to take the hints." Giggling, she added, "I actually thought you were brain damaged." I stayed silent as she continued. "But we kept seeing each other at that pavilion; whether if the sun shined, it rained, it snowed, every day I went you were there." I felt her hand on my arm as she pulled it backwards, making me turn back around to face her once again. She then turned me a little more to the left as she began to gently pull the bandage on my side off, exposing my wound.

She dunked the rag and began tapping it around the large, stitched closed slash as she kept telling me her story. "I began looking forward to our interactions until you invited me to your friend's party. I was so nervous and angry with you, and I had no reason to. And then I was even miserable to you and your friends at the party, but the next day you still showed up at the pavilion; you didn't give up on me."

As she finished cleaning my side, she pat dried the area with the towel, then grabbed the bandage from the couch and placed it on my side, covering my injury once more. She then stood back up and looked me right in the eyes and said, "It meant everything to me, Sam. And even after I explained to you why I had my walls up, you refused to let that deter you from getting to know me. I knew then I was in love with you." I suddenly felt my pants being unbuckled as Gina never looked away from my eyes. Once my pants were completely undone, she slowly lowered them to the floor as she kneeled with them until they were around my ankles.

She tossed the washrag into the bucket once again as she placed her hand on my left calf, making me lift my leg into the air as she pulled my sneaker, sock, and pant leg off me before allowing me to set it back onto the floor. She then repeated the same thing with my right leg. Once my pants were completely off, she threw them over towards where my shirt laid as they also hit the wall and slid down to the floor. All I had left on my body were my boxers as she dunked the rag into the warm water and squeezed it out before she started to slowly rub it on one of my legs.

"Gina?" I said again softly, but my voice had a small tremble to it. She again ignored me.

"We had our difficulties, but you were always there for me. Even when I had to continue my schooling for my medical degree all the way to my doctorate; you never once batted an eye. It was you who sacrificed everything for me, for my dreams. You worked long hours at jobs you hated just to make a living for us so I could chase my dream. Sam, you do not know how much that meant to me."

As she finished cleaning my legs, she placed the rag into the bucket. As she stayed on her knees, she looked up at me and said, "And even after I got accepted to a great program, you upped your entire life and moved to another city with me so that I could follow my dreams and get my dream job. We had such a great life, but there was something missing, and then you asked me to marry you." *What! Married?*

She reached up and dragged my boxers down from around my waist, exposing my partial erection until my boxers were resting on the floor around my ankles. She then repeated the same actions to get them off me as she did with my pants. After they were removed, she squeezed out the rag once more and began to slowly clean me around my crotch and underneath as she went on. "But that's just you Sam. You always looked out for me, you always supported me, you always encouraged me, you never gave up on me, and most importantly, you saved me, Sam, my love."

As she finished cleaning in between my legs, she tossed the rag into the bucket, then pat dried my legs and crotch before she returned to her feet. Once standing, she pushed me backwards until I fell back, sitting on the couch completely naked. She slightly lifted her shirt up in the air just enough that I could see that she was not wearing any underwear as I got a full view of her pussy. She slowly climbed on top of me as she sat on my legs, but mere inches from pressing up against my now fully erect dick. "Gina?" I said once more, but she again did not respond to me as she placed one of her hands on the side of my cheek as she leaned in so close to my face.

"I want to say thank you, Sam," she whispered softly to me while looking deep into my eyes.

"Thank me? But for what?" I answered back to her.

"Thank you for everything you did; everything you do. Thank you for waking up every day and doing what needs to be done without question or thoughts of return. Thank you for working a job that I know you don't like so that I could achieve my goals and live my dreams." I sat staring at her as what she was saying to me, though very intimate, felt like I heard it before. "Every single day, I miss you every single hour that we're not together. Tonight, let me show you how much I appreciate you, how much I love you. Tonight, my body is yours."

Before I could say anything, she reached down with both of her hands and grabbed mine, slowly wrapping them around her and sliding them underneath her shirt until both were resting against her ass cheeks. I gave her a slight squeeze as she let out a small moan and smiled while biting her bottom lip. Slowly gliding my hands upward along her back, I lifted her shirt up over her head until it was removed, exposing her now completely naked body. I tossed the shirt across the room near my clothes as it slid across the wall and hit the floor.

Gina giggled a little as she reached down between my legs and massaged me while I returned my hands to her ass. Her touch was intoxicating as I breathed heavier while she continued to look into my eyes. After a little over a minute went by, she slid forward a little more as she lifted herself up in the air on her knees. Moving one of her hands to my good shoulder and still holding onto me, she slowly lowers herself onto my dick as she pushes me inside of her.

Her moans excite me so much as she lets out a loud ecstasy filled gasp, letting go of my dick so she can finish pushing me all the way inside of her. She places her now free hand onto my cheek as she leaned forward, pressing her breasts against me; her hard nipples pushing against my chest. She sits there holding onto me as she lets her muscles stop spasming before she slowly slides her hips back and forth while I feel her grip on my shoulder tighten in between each little moan she lets out.

The warmth of her body is so incredible as I hold her so close to me while she moves. She continues to look deep into my eyes as our lips are just inches away from each other. A strong feeling pushes itself from my head to my mouth as in a small, moaned sigh I said softly, "I love you."

In a small, exhausted breath, she said back to me, "Sam."

"I love you," I said again without missing a beat. She pressed her mouth against mine as we began kissing passionately. As my lips tasted her incredible embrace, my brain suddenly felt a massive push of clarity. *She is so incredible; and yet her touch is so familiar. This is the first time we are getting intimate and yet, could this be?* I suddenly remembered the dream I kept having. *Oh my god, that wasn't a dream; it was a memory! It was her in the dream! All along, it was her!*

As she pulled away from our kiss, I felt a rush of passion rush over me from the top of my head to the bottom of my toes. Looking into my eyes once more, she says to me, "I love you, Sam."

"I love you too," I replied to her. She increased her rhythm of her hips as she goes to lean in to kiss me once more before I suddenly said, "Amy."

Without warning, she stops and slowly leans back with an expression of shock. As her eyes suddenly filled up with tears, she asked me, "What?"

"Amy," I said again as I too felt a sudden sense of shock.

"Wh… who… who's Amy?"

Looking into her eyes, I said, "My wife."

Chapter Twenty-Seven

The sudden outrage and confusion came over Gina like a flood as she jumped off me and stood in front of me. "What the hell do you mean, your wife, Sam? I'm your wife!" she said in anger as she looked around for her t-shirt. I truthfully did not understand myself. From the moment Gina started telling me her story, I knew I had heard it all before. The way she touched me, I felt it before. Everything in those moments of intimacy we were having together felt so right and familiar, but in the end, it wasn't Gina that my mind was associated with all of it.

"I don't know, honestly. I don't know why at that moment I said Amy's name, but I did. And the more I thought about it, the more my head was convinced that Amy was my wife."

Finding her shirt, she bends over and quickly grabs it and puts it on, then said, "So what, are you cheating on me, Sam? Is that what this is?" Before I have time to answer, she takes another couple of steps back from me and wraps her arms around herself like she had just been violated.

"What? No! I'm not cheating on you, Gina. You're not my wife." I could see the pain in her face as she paced back and forth while placing one of her hands on her forehead, trying to figure everything out.

"But it's you Sam. You are the one in my memories. It's you I fell in love with. It was you that proposed to me. Maybe, maybe you're just having a tough time remembering. Maybe you have a concussion, and your memories are scattered."

As I pulled my boxers back on, I said, "I don't know Gina. I really don't think that's it."

As soon as I finished my sentence, Gina turned towards me and screamed at the top of her lungs, "Then what is it, Sam? Either you have a head injury or you fucking cheated on me! And now you are remembering her before me! So, excuse me if I'm having a very hard time handling all of this right now!"

I just had no idea what to say. The details of her story were in my memory. I could remember meeting her at our campus pavilion, I could remember that party, I remember proposing to her, all of it. The only problem was the only detail that I just simply could not remember was her. I knew there was the girl of my dreams there, but I just could not picture Gina.

Tears in her eyes, she said, "Do you remember proposing?"

Sitting in the chair off to the side of the couch pointing towards her, I said, "Every detail."

She quickly sat down on the couch cushion farthest from me and said, "Okay, maybe it's a memory problem, a head injury that you suffered?"

"Gina, I…"

"Sam, please!" she screams out at me. "Can you tell me about it?"

I took a deep breath and told her what I could remember. "It was your birthday. I had been planning on asking you for some time. I had the ring all picked out for a while and had finally paid it off weeks prior. My first attempt didn't work out like I had hoped. I tried to get together with your small group of college friends, but it fell through, so I had to hold on to the ring for a few weeks until your birthday."

She lifted one of her legs onto the couch as she hugged it while I talked. Looking at me, she asked, "Could you tell me about the ring? What did it look like?"

"It was white gold, because you had told me in a past conversation that you didn't like yellow gold. It had a center pieced enormous diamond held in place by six points, with two smaller diamonds on either side of it."

"Tell me about the moment you proposed?" she asked me with a small tremble in her voice.

With a gigantic sigh, I continued. "Your schedule was so crazy with your job. You had so much going on with classes and training and tests, all your free time was gone. I convinced you to give me a couple of hours so I could take you to your favorite restaurant. Plus, it was your birthday, and I just wanted to celebrate. So, with the ring in my pocket, we were off."

With a small stream of tears running down her cheek, she asked me, "What was the plan?"

"The plan?"

"Yes?"

"I had contacted the restaurant prior so they could seat us at a table near the middle of the restaurant. I wasn't one really for public displays of affection, but I wanted the whole restaurant to see who I wanted to spend the rest of my life with."

Giggling, she said, "It didn't work out that way, did it?"

"Not at all. When we got there, instead of sitting us at a table in the middle, they put us in the smallest booth they had all the way in the back corner." She giggled again as I kept talking. "There was no way I was going to pull the ring out and get on the floor to propose since I was having a challenging time, even getting in and out of the booth in general."

She smiled more, though more tears kept running down her face. "You made me think you didn't want to get married all night long."

"Yeah, I had this stupid idea that I would talk down marriage, so when I finally asked you, you would be shocked."

Sniffing tears back, she said, "It worked. Near the end of the meal, I started thinking to myself how I couldn't believe you thought like that. And to tell me on my birthday of all days!"

"We finally went to leave, and we were standing in the parking lot walking to my car when I did it." The reflection of the light from the lamp in her tear-filled eyes was hard to look at as I continued. "You know what? Everything I said tonight? Fuck it!"

"You got down on your knee in the middle of the restaurant's parking lot and said to me…"

"I know our journey has been long and had so many twists and turns in it, but would you do me the honor of being by my side for the rest of the way through the rest of my life? Would you make me the luckiest man alive? Would you marry me?"

Gina's tears couldn't hold back anymore as she burst open, crying as I finished. I could not tell if her tears were from sadness at me saying Amy, or from her joy that I remembered how I proposed. "That's it Sam, that's exactly how it happened." She stood up from her spot on the couch and walked over to me. Sniffing her tears back again as she bent down to hug me. As she embraced me, she said, "So it's a memory problem, then. We can work on it to help you."

I suddenly grabbed hold of her and pushed her back away. As she looked at me, confused, I said, "I'm afraid there's nothing to work on. There is only one problem, but I remember it all. I didn't say, 'Gina, will you marry me?' I said…"

Jumping back away, she smacked my hands back and screamed, "Don't you dare say her name!" Turning away from me, she aggressively stomped towards the bedroom. Before walking through the door, she yells to me, "Just get the fuck out of here, Sam!"

Standing up from the chair, I pleaded, “Gina?” Without a word, she charges into the bedroom and slams the door closed. In the low light of the room, I could hear her collapse onto the bed and just a full-on cry. She was in such pain and heartbreak, and it was all my fault. *I promised her I wouldn't let anything happen to her, and I was the one that hurt her in the end.*

I quietly got myself dressed once again and laid down on the couch as I just listened to her cry. After some time had passed, I could not hear her crying, thinking to myself that she must have cried herself to sleep. I laid on the couch trying to fall asleep myself, but my mind would not stop racing about my past. I kept trying to convince myself that it was indeed Gina and not Amy that I was remembering, but it was to no avail.

I could remember everything about meeting her in college, about going out on dates, moving to the city for her job and schooling, asking her to marry me, getting married, all of it. I could remember every single detail but one. The woman in front of me was not clear to me. I could not tell if it was the Gina that I know, or the Amy that I can't remember any details of.

And then I thought to myself about the small moment of intimacy that Gina and I were sharing with each other. Everything about our encounter, the touching, the kissing, the way she felt when I was inside her, it was all in my memory of experiences, but

I still could not picture either woman. Even thinking back to that crazy dream, I could remember everything in detail except the woman that was in front of me; the woman that I was making love to. *Maybe my brain is damaged.*

I soon felt a blinding light hit me in the eye as I glanced out the window to see the sun rising in the distance. *Wow, it's morning already.* Getting up from the couch, I walked over to the closed bedroom door. Standing in front of it, I could hear slightly small sobs from Gina as she must have at some point woke up and cried once again.

I raised my hand to knock on the door but paused. As I held my hand in the air, I felt a sudden sense of anger and disappointment in myself. As I tried to shake it off, I softly knocked on the door. "Gina?" I called out, but I got no response. *Are you surprised she doesn't want to talk to you?* Lowering my hand, I shook my head to clear it, then spoke to the door.

"Gina, listen. I'm sorry. I'm sorry about last night. I'm sorry about upsetting you. That was never my intention. But there's still things I need to figure out with my memory, and I think that for me to do that I need to go. I'm sorry that I hurt you. I hope you know I never meant to do that. I do care for you Gina, before I left, I just wanted you to know that." The other side of the door was silent. *Gina, I love you. I'm just not in love with you.*

Turning away from the door, I walked over to the front door and opened it. As I stepped out of the room, I turned around and looked back at the bedroom door one last time. She still didn't come out. I let out a heavy sigh and closed the door. Standing outside the hallway, I placed my hand on the door while feeling this rush of sadness come over me. *Goodbye, Gina.*

I turned down the hallway and made my way to the elevators at the other end of the floor. I knew I was leaving, but I did not know what was next for me. William was gone and his complex vanished in the fog. James had said that all the people in the city had all been sent away, so Remembrance was going to be completely deserted. It appeared there were stranded members that were all regaining their memories, so I had hope for myself. I had some memories return to me, though they were incomplete and caused someone close to me pain. *Maybe I don't want to remember after all.*

Pushing the call button for the elevator, the doors opened almost immediately as I stepped on and hit the button for the lobby. As the doors closed and the elevator started moving, I started thinking about all the areas of the city I had yet to see and explore. *With no threat of Justices coming after me, I should have more freedom to look around and try to discover a way out of here. Perhaps even regain my memory completely.*

As the elevator stopped moving and the doors opened, I spotted Austin sitting on one of the benches eating a bag of heavily powder cheese covered tortilla chips. "Hey, good morning, man!" he called out as I stepped off the elevator.

"Hey Austin," I replied. I could see the orange powder covering his fingertips as he waved at me. "What are you up to this morning?"

"I felt this urge to come down and grab some breakfast, but they're still cooking it, so I grabbed a quick snack beforehand?"

Slightly grinning, I said, "Wait, you're eating before you eat? How the hell are you in such good shape?"

As he finished crunching down a few more chips, he smiled as he chewed and raised his one arm in the air and flexed his biceps before he said, "It's genetics, and I'm a freak of nature." We both laughed for a few seconds before he asked, "So, where's Gina?"

My smile quickly went away as I turned slightly and glanced back at the elevator doors as they closed. "She's still up in her room."

"Her room? Didn't you two stay in the same room?"

"Yeah, but we had a huge argument. All my fault." I looked towards the front door before I said, "I gotta go, Austin."

"What? No, not yet. Aren't you going to stay at least for breakfast?"

Shaking my head, I replied, "No, it's for the best. Just do me a favor, look out for everyone here, will you? Make sure everyone gets home." His smile disappears as he sets the bag down on the bench and stands up before hugging me.

"Take care of yourself, Sam. I know you need to go. Just be careful."

Pulling away, I said back, "You too, Austin. I guess we might not see each other again."

Shrugging his shoulders, he said, "You never know." He picked up his bag of chips and tapped me on the shoulder before he turned and walked away towards the restaurant. Once he disappeared around the corner, I turned and headed for the front door of the hotel.

As I pushed the front door open, I hear the ding of the elevator doors opening and a frantic voice from behind me. "Sam!" Gina yells out.

"Gina?" I said as I twisted around to see her running towards me. Stopping in front of me, she is completely out of breath.

"Sam, wait!" she barely gets out as she tries to suck air into her lungs. As I stood there, she took a couple deep breaths and said, "I'm sorry Sam, I didn't mean to make you feel like you did something wrong. Just please, don't…" She stops before she finishes her sentence and quickly reaches out and hugs me so tightly. I grabbed her and returned the hug as I could hear her cry once more.

We stand there hugging each other for a few seconds before letting each other go. As she looks up at me, I wipe her tears away from her face as she smiles. "I'm so sorry Gina."

She shook her head and said, "No, don't be sorry, Sam. I know you need to go; that's what the uneasy feeling I told you about in that alley was. I ignored it at first, then I didn't want to believe it. You need to get to your wife. I just wanted you to know that I love you so much." She reaches out and wraps her arms around the back of my head as she pulls me in for a very intimate kiss I don't resist. After she pulls her lips away from mine, she releases my neck and wipes more tears from her face, but she is smiling. "Now, go Sam. Go to Amy."

I take a step out of the hotel and turn away. After a few more steps, I hear the door to the hotel close as I turn around to look at Gina one more time, but suddenly see the lobby fill with fog. "No!" I screamed as I charged towards the hotel. Before I could reach the door, the last thing I saw was Gina standing on the other side of the door, smiling at me before the fog swallowed her completely.

"No! God damn it, no!" I scream at the top of my lungs as the entire inside of the hotel is filled by the orange glow and heat from the fog. I take a couple of steps back from the heat as I scream out, "Gina! Austin!" I got no response. The hotel was gone, everyone that was inside the hotel was gone, and there was nothing I could do.

Taking a few more steps back, I suddenly felt so weak in my legs as I collapsed to the ground on my knees. The fog surrounds the entire hotel until it is gone. I looked around as all the buildings, street signs, light posts, cars, everything disappeared behind the fog, leaving only me and the paved surface under me. I slam my fist down onto the asphalt in anger. *I'm all alone now.* I pick my fist up and slam it down on the asphalt once more. *Why is this happening?* I pick my fist up again and slam it down on the grass. *What?*

I slowly open my fist as I run my fingers through the grass that just magically appeared under me. I could smell the fresh cut as I looked around, watching the fog back away from me and revealing more and more field. A hill that climbs upward to the left of me is growing trees at all ends. Looking in front of me, I suddenly see the fog revealed a house at the end of the grass.

It was a two-story home; the bottom floor was a concrete foundation that was partially hidden away into the side of the hill while the top portion of the house was covered with an ivory siding. From my angle, I could see two doors to enter the home. One was on the side of the house that led into the basement, while the other was at the front of the home, at the top of a flight of steps to a small porch made of wood.

Standing up off the ground, I made my way over to the home until I stood just outside the door leading into the basement. A strange feeling crept up my spine as I reached my hand out to the doorknob. *This feels so familiar.* Turning the knob, the door pushes open with a loud *strip* noise from the rubber seal that went around the edge of the door.

Stepping into the home and closing the door behind me, I was standing in a large family room. Directly to my left sat an old coal stove standing on top of stone tiles in a large rectangular pattern with three five-gallon buckets filled to the top with coal.

The stove was not lit. In front of me sat a large sectional couch that was wrapped away from the wall to my right, allowing the sunlight to shine in the two small windows imbedded in the wall. In the corner angled towards the couch was an old free standing large screen television with an assortment of old video game consoles sitting on the floor.

As I took a few more steps into the room, I then saw a large pool table that was at the far left of the room near the other wall; a small stand that held multiple cue sticks was attached to the wall almost centered with the table. In the wall's corner, next to the pool table, was a small white refrigerator while a box with a picture of pool balls on the cover sat on top. Slowly making my way past the table, I noticed a door to the left that was open. Looking in, I saw it was a small bathroom with a large sink countertop and a standing blue shower in the corner.

Across from the bathroom was a set of stairs that went up where I could see the other door that was at the top of the small wood porch from outside. A small hallway to the right of the bathroom went forward to two more rooms. The room directly ahead was a small utility room that had an electrical panel along with the water heater that sat in the corner directly to the left of the doorway.

The other room was an exceptionally large bedroom. A queen-sized bed was at the far end in the middle of the wall with a dresser to the left of the bed that had a small television sitting on top of it, along with a video cassette recorder and another video game console attached. A small shelf sat next to the dresser that had different books, science fiction figures and vehicle toys, and sports items spread across all the shelves. At the other far end of the room, across from the bed, was a small drum set that was set up in the corner next to the closet.

I slid my finger across one cymbal as a small layer of dust came off onto my finger. *What is going on? Why am I here?* "Why is…"

"No!" I suddenly heard a woman's voice scream at the top of their lungs from above me.

Running out of the room, a ran to the edge of the steps and yelled up, "Hello?"

"No!" the voice screamed out again.

"Amy?" I shouted up the steps as I immediately ran up the stairs to the door and turned the corner to climb another set of stairs. After running up the second set of stairs and reaching the top floor, I saw to my left was a living room with the television on some news channel, in front of me was the kitchen, and to my right was a long hallway that led to more rooms. "Amy!" I called out once again, but I didn't see anyone.

"No!" the voice called out once more, but I heard it come from down the hallway.

"Amy!" I screamed as I ran down the hall towards the voice. I passed a couple of sets of closet doors before I came to a quick intersection in the hallway. On the right was another bedroom, and to the left was another bathroom and one more bedroom.

"No! Why?" the voice screamed out one more time from the bedroom on the left. Running into the room, I see a woman lying on the bed that was directly in front of the door with its top pressed against the far wall. She was lying on the bed covering her face as she cried uncontrollably.

"Amy? Amy!" I called out to the woman, but she didn't respond to me at all. As I took a step forward towards her, I glanced down onto the bed to see her cell phone sitting on the edge of the bed. Leaning down, I see the phone was opened to the phone app, and it was on the last voicemail message. The predictive text message said, "Unable to Translate Message." I then noticed the missed call was from Sam. It was from me. "Amy?" I asked once more to the woman, but she again does not respond to me, she just continued to cry.

Looking at the screen, I felt an incredibly intense feeling of anxiety as I pressed the message playback. The message plays with a bunch of static and loud noises in the background. I quickly realize that the noises are loud banging and what appear to be explosions, along with screaming from a bunch of people. *What is this?*

I suddenly could hear my voice come across the voicemail as I say in the message, "Amy! Amy, it's Sam! Baby, I'm so sorry! I'm just so sorry! I didn't want our last conversation to be a fight! I love you! Please know that I love…" There was unexpectedly a loud explosion and then the message ended.

I dropped the phone and walked out of the bedroom in complete shock. Making my way out of the hallway, I looked at the television that was on and I realized what the news program was reporting on. The image on the screen was an aerial camera shot of a plane crash in the middle of a field as flames shot all over the field and from the plane. I then made out what the anchor on the program was saying as I sat down in one of the chairs in the living room.

"Again, we are reporting a plane crash shortly after takeoff from McCarran International Airport. Emergency crews are on route as we speak. We have no reports of survivors at this time, but we will keep you posted as we learn more. The flight lifted off shortly after nine local time and…" The voice drowned out in my head as I looked down at the floor in disbelief. *Was I on that plane? What was that message? What the fuck is going on?*

Knock, knock, knock.

I lifted my head up in the air and looked to my right out into the kitchen as I could see another door leading outside. On the other side of the door, I could see someone standing there. Rising to my feet from the chair, I walk out to the kitchen and open the door and am suddenly shocked to see who was standing in front of me.

"Hello, Sam," she said in a very calming voice.

"Shaelynn?"

"Can I come in?" she asked as she points into the house. Immediately I notice that her accent is no longer present as she spoke perfect English. I take a step back away from the door as she walks into the house. She grabs the door and closes it behind her. As she turned back around, she looked at me and said, "How are you doing, Sam?" I just look at her and shake my head in complete disbelief. She slightly smiled and placed her hand on my shoulder and said to me, "Why don't we go sit down, Sam?"

I look towards the living room before looking back at her, then nodding my head. We both walked into the living room as she sat in the chair across from the chair I was just sitting in as I sat back down in it and just stared at the television. She looked at the television and then said to me, "Sam, why don't you mute that?" I look over at the remote sitting on the couch away from me as I get out of my seat once more, pick up the remote, and mute the television.

"There, that's better. Now we can talk, Sam."

"Talk? Talk! What in the world could you possibly want to talk about Shaelynn? I had absolutely no idea what was going on these last few days and now that I know, I don't believe any of it!"

Calmly, she said, "I know you are upset, Sam, but that's why I'm here now. I'm here to help you."

"Help! Help me! What can you help me with?" I scream as I placed both my hands on my head.

"Well, with that, Sam," she answers as she points at the television. "Let's start with that. Do you remember anything about that?"

I turned away from her, then halted. As I slowly turned back towards her, I removed my hands from my head and said, "I remember, I remember everything."

Chapter Twenty-Eight

The airport was crowded, yet manageable to maneuver around as I walked away from the security check. Once I finished tying my shoes and standing up off the floor, I made my way towards my terminal. I was not angry or upset. I felt surprisingly excited. I perhaps just committed career suicide, but I just did not care anymore.

I was in Las Vegas for a conference for the company I worked for. It was a yearly event, but for the most part, the formalities were always the same. The company brought together all the executives to the department managers for each region across the country to celebrate the company's successes and accomplishments throughout the past fiscal year. For the region I worked in, however, it was more of a formality since we were always at the top of the company year after year.

Ever since I became a District Manager for my region, we have seen extreme successes in all aspects of our growth that it was almost a forgone conclusion that we'd do it again. Yet, every time the company released the official numbers, I celebrated with my managers, thanking them for everything they did to continue to keep morale at its highest point. I never assumed that we were going to achieve our consistent level. I always coached my teams to push them in their areas of their strengths. This year was no different, as we hit all our goals one more time.

Yet even though my team consistently hit all the goals I set; I was constantly getting flak from the regional manager. He always told me and the other district managers that our teams were not performing to *his* expectations and that we should push our managers to cut them from their staff and hire new employees. Our region was number one overall every year, yet that was not good enough for him. If there were any other region but us in any category of the company, he had a shit fit. Over the last few years, we lost a lot of good people that worked hard but they were let go due to pressure from him or they quit because they could not handle the unnecessary stress that was laid on them.

The one thing that I always found odd was the fact that he would compare our region to a city. It was strange as hell, but listening to him explain his vision, you could not help but be impressed and motivated. He would always talk about this goal of perfection in his *city* that most of the other district managers always scoffed at behind closed doors. To be honest, I did too a little, but I still admired the dream. I always found better ways of reaching my goals without dipping down to his methods of firing these people that did nothing wrong and essentially ruining their lives.

So here I was, once again on my way to Vegas for yet another conference for the company, but this time around was different. My wife, Amy, always supported me in my successes with this company ever since I got this job. We moved a few times because of her training and job offers in her career. She was an incredible trauma surgeon and was sought after by many different hospitals across the country. She always strived to better herself, adding tiers to her expertise, and I was there with her every step of the way without cause. Each time she got an offer she could not refuse, I without question packed everything and moved with her to the next new city.

Her profession took her away from our home at all kinds of hours of a day, sometimes days at a time. I would find a job that would keep me busy to help support our lifestyle, but I would also do everything I needed at home so that Amy would have no worries when she came home of needing to do anything. I did it all without question. That's how much I loved her.

A few years ago, she was feeling overwhelmed and decided that she wanted to step down from the major hospital network she was working for and wanted us to start a family. We talked about it before, but her work schedule did not really give her the flexibility she would want to raise a family. But she always told me I reminded her of her father, and she told me she always felt like I would make a good dad. It was a shock to us both when we found out she was pregnant.

It forced us to decide to move back home, which we were both happy about. She immediately got an offer from the local hospital in the city and my best friend from college, Austin, got me an interview for the company he was working with. Everything was set for us until the worst thing could happen. After moving back home, a few months later, she lost the baby.

She was heartbroken for such a long time. I'd find her crying at night in the nursery of our apartment we made. I was convinced that her stress from work messed with her body so much. I was determined to never let that happen to her again.

I went full speed into my new job and quickly climbed the ranks and eventually became a district manager. The money was significant, and it allowed us an extra cushion financially to allow Amy to take a step back if she wanted, which I told her several times to do so. I would do anything for her.

And then comes along our regional manager, Anthony Williams. He was the one that convinced me to go one hundred fifty percent into my career, to better my work life balance. To improve my district, to make the region better, which would make my home life better. I was so bought in to his vision that I never realized that my work life balance was disappearing, and it was becoming only about work. Amy saw this, and she tried to tell me time after time, but I would not listen.

We had so many arguments over the last few months about me working so much, about me killing myself, about me forgetting about her, and about me not wanting to try again for another child. I think that's the one that scared me the most. Being a father was not something I was afraid of. I was afraid of putting Amy through that trauma all over again. So, the more she talked about it, the more I dove into work.

Even on the day I was leaving for Vegas, we argued until I walked out the door. I was supposed to take a vacation. She wanted to go spend some time at my parents' old home, she just wanted us to spend time together. She even said she forgot what it was like to spend some time with me because I was working so much.

"Yeah, well, what about all those years I spent taking care of everything so you could chase your dream? Why do I have to sacrifice again to make you happy?" was the last thing I said to her as I walked out the door to head for the airport. As I drove away, I pushed it out of my mind and just focused on the trip and the conference.

The conference, as expected, went without a hitch. Our region once again won for the top region in the company for the whatever time in a row, but I this time won best overall district and district manager in the company. I received so many praises and congratulations and handshakes galore from my colleagues, but I just for some reason felt like I won nothing. I could not put my finger on why I was feeling this way, but I put that out of my mind as well as we learned the winner of the best regional manager. Even though our region won best overall, Anthony did not win the best regional manager.

He was furious. So much so that he called and held a meeting hours later in a separate conference room at the event, but I found out only later, once I got there, that he only ordered me there. Once I arrived, he immediately went in on the changes he was making. "This is completely unacceptable! There are too many people in this company under MY district managers that are not adding anything into my perfect city!" he shouted at me.

"But we won the best region. How is that not an input?"

"How? I didn't win, Sam! I am striving for the best; I want MY city to be perfect. Every part is important and if one person messes it up, I want them cut out! I want the best working for me moving forward!"

"But Anthony, if they did nothing wrong, we can't just fire them for no reason," I tried to reason with him, but he just was not listening to me. He kept smoothing his long hair back with both his hands, even though it never came forward.

"I want a complete overhaul of every district. I want every manager reevaluated and if I don't approve, I want them moved to another department or cut out completely," he ordered me with a crazed look in his eyes. He was so different from the many times I talked to him in the past. Losing the award made his true colors come out, and I wasn't liking what I was seeing. And then he came at me.

"And I don't want you working with these people anymore!" His raspy deep voice cut quick as he spoke.

"Wait, what are you saying?"

"You heard me, Sam! I know you tried to work with your underperforming employees to help them. I want all of that to stop! I need to know if you can make tough decisions when it counts. If they don't get it right the first time, I want them cut out! Understand?"

"Anthony? I will not ruin someone's life because you're upset you didn't win some award. These people work hard for me, and they have made this company a lot of money."

"I've tried that all before myself. Watching you always reminded me of my old sedan I had when I was a teenager. I would put so much work into it, keeping it running well past its time. Getting all those looks from people pitying me. I realized then, if it doesn't work right from the start or stops working right after a while, don't fix it, get rid of it!"

I shook my head as I said, "But this is people we're talking about. Team members with families, loans, mortgages, people that have lives because of this job. I can't just take that away from them unwarranted. I won't."

"Are you saying you're defying me? That you are trying to impeach me out of my city?"

"Anthony, it's not an actual city, for fuck's sake. I think you need to just sleep on it and get a rational mind before you make any grave decisions that are going to hurt many people."

"Hurt people, huh? Sam, you are my best DM in the region. I need you to help me make my city perfect. I'm sure you wouldn't want anything to happen to Austin, though, would you?"

"Wait, what?" I asked him, as I could feel my anger crawling up my spine.

His deep raspy voice curled as he said, "I know Austin White got you this job before I became the RM, but he hasn't been performing like he should. If you don't help me, get my city in order, then perhaps he can go find another job."

It completely threw me back; I could not believe what I was hearing. "Are you seriously threatening me with his job?" I asked him as I stood up from the chair, I was sitting in.

"Don't be so dramatic Sam, it's a simple question. I already told you I need you to help me fix the mistakes of everyone else in the region, don't start making your own mistakes." As he walked closer to me, he placed his hand on my arm and said, "Or maybe I don't need you and you'll lose that comfortable paycheck to take home to your wife." The anger boiled over into my face as I could feel so much heat below my skin. He then added, "It's not that hard of a decision here, Sam. Are you focused on your career or your family?"

I smacked his hand away and said, "So you're trying to make me choose between my friend and my wife? What the hell is wrong with you?" I turned around and walked out of the conference room.

"Where are you going, Sam?" he shouted.

Stopping, I turned around and said, "You want to know what the problem is with this fucking vision of a city you got? It's you!" Once I stormed out of the conference room, it took me no time to reach my hotel room on the fourth floor, gather my things, and leave. As I was making my way to the lobby, I ran into Austin talking with another district manager, Henry Sagal, as I was trying to change my flight on my phone.

"Hey man, where are you going?" he asked me.

"I'm outta here dude. Anthony is fucking out of his mind!"

He grabbed my arm, stopping me, and asked, "Yo, what do you mean?"

Henry added, "Anthony is a little over climactic, but I don't think he's that bad."

"Henry, you didn't hear the conversation I just had with him. So why don't you go pray on that and please don't give me your two cents," I snapped at Henry.

"Yo man, what the hell?" Austin jumped in.

Shaking my head, I said, "I can't really get into it here, but I am leaving. I'll talk to you later."

Before I could pull my arm from his grip, he tightened his hold on my arm and said, "Well, wait a minute, I'll go grab my stuff and come with you."

"No, don't. I can't change my ticket; I need to purchase another which I'm fine with, but I don't want you to waste your money." As I released my arm from his hold, I added, "Just come home as scheduled and we'll talk as soon as you get home." With the expression on his face, I could tell he was concerned, but all I was thinking about was getting home.

"All remaining passengers, please proceed onto the plane." I shook the thoughts of the last few hours from my mind, never realizing that they had allowed people onto the flight. Looking away from the boarding gate, I remembered I was holding my phone in my hand; Amy's name was showing to start a call. I backed out of the phone app and switched my phone to airplane mode.

As I boarded, I got my boarding pass scanned and ID checked, shown down the chute that was attached to the plane, the boarding pass checked once more, and shown to my seat. No longer needing them, I tucked my ID and my boarding pass into the pocket of my side bag I had with me before storing it into the overhead bin. I had my tablet in my bag, but I figured since I could not use it until the plane was in the air, I'd just wait and leave it be. I also removed my jacket and tucked it into the overhead, leaving only my phone in my pocket as I took my seat.

My original ticket was for first-class, but all I could get on such short notice was an economy class ticket, and that was perfectly fine with me. I honestly did not care. I just wanted to get back home as fast as I could. *I didn't pay for the first-class ticket anyway, so the money is no loss to me.* I sat down in my seat and just left my mind wonder.

I started finding myself getting lost in thought as passenger after passenger walked past me, looking for their seats as the plane filled with people. I was not paying any attention to them as they walked by or sat in the seats in front of me as I still was having such a challenging time wrapping my head around Anthony and his sudden outburst. *Was he faking his civility this whole time that I'd known him?* The idea that he would threaten an employee's job just because he lost a company award was almost unbelievable to me. I then remembered overhearing a conversation that some of the other district managers were having where they mentioned he had already been divorced three times because he was more focused on his job, on his *city*, than his home life. I did not know if that was true and at this point; I did not care.

"Excuse me? Do you mind?" I turned my head to see a young woman standing in the aisle next to my seat. "My seat is over by the window; I don't want to step on you."

"Oh, wow. I'm so sorry," I said apologetically as I stood up out of my seat to allow her to get by. She was very attractive, she was a short woman, probably twenties. She had on purple yoga pants with a matching jacket she had strung over her arm and a black t-shirt. From what I could tell, she had on a black sports bra supporting her large breasts since I noticed the strap sticking out ever so slightly from the back of her shirt as she walked past. As she sat in her seat, I also noticed her freshly pedicured toenails showing since she was wearing flip-flops. *I bet that makes it a lot easier going through the security check.*

"Good afternoon, captain," I heard from near the front of the plane. Glancing up, I saw the Pilot and Co-Pilot walk onto the plane as they both headed up towards the front. *They both look freshly rested. That's always a good thing.*

As I sat back in my seat, the young woman says to me as she was fixing her long blonde hair back into a ponytail. "I'm so nervous." I did not think she was saying it to me as much as she was just saying it out loud to herself. To be on the safe side; however, I figured I would be polite back.

"Excuse me?" I asked.

"Oh, no, I was just saying to myself that I'm nervous." *Thought so.*

"Of flying?"

"What? No, not just flying. I'm heading home to see my parents. I haven't seen them in a few years. I'm just a little nervous."

Smiling, I said, "Oh, I'm sure it'll be fine. You've at least talked with them, right?"

She slightly frowns as she replies, "Well, not really. I'm actually coming home for a surprise. I haven't really talked with them since I moved out here to work at one of the casinos. I'm a dancer."

"A dancer? That sounds like a pretty amazing job. I wouldn't see why they'd have a problem with that."

"Naked dancing?"

I paused for a second as I just stared at the back of the seat in front of me. Clearing my throat, I said, "Even naked. Parents want only what's best for their children, and sometimes they worry about them even when their children have their life figured out or are still trying to do so. Will it be tense? Yeah, maybe. The important thing to always remember is they want what's best for you."

She smiled as she sat back in her seat before she said, "Wow, thank you. You are a real walking public service announcement, aren't you?" She laughed at me as I sat back in my seat and buckled my belt. "I'm just teasing you. I'm Jennifer, by the way."

"Sam."

"Nice to meet you, Sam. So, you heading off on some business trip looking all handsome in that fancy suit of yours?"

"Heading home, actually," I replied as I straightened my tie.

"Really? Gonna see your girlfriend?" she asked as she leaned closer towards me as she glanced at me with her blue eyes.

"Nah, I'm heading home to see my wife."

"Oh," she said as she sat back once again in her seat. "I didn't realize you were married since you had no ring on." I glance down at my hand as she points at my empty ring finger.

"Damn it, the security check." I stood up from the seat after unbuckling my seat belt and reached into the overhead to get it from my bag. As I closed the overhead, the plane moved to get into its position for takeoff. *I have been so distracted that I never even noticed they went through all their preflight instructions.* As I returned to my seat, I slid the ring back onto my finger and buckled my seat belt once more.

"That's too bad," Jennifer said as she turned her head away from me and looked out the window as the plane picked up speed down the runway and lifted off. The steep incline of the plane only lasted for a few minutes before the plane leveled off. I could hear a unanimous sigh of relief once the lighted seatbelt sign turned off.

After roughly a half an hour had passed, I leaned over towards Jennifer and asked, "Why?"

Removing her headphones she put in her ears shortly after takeoff, she turned towards me and said, "Why what?"

"Why too bad?"

Giggling, she replied, "Too bad you're married? In my line of work, I get hit on by so many guys," she leaned a little closer as she whispered, "and girls." My eyes widened a little as she continued. "It's just hard to find a good person to, oh I don't know, hang out with." Her devilish smile left me believe she did not mean *hang out* as you would normally think of it. "And then I happen to randomly meet a guy that looks like he's got himself all set up, and he's married."

Shaking my head slowly, I said, "Don't let the exterior fool you. I'm not as together as you think. The last conversation I had with my wife before I came here, well, we had an argument. I left my conference early because I realized that's not how I want her to think of me when I'm gone."

"Gone?" she asked me.

"I mean, when I leave on a trip, I don't want her to think of the anger as the last image of me before I see her again. I want her to know that I still love her. I couldn't wait two more days for my conference to be over to tell her that. So, here I am."

She looked at me with a small tear forming in the corner of her eye as she said, "Wow, see that's what I'm talking about. The good guys are always taken. She's so lucky to have you." As I smile, the plane suddenly shakes hard as the inside seemed to almost buckle, loud bangs could be heard from the underbelly. We both straighten back into our seats as she grips her armrest tightly.

The plane seems to level out smoothly before it does it again, forcing some of the overhead bins to pop open. "Everyone, please remain seated!" One of the flight attendants called out to the passengers as she walked down the aisle, closing the bins that had opened.

We suddenly heard the loudspeaker come on as a voice said, "Ladies and Gentlemen, this is your captain speaking. We are experiencing some unexpected turbulence. Please remain seated and follow the instructions from the crew. We hope to be back to…"

He was immediately cut off as another hard shake hit the plane as metal seemed to scream from the sides of the plane through the walls. "Oh, my god!" someone screamed out. "The engine!" We glanced out the window to see one of the two engines under the wing was shaking horribly. The fan blades inside the engine seemed like they were spinning at an odd angle.

BOOM!

The engine suddenly ripped apart from the front as smoke and flames shot out as metal pieces flung from the frame in all directions. "Holy shit!" Jennifer screamed as she jumped back away from the window when one of the metal pieces slammed into the side of the hull near the window.

The loudspeaker came back on as the captain ordered, "Ladies and Gentlemen, this is your captain speaking. We need to make an emergency landing as we are turning back to the Las Vegas Airport. Please remain seated. Do not get out of your seats. Please make sure you have your seatbelts securely tightened and please try to remain calm."

Jennifer reached over and grabbed my arm before she said, "Can we make it back to the airport without an engine?"

I nodded as I answered, "This plane has three remaining engines. It should be able to get us back as long as…" Another rumble of metal erupts from outside as the engine next to the damaged one also abruptly explodes. Passengers on the plane screamed in terror, as we could feel the nose of the plane point downward. Jennifer's hand flew from my arm as she screamed uncontrollably as the skyline outside the window shifted at an awkward angle. *Pull up, pull up, pull up, PULL UP!*

I grab my phone out of my pocket without reason and in the shaking and bangs and screams; I wake it up and switch it back to cellular. As the phone regained the signal, I opened the phone app and swiped to my favorites and pressed the first name on my list. *Amy.* I can barely hear the phone ring with all the horrible noise around me, but I just can make out her voice as I realize it went to her voicemail.

With a sigh, as soon as I heard the indicator beep so that I could start talking, I said, "Amy! Amy, it's Sam! Baby, I'm so sorry! I'm just so sorry! I didn't want our last conversation to be a fight! I love you! Please know that I love…" The phone was thrown from my hand as I could hear a loud twist of metal and an even louder groan of steel as the entire plane began to violently shake and thrust. The floor pressed itself up and throws us all around as I faintly hear a loud explosion and a quick flash of orange and red across my eyes along with an intense feeling of heat before everything goes black and silent.

Chapter Twenty-Nine

I collapsed back in the chair as I placed my hands onto my face. Slowly dragging them down, I can see Shaelynn sitting in the chair across from me. "Sam?" she asked as I just looked up at the ceiling above her without saying a word. "Sam, I need you to focus."

"Focus?" I whispered as I pulled my hands the rest of the way off my face. "You want me to focus? On what, exactly? On the fact that I'm supposed to believe that I am remembering now that I was in a plane crash. That all of this isn't real? Is that what you want me to remember?"

She sighs as she shakes her head. "Sam, this is real. It's as real as your mind is making it."

"My mind? Shaelynn, I'm dead!"

As she smiles, she asked, "Are you, Sam?" I look at her, confused, as she stands up and heads out to the kitchen. "Sam, you remember only what your mind can at the moment. It's all there, it's just out of order."

"Out of order? What, like a fucking bathroom stall? Like…like some fucking fast food restaurant's ice cream machine?"

She chuckles. "Not exactly. Think about it, Sam. Everything you remember, not just from the plane crash, but your entire life. It is all out of order. Your mind is trying to put everything back in its place."

I get up from my seat and join her in the kitchen as she reaches into the refrigerator and pulls out a glass pitcher of lemonade. "I'll give you an example. Me, for instance. Do you remember me?" She then walked over to a cupboard that was next to the entrance and pulled out of it two glasses before setting them down on the countertop.

"How can I not? You were the first person I met when I woke up here." She poured some of the lemonade into a glass and slid it across the counter towards me.

"Not exactly Sam. You know me from further back than that." She poured herself a glass of lemonade as well.

"I don't understand. I've never seen you until I woke up here."

She chuckles again as she places the pitcher back into the refrigerator. "Oh Sam, I thought you were much more observant than that." As she closed the refrigerator, she picked up her glass of lemonade and walked over to the small table off to the side next to the outside door and sat down. "Have a seat, Sam," she said as she pointed to the chair across from her.

With a heavy sigh, I picked up my glass of lemonade and sat down at the table as she asked of me. "I'm just not getting what you are trying to tell me. I remember you from when I woke up in front of your house…"

"Was that really my house, Sam?" she asked as she cut me off.

"What? How am I supposed to know that? You sat on the porch, you offered me water, so it's easy to assume."

She chuckles again as she sips some of the lemonade. "I really do love lemonade. Okay, Sam, what about the church? Do you remember the church?" An image quickly flashes into my mind as I recalled Henry before the entire church was swallowed by this fog. I lowered my head as I said, "Why would you bring that up?"

"Well, why not?"

"Why? Because I failed. Because thanks to me it was destroyed, and Henry is gone."

She shook her head as she said, "Sam, you can't blame yourself for something that didn't happen? But I'm not talking about Henry; what about the church itself?"

"What are you getting at?" I asked as I got more and more frustrated with her questioning. I spun the glass of lemonade in my hand but had yet to take a sip of the drink.

"Alright Sam, how about Gina?"

My eyes widened as I slammed the glass down on the table. "Don't bring her up."

"But why Sam? Why don't you want to think about her?"

"Because I hurt her too. She told me she loved me, that I was the love of her life, but I couldn't tell her the same."

She nodded her head as her eyes got a little wider. "And why is that? Why couldn't you tell her you loved her?"

"Because I love Amy!" I screamed as I slammed my hands on the table before I jumped up out of the chair and stomped back into the living room. "Why are you doing this to me?"

"Sam, sit!" she yelled at me as she stood up and pointed her finger at the chair I just left. I stood for a few seconds as I stared at her. She pointed at the chair once more without saying a word to me. I slowly walked back over to the table and sat back in the chair. As she sat back in her seat, she then said, "Take a drink Sam and cool off." I slowly grabbed the glass as I put the drink to my lips and took a large sip of the lemonade. As I lowered the glass from my mouth and placed it on the table, I looked at Shaelynn as she smiled and said, "There. That's better."

I felt myself calming a bit as the pounding in my head that was just forming was trickling away. Shaelynn leaned onto the table with her elbows and said to me, "Now listen to me, Sam. I'm not trying to hurt you; I'm trying to help you, but if you keep fighting me, then you will never understand."

Nodding my head at her, I said softly, "Okay, I'll try."

Sitting upright in her seat, she said, "Now, Gina?"

"But can we please…"

"No, Sam, you need to face it." She snapped at me, cutting me off. "Gina said she loved you and you could not say it back because why?"

"I'm in love with my wife. I'm in love with Amy."

"Okay, but there was something about Gina that was strange, wasn't there?"

"I don't understand what…"

"Sam, please." She said, cutting me off once again. "What was it about Gina?"

I sat for a few moments before I frustratingly said, "Because she reminded me of Amy."

"Of your wife? What was it about her that reminded you of her?"

I struggled to speak as I said, "Her memories about me, about us, they were never 'us', they were of Amy and I."

"And doesn't that seem strange, Sam?"

"Well, of course, that's strange. Why would a person I never met before telling me something about her life that I was never part of?"

"You weren't? Or maybe she wasn't?" I thought for a minute about what Shaelynn had just said. *Gina's memories about me I remember them like they actually happened to me, like I was actually there. But I wasn't there! That wasn't me! But… but was I?*

Looking at Shaelynn, I said, "But I was there."

Smiling, she looked at me and asked, "So if you were part of her memories, then who wasn't?"

"Gina. Gina was never there."

"Because?"

"Because it wasn't Gina, it was Amy!" She leaned back into her chair, smiling as she took another sip of lemonade from her glass. I, on the other hand, placed my elbows on the table and rested my head in my hands. Sighing, I said, "So Gina was never real?"

I hear Shaelynn's glass tap on the table as she answers, "Oh, she's real. She's just not who you think she is. But you're doing good, Sam."

I lift my head out of my hands as I look at her with a disgusted face as I said, "Doing good? I still don't understand what I'm supposed to be trying to do here."

Shaelynn nodded her head as she stood up from her chair. "Okay, Sam, let's try this. You said you don't know what you're doing here, right? Then let's talk about here."

"What are you talking about now? My head hurts so much."

"I know, Sam, but this is important. Now, where are we?"

I looked at her, so confused. I knew exactly where we were. "Why are you asking me that? This is my house."

Smiling at me again, she asked, "Right, this is your house. Is this your home, though?"

A sudden feeling of shock came over me as she asked me that. I slowly stood up and looked around at everything in the house. Without a word, I walked into the living room and studied everything in the room; the chairs, the couch, the television, all of it. I remembered all of it. I walked over to the wall where a collection of different pictures and photos were in a frame as I got choked up. As I turned around to look at her, she stood behind me. "I remember."

"Good Sam, so where are we?"

Looking around the room again, I said, "This is my house I grew up in. This was my family's house, my parents' house." I turned back around and looked at the photos again. "They died in a terrible car accident before I was a teenager. So, my grandparents became my guardians. They sold their small home and moved into this one, so I didn't have to move. When they eventually passed, they left it to me, but I just couldn't sell it." I turned around and asked, "Why am I here?"

"So, you remember this house, then?" she said.

"Yes, I remember. But I still don't understand."

She nodded her head and walked over to the couch and sat down. "It's your memory, Sam. Your mind."

Walking over to the coffee table and sitting down in front of her, I asked, "What do you mean by my mind?"

"Your mind is trying to put itself back together. The more you remember, the better. All of this, this was all made from your memories."

Shaking my head, I said, "My memories? Now I really don't understand."

"Okay Sam, how about this? Who am I?"

I looked at her with a snicker as I said, "What are you getting at here Shaelynn? We already went over this; I already know who you are."

"Yes, you do. Who am I?"

Throwing my hands into the air, I said, "Alright, I'll play along. You are Shaelynn."

"Sam? Shaelynn what? What is my last name?"

A frown replaced my snicker as I said, "How am I supposed to know that? You never told me!"

"I never needed to; you already knew who I was. Think about the church Sam, who am I?"

Shaking my head in anger, I said, "I'm tiring of this."

"Sam, please, who am I?" she pleaded with me.

"Oh, my god. I don't know! You are Shaelynn…" I suddenly paused for a second before a word found its way onto my tongue. As I looked at her in shock, I said, "Tibbs." An enormous smile found its way onto her face as she heard my answer. "You're Shaelynn Tibbs; you are Pastor Tibbs!" My hands covered my mouth as if I could not believe who was sitting in front of me. "Wait, why did you have different accents every time I saw you?"

She chuckled as she said, "Your memory of me wasn't completely there just yet. I guess you forgot for a moment what I sounded like."

I paused for a second before I asked, "But I don't understand; how are you here? You died so many years ago."

"Sam, this is what I've been trying to convey to you. We are all here because of you. This is all from your memories. The house, me, you, everyone, and everything is from your memories. But your memories are scattered and incomplete. Your mind has been trying to place everything back together since…" She suddenly pauses and glances over at the television.

I turn around and look at the screen to see the muted news coverage of the plane crash. A sudden grief came over me as I turned back around. "So, it's true?" I asked her.

Leaning forward, she placed her hand on my shoulder and said, "I'm afraid so."

My grief turned into a much deeper sadness as I said, "So, I am dead?"

Smiling slightly, she said, "Death is only in the perception of people, Sam. Some people can physically be fine but be dead on the inside, while others could be long gone and turned to dust but live on in infamy." *That doesn't really make me feel better.*

"Wait," I blurted. "That girl on the plane, she was wearing the same clothes that Gina was wearing the first time I met her, right? But that definitely was not Gina. But then Gina has Amy's memories?"

Shaelynn nodded her head as she said, "So, perhaps you are finally beginning to clear some of the gray out of your head."

"Gray?" I asked as I was confused.

"Yes Sam. Everyone calls it an expression or figure of speech, but it is neither; It's an actual thing. Every time someone has an issue remembering something, they always say, 'Oh that's just a gray area' or 'The facts on the matter are a little gray.' The gray in someone's mind is an actual thing, preventing them from remembering, and in turn, causing them to forget. Your mind, however, is trying so hard to remember everything. Your head is desperately trying to hold on to your memories and place them back in order."

"So, the fog? The Justices?"

"Is the gray." I slowly stood up from the coffee table and walked away from Shaelynn as I tried to grasp everything she had just told me. "Sam, the more you remember correctly, the more the gray leaves your mind."

My head hurt significantly as I thought about grasping what she was telling me. After a few seconds, I asked, "But what about the city? What about Remembrance?"

"Remembrance? You created it. Well, your mind did."

"My mind?"

Nodding, she said, "Yes. The gray shrouded over everything that your mind tried to correct and remember. What better way to self-contain everything wrong than within a place that your mind could focus on? As you remembered, or saved, they faded away." She chuckled a bit before she added, "That fool William and his crazy city ideas gave your mind the perfect creation to help you heal."

"But the fog swallowed and killed Henry, Austin, Gina, everyone; the entire city!"

"Did it swallow them, or did it get rid of what wasn't real?" A look of shock came across my face. She added, "Where did you see Henry and Austin last?"

I thought for a second before I said, "They're at the conference!"

"So, did they die by the fog?"

"No, no, they didn't. But what about all the other stranded?"

"Do you know the stranded?"

"I don't think so."

"Then perhaps they're just random people from your memories. Like the people of the city, can you remember ever meeting them? Knowing any of them? Or are they just random people you've seen throughout your life?" I thought for a minute as I tried to remember all the people from the city. I can remember the outfits, looks and styles of what the people were wearing, but nothing specific of their faces. *They were all just random people.*

"Okay, okay, what about the sandwich shop and the shoe store? I can remember those workers from those places. What about them?"

Nodding her head, she said, "Okay, Sam, what about them? What do you remember?"

"I… I don't… I don't," I kept stuttering as I tried to think and talk.

"Sam, the shoe store? What do you remember about the shoe store?"

With a sad look, I glanced once more over at the picture frame hanging on the wall and looked at a picture of my parents. "The shoe store is the last place my mom took me before she died."

"And the sandwich shop, Sam? I know it's hard; what do you remember about there?"

As a tear rolled out of my eye, I answered, "The last place I went with my dad." As I wiped the tears from my face, I said, "The ice rink; that's where my grandparents took me a lot when they had to raise me. My grandfather loved hockey; I acted like I didn't because I was being rebellious, but I secretly did." Looking back at Shaelynn, I added, "And that's how I met you. You were the pastor at their church, and somehow you always knew I was keeping pain deep inside me. You could always get me to open up and talk. Even when you stopped being a pastor, you still helped me when I would visit you at your home in my later teenage years."

I paused for a second and said excitingly, "That was your church. That was the church my grandparents took me to when they first became my guardians. I didn't see myself as religious and they didn't force me to continue to go when I made my choice, but they raised me to be who I am, until I lost them right before I went to college." Walking back over, I sat down in front of Shaelynn again on the coffee table.

. "And even after they died, you were there for me until," I paused for a moment and then added, "Until you died." I paused again as I looked at her and said, "You passed away shortly after I graduated from college, but I couldn't come to your funeral because by the time I learned about it, it was too late." She closed her eyes, grabbed hold of my hands as I continued. "I'm so sorry Shaelynn."

"It's alright Sam, there's nothing to be sorry about, there is nothing to forgive you for." She took one of her hands and softly tapped the side of my face, wiping one of my tears away from my cheek with her thumb. "Now, this house; is this your home?"

Looking around the room once more, I said, "It is my house because I own it, but it's not where I live. I couldn't bring myself to sell it, so I just continued to pay the taxes and utilities to keep it running." Laughing slightly, I then said, "Amy convinced me to keep it a few times. She said she always loved it because even though I lost both my parents and grandparents, the house gave me so many wonderful childhood memories. We have even come here a few times over the years to vacation in it just to get away from the city. She's told me how much she loves this house, but with our jobs, there was no way we could live here."

Suddenly standing up, I looked down the hallway towards the crying woman. Though now, at this point, I could no longer hear her. "Oh my god, Amy! I was on my way home to Amy. Our last conversation was an argument as I stormed out to go to that stupid conference for work."

"What was the argument about Sam?" Shaelynn asked.

"She wanted me to take time off from work. To spend more time at home because I was gone all the time. She wanted to try for another child, but I just kept working." Turning to Shaelynn, I added, "I was so scared of losing her. The stress she was under from her profession caused the miscarriage, and I wanted to make sure she never went through that again. I never wanted to see her in that kind of pain again."

"And you forgot about her?" I was suddenly shocked by her statement. "You were so focused on protecting her, you completely forgot she was a grown woman."

Nodding my head and as more tears crawled down my face, I said, "That's why I wanted to get home to her. I wanted her to know that I loved her so much and I was sorry for making her feel any less important when she has been the most important thing in my life."

Shaelynn stood up from the couch, looked right at me and said, "Good, Sam. I think you finally remembered what is most important to you." She started walking away from me and heading for the kitchen.

"So, what now?" I asked her.

"Now, now it's time to go, Sam."

"What. What? Time to go, but?" I glanced over at the television as I once again saw the image of the airplane crashing and in flames. *I forgot; I'm dead.* Turning back towards the hallway, I said, "No, can't I just see Amy one more time?"

"I'm afraid it doesn't work that way, Sam. You need to go before it's too late."

Standing in the hall torn, I said down the hallway, "Amy, I'm so sorry. Just know, I never meant to hurt you. I loved you; I will always love you." Turning away from the hallway, I saw Shaelynn disappeared before I heard the door to the outside open. Walking around the wall and entering the kitchen, I saw her standing next to the door, holding onto the doorknob.

"Okay Sam, time to go." Walking over to the door, I paused in front of it.

"I'm scared," I said to her softly.

Smiling at me, she said, "Then you know you are ready." With a heavy sigh, I stepped out onto the wood porch as I stared at the thick gray fog just at the edge of the two steps off the porch that led to the ground. Taking one last look behind me, I see Shaelynn as she looked on with a big smile on her face. As I looked forward, I took the first step, then the second step, off the porch.

The thickness of the fog quickly surrounded me as everything around me turned gray. I held my hand up in the air in front of my face as I watched it fade away into nothing but gray. I tried to breathe calmly as I watched everything go gray, to white, then finally to dark.

Chapter Thirty

Crackle, crackle, crackle

The pain across my entire body is so intense. As I tried to open my eyes, the only thing in my vision was an extreme blur mixed with colors of dark browns, grays, oranges, and reds. Trying to take a breath through my nose, I could smell thick aromas of alcohol, burning fabric, smoke, and other random scents, all mixing. The taste in my mouth was thick, bitter, and metallic as I felt liquid dripping out of the corner.

Snap, crackle, snap.

Realizing I was sitting in a chair, I tried to sit up straight, but a sharp pain in my side and around my waist immediately stopped me. Trying to lift my left arm, I am suddenly stopped by excruciating pain that shoots from my shoulder all the way to my fingertips. As I try to move my right, the pain in my side gets more intense as I pulled it to my lower stomach as I touched a strange metal clasp. Sliding my fingers around it, I feel a square plastic piece that almost has a spring to it when I press on it. Pressing the plastic, I hear the metal click to the side and fling out suddenly as I fall out of the seat and hit the ground headfirst.

Trying to sit myself up, I look straight up in the air and see my seat directly above my head. I glanced around as my vision improved as I recognized the image before me was the plane's cabin. Except, the image differed from before. Besides noticing that the lights inside the cabin were out, or that there were horrific smells all around me; perhaps the most noticeable thing I realized was the plane cabin was upside down.

As the blur in my vision cleared a little more, I noticed the thin arm off to the side hanging down next to my seat. *Who is? Jennifer!* Slowly lifting myself up off the floor, I try to make my way over to the dangling woman as she was stuck in her seat just like I was, held in by her seatbelt. Getting myself directly below her, I tried to support a little of her weight on my good shoulder as I reached up and grabbed her seatbelt, getting it to release.

Her limp body falls out of the seat and collapses across my shoulder, then her one knee strikes me in the back, causing me to fall to the ground. As we both bounced on the floor, or the ceiling, I rolled her to the side and tried to wake her. "Jennifer? Jennifer?" I said as I shook her. I quickly noticed that she had lost both of her flip-flops during the crash, but it was nothing to worry about right now. I placed my fingers against her neck and I'm relieved when I felt a pulse. Looking around the cabin, I felt disoriented as my mind accepted the reality that the plane was upside down. *How did this happen?*

Small sparks shot out from all over the cabin and flames were running along the floor above my head every so often as I tried to find a direction to go. About halfway towards the front, or at least what I thought was the front, flames surrounded the entire walkway, blocking our path. The way the cabin was filling with smoke, I knew it would not be long before we would become unable to breathe. I picked her up once more and made my way towards the back of the plane.

It was not long before I came upon another wall of flames blocking the way towards the rear of the aircraft as well. Setting Jennifer down, I looked for a way to get past the fire when I spotted the rear exit door just on the other side of the flames. Jumping past the flames could cause more injuries, and I knew I might not reach the blankets stored under the seats with them all the way above my head. *Especially since one of my arms is barely working.*

Looking to my right, I saw the door holding one of the plane's fire extinguishers as I broke open the compartment door and pulled it from its holder. Pulling the safety pin, I point it at the flames and pull the trigger to have nothing come out. *Tell me this fucking thing is broken, too.* After pulling the trigger multiple times to no success, I angrily threw the extinguisher against the side of the cabin as I screamed, "Fuck!"

When the extinguisher smacked the wall of the cabin, the trigger fell off, causing the extinguisher to launch forward into the flames as it sprayed Halon all over. Part of the flames went extinguished as I picked Jennifer up and carried her to the other side of the flames just next to the door. Spotting another extinguisher, I pulled it free from its holder and sprayed the rest of the flames out.

Dropping the now empty canister on the ground, I reached out and grabbed hold of the door mechanism as I tried to push the door open. As the door swings open, I am immediately blinded by the light of the sun and the smell of fuel. *Jesus Christ, are you kidding me?* Kneeling on the ground once more, I attempt to wake Jennifer one more time. "Jennifer? Jennifer, wake up!" She slowly opened her eyes and quickly screamed as I tried to grab her. "Jennifer, it's Sam!"

"Sam? Oh my god…"

Quickly cutting her off, I said, "Look, look! The exit is right here. I need you to climb out of this plane and get as far away as you can. You think you can do that?" She grabs hold of my one arm and nods her head, as I can see she is still a little foggy. Once she is standing, I help her climb out of the plane, using my arm to hold on to as I try to lower her as close to the ground as I could.

"Sam! I'm not on the ground!" she screams up to me as she holds on so tightly to my hand. I glance down and see she's not that far up in the air, figuring it was maybe a four-foot drop to the ground. Th*e more important thing is that she gets as far away as she can.*

"I know. I need to let you go."

"Sam! No! Don't let me go!"

"I need to help more of the passengers on the plane, Jennifer. It's not that far of a drop. I need to let you go. Just run as far away as quick as you can. Look, I'll count down, okay?"

"Sam?"

"Three, two, one!" Once I opened my hand, she screamed out as she fell the short distance falling on the ground the moment she landed. I waited a few seconds as I saw her run away from the plane as I told her to do. Climbing back into the cabin, I realized she had pulled my watch off when she fell, as I could see the brush mark on my skin. I try to gather as much strength as I could to get back onto my feet and go help another passenger.

One by one, from the closest to the door, I began trying to release passengers from their seatbelts and carried them back to the door. Some of them, however, that were hanging were just like some of the other passengers that were free from their seats and laying on the ground, unfortunately dead. The more I got down, carried, or dragged towards the door, the more the smoke and flames got thicker at the other end of the cabin. I am not even sure how many I dragged to the back as some of them even began climbing out of the plane without me saying anything to them, but also, none of them tried to help me rescue more people.

Soon the flames were so hot and had grown so strong that I had two people left to drag to the back and I could feel my skin burning without touching the fire. I checked one passenger and felt no pulse, so I reached out for the other and got a faint pulse. Reaching up and clicking their seatbelt free, their body fell lifelessly into my grasp, but I suddenly felt a tug on the back of my shirt.

"Help me!" the man still hanging in his seat screamed as he yanked me backwards. With my strength sapped, I fell to the ground as the other passenger pinned me to the floor, causing me to smack the side of my head on one of the metal framings of the roof. "Get up! Help me!" the man in the seat screamed at the top of his lungs as he flailed his arms all over the place.

The sharp throbbing in the side of my head made my vision go blurry once again as I tried to push the other passenger off my body, but they barely moved. Suddenly, I glanced up at the seat as the man screamed in terror and pain as his sleeve caught fire and burned him. He frantically flung it through the air, trying to get it to go out, but just made it spread more. "Fucking help me!" he cried out once more.

With every ounce of what little strength I had, I pushed the other passenger off me as their body rolled to the side but fell right into the flames that had now spread along the floor close to us. I stood up as quick as I could and hit the button to release the screaming man's seatbelt as he fell out of the seat. As he landed on top of me, he pushed me to the floor once more, pinning me underneath him. Without a word, he immediately crawled off me and ripped his shirt off to get the flames off his burning skin. "Help me!" I screamed out as I tried to pull the other man from the flames.

Without looking back towards me, he climbed back onto his feet and ran for the exit door. "Hey, help me!" I screamed out again, but he was gone. I grabbed someone's jacket that was laying off to the side and wrapped it around my one hand as I reached into the flames and pulled the man from the fire, quickly patting all the flames out as fast as I could. However, I knew at that point he would have serious burns on his body.

Once I got the last flame out on the man's body, I dropped the jacket on the floor and tried to drag the man towards the back. Blood was running down my face, from my shoulder and arm, from my side, and I was sure from the pain in my leg that I was bleeding from there as well. I could see the sunlight coming in the door before I felt my legs' energy sap as my knees buckled under my weight. Suddenly, to my left, I heard a small electrical spark from the light paneling as a small explosion forced me sideways as I collapsed to the ground, letting the last passenger go.

As I bounced against the floor and side of the cabin, my vision became blurrier as I could no longer focus my eyes on anything. I reached for the door, trying to find any more strength that I had somewhere in my body, but there was none. Unable to keep them open, I closed my eyes as I started becoming delusional. I thought I started hearing the voices of other people, but I could see no one. As everything became dark, the same thought kept repeating in my mind until I said it out loud with my last breath, "Amy, I'm sorry."

Chapter Thirty-One

What is happening? Flashes of sounds and lights kept rushing past my vision, filling the darkness with random images and echoes of dreams, or hallucinations, or memories. Random voices came and left, saying words that sounded familiar, but I could not decipher them, leaving me with more questions. *Who was that? What did they just say? Where am I?*

I could not feel any part of my body; I only felt pain and agony. My fingers; pain. My feet; pain. My legs and arms were in more pain. Then, just as much as I felt everything, I felt nothing. Just as I saw visions of lights, there were none. As soon as I heard repeated random noises and sounds, there was no one. The silence became my new current reality.

The darkness drove me mad. There was no end, no beginning; there was no start and no finish. I could hear my breath, but when I tried to scream, there was silence. I tried to understand the direction, but I could not figure out which way was up, and which was down.

Who am I? My thoughts concentrated on that question in my mind as I tried to focus on one simple thing. *Who am I?* The more my mind wandered away from that one simple question, I lost focus, and I filled my mind with an endless cluster of thoughts. I focused more intensely on that one question. *Who am I?* My brain pounded so incredibly excruciatingly as I thought more and more about the answer. My lips, so dry and weak, separated in the darkness as a quick gust of air pushed out of my lungs as a fragile, scratchy echo crawled past my tongue and said, "I… am… Sam."

As soon as the answer was in my hands, a new and stronger image pushed its way into my line of thought. I felt a strange but strong feeling of warmth wash all over my body the more I focused on it. I remembered who I was, and now my mind became addicted to the thoughts and determination of this new image. My heartbeat became even stronger behind my ribs as my pain seemed to push its way out of my body through every single pore like sweat. I felt my lungs expand on either side of my heart as one more gust of oxygen pushed out of my throat into the universe, pulling out of my mouth, "Amy."

The surrounding darkness brightened as it all became a grayish blend of black and white. I could feel my balance return, as if my equilibrium had turned my mind forward. The gray faded more as my surroundings became more of a white hue. A soft sense of relaxation came over me as the hue grew brighter and brighter, then faded to nothing as the darkness returned.

In the darkness and silence, a sudden small and faint beep could be heard. I still could not move, but the sound felt like it was approaching me. As I focused on the beep, a new sliding shuffle in the distance from another direction approached me as well. *What is that?* As the sounds came closer and closer, I suddenly could hear the faint voice of someone speaking as I struggled to listen.

"Authorities are still investigating the cause of the mechanical malfunction of the aircraft, but they are crediting the pilot for his training and quick thinking to get the plane to land in that field with minimal casualties. We have also learned from some survivors that many of the passengers pulled together to help each other save one another and pull as many as possible from the wreckage. As the investigation continues, we will bring you more information as it becomes available. Reporting live, this is…" the voice faded out as I tried to listen to more sounds that became familiar.

Small flashes of dim whites and grays blurred across my eyes as I finally felt my eyelids opened. As my eyes tried to focus more, the image they formed I was stunned to see. Once adjusted, I was staring at rectangular light fixtures with halogen tubes in them in between a handful of rectangular ceramic tiles before I saw another light fixture, then they repeated. The lights were turned off, however. The little brightness in the room was coming from a small rectangular light that was attached to the wall behind my head.

I also noticed metal tracks that were strung in a circular direction around me with a light greenish drape hanging down from the track; the drape was pushed all the way to the end of the track. Hearing the sliding noise once again, I glance to my right as I see people walking back and forth in front of and behind a large wood-stained desk, answering phones and carrying computer tablets. They were all dressed in all blue, all green, all navy, and all white uniforms as they passed by. Watching one of them come out of a room, they closed a sliding glass door to the room that produced the noise I was hearing. *Wait? Am I?*

I suddenly could feel the texture of soft cloth in between my fingers on my right hand when I glanced down to see that a blanket covered me, as my head was resting on a plush pillow. I tried to lift my left arm, but pain immediately stopped me in my left shoulder, so I left it be. Raising my right hand to my face, I could feel the rubber tube that was placed under my nose with two vents blowing oxygen into my nostrils. As I felt the tube, I turned my right hand so that I could see the top of it. Taped down, I saw a needle stuck in my hand as a rubber hose hung down my arm and went up to a bag that hung high off to the right of the bed, I was laying in.

Next to the bed was a small machine that the beeping noise was coming from. The screen showed a variety of numbers and charts monitoring me as two wires ran off that machine. One of the wires was attached to a clip that squeezed my index finger on my right hand while the other attached to a cuff that was wrapped around my upper arm. Looking down towards the far-right corner of the room next to the opening of the doorway, I saw a small television that was on a news program attached to the wall at the upper part of the corner pointing down towards the bed. *How did I get here?* I tried to sit up, but my side and legs hurt badly along with my shoulder as I clinched my eyes tightly, trying to get the pain to back off.

"Sam?" a voice said from someone that had just entered the room. Turning my head to see who it was, I saw a black man standing in the doorway holding a small brown bag and two paper cups with plastic lids on each. He was wearing a blue t-shirt that depicted a video game character but showed off his fit biceps, black jeans, and white sneakers.

"Austin?" I barely got out of my mouth as he sat the bag and drinks down on the end table next to the door. As he approached the bed, he kneeled and grabbed my hand.

"Jesus Christ Sam, Jesus Christ," he kept saying softly as he squeezed my hand hard.

After a few moments, I asked, "How did I get here?"

Getting up off the floor, he grabbed a small chair that was pushed off to the side and moved it to the edge of the bed before he sat down on it. "The first responders found you inside the plane near the exit door. Apparently, you saved a lot of people." He paused for a second and shook his head, smiled, and added, "But they didn't know who you were because you didn't have any identification on you. It took the one girl you saved to tell the medical crew your name was Sam. They eventually matched it to the manifest of the plane."

Weak, I said, "I put my wallet in my bag. Didn't think I'd need it."

Still smiling, he said, "Well, let that be a lesson to you, asshole. Always keep your wallet in your pocket."

I looked back towards the television. *I can't believe I survived that.* Still weak, I asked Austin softly, "What happened?"

He turned his head and looked at the television too before he said, "They still don't know yet. All they know is the one engine had a malfunction and blew up. When the plane tried to turn around, a second went out on the same wing and damaged it badly. The pilot tried to get the plane to emergency land in a large field, but the damaged wing broke off. Authorities said he was able to keep the nose up long enough that the plane didn't crash headfirst, but the damage was done and the plane split in half. You were in the section closest to the damaged wing, so your section actually flipped over in the field."

Glancing at the ceiling, I softly said, "I remember the cabin being upside down. I got free and just didn't think twice. I had to help as many people as I could."

Looking back at me, he said softly, "People died, but because of you, many people lived with several walking away." Leaning forward, he chuckled as he added, "But you should've waited for me, stupid."

Slightly smiling, I said, "Your wife would've killed me if you would have been on board."

"Gina? You ain't wrong about that," Austin said as he sat back in his chair.

I looked at him for a few seconds before I asked, "How did you know I was here? In the hospital?"

"Well, it wasn't easy. It was a couple of days of waiting before we learned where you were. You were in no condition to tell them. Like I said, one of the other passengers said your name was Sam, but it was a few days before they learned your last name from the manifest of the plane. Once the hospital reached out, we came as soon as we could."

"No condition?" I asked.

"Yeah, you've been unconscious for a few days. You had to have a few surgeries before they stabilized you enough to put you in this fancy hotel room."

I chuckled a little before I coughed, "No don't, my guts." Austin started laughing harder at my pain. Once I stopped coughing, I thought about what he just said and asked, "You said we?"

"Right."

"Who's we?"

"Who do you think?" He pointed across me to my left side. Turning my head to the left, I saw her sitting there curled up in the large, cushioned chair, sleeping. I couldn't help but stare at her as my eyes filled with tears. She had kicked her shoes off as they lay on the floor at the front of the chair. She had her legs pulled up to her chest as she had herself tucked into a ball in the chair to stay warm. As she slept, she wore an oversized maroon hooded sweatshirt and black and brown patterned leggings. Her brunette hair hung down across her shoulders as her head was tilted to the side, but I could still see her freckles across her nose and cheeks and her small nose ring in her left nostril. I found an enormous amount of energy as I opened my mouth and called out, "Amy!"

She opened her eyes and as soon as her beautiful green eyes saw me, she jumped out of her chair as she screamed, "Sam!" She immediately ran to the bed, leaned over the bed, and hugged me as she kissed my neck and face before she cried. I didn't care that she pressed against my left shoulder. All I knew was I needed to tell her.

"Amy, Amy," I said as she stood back up.

"Oh my god Sam, I thought I lost you," her tears were causing little dirt marks on her face, but I still thought she was so beautiful.

“Once she got here, she tried everything she could to take over your care, but they refused to let her near you,” Austin said. “But they didn’t know who they were messing with.”

Wiping her tears on her sleeve, she said, “Once they knew who I was, they let me help with their other patients, but I told them they had better not let you go.” I smiled without saying a word to her. I just didn’t want to look away from her.

Austin reached out and tapped Amy on the shoulder as he said, “I’m gonna go call Gina and let her know Sam’s awake.”

Amy nodded her head and mouthed the words, “Thank you,” as he walked out the door. Once he was gone, she reached down the side of the bed and lowered the side railing a little more than sat down on the edge of the bed. I gingerly slid my whole body towards my right to give her more room on the bed. “Sam, what are you doing? Don’t move around like that,” she ordered me.

As I got myself over as far as I could, I looked up at her and said, “Please, just lay down. Be close to me.”

She spun herself around as she laid down on her right side but draped her left arm across my chest and left leg over my leg. We laid there for several minutes in silence as I listened to her fight back crying before she said to me softly, “I really thought I lost you when I got your call. Why did you leave early? Austin told me what he knew, but it wasn't much."

Looking into her eyes, I answered, "I think I quit my job. Anthony was talking crazy and threatened me, and I just realized that you were more important to me. So, I decided all I wanted to do was come home. All I needed was to see you."

"Sam," she whispered as she smiled, brushing her hand through my hair slowly.

Softly, I added, "I didn't want the last time we talked to be that stupid argument."

Tilting her head to look at me, she said, "I know Sam. I'm so sorry. I was being selfish and demanding. I shouldn't have gotten so angry at you."

"No, you weren't," I replied softly. "I am sorry. You weren't being selfish; I wasn't being a good husband. My home life was being dictated by my job. I wasn't being fair to you."

She sat up on her side as she looked at me and said sternly, "No, you weren't. I got so used to you sacrificing everything for me, I just expected you to be there without question. And then you got your job because of me and the stress I was under. Sam, I never once took what you wanted into any of my decisions. You just went along with what I wanted. The moment you weren't where I expected, I got mad."

"Amy, stop." She closed her mouth as she looked at me, waiting for me to speak. "What you're saying isn't wrong, but it was my choice. I chose to sacrifice for you. You wanted to achieve your dream; I was already living my dream. I had you." Her eyes filled with tears again as she leaned over me and kissed me so passionately. *It feels like forever since I've tasted those lips.* As she pulled away from me, she curled herself up more against me as she pulled the blanket out from under her and crawled under it to lie with me in the bed.

I took a deep breath and finally felt myself relax. I turned my head towards Amy, kissed her forehead, and said softly, "When we get out of here, we have a lot to decide and discuss."

"Okay," she whispered as she hugged me tightly. Even though I was still in so much pain, I knew I was where I belonged; I was with Amy.

Epilogue

With the radio off, I could hear the outside better. The hum of the SUV I was driving was relaxing. As I drove along the highway, I admired the colors of the fall foliage in the trees that grew along the road. The randomness of the reds, browns, and oranges was such a beautiful sight that I had forgotten about them living in the city for so long. Looking at the passenger seat, Amy gazed out the window, admiring the trees as well. Looking down at my center console, our hands clasped together with our fingers wrapped around each other's.

We had been driving for nearly an hour, but we were only minutes away from the house. It took us a long time to finally come to a decision on my family's old home, but we were happy with the end results. I did the last of the paperwork we needed to fill out, and now this was going to be our last trip from our apartment in the city. Admittedly, I was still feeling uneasy about everything, but I knew it was the right thing for us to do.

It has been a long year and a half since the plane crash. After the investigation was concluded, they still were unable to determine what exactly caused the malfunction in the engine. The plane had just passed a safety inspection with excellence, and yet this still happened. The airline and the media continued to praise the pilot for, saying the crash could have been so much worse if it was not for his quick thinking. *I'm not sure how much praise I can give the pilot when I was hanging upside down honestly.*

Austin told me that many of the passengers had said that they were thanking me for saving their lives, but I never heard it. Not once did the media or the airline mention that, and I was perfectly fine with it. In the end, they gave everyone that was on that flight a settlement, partly for our pain and suffering, but also for our silence. No amount of money could ever bring back those people lost in the crash, but I always keep thinking that it could have been much more tragic.

The settlement, on the other hand, made it much easier not to return to work. I never went back, even though Anthony reached out to me several times once I finally made it home with Amy. The man just could not grasp the idea that I had a lot of rehab and physical therapy to go through, not just physical but mental healing, before I could even think of returning. But after that conversation in Vegas we had, I never wanted to return either. But Austin gave me such good news that made me feel so much better.

Shortly after the convention concluded, Austin reached out to the divisional vice president about Anthony's conduct. He told him about the things he said to me after the awards ceremony, so they started their own internal investigation. Turned out, many of the things that he was doing were against company policy. Plus, they really did not like his whole fire people for no reason mentality, so they turned around and fired him instead. Right after they did it, the DVP called me to tell me what had happened and to offer his deepest condolences.

I had met him a few times. James O'Keith was his name. He was a big guy; I think he was Irish too, by his accent. He told me they had felt for a long time that the high ups wanted me to move up in the company and when I was ready; they wanted me to take the newly vacated regional manager position. I was humbly flattered, but I told them I had made up my mind and was still ending my employment with the company.

"I'm really sorry to hear that fella, but I respect ya decision," James said to me over the phone. "But just so ya know, if ya ever change your mind and want your job back, just give me a holla."

"Thank you very much, sir. I really appreciate you saying that. But I know there are much better and more qualified candidates in our region you can look at."

Laughing over the phone, he replied, "Ya know what Sam, I think ya are right about that." It actually made me feel better to know that someone else was going to get the well-deserved position than if I had taken it. But I had many more important things to focus on.

As we pulled down the street that approached the house, I started feeling a little anxious. Amy squeezed my hand tightly, as she could tell I was nervous. While still holding my hand, she used her other hand to rub it up and down my arm, her fingers gracing across the goosebumps that had formed on my arm. Pulling the truck to a complete stop and putting it into Park, our journey was done. Taking a deep breath, she looked at me and said, "We're here. Are you excited?"

"I'm not sure. Excited, nervous, anxious, all the above." Turning my head, I looked her in her eyes and said, "But as long as you are okay with this decision, then the only thing I am is happy." As she smiled at me, she leaned over the center console and kissed me ever so softly.

After a few seconds, she pulled herself back and asked, "Are you ready?" I nodded my head as I took a deep breath and blew it all out. "Okay, let's go," she said as she opened her door. As I stepped out, I could not help but stare at the house as I closed my door after getting out of the SUV.

Standing in the driveway, I just looked at the house all over. On the side of the house, there was a large wooden porch that led down the hill towards the basement door. I looked at the giant tree that had its limbs growing over the top of the porch and part of the roof offering natural shade to whomever sat outside in the past. I looked at each window, imagining all the times someone from the inside looked out those windows and smiled.

I could not help but think about the people I lost in my life that lived in this house for all my years I had lived here. But that was quickly replaced by all the wonderful memories I had of all those people while they were alive. And now I could not help but think about all the new memories this house is going to offer to someone new.

Honk, honk!

I turned around and quickly smiled as another SUV pulled up in the driveway next to me. As the passenger window rolled down, a man's voice shouted out from inside, "Delivery!"

"Austin, you asshole!" Amy yelled out as she walked around from the other side of our truck.

"Oh, I'm sorry," he said as he turned off his vehicle.

The woman in the passenger seat smacked him on the arm. As she got out of the truck, I saw she had black hair cut just below her ears and tanned skin. She was wearing a black coat, a purple top, and black jeans with black boots. "Austin, if you woke up that baby, so help me god," she said as she pointed her finger at him.

Laughing, Amy said, "No, it's okay Gina. She's still asleep." Turning around, I saw Amy carrying a car seat that had a large handle that folded up, so you did not have to remove the child from the harness. In the seat was a little baby girl wearing a little pink, white, and orange onesie with a small pink hat that covered the top of her head. "Long car rides tend to just knock her out."

As he walked to the other side of his SUV, Austin looked at me and asked, "So, you're really going to do this?"

"Yeah, we are. It's just the right move for us," I answered.

"I just love this house, Sam. I'm really surprised you kept it for this long," Gina added.

Amy looked at Gina and said, "There was always something telling him to keep it. And now, it just seemed like the perfect opportunity to finally do something with it."

Austin then asked, "So, you think you two are going to miss living in the city?"

"Maybe a little," I answered. "But with little Lynn here, our priorities changed."

"Not to mention, with me taking the Chief of Surgery position at the local hospital in town, the commute was going to be crazy. And I just wanted to spend as much time as I could with these two as possible," Amy added.

"I just love my little Lynn," Gina said as she bent over and picked up one of the baby's hands and kissed it repeatedly. Her voice was exaggeratingly high pitched and almost childish as she spoke. "I'm going to come see you so much. You're gonna get sick of your Aunt Gina, yes you are."

"And you said I was going to wake her up?" Austin scoffed as he slapped his wife on the butt with her bent over the baby.

"Well, we are going to take little Lynn inside and put her in her crib. You think you guys can manage to bring the rest of our stuff inside? Plus, I want to get dinner started," Amy said as Gina and her started walking towards the house.

"Not a problem honey, we gottcha covered," I answer her as I open the rear hatch of our SUV.

Austin leaned over and grabbed one box before he said, "So, have you figured out what you are going to do with yourself? You gonna be a stay-at-home dad?"

"I don't know yet. Maybe. There's no rush right now for me to figure that out."

"You know, you could always come back and work for me," he said as a gigantic smile showed itself across his face.

Laughing I said, "Nice try Mr. Regional Manager, but I'll pass." As I closed the hatch, I could not help but to continue laughing as I added, "Besides, I've had enough city building for one lifetime."

"That's fine. It doesn't need to be a city. How about we just start with a town?" I grin at Austin as I walked away from him and headed for the house. "Okay, fine, how about a suburb? A neighborhood?"

"Dude, I get it, you can stop."

As I stepped up onto the porch, he then said, "Help a brother out, man. How about just a street?" As I opened the door and walked into the house, Austin ran up the driveway and jumped up onto the porch before he pursued me inside the house.

The End

www.ingramcontent.com/pod-product-compliance
Lightning Source LLC
Chambersburg PA
CBHW020945310726
48980CB00001B/59

9798992586527